CALLED BY FATE

DEMI WARRIK

Called by Fate: Fates Mark #3
Copyright © Demi Warrik 2022
All rights reserved
First published in 2022

No part of this book may be reproduced, stored in a retrieval system, or transmitted in any form or by any means whatsoever without written permission except in the case of brief quotations embodied in reviews or articles. All characters in this publication other than those clearly in the public domain are fictitious, and any resemblance to real persons, living or dead, is purely coincidental.
The unauthorized reproduction or distribution of a copyrighted work is illegal. Criminal copyright infringement without monetary gain is investigated by the FBI, is punishable by fines, and federal imprisonment.

Editing: Proofs By Polly
Proofreader: Raven Quill Editing, LLC
Cover: Ryn Katryn Digital Art

AUTHOR'S NOTE

Hey there lovely reader! I'm so glad you made it to the end of Sadie's series. As with books one and two, there will be themes some readers find triggering. This book will contain awesome fight scenes, steamy sexy times, loss, and lots of cursing. I turned up the heat for this book too so be prepared. ;)

As always, please take care of yourself, and thank you for reading Sadie's journey.

Enjoy the ride!

For all of us who dare to dream. The stars are in reach, grab them and don't let go.

1

THE NIGHT OF THE CHALLENGE

No matter how hard I try to stop it, the blood won't stop flowing. There's so much of it covering the ground, my hands, staining the rug in the foyer. It's an endless flow. My mouth is moving but I'm not sure I'm even aware of what exactly I'm saying.

Vinson's heart starts beating erratically, then slows. Time is running out and I can't seem to do anything but watch. His beautiful features go slack, no longer pinched in agony before his heart stops completely. Just ceases to beat and doesn't restart no matter how much I plead for it to. No matter how much I plead for Kaos' magic to work. Nothing happens.

The room around me is completely silent, or hell, all hell might be breaking loose around me. I'm not sure if the Elders followed us from the garden or if I would hear anything over the roar of my own heart pounding in my ears.

My still beating heart.

I'm not sure how I know, maybe I'm borrowing one of Elian's seemingly endless abilities, but Vin's once bright—

now completely dull—soul rises from his body and starts to fade into the ether.

Looking back down at him, I try to do something —*anything* to stop him from leaving me when something black catches my eye. Anguish rips through me all over again as I stare at the black blade protruding from his chest, my black shadestone blade Reginald plunged into his chest.

My shifter.

My Vin.

Dead.

How do you come back from death? How do you come back from something so final? Something so finite that, until recently, I thought was absolutely inevitable. Weavers and shifters alike can live almost infinitely and yet, Vin's life was torn from him way too soon.

Because of me.

Tears drip from my cheeks as I lean over him, brushing one of his brown locks out of his face. His skin is already starting to cool. Which is insane considering how hot shifters normally run.

A strong pair of arms wrap around my middle and for the first time, I realize I'm screaming. They try to pull me from my shifter, but I throw an elbow into their stomach so they'll go away. Some distant part of my brain recognizes I'm in shock, but everything is so dull, so muted. Everything except for Vin. He can't really be gone if I don't let go of him, right?

The arms try to move me again and my first reaction is to elbow them again. When they don't let up, I turn around and snarl. The anguished look on Reed's face is enough to snap me out of it though as the sounds around me start rushing in, going from dull as if underwater, to clear as if I break the surface.

"I'm so sorry, Love, but I couldn't bear the pain in your

screams any longer," he says, and guilt floods me alongside everything else.

"I'm sorry, Red." My response is automatic, robotic even. It's as if my brain is going through the motions without bearing in mind the agony that I'm in.

This time when Reed reaches for me, I allow him to pull me away, but not too far. I can't leave Vin. Reed gets the message and sits on the ground, pulling me into his lap. He cradles my head to his shoulder and slowly rocks back and forth, trying to soothe the turmoil inside of me.

Through my tears, I find Elian still passed out, but not dead. Thank the Goddess. He may be a brooding asshole, but he's still someone I'm also developing feelings for, despite his nature.

Gods, I can't even imagine the power it must've taken to pull us through the shadows to safety, considering he said he couldn't transport us when we were getting attacked in the car. That feels like a lifetime ago, even though it hasn't been. Either way, I'm grateful for him getting us out of there, even if we left Ash behind. I can't think about that now though. My mind can't handle the betrayal.

Kaos is bent over my prickly mate, a black glow emanating from his hands while Dante assists, lending Kaos some of his strength. Now that I think about it, I can feel Elian subconsciously draining the others through their Circle bond and, in turn, me through them.

Reed kisses my temple and smooths my tangled, and probably bloody hair out of my face, distracting me. Until recently, I had no idea I felt so strongly for the sweet shifter, but something changed the night he carried me home from the party. Or maybe it was one of the times in the kitchen, his flirty smile at dinnertime, or when he didn't leave me behind when the Elite attacked after our shopping trip. It doesn't matter because the truth is, I do care for him. And this… well, it's breaking something vital inside of me.

A broken whisper falls from my lips. "Please, Goddess, don't take him from me." My throat is raw from screaming.

I once said that some people in this world are important, you don't always know how or why. Vin is important. He's damned important to me and my future. I won't accept the finality of his death. I can't.

Just when I think the Goddess won't appear, the same bright glow from the meadow blinds me, and she appears, floating over Vin in the middle of the foyer. She is as luminous as ever, beautiful in such an ethereal way there's no mistaking her as anything other than distinctly *otherworldly*. She looks upon the scene with sorrow etched across her delicate features.

The Goddess stares at Vin for a long time, so long it feels like an eternity before she turns those ancient eyes to me, filled to the brim with sadness. "As much as I'd like to assist you, my dear, I'm afraid I cannot interfere. To do so would break my sacred oath to allow free will."

I scramble out of Reed's lap and plant myself on my knees in front of her. "Please, I will do anything, *anything*, to get him back."

The Goddess' long, black hair flows all around her, floating on an unknown breeze, painting a beautiful picture of her. She motions for me to stand. "Rise, Sadie Sinclair. You need not bow before me."

Reluctantly, I push myself up into a standing position, wiping my bloodstained fingers on my dress that I realize is also soaked in blood, stained red with his life force. My heart aches so fucking much.

"There has to be a way for me to bring him back," I plead. "Without breaking your oath," I add, staring into her eyes despite the urge to look away. I shiver when Reed places a hand on my back and it tingles through the fabric, lending me some of his strength.

She looks contemplative for a moment before one of her lovers appears at her side. If I'm not mistaken, he's the God of Light, judging by the faint, golden glow emanating from his skin. He's wearing nothing but a leather-type contraption over his nether regions that certainly doesn't hide any of his muscles. But at least it hides his dick, although I wonder…

Reed nudges me, and I blush, remembering he can hear my thoughts. Even as distraught as I am now, I shouldn't perve on his God.

The God of Light takes the Goddess' hand and brings it to his lips. Her eyes soften at the intimate gesture.

"My love, if I may?" The Goddess nods for him to continue. "Sadie could go to our realm with us," he offers, and a spark of hope ignites in my chest. Judging by the way Kaos and Dante's shock brush up against me through the bond, what the God of Light is offering is a huge deal. Even Hemsworth's eyes widen from his place at my side. I hadn't noticed him until now. "We could escort her to the gate to retrieve the shifter's soul. What she does after that is up to her, but I think we owe her this chance."

The Goddess places a hand up to stop him from saying anything else. "No. It's too risky. Sadie could get trapped there and she's far too important. The fate of this world rests on her shoulders."

Jeez. No pressure or anything. Reed cracks a small smile despite everything as he hears that thought.

I clear my throat and straighten my spine. "No offense, Goddess, but that is my choice to make. What about *my* free will?"

She sighs and it sounds more like a tinkling wind chime than anything. "When it comes to matters involving my realm and the afterlife, I have total domain over those choices. Here on Earth, I promised to always allow you to make your own choices. You, my dear, are so precious. More so than you know." Her lip curls and it's the only subjective gesture I've ever seen her make. "The Elders have perverted everything sacred. You have to be the one to stop them. It's been foretold in the stars."

"And I will do everything in my power to stop them, believe me, I want them to pay more than anything, but..." I glance over to my other mates, giving each of them a broken, tender smile, including Elian who is just starting to come to, and Hemsworth sitting at my side. "Vin is a part of us. A part of me, and to do that, I need him with me. I feel it in my very soul that he's important to all of this."

"At least let her try, my love," the God of Light interjects softly.

After a long and tense silence, the Goddess' shoulders slump—a tell that she's very worried about this, which means I definitely shouldn't take it lightly. No, if the Goddess is worried, then something very bad is in our future.

Kaos wraps his hand around mine, pulling my attention to him. "Sorry, Goddess, would you mind if we had a word with our mate?"

"Not at all, dear."

Kaos pulls me to the side and my Sworn circle me, acting like this is a football huddle. "My Flame, have you considered the implications of this? Even the Goddess is worried for your safety." Reflected in his eyes is the weight of judging every pro and con and every possible scenario.

"Why would you risk your life for the shifter?" Elian asks and, surprisingly, there's no bite to his tone. "Do you love him? The shifter?"

"I—" I pause and take a moment to think about it. "I think I was starting to," I answer truthfully because, while I have strong feelings for Vinson, it's not love yet. Love is too strong a word for me to throw around without absolutely meaning it with every single ounce of my soul.

"Then we'll stand beside you," Kaos responds.

There's another flash and the other two of the Goddess' men appear. Like in the meadow, one is surrounded by stunning russet-purples, the color reminding me of sunset, and the other in the pre-dawn light of a gorgeous morning. They have a mischievous glint in their eyes as they surround the Goddess and caress her, whispering something in her ear. Totally thanking my lucky stars that the Gods are on my side right now. I think the Goddess is too, and she's right to want to protect this world, but I need to get to Vin. Being without him forever would… destroy me. I feel it in my very soul.

The Goddess looks to her lovers and back to us, understanding shining in her eyes. "Then you should do everything in your power to get him back. My consorts and I may be eternal, but I know if anything happened to one of them… Well, I'd be doing the same thing as you. You're important to this world, but something you've taught me, by watching you, is that family is more important than anything. Go after him, Sadie, and do not let anything stand in your way."

My mates nod their heads in agreement, murmuring soft words of encouragement and stroking our bonds with love. I'm so grateful for them and their understanding.

Hemsworth nudges my leg. "I'll stay and protect his body for you. Go get that shifter. He owes me a steak."

Classic Hems. If the situation were different, I might even laugh.

"You should go after him," Dante agrees and he's usually the most jealous of them all, so for him to say that…

Relief pours through me, and I smile, but the Goddess holds her hand up. "You should know that it won't be easy. I can see his soul fighting, straining to come back here to you, but the spirit realm is designed to not let souls go. He was killed with your shadestone dagger, which was forged from a substance in my realm for *you* to use. Elder Reginald never should've been able to touch it, let alone wield it, but something is protecting him from harm. When you return, you'll have to figure out how to put an end to whatever that is because it is not natural. You won't be able to stop them otherwise, I'm afraid."

"You're right. Something is helping them stay invincible, and I damn well intend to get to the bottom of it and what my uncle is up to. But first... Vinson. Is there anything else we should know before going in there?"

"Yes... and your mates aren't going to like it."

Oh hell.

2

The Goddess' image flickers, and she reaches her hand out for me to take. "Come, my dear. I will explain more once we get there. We must act quickly. The longer we take, the more Vinson's soul will bond to the In-Between which is where souls with unfinished business go." She looks over at my Circle. "Place a hand on your Link and I will transport you all in one swoop. Is everyone ready?"

A chorus of yeses reaches my ears, and they might as well be my favorite song.

Reed steps up behind me and places his hand on my shoulder. Dante steps up to my side and takes my right hand while Kaos helps Elian from the floor. He doesn't sneer or make a rude gesture like I've come to expect. He looks impassive as he lays his hand on my other shoulder, but I'm starting to think that's just how he is. He's a dick, yes, but he has his reasons and I plan to get to the bottom of it one of these days.

Kaos grabs my left hand, bringing me back to the present. Once we are all connected my body sings and buzzes with energy, and I realize I haven't only been falling for Vinson... I'm falling for all of them—each in their own little ways.

And that thought doesn't scare me. Not even a little bit.

The Goddess winks at me as if she reads that thought before closing her eyes with a look of concentration. I watch as she waves her hand in an infinity pattern, sparks of black and gold trail the movement before there's a flash, and in the next instant my stomach bottoms out. Our bodies phase out of our world only to be planted into her realm.

Taking a look around, my jaw drops, because absolutely everything is different. A purple hue covers the world around us, including the soft grass beneath our feet. It's night out and the stars are shining so brilliantly that almost everything is illuminated. *We're really freaking here.*

The guys are wearing varying degrees of shock and awe on their faces. They've known about this realm their entire lives and now they're here. Though I do wish the circumstances surrounding our visit were different. There's an ache in my heart that's not going to go away until Vin is back in our world.

The God of Dusk and Dawn didn't follow us, so it's just the God of Light and the Goddess. If I thought she looked ethereal in our world, it's nothing compared to now. She is absolutely radiant on her turf; her hair is shinier and her skin glows like moonlight.

She releases my hand and looks me up and down, shaking her head. "These earthly clothes won't do here." The Goddess snaps her fingers, and in a flash, my Sworn and I are wearing different clothes.

The guys are now dressed similarly to the Goddess' consorts with leather straps that are strategically placed across their chests and nether regions, and holy damn. Forgive me for ogling, Goddess, but thank you for blessing me with these fine ass men.

I glance down and find my attire similar to the dresses the Goddess herself wears. I'm sporting a long, shimmering, purple dress that moves with me perfectly. It's sheer but somehow not in the places that matter, and it's so fucking soft. Much better than that bloodstained dress that reeked of betrayal.

Don't think about that now, Sadie. I shove the thoughts that want to bubble up down, locking them up tightly in my little box of *fucked up shit I'll have to deal with later*. Our feet are bare but I prefer it that way honestly. I can feel the magic pulsing through the land beneath us, alive and buzzing with power.

With a nod of satisfaction, the Goddess and the God of Light start walking down the dirt path we're on and my mates follow close behind. I notice every ten steps or so there are beautiful, glowing flowers that help illuminate the path even more than the stars. The colors range from vibrant purples to brilliant blues, and softer colors in between. It's truly a sight to behold.

"Before we get started, you need to know that time works differently in my realm." Her strides never falter, and I quicken my pace to keep up with her. "A few weeks may pass here but on Earth, only a few minutes will go by. Which works in our favor in this instance. My Brilliance" —she gestures toward the God of Light— "and I will lead you to the grotto where the entrance to the spirit realm resides, but you'll be on your own from there on out. You will have to go in after the shifter alone."

"Oh, I thought my mates would be going in with me?" I ask as a spike of nerves shoots through me.

The Goddess shakes her head. "Only to my realm and the gate, I'm afraid. If they went in with you then no one would be here to keep you tethered and protect your body. There would be no thread to pull on if you needed it."

"What do you mean 'protect her body?'" Elian demands, slight venom lacing his words even though he's talking to the freaking Goddess herself. Reed, Kaos, and Dante also look anxious at the thought of me going in alone.

"Sadie's soul will have to be severed from her body to allow her to go in and rescue Vinson. That will leave her extremely vulnerable, as you can imagine. You four will have to protect her body while she's in there. Or, if something goes wrong while she's on the other side, it'll take all of you to pull her back."

None of my mates like that answer at all, judging by the snarls and tension lacing through them. But none of them say they're going to stop me, for which I'm thankful. Not a single one of them could say they'd do this differently if the roles were reversed. It's written on all their faces.

"I don't like it," Kaos says softly, reaching out to hold my hand. "There are too many variables."

"Me either," Dante agrees and lays a hand on my shoulder in support.

"We can keep her safe," Reed vows.

"I can do this, guys. I'll go after Vin and bring him back from death. No biggie, right?" I mutter the last part under my breath.

The Goddess' lips quirk as she glances over before growing serious once more. "You are connected to him even though you are not mated yet." My eyes widen with that admission. Is she saying we're fated? "To ensure his soul heals, you will have to give him a part of yours, which will weaken you for a bit. Are you okay with that?"

I don't even have to think about it. "Yes."

"I figured as much. I should also warn you it seems Vin isn't the only one in the afterlife waiting to speak with you. Several others have been waiting for this moment to come."

A chill shoots through my body at her words.

"Who?" I ask. There are so many possibilities and even more people I'd like to see. So many answers I could receive...

"You'll see," she replies cryptically. "Now, after giving Vinson a piece of your soul, when you are ready to send him back to your world, all you need to do is give him the shadestone Bedi gave you and it will transport him to his body. I've taken the liberty to add a special pocket to your dress to store it in. And such a special little stone it is."

I stop in my tracks, retracing her words. "Wait, so that means Bedi knew I'd need this all along?" That damn seer. She's always one step ahead of everything and it makes me nervous as hell. What else does she know?

What else has she been preparing me for?

The Goddess nods. "She is a seer, after all."

"Right. What's the deal with her, anyway? She's apparently been with me my whole life, even if I didn't know it, but she seems so hot and cold."

The Goddess shakes her head. "That's a conversation you should have with her, but you should know she's always had your best interests at heart. Knowing the future and how things will play out is not an easy task, I'm afraid."

That sounds ominous as fuck but sensing I'm not going to get a better answer than that, I drop it. For now. We don't have all the time in the world, and I'm itching to get to Vin.

A heaviness settles over us as we draw closer to the spirit realm portal, and something starts to tug on my chest in the same spot I feel the rest of my mate bonds. We reach the top of a hill that overlooks a meadow with every color of flower under the sun, or, in this case, the moon. In the middle, about fifty yards away, is a swirling blue and black portal with a fearsome looking wolf standing next to it, guarding the entrance.

The Goddess tenses. "Something urgent has happened that requires my attention, so this is where I must leave you, child. Talk to Keros, the portal guardian. Tell him you have my blessing to enter the portal and he should let you through without issue." She turns and places a hand on my shoulder, a certain fondness in her eyes. "Please, be careful and don't dawdle too long. Do you understand what needs to be done?"

"Yes." The Goddess leans down and places a kiss upon my cheek that feels the way my shadows do when they surround me, and then she turns to walk away. "And Goddess? Thank you for allowing me to do this."

"Certainly, my dear. Now go get him." In the blink of an eye, she and the God of Light disappear into thin air.

Kaos clears his throat and I turn to him, gazing into his soft, blue eyes. I turn my attention to the rest of them as they surround me. My heart squeezes at the sight of my mates looking so unearthly and badass. Not to mention super fucking hot. I'll have dreams of them in their outfits for years to come. "Are you all upset with me?" I ask when the silence drags on.

"Oh, Sadie. You think we'd be mad at you for this? Vin may be a shifter, but he's a great guy and we respect him. For Goddess' sake, the man took a blow for you and almost died." He winces. "Then actually died. Dude is definitely mate worthy material."

"If you want to rescue the shifter from death, we'll be with you the whole way, Love. You can always count on us," Reed adds.

Dante nods his agreement. "We'd follow you anywhere, Angel. Even death."

Tears spring to my eyes again and I let them fall. Tears are for the weak? No, tears are for those who have been so strong for so long and need an outlet to let it all out. Fuck those who think they're a weakness, and fuck my uncle for ever putting that notion in my head.

"Besides," Kaos continues, "don't you know that each of us

would do anything to keep you happy, including following you to the Goddess' realm to protect you?"

"Or, you know, in this case, the door to the afterlife," Dante quips with a nonchalant shoulder shrug, being the comedic relief that he always is. "Not to mention, I need more of that man's cooking. How else am I going to get fat and lazy without him around?"

I crack a small smile and launch myself at him. Dante catches me with an oomph and a chuckle. He runs his hand down the back of my hair, digging his fingers in before bringing my head to his chest. His very bare chest. Goddess, give me strength. I inhale his smokey scent, loving how comforting he always is.

Sudden warmth at my back clues me in to Kaos joining in on our hug. He plants a kiss on the spot where my neck meets my shoulder, sending a tingle down my spine. So much skin touching. Everywhere. My body is buzzing, singing in their presence.

Not to be left out, Reed joins the circle, spinning me toward him so he can give me a hug next. While I'm close to his ear, I whisper, "You and I are completing our bond when we get back to our realm." I pull back so I can look into his eyes. He looks slightly pained, which is not at all what I expected.

"I don't want to tell you to hurry back because you need to take your time with the shifter... but fuck, hurry back to me, Love," he responds, pulling me in for a passionate kiss, telling me with every brush of his lips exactly how he feels about completing the bond with me. I'm completely breathless and panting when he pulls away. Yeah, definitely completing the bond. These men are mine and it's about damn time I claim them.

Elian clears his throat, and I reluctantly pull away from Reed, but not before planting a kiss on his cheek.

"Could I have a word with you before you go?" Elian asks as I approach him cautiously, like one would approach a feral cat who has been known to claw you before.

"Sure, what's up, Elian?"

He looks away from me, but not before I see the pain flash in his eyes. He runs a hand over the small scars on his arms and, with his new attire, all his tattoos are on display. He looks glorious, yet so vulnerable. I hold my breath, waiting for whatever he's going to say.

"If you see my mother and sister on the other side... would you tell them I'm sorry I failed them? I—" He pauses to take a deep breath and gather himself. "I need them to know I'm so fucking sorry, and that I finally killed him for them. All those years pretending to be his protégé nearly fucking ruined me, but I did it."

He breaks off and returns his gaze to mine. It doesn't take a genius to know he's talking about his father, Elron. "And I'm sorry to you too, Sadie, but I don't regret killing him. Even if you're not much safer than you were before, at least you are a little with him gone."

I take a moment to ponder everything he's telling me because I can tell this is hard for him to say, let alone admit. I'm not sure how to feel about it. It's a side I've never really seen in Elian, but I'm glad he wants me to do this for him. I choose my next words carefully, hoping not to spook him. "Are they why you did it, why you killed your father?"

He nods. "I saw an opportunity and took it. I'm sorry it was at your expense."

"I forgive you, Elian. Thank you for getting all of us out of there safely." I place my hand on his cheek and he wraps his around my wrist. All I see is a broken, lost man played by the machinations of a cruel father. "And yes, if I see your mother and your sister, I'll tell them all about the man you're becoming."

Elian grips me by the back of the neck with his other hand and slams my mouth to his. His kiss sears me from the inside out, setting every nerve ending in me ablaze with passion. We're two souls intertwined in that moment, and I feel a part of myself heal inside with his mouth on mine. We could understand each other more than anyone if only he'd let me in. Hopefully, this is the start of that.

When we come up for air, he backs away. "Go, go get your shifter, and then return to us so we can prepare for war."

"Yes, sir," I respond, saluting him and watching as his eyes heat.

I tuck that little piece of information away for later.

3

When we reach the portal, the wolf guarding it spots us immediately—his yellow eyes zeroing in on us. The hair on the back of his neck rises and he snarls.

Fuck. What was his name again? K something... Keratin... Kerosine... Shit, why am I so bad with names?

Reed coughs. "Keros."

I shoot him a small smirk. "Thanks."

He winks. "Don't mention it."

Giving my attention fully to the wolf, I decide to address him confidently, but appropriately in hopes to *not* piss him off. Because a giant wolf is a little fucking intimidating. Like, he could swallow me in one bite. "Keros, guardian of the portal, my name is Sadie Sinclair and I come with the Goddess' blessing to cross over to the other side and retrieve my mate, Vinson Meadows."

He sniffs the air and snarls at us once more. His eyes shift from the molten gold they were a moment ago to a blazing blue—the same blue as the swirling portal behind him.

"Prove it!" he booms in a dark, otherworldly tone that

resonates like there are different voices layered within, echoing around us, even when it shouldn't.

Honestly, you'd think having my own talking familiar would prepare me for a giant talking wolf, but I don't think anything quite can describe the sight.

"The Goddess said I only have to tell you that I have her blessing." I warily turn my head to look at my mates like, *what do we do now? Ram this thing and hope for the best?*

Keros lets out a soft whine and I turn back to him to notice he's staring at my cheek. Confused, I bring up a hand to touch it, wondering what's making him stare at me like that. Oh right, the Goddess kissed me there.

He shifts into what I think might be his human form... Or at least, I think he's human. Other than the bright blue hair and swirling eyes, he could certainly pass for one.

Oh wait, nope, he has horns. Those are definitely tiny horns protruding from his forehead. Is he a… "Demon, yes," he says with a quirked brow, watching my reaction. And he's also reading my mind. Cool. Sweet. Kewl.

Don't freak out, Sadie. You already knew magic is real, why not add demons to that list?

"You have been marked, Shadowbringer, and therefore you may proceed." His voice is more normal when he speaks this time but is still a deep baritone. "I offer you my apologies for being cautious. Many before you have tried to cross this gate with unsavory intentions. It is my duty to keep the spirits safe. I will not fail them again." His face is pinched in anger with that last admission.

I look around in confusion. "Who else would be able to access the gate from this realm? It's not like you can just portal here. I don't think so, anyway…" I add the last part because I'm not exactly sure myself.

"You are right. You cannot, but this gate sits in many realms, Shadowbringer. Not just the Goddess' eternal realm.

For instance, it's under a lake in the realm you call Earth and next to an apartment complex in the demon realm. And it's mine and my brothers' duty to protect them."

Yeah, I'm not even going to try and comprehend the whole *this gate sits in many realms thing.* Nope, that one is way above my pay grade, and besides, talking to him is wasting time. Vin needs me. Even if time does work differently here, who knows if it does on the other side of this thing.

"I'm sorry, Keros, but I'm kind of in a hurry with trying to save my dead mate and all. So, if you would be an awesome protector and let me through, I'll get out of your interdimensional demon hair."

"Tell me again who you are going after?" Keros inquires, tapping his chin.

"His name is Vinson Meadows and he's a shifter."

He tilts his head skeptically. "And you said this Vinson is your mate?"

"Yes, we" —I gesture to my Circle— "seek to bring change in our world and peace between the Weavers and the shifters. Eventually," I add. I mean, Rome wasn't built in a day, and I'd be crazy to think years of prejudice would simply disappear overnight.

Keros looks thoughtful and then he smiles wolfishly, flashing his sharp demon teeth, suddenly dropping the formality for a more familiar friendly disposition. Somehow his teeth aren't scary though. They suit him. "Well, it's about damn time. We've been waiting for this change to come for what seems like ages. You've got a good head on your shoulders, Shadowbringer. Make sure you keep it that way. There are powerful forces at play in your world currently."

"Don't I know it. Wait… How do *you* know that?"

"Because I hear the whisperings of the dead. You've pissed off those bastards you call Elders. Royally. And they're gunning for you. But I quite like you, so stay alive. The

Weavers and the shifters have been separated for far too long. It's no wonder your magic is dwindling... But, ah, I've said too much." He turns and heads for the portal. "Come, it's time for you to go after your mate."

Finally! Not that the conversation hasn't been interesting, but I'm dying, soon to be quite literally, to get to Vin. The longer he's gone, the less I can feel him. I hurry along after Keros, trying to keep up with his steady pace. "Your Circle will need to stay on this side to protect your body. I'm assuming the Goddess has already warned you of the liabilities should anything happen to you or your body?"

"Yes, and I'm willing to take the risk."

"Impressive, given you will need to give him a piece of your soul, one you can never get back. This shifter must really mean a lot to you."

"I'd give it to him in a heartbeat. Not even death can take him from me."

"Aww, I totally ship it," Keros responds, and I gape at him. "What? I do spend days in the human realm from time to time protecting that gate with my brothers. I've picked up on a few human sayings."

"This guy just keeps getting more interesting," Dante mutters under his breath, making us all chuckle.

Keros watches us in amusement, but there's also a wistful expression on his face, like he longs for something more before it disappears in a flash, as if it were never there at all.

He comes to a stop before the portal, and I find myself entranced by it. Up close, it's even more mesmerizing. From far away, the black and blue looks like swirls, but up close you can make out some of the souls' features as they pass by.

"Stay focused on your task, Shadowbringer, and good luck."

Without another word or a warning, Keros pushes me into the portal and off into the land of the dead, simultaneously cutting my soul from my body as he does so. It happens so fast, there's no time to even process it before I'm being sucked into the In-Between. Before I'm thrust away, I hear the guy's protest, but there's no time to waste. I'm off to find my wolf.

This whole endeavor wasn't on my bingo card either. Man, I really need to start putting "expect the unexpected" on those. Maybe then I'd actually get a bingo.

4

The frigid air is the first thing to greet me on the other side, nipping into my skin and making goosebumps rise. I wrap my arms around my chest to try and hold in my warmth. This dress the Goddess put me in sure as hell isn't very warm, so I call the shadows to me and wrap them around me like a cloak, keeping the chill off me then I take a deep breath and crack my knuckles.

It's time to find Vin.

But first, I pause a moment to take in my surroundings. Everything looks deserted, cracked, and barren as far as I can see. It's dark, with barely any moonlight unlike the Goddess' realm, and everything has a blue hue to it, making the entire landscape seem more like a mirage than anything real.

Except for me. It seems I'm the only thing with any sort of color in sight. Which makes me a target if there's anything dangerous here, though my intuition isn't tingling yet. If my shadows weren't around me, concealing me, then I might as well be wearing a flashing neon sign that says, *I'm not from here!*

Perfect.

Wasting no more time, I close my eyes and find my center, concentrating on nothing but my mate bonds. Kaos and Dante's cords shine brightly while Reed and Elian's are there, but muted and have no color. Vin's is nowhere in sight and my heart plummets to my toes. Has he already moved on?

Surely not, or Keros wouldn't have let me into the In-Between, right?

Wait!

There it is—the faintest light. It starts to grow beside the others, and I stroke it, trying to imbue it with my energy, coaxing it back from the brink. Once it stops flickering and the energy strengthens, I pull on it and beg my magic to take me to Vin. My body jolts forward, faster than my eyes can track. I jerk to an abrupt stop, and the sight before me almost brings me to my knees.

"What? How? How are you still here?" I choke back tears, barely believing my eyes.

"Oh, kiddo," my dad breathes. "You look... so grown up."

I can't believe I almost forgot what he looks like when we share the same cheekbones and facial structure. Even his beard is still scruffy, which I remember always prickling me when I hugged him. Seeing him is like a punch straight to my gut because I've missed him so damn much.

"That's because I am," I respond and rush forward, not able to take the distance any longer. My dad was always a hugger. I attempt to wrap my arms around him, but I pass right through him, making him laugh.

"Hey, that totally tickled." When he sees my tears starting to fall, he sobers. "I'd love nothing more than to wrap you in one of our famous bear-hugs, kiddo, but I can't. I've been here too long to have any substance left to me."

"Why are you *still* here, Dad? I figured you would have already moved on..."

He smiles sadly at me and reaches his incorporeal hand up to stroke my cheek. The chilly air his hand feathers across my face brings me a small amount of comfort. "Unfinished business, tiger. Your mom knew you'd have to come here one day."

Tears sting the back of my eyes, and I open my arms for him again. He gets as close as he can without passing through me, and I pretend to lay my head on his shoulder like I used to when I was little, and he'd pick me up into his arms. "Oh, Dad. I've missed you so much. How could you just leave me like that? Especially with him?" My words surprise me as I thought I'd shoved those feelings deep down in my mental box but seeing him brings them all to the forefront of my mind.

His jaw clenches and he glances away. "Your mom and I suspected danger would follow you and Skylar, which is why we tried so hard to keep you both safe. You two were never supposed to end up with that bastard brother of mine, but he—he killed your mother. After that, I knew I had to do everything in my power to keep you and Skylar safe, but it still wasn't enough. Your brother filled me in on the details when he passed, and it enraged me. Your uncle wasn't always this way…"

I gasp, stuck on the part where he said Mickey killed my mother. "He *what?* Dad, I thought Mom died giving birth to me? This doesn't make sense."

Another spirit appears behind my father, and I'm rendered speechless at the sight of her. We look so much alike it's not even funny. Even with the blue hue tinting her features, I can tell we have the same bright, green eyes and wavy, blonde hair. Hell, even our posture is the same—like we're ready to take the world on at a moment's notice.

"Mom?" I question, even though I already know the answer in my heart. "Is that really you?"

She smiles sadly at me and it's like looking at a freaking mirror. "It's me, sweetheart." Her voice is soft and sweet—like a mother's should be.

"I've never even heard your voice..." I whisper, bringing a hand up to touch my own lips.

"It's so wonderful to finally meet you, but I need you to listen to me very carefully, okay? In my former life, I had the ability to see the future." She puts a hand up to stop me when I open my mouth. "Nothing like the seers. I can only see some details and aspects concerning my life, and the path I was supposed to take. Things have changed. The Elders and your uncle have upped their game and are more powerful than they were before."

"I don't understand. How do you know all this? Why—"

"The dead talk, Sadie. Staying here has given us access to this information and the ability to help you."

"Okay, I'm still confused though, so can someone break this down for me? Barney-style it or something?"

My dad chuckles. "You always did have quite the sense of humor, tiger. Long story short, we had to keep your mother's heritage from you and Skylar in order to keep you both safe. Bedi helped us lock your powers away and was supposed to help watch over you in the event we couldn't."

And what a wonderful job she did, I think with an eye roll.

"The past is the past. It's time for you to find out the truth, Sadie. The *whole* truth of who you are," my mom says.

"You mean the part of me that's still caged?" I ask, thinking of that small part of myself that's always been there, but I've never been able to access it.

"Yes." She pauses to inhale deeply while I hang on her every word with bated breath. "Your grandparents were a Light Weaver and a shifter, and they were true mates, against all the odds." Whoa, talk about a total fucking *bomb*. She doesn't give me a chance to say anything before continuing.

"I am half Light Weaver, half shifter, and your father is a full Night Weaver, which makes you the only known living Triad in existence. And since he was full, it makes sense that your Night Weaver abilities would be the most prevalent," she says, taking in my cloak of shadows with a certain fondness in her eyes.

"I'm a… *what?*" I demand, still stuck on that part. She can't drop something like that and continue without an explanation like she didn't reveal that I'm something new— something unheard of. For fuck's sake…

"A Triad," she repeats. "Part shifter, part Light Weaver, and part Night Weaver. The combination of powers mixing is a potent bunch. That's why the Elders and your uncle are so wary of you. You have a chance to stand up to them and have the power to back it up. There has been a lot of plotting and conniving on their end to bring us to this point. Which is why we hid all of this until it was time."

"But what about Dad? If you had magic, wouldn't I remember?"

My mother shakes her head. "Your father hid his powers from you. We also had Skylar's powers locked away because we wanted to give you both a normal life. It was safer that way, and the reason we hid in the human world. We even erased the archives of any mention of the Sinclair family. Back then, the world wasn't ready to know the truth of your existence. I'm still not sure if they are now, but it's time."

I finger Skylar's necklace for comfort and it makes me miss him. I wish he were also here because he always knew what to say when things were crazy.

"That's… I mean… This is a lot to process," I respond, not knowing what else to say. I mean everyone keeps telling me I'm supposed to be powerful, but to actually hear it from my own parents?

"When your uncle killed your mother and tried to absorb

her power," my dad starts. "I knew then that I had to do something to protect you both, because he'd come for you next. I went to Bedi, and together, we found an ancient spell to conceal both your and Skylar's magic. It would've worked if Mickey had never gotten his hands on you two. The spell hiding your brother's power broke under all the stress, and that's when Mickey knew and killed him. When yours never surfaced, he thought you were a dud and moved on."

I clench my fists. "That bastard!" I want to rage now that I know, not only did he kill Skylar, but my own parents too. That flame of anger inside of me burns brighter with each revelation that comes to light. Heads will roll.

I look at my dad, betrayal simmering in my eyes, which he doesn't miss since he's always been attuned to my emotions. How could he, of all people, hide something this huge from me? "Why, Dad? Why lie?"

"I'm sorry, kiddo, but it was the safest thing to do. There were many paths your mother saw that your life could take, and this was our best option." He tries to place his hands on my shoulders but sighs in frustration when they pass through me, and I shiver from the cold brush of air.

With that one defeated breath, I can tell he thinks he should be carrying the weight of the world on his shoulders, but he shouldn't. Not when he's supposed to be dead, partying it up with Mom and Skylar in the Goddess' realm. He shouldn't be here in the In-Between waiting for me with her.

My mother draws my focus back to her. "It's important for you to complete the bonds with all of your mates as soon as you can," she continues. "In the long run, it will keep you safer, since you will have their full strength to draw on."

Something occurs to me when she says mates as in plural. "Wait, if Night Weavers normally have harems, why don't I have more dads?"

She shrugs. "That, I'm not entirely certain of. If I had more mates out there, I never had the chance to meet them."

Fair enough.

My dad still looks guilty. "I'm sorry for all the things my brother put you through, Sadie. Not a day goes by that I don't wish I could've changed everything. Do you hate me?"

Do I?

Even with all the bullshit and the lies, I don't think I could ever hate him. From what I can tell he tried everything in his power to protect me and Skylar—even if I think some things could've been different.

"I could never hate you, Dad."

He smiles through his tears, a look of pure pride in his eyes. "I'm so fucking proud of you, tiger. And as much as I hate everything that you went through, all of it shaped you into the strong, take-no-shit woman you are now."

"Damn right it did."

He chuckles and doesn't bother to wipe his tears. "The best part about raising you outside of the Weavers community is now you don't have the same ideologies as them. Change comes with an open mind and thank the Goddess you have one of those."

"I mean, I'd kind of have to have one with five fucking mates and all."

He grimaces. "Yeah, I didn't need that mental image. Thanks for that."

"You didn't get to scare off any of my suiters with a gun, Dad. That was just payback."

My mom starts fanning herself. "Those men of yours… Phew, I couldn't have handpicked better ones for you." I laugh and she smiles at me. "I'm also proud of you, sweetheart. Don't let Mickey and the Elders get away with this. They weren't always as powerful as they are now. You only have to find what's giving them their strength, because it's not something they're getting from the Goddess."

"I won't let you down, Mom. Any of you. As long as I'm breathing, none of you will have died in vain."

"You could never let us down," she says. "We have the utmost faith in you." There's a shift in the air behind me, and I turn. "Ah, I was wondering when he'd show up. There's someone else here who'd like to say hello."

I'd recognize his energy anywhere. I whip around and face my brother. "Hey, little sis," he says and opens his arms for me.

I gasp and rush forward, forgetting they don't actually have bodies anymore, and flounce right through his incorporeal self, tripping and falling to my knees with an *oomph*. "Dammit, Skylar. You're such a dick," I say, standing and wiping my hands down my dress to straighten it.

"Aww, come on, little sis. I have to have some fun now that I'm dead," Skylar quips with a devious grin on his face, like always. He was always scheming, always had something up his sleeve. Like the one time when he came up with an insane plan of distracting the security guards at a concert by releasing squirrels he had been catching and training for days, only for it to backfire with those squirrels biting him and running away in the opposite direction. We definitely got kicked out of that one, but he ended up finding us the perfect spot to sit outside and listen. We made it our own mini concert instead.

His strength and resilience are why I am the way I am.

Moons, seeing him again makes me want to drive a stake straight through Mickey's cold, black heart.

"I can practically see the gears turning in your head from here, sis. What are you planning?"

Okay, so maybe we're not that different.

"I'm thinking about what I'm going to do to Mickey when I finally get my fucking hands on him," I respond.

Skylar smiles. "Make him pay, will you? This whole being dead thing sucks, but hey, at least I wasn't a virgin when I died, right?"

My mom's nose scrunches and Dad admonishes Skylar by smacking him upside the head. Since they're all spirits, his hand actually connects instead of going through. "Your mother and sister didn't need that information, son." He grimaces. "Frankly, neither did I."

I shake my head, extending a hand for Skylar to fist bump, then realizing it's pointless. "This whole being see-through thing is bullshit, but props, bro. And hey, now I'm not either." I cackle as he and Dad both grimace.

My dad's image starts to flicker around the edges. Now that I'm paying attention, they are all starting to flicker. "I'm afraid my strength is waning, tiger."

"It's time for us to move on. You'll have to handle the rest on your own," my mom adds.

"And, while I could spend eternity catching up with you, sis… Don't you have a shifter to save?"

"Oh my Gods, yes! His name is Vinson. Gah, you would love his cooking, Sky. He's a freaking genius with food."

"A good cook he may be, but the reason I'm quite partial to him is because he stuck with you when that ex of yours came after you," Mom says.

"You had an ex come after you?" Dad demands, his voice slightly warped from his form flickering. "Why didn't I know about this?"

"Yeah, he tried," I admit, thinking about the crazed look in Tyler's eye that day. I shove the memory away before it can overtake me. "But I killed him, don't worry."

My dad's jaw drops and then he beams at me with pride in his eyes. "That's my girl! You always were so independent."

Wait. He's... happy that I killed someone? Glancing around, I take in everyone's ridiculous smiles at the fact that I killed my ex, and their faces mirror Dad's.

Ah, family bonding over murder. So fun.

Each of them flickers out of existence completely, and my stomach drops to my toes until they return. I've missed them all so much, even my mom, who I never knew. Now that our time is truly coming to an end...

"Don't leave me alone again. Please," I whisper brokenly. "It feels like I'm losing each of you all over again. I can't take it. I can't let you go a second time."

"You're so much stronger than you know, tiger. It's time for you to embrace your destiny. But first, save your shifter and bond with your mates. Then go take down those bastards. Don't make any stupid choices, okay? The Elders and your uncle are powerful and have a whole army backing them. You're going to have to be smart about this." He sniffles but covers it up with a cough.

"Mom, I don't suppose you've had a vision about how to bring them down?"

She shakes her head. "Even if I had, I couldn't tell you or it might change the outcome."

"I understand," I respond, because I do. It also makes me a tad more sympathetic to Bedi. Besides, this is my last opportunity with my mom, and I'll be damned if I'm going to have my last moments with her be angry ones.

A portal pops into existence behind my family, but they're not paying attention to it. They already know it's time. Everyone's attention is on me, looks of sadness coloring their features—the same one's probably reflected in my own.

"I've cried enough today. I know it's time for you all to go, and it sucks, but I'm happy you're going to be moving on. Let's not say goodbye. I'll see each of you again one day. For now, though, I have unfinished business back on earth." I crack my knuckles as my words bring a smile back to their faces. My dad and mom give me another air hug before stepping inside the portal.

Skylar tries to ruffle my hair, but all he manages to do is to send a shiver through me. "It's nice to see you keep me close," he says, nodding to my necklace with a smirk on his face. "Even if it's a little macabre."

"You've kept me sane in so many scenarios, you don't even know, bro."

"I'll always be with you, sis." He steps into the portal where all their color returns, making them as bright as the sprawling landscape behind them. It's so wonderful to see them all looking vibrant again that it makes tears fall down my cheeks.

With one last look, they disappear, taking a part of my heart with them.

I wipe away the tears and focus on my center again, knowing I have a purpose here. I need to get to Vin. Picturing the threads that connect me to my Circle, I find Vin's which is glowing more than it was earlier. It gives me hope that he's hanging on. Maybe he wants to come back to me as much as I want him to. Wrapping my essence around Vin's again, I encourage it to take me to him.

This time, when my body comes to a stop, all the air leaves my lungs.

5

VINSON

I'm... dead.

My memories are quite hazy, but that's a fact I remember clearly. Alongside the Elders... the blinding pain... Sadie begging for my life... *Sadie.* A sharp pang of longing shoots through me at the thought of her. Her bright, beautiful eyes, her gorgeous smile, her tantalizing scent. All the moments I've protected her in her dreams... even though she doesn't remember those.

What I wouldn't give to be able to do things with her differently. I wouldn't hesitate at the chance to see if my hunch about her being my mate is... was correct.

My wolf sure seemed to like her anyway. A smile comes to my face when I think about him jumping and wagging his tail in my mind every time she was near. Combined with that delicious scent of hers and his insistence she was the one... It was all I could do to not lose control around her and say fuck the consequences.

I'd lose that control if I could go back.

Speaking of my wolf, a hollow feeling blossoms through my chest when I try to mentally reach out to him and find him gone. And man, it's fucking empty without him. Technically, I've never met him in person, as shifters can't shift before they meet their mate, but he was with me mentally for as long as I can remember.

His loss is staggering, reminding me of what's happening. I need to focus and figure out where I am and how to get back to Sadie, if I even can, because this whole death thing is bullshit.

Unfortunately, everything after Sadie begging for my life is blank. Obviously, I'm dead, but these aren't the beautiful meadows I'd pictured from the stories of the Goddess' eternal realm, so where the hell am I?

Why am I here?

And how do I go about defying death?

Taking in my surroundings reveals absolutely nothing. It's an empty wasteland as far as I can see. The scents are as dull and muted as the barren landscape. My sense of smell when I was alive was quite strong but being dead must've changed it. I look down at my body and find I'm tinted blue but still solid, which is strange. I figured I'd be more... ghost-like?

I might be wrong, but I don't think I made it to the Goddess' realm. Hopefully I'm not being punished for something and ended up in the bottomless pit of the underworld. That would really fucking suck. Even so, I'd still fight every demon, clawing my way out to get back to Sadie if that's what it takes.

Can one fight their way out of death?

Guess I'm going to find out.

I can't stand here forever. I need to get a move on and see if I can figure out what's going on. The best way to do that is to find someone or *something* who knows.

I don't make it more than six steps in the direction I picked before something tugs on my chest, which still feels really, well, *alive* for me to be supposedly dead. The tug reminds me so much of Sadie that it hurts. What I wouldn't give to see her again, to touch her, to go back to that moment of her walking down the stairs in that divine dress and kiss her senseless.

I rub my hand against the phantom ache in my chest, trying to ease it, but it's no use. Her essence is firmly wrapped around me and it's not letting go. When the feeling eases enough for me to focus, I continue walking toward the pull, letting my instincts guide me.

I'm getting out of here. One way or another.

I have no idea how long I've been traveling aimlessly, but I haven't come across a damn thing so far. There aren't any other souls in sight either, which is strange.

"Goddess?" I call out. "Can you hear me?"

No answer.

I run my hands through my hair in frustration. How am I supposed to get back to Sadie and my wolf if I can't get any answers?

The tugging sensation grows in my chest and this time I close my eyes, concentrating on the feeling. Sadie's comforting scent wraps around me like a lifeline and I latch onto it, letting everything about her consume me until it almost feels like I'm with her.

"My Moon, I miss you so fucking much. Even in death, your sweet scent taunts me."

"I'm here, Vin," her voice says in my mind, and I curse it for seeming so real.

"As much as I wish this was one of my dreamwalks, I'm afraid that's not possible. Unless you were dead, and in that case—"

My eyes snap open to find a radiant Sadie standing in front of me. She looks absolutely stunning in a dress that resembles something the Goddess would wear. She's beautiful, but if she's here, that can only mean one thing…

"No, no, no… you can't be here." Shock and despair wrap around my heart like a vise, warring with each other. "You can't be dead, Luna. I was coming back for you, not the other way around!"

Sadie chuckles, confusing the shit out of me, and wipes the tears from her eyes. I hate seeing her cry and it makes me want to brush them away. "Vin, I'm not dead. Technically, anyway. It's so damn good to see you."

"It's good to see you too, my lovely Moon," I say breathlessly, hoping her statement about not being dead is correct. "But I don't understand. If you're not dead, then how are you here? Where are we?"

"We're in the In-Between," she explains. "As for the other half of your question, let's just say, it's a good thing I'm favored by the Gods." She rubs her thumb along her necklace, which is a sign she's nervous. I can only imagine the pressure she's under. I'd give anything to take it away from her and put it all on me.

I reach out to smooth the wrinkle out of her brow and she tenses, so I pull back, but not before my skin grazes her cheek and we both suck in a sharp gasp. It's as if an electric current slams into us both and she throws her arms around me. It's all I can do to open mine in time to catch her.

"I thought you would be see-through like my family, but you're solid!" she exclaims.

I have no idea what she means, but I don't question it. Instead, I thread my fingers through her hair and cradle her head to my chest. "I never want to let you go again, Luna."

"Then don't," she whispers. "And don't fucking die on me

again. I'm, like, ninety-percent certain this" —she gestures between us— "is a one-time deal."

"What's a one-time deal?"

She looks around like someone might be watching us, but when she doesn't see anyone, she returns her attention to me. "The Goddess and her consorts allowed me to come in after you."

My heart starts to beat wildly in my chest. She wanted to come and get me as badly as I wanted to get back to her. "There are so many things I wish I had done differently with our time together. Like, I would've kissed you that first time in the kitchen when you had jam on your face."

The memory makes her smile. Goddess, she's so damn beautiful. Her smile alone is enough to make my heart race.

"I guess what they say about not knowing what you have until it's gone is true, huh?" she replies softly.

"Extremely. And I'd do anything for you, my Moon," I tell her with complete conviction.

She pulls back to look at me while tracing my lips with her fingers, making me utterly aware of every place her skin is touching mine. My mouth goes dry, and I lick my lips. She follows the movement with her eyes, focusing on my mouth. If only we weren't in a barren landscape, I'd take her right here.

Sadie's nose scrunches, and I find it so adorable that I have to stop myself from booping it because I remember she doesn't like it when Dante does it. "Why does that nickname seem so familiar, yet I don't remember you ever calling me that?" she asks, still not moving her gaze from my lips, like she's picturing how they'd feel against hers.

"Ah, well... That night at the pack party, you might've mentioned to me that you have horrible nightmares almost every night. Then you fell asleep in my arms." I pause, thinking back to that night and how it made me feel. "The fact that you felt safe enough in my presence to fall asleep was something I never dreamed of. I was overcome with an urge to help you in the only way I knew how."

She gives me a confused look and my admission breaks her focus on my mouth. Her green eyes return to mine, almost taking my breath away. "How was that?"

I open my mouth to explain my secret power to her, then stop myself. I've never admitted this to anyone but dying has put a new perspective on my life, and I decide to say fuck it. Besides, she's my mate. I know it in my heart.

"I have this special power when it comes to dreams," I admit out loud for the first time in my life. "When I visited you in your dreams that night, I called you my Moon, because of your Night Weaver powers."

"How did you discover you had this power?" she asks.

I think back to the first time I discovered dreamwalking. I had to have been about sixteen at the time and had a crush on this girl from my former pack. "Ah, it's kind of an embarrassing story." My face heats, and Sadie chuckles.

"Tell me anyway. I want to know everything about you."

"Well, I had a crush on this girl at the compound and wanted to know more about her. When I went to bed that night, I immediately knew something was different. The dreamscape I was sucked into was completely disorienting and nothing like normal, but then instinct kicked in, and I figured out what was happening. I was going to use this chance to find out what she liked, but she was taken away a few weeks later, and I heard she was killed."

"I'm so sorry, Vin," she says, sorrow tinging her tone. There's not even a hint of jealousy in her eyes.

"It's all right. It was a long time ago and she wasn't my mate," I tell her softly. "After that, I started to use my connections with my pack to explore dreamwalking, trying to find out what all I can do… Until I realized it was unheard of for a shifter to have power, so I stopped. I hadn't dreamwalked in years before I slipped into yours.

"What I have figured out is that I can only do it with people I have strong feelings for and connections with. Even though I haven't done it in years, I tried pushing myself to learn more about the Elders through their dreams, but since I hate them and have no relationship with them, I've never been able to get very far. I promise I've tried to help you in whatever way I can, my Luna."

Sadie looks contemplative, like she's trying to digest what I'm saying, and my heart starts to sink. Is she going to accept me and my strange ability?

"Are you the reason why I haven't had many nightmares lately? That was because of you?" she asks.

I nod, watching her sort through her emotions. She has one of the most expressive faces, and I fucking love it. I love knowing exactly how she's feeling. It's like she's an open book. "I've visited you almost every night since then to keep the nightmares at bay."

A huge grin breaks across her face at my admission and she throws her arms around me again. "Thank you, Vin. Seriously, those nightmares are a bitch sometimes. Sleeping beside someone usually helps, but not always."

"It was my pleasure," I murmur. "I knew I couldn't afford to show you affection during the day for fear of the repercussions, so I felt like I needed to do something for you at night. Honestly, it's the least I could do for my mate."

She grins. "Mate, huh?"

"Er, yeah," I admit. Saying it out loud feels right. "I never should have doubted it, but I didn't think it was possible between a shifter and a Weaver. I feel drawn to you in every way there is. As soon as you came into my orbit, I knew you were going to be trouble, and yet, my wolf and I didn't care.

We wanted you. We *want* you, Sadie Sinclair." Finally saying all of this out loud is like a weight lifted off my chest.

Hopefully, she has a plan to get us out of here alive because there's no way I'm giving her up now. She's mine.

Sadie cups my cheek. "Well, that's a good thing, Vinson Meadows, because I want you too."

Our gazes lock and our mouths inch toward each other. I glance down at her plump lips, and ask, "Can I kiss you?"

"Yes," she breathes against my lips. We are so close, it would've been impossible for me to pull away if she had said no, so thank fuck she said yes.

That's the only invitation I need. I descend onto her mouth like a madman starving. She gasps and I take the opportunity to slip my tongue inside as she kisses me back just as fiercely. She tastes amazing, almost exotic, and her sweet flavor is enough to drive me wild. I've wanted to kiss her forever it feels like, and it's happening. Like fate has finally led us to this moment. I never want to let her go because kissing her is like fucking nirvana. I wrap my fingers through her hair and tilt her head while I continue to kiss her senseless.

When we both need to come back up for air I pull away, but only slightly—enough that I can look into her eyes. "You are perfect, Luna. Thank you for coming to rescue me."

"I'd do anything for my mates," she responds and captures my lips again.

6

SADIE

As much as I want to feel Vin's lips against mine forever, I pull back with a sigh. "We probably shouldn't linger here much longer. I don't want you to bond with this place and be stuck here."

Vin shivers. "I don't either. I want to kiss you more when I'm alive again, my Moon, so how do we get home?"

"In order to bring you back, I need to give you a part of my soul," I explain, watching his reaction. His eyes widen, but I don't give him a chance to say anything. "I'm ready to do so if you are."

Vin contemplates my words for a moment, staring at me with those golden eyes of his. "Is it dangerous to do this? Will it hurt you?" he asks, always more concerned with my safety than his own as he cups my cheek.

"It'll only weaken me for a bit, according to the Goddess." I place a gentle kiss against his lips. "For you, it's completely worth it. I'd give all of you a piece of me if you guys needed it."

"You've given us that and so much more," he responds. "I'll gladly take a piece of your soul, Sadie, but only if you allow me to give you a piece of mine in return." He punctuates his point with a soft poke to my chest.

I shake my head. "I couldn't, Vin. Your soul needs to heal, whereas mine is fine."

"I'm not negotiating on this, Luna. I want you to have a piece of me too." I can see in his eyes how determined he is about this. It's mixing with the love and adoration on his face.

Even though we're on a time crunch, I decide to go along with it, knowing he's not going to change his mind. "I'm not exactly sure how to do this, so bear with me, okay?"

"All right. Let's do this," Vin agrees.

I close my eyes to concentrate and let my magic guide me, urging it to give a piece of myself to Vinson, forever. I open my eyes to catch the shadows wrapped around me come to life, swirling as they form themselves into a ball. Opening my palm, I beckon that part of myself to me and instinctively place the shadows over Vin's heart, watching as they dissolve into him.

The expression on his face can only be described as awe. He looks up from where the shadows—a piece of my magic and my soul—went into his chest and his face lights up like he's feeling me inside of him. I've never seen him look so happy as he does in this moment, and it makes my heart leap for joy. For him.

Vin does the same for me, but instead pulls the power from his head. It's golden, like his eyes. When he places the ball over my heart, I feel his essence enter me and it's a shock to my system. For the first time, I can *feel* him inside of me. A piece of his soul, so wild and untamed. His foresty scent wraps around me, gifting me with his adoration. I love feeling him inside me like this. It's foreign, but also not.

I know why he looks as happy as he does, because now I feel it too and it's… unlike anything I've ever felt before.

So perfect. So beautiful. Mine, I hear him say in my head, and I blush.

"Ready to go home?" he asks aloud, and I nod, still giddy with the feelings coursing through me.

I bite my lip. "Wait, I have a question."

"Ask me anything, Luna. I'll answer it if I can." His face is soft and caring as he gazes at me. It makes my heart swell knowing he means it.

"Do you think the shifters will follow me?" I ask, a certain vulnerability in my tone. I know it's not solely my responsibility, but I want to atone for what they've been through. They deserve better. Plus, they're my people too, and I'll fight just as hard for them as I will for the Weavers.

Vin strokes my cheek. "I know they will," he responds with complete conviction. "Some of them will choose to stay with the Elders because that's all they've ever known, but a lot of us want freedom and our salvation."

I glance away from him. "I'm afraid, Vin."

He brings my gaze back to his. "Of what?"

"Failing," I admit softly.

"I've never known you to be a quitter, Luna. Or a failure. You can do this. You have a whole Circle of Sworn rooting for you. We won't let you fail."

"You mean it?"

"Of course, my Moon." The firmness of his statement fills me with joy because he doesn't even know I'm part shifter yet. So the fact he has such confidence in me before knowing is a testament to his faith in me. "Now, how do we get out of here?"

I pull out the small chunk of shadestone Bedi gave me after my ceremony and stare at it. Confusion rocks through me at how this small stone is both my ticket to home and a weapon of destruction. I'll never forget how Elder Reginald used my own dagger to kill Vin.

That's something else I haven't been able to figure out. How was he able to handle it? I thought only those who were considered worthy could wield it. And it certainly burned Elian's father when he tried to use it against us, so why not Reginald?

What are we missing?

"You're staring at that piece of shadestone like it holds the key to the universe," Vinson softly interrupts my mental thoughts, stroking his fingers down my arms.

I sigh. "Yeah, it's... Well, nothing makes sense. Reginald…" I have to pause and crush down the grief that wants to well up inside of me thinking about Vin's death. "He killed you with a shadestone dagger—*my* shadestone dagger," I correct, guiltily.

"Don't," he says, imploring me with his eyes to listen as he rubs his hands up and down my arms. "Don't do that to yourself, my Moon. It wasn't your fault." When I look at him, there's nothing but honesty written on his face.

"But wasn't it?" I whisper.

"No," Vin affirms, pulling me into a bone-crushing hug. "They planned this. They had everything ready to make you submit to them."

"I could've been stronger—I could've made my move when they were distracted with Elian and Elron. I could've reacted faster, maybe grabbed my dagger back before they did. I was just so shocked by Elian's outburst..."

Vin pulls back so he can look me in the eyes. "Nothing would've changed. What happened that night was meant to happen. I don't blame you and you shouldn't blame yourself either." He lifts my face to his, placing a soft kiss on my lips. "So, don't beat yourself up, okay? You came after me. You, a Night Weaver, actually came after me, a lowly shifter."

I smack his arm playfully. "None of that lowly crap, you

hear me? You and I are equals. We're mates. You can't really get on more equal footing than that."

Vin's eyes heat when I claim him as my mate again. He smiles down at me and pulls me into a breathtaking kiss, bending down to capture my lips, and I rise to my toes to meet him. I love how all of them are taller than me.

"Gods, I'll never get tired of doing that," he rasps against my lips. "And as much as I'd love to continue, I think we should get going. We can resume this later."

My lips form into a pout that makes him grin. "Yeah, yeah, you're right," I agree reluctantly. I could spend forever in Vin's arms, but it's time for us to go back. Something tells me we're needed. "The others are probably ready to come in and yank me out at this point."

"I'll bet they are. Come on, let's go home, Luna," Vin says, and I make sure he has the shadestone before reluctantly stepping away.

"Since your body is in our realm, but mine and the others are in the Goddess' realm, I'm going to send you back first. Then I'll use my tether to get back to the guys. Hopefully, since time works differently, you won't even know I'm not there."

"Sounds like a plan, my Moon."

"Okay, close your eyes and concentrate on home... on your wolf... on me being there to greet you in person." His lips quirk with that one. "And then let the magic within the stone guide you there."

Vin pops one eye open, and says, "I'll see you soon."

"See you soon," I echo, and then he's gone.

I can't believe I actually did it... I brought Vin back from the dead.

Now it's time for me to get the hell out of here too.

Focusing on my own magic, I picture my tethers connecting me to my Circle for the third time, stroking each bond with my mental finger, shivering when I feel their answering strokes. "I'm coming home, mates," I whisper.

"Actually, before you go, we'd like a moment of your time, if you don't mind," a familiar voice says.

Huh?

I whip around to find Jimmy and Nicole Campbell, Ashley's parents' apparitions standing behind me. "It's so good to see you again, Sadie," Ash's mom says quietly. She gives me a small smile, but that's not what I'm focusing on. She looks extremely worse for wear. They both do. Instead of being a blue tint like my family was, she and Jimmy are a sickly green color.

"What—How? What's wrong with you two?"

Ash's dad sighs heavily, rubbing his temples. It's something he did a lot while he was alive and the movement brings me back to all the meals sitting around their dining room table, all the game nights we shared together, everything. But thinking of those nights and about Ash's betrayal is enough to drive a stake through my heart.

"That's actually what we're here to talk about," he says at the same time I speak.

"I can't believe she betrayed me."

"Oh, honey, I know, but you must understand... Your uncle is controlling our corpses. His magic is strong enough to reanimate us for short periods of time and yank our souls from peace and into the In-Between. Everything about it is perverted and wrong, but Ash thinks it's real." Her face twists with anger. "She's overcome with a need to get us back even though it's not possible."

I look at Jimmy and he nods, looking exhausted and defeated. "You have to convince her to let us go. We are well and truly dead. The bodies Mickey is controlling to force her compliance are not us, but he has somehow convinced her they are. It's hell for him to do this to us, the pain he puts us through each time is excruciating."

"She's not going to believe me when I tell her all of this. I know how she is, and I know how much she loved you both. If she thinks you're back…" I trail off.

Jimmy nods like he expected as much. Ash gets her hardheadedness from him, that's for sure, so he likely understands more than anyone. "I figured. That's why we came up with an idea. Tell her the memory of us debating pancakes and waffles over brunch the morning of our crash. Say waffles are just pancakes with abs and she'll know."

My mouth pops open. I'd never thought of it like that but dang, waffles really are pancakes with abs. The memories from when I lived with them pop into my mind, and I think about all the breakfast foods we used to eat. That was their favorite meal of the day. The loss makes my heart ache. "Okay, I'll tell her," I respond, pulling myself from those thoughts.

Nicole sniffles. "You must stop him, Sadie. Please, let us rest in peace. Tell Ash the truth."

"I'm so angry with her." I run my fingers through my hair. "Why didn't she come to me about this? I could tell something was off, but... it's so much worse than the normal drama I expected. I thought she needed space after what happened. I never…" I let out a breath. "But after I saw your graves had been disturbed, I should've known. *Fuck*."

After having to leave my family behind for a second time… the anguish of having to say goodbye again. Well, I think I understand Ash's motives, even if they still pain me to no end. If I thought I could get my parents or Skylar back, would I jump at the chance?

I certainly jumped at the chance to get Vin back.

Ash's grief-stricken face invades my thoughts. I can't help but wonder where she is. I need to see her again if only to at least try to make her see past her grief. To tell her about her parents and Mickey's warped magic. It's the right thing to do.

"You have every right to be upset with her," Jimmy says softly. "But you should also know everything. Mickey put a geas on her so she can't speak about us, or what happened to her when she was abducted. We heard him put it on her when he brought us back the first time. He tries to pull our souls back too, but that goes against the laws of nature, so it only ends up torturing us, but it's convincing enough to fool Ashley."

Anger courses through me. "I swear when I get my hands on him..."

They both chuckle. "He deserves whatever punishment you dish out for him."

"I've missed you both," I admit, wringing my hands together. Seeing so many of my loved ones I grieved in the past is taking a toll on me. Without Vin to distract me, I'm feeling quite melancholy and guilty for my uncle's actions.

Ash's mom's face contorts with sadness. "We've missed you too, sweetie. Both of you. I've always counted you as my second daughter."

"Our time together was short, but you made such an impact on our family," her dad agrees, then suddenly turns and looks behind him, nodding before he turns back to me. "I'm afraid it's time for us to go, kid. Tell Ash the truth. Make her understand."

Nicole starts to weep silently. "If anyone can get through to her, it's you."

I nod. I may still be angry with Ash, but I know her better than anyone, and I'm not willing to throw our friendship out yet. We've been through too damn much together for that. My distrust won't go away overnight, but I need to give her the chance to make amends because that's what family does.

"I'll do what I can because she's like my sister."

Nicole smiles. "I think it's time you head back too, hun. Your mates are starting to get antsy. If you're not back soon, they're going to send in the cavalry." She winks at me, and I give them a small smile of understanding. One second, they are there and then the next, they're gone and I'm left fucking confused as hell.

My uncle, Mickey, is a necromancer.

Apparently a powerful one too. Just when I think I've found out the important stuff about magic, the universe throws a crazy, body snatching, soul ripping, psycho my way.

Fucking great.

Before I can leave, I have one more piece of unfinished business. Even though Elian's mother and sister aren't here physically, I decide to say it into the void. Hopefully, wherever they are, they can hear me. I tell them about how we met, about how he killed Elron, and all about the man he's becoming.

I never thought I'd say this, but I'm falling for the brooding asshole. It makes me chuckle slightly. Women always fall for the bad boys, don't they?

When I'm finished, I feel the need to add, "I promise to look after him since you can't anymore. Elian deserves a little love and happiness in his life after all the shit he's been through."

The featherlight caress is all the answer I need as to whether they heard me or not, and it feels distinctly like a *thank you*.

7

SADIE

Getting out of the Goddess' realm was a lot easier than I expected. I used our tether to get back, and my mates were exactly where I left them, waiting for me at the entrance to the In-Between. The God of Light popped back in to escort us out and bam, we were home.

I told them everything that happened while I was gone, literally everything from my new Triad status, to Vin, to what Mickey is doing to Ash's parents. They were shocked, but at least now we know what I am and have a tad more information.

"Dammit! Why isn't he awake?" I demand, pacing the floor in the foyer of their estate.

Thankfully, while we were gone, someone cleaned the blood from around Vin's body. If it weren't for the stains on his clothes and the dagger in his chest, I could almost forget it ever happened. Except he's not awake, and Hemsworth is missing.

I'm close, don't worry, Hemsworth speaks into my mind, and it makes me suspicious. What is that dog up to?

"We've only been back a little while, Angel. Give it some

time. You remember the Goddess said time works differently in her realm. It seemed like ages there when only an hour or two passed here."

"Gods." I let out a breath. "I hate when you're right."

Dante smirks. "I know."

I smack his arm lightly for his cocky remark. "Watch it, Blondie. I'll make you put your money where your mouth is."

He places a hand over his heart and pouts. "Oh, Angel. You wound me. You really should kiss me to make it all better."

"Nuh-uh, you've used that line on me before... Wait, his heart!" I turn, studying Vinson once more. "Should we take the dagger out?"

Kaos kneels next to him and seems to contemplate what to do. "Maybe the shadestone resonated with the bit in his heart and brought his soul back, but we need to do the rest. Good thinking, Little Flame."

Suddenly, there's a loud crack, and as if speaking the words aloud causes the dagger itself to act. It flies out of Vin's chest and clatters to the floor next to him, now in several shards.

Reacting quickly, Kaos places his hand over Vin's wound, and it immediately starts to glow black as the familiar sight of his magic enters his body, and this time... it actually seems to be working.

Relief flows through me when he says, "The chest wound is healing." That tiny sentence is enough to make me feel like a lead weight has been lifted off my shoulders. But I also notice the black veins scrawling up his neck are still there, so I add my own magic to the mix, hovering my hands over where he took the blast, watching as the lines slowly begin to dissipate. Thank the Goddess.

Another crack splits the air, but this one is different. This one is like bones breaking and grinding together as they try to realign themselves. The sound sets me on edge and my eyes snap back to Vinson as his body contorts.

Kaos and I are forced to scramble away when there's a blinding flash of light that surrounds Vin. The next thing I know there's a giant black wolf—almost as tall as me—in Vin's place, surrounded by writhing shadows. He looks intimidating as hell, with his eyes a molten gold, meaning the wolf is in charge. He's twice as big as the other wolves I've seen.

"Holy fuck. Is he smoking?" Dante asks, looking from me to Vinson.

"No… those are my shadows," I whisper in awe, studying the magnificent creature before me. "Fuck. Yes."

"What the hell?" Elian asks, eyes flickering between us. "Why did he shift?"

"When mated shifters are severely wounded, we shift to help heal the wounds," Alpha Darren says, strolling into the entryway, startling me. Apparently I'm not the only one startled as we all jerk to look at him. The man is so tall he almost takes up the whole doorway. His beta, Carter, trails in behind him. He's a tad smaller than Alpha Darren, but not by much. I can see why Ash was struck by him. He's cute, but he doesn't hold a candle to my mates.

"How did you know he shifted?" I ask.

"I felt his wolf starting to emerge as soon as his soul snapped back to his body. I am his Alpha after all." He pauses, and a smile plays on his lips. "Not to mention, Hemsworth showed up and said it was urgent, so I came right away."

Hems struts out from behind Alpha Darren with a little shit-eating grin, showcasing his teeth. "I'm glad to see you accomplished the mission, Weaver." He trots over to my side and stands on his hind legs to give me a lick on the cheek. I wrap my arms around him and squeeze. "Mhpmh—" he mumbles.

"What?" I pull back so I can hear him.

"I said you were suffocating me, jeez."

I ruffle his fur, making sure to give him an ear scratch since I know he loves it. "I missed you, you little shit."

"You were only gone for, like, two hours," he points out.

"It felt much longer than that. I'm glad to be home, and I'm glad I could save him."

Alpha Darren clears his throat. "If you two are done, I'd like to focus on the matter at hand."

"Of course. Sorry," I apologize. "Do you know how long he will stay shifted?"

"It's hard to say—"

The wolf version of Vinson lifts his head, and those golden eyes zero in on me like I'm a juicy steak and he's starving, which he probably is after expending so much energy. Well, and being dead, but we're not going there.

He pushes up from the ground with his massive paws, stretching, testing out the waters before his eyes lock in on me once more and he descends into a crouch, lowering his head to the floor and prowls toward me. One step after another. The shadows swirl and coalesce around him with each step.

Alpha Darren tenses, and says, "Don't move, Sadie. His wolf is testing you."

Pfft. Easier said than done. Vin's wolf is enormous. Seriously, his head is to my chest. It's hard not to feel a little intimidated, even if I know the human version would never hurt me. The beast is very different.

When Vin's wolf reaches me, he pounces, tackling me to the floor. A very unbadass-like squeal escapes my lips as I hit the hard floor with his wolf on top of me. He nudges my cheek to the side with his snout and proceeds to... lick me.

He freaking licks me with his rough ass tongue and sends

an echo of his adoration for me through our newly formed soul bond.

"Jesus, Vin! Get off me, you big oaf. Your tongue is a lot rougher than a cat's!" Not to mention it kind of tickles and I'm laughing like a loon in the middle of our foyer.

His wolf seems to pout and huffs a breath in my face then his eyes return to their normal golden color, one I know well. Vinson is in control. Our mate bond sizzles between us, stronger than ever, like it's reminding us it's there. The feeling is intoxicating.

There's another bright flash of light and a totally naked—totally human—Vinson now rests on top of me in all his glory. And damn if it isn't glorious. Abs on display for days, giant… ahem, package dangling, ripe for ogling.

Am I drooling?

Eh, wouldn't be the first time I'd drooled over a man. No shame.

"Hey, wolf," I say to him playfully.

He leans his body weight off me with one hand and with the other he reaches up to caress my cheek. A spot on his wrist captures my attention and I pull it toward me to get a better view. "Holy shit," I breathe. "You have my mark!"

He looks down in confusion, but when he sees my mate mark on his wrist, complete with a wolf connecting my moons, his entire face lights up like it's Christmas morning and I'm his present he's been dying to have all year. I wonder when he'll unwrap me…

"This is amazing," Vin says in astonishment. "I wonder if you'll have a wolf too…"

But I'm no longer focused on our mate mark. Nope, something larger, quite naked, and at full mast has captured my attention.

Godsdamn, he is packing. Is that thing even legal? There's no way it's fitting inside me, though I do love a challenge…

I must project my thoughts to him because he looks from me to his package, to the others around us and smirks. "Shifters are normally okay with nudity, but I'll uh, go put some clothes on for everyone else's comfort."

"Aww, don't ruin my view." I pout and look at the rest of my Circle. "Actually, I wouldn't mind getting all of you naked."

Whoa, where did that thought come from?

Alpha Darren makes a choking noise and Hemsworth groans, reminding me we're not alone. "Okay, fine. Not the time or place. I get it. Go get changed, Vin. I think we have a lot to discuss."

He winks at me and heads off in the direction of the room he was staying in before everything went down. I *totally* don't watch his tight ass as he disappears down the hallway. Nope. I'm paying attention to whatever Alpha Darren is saying.

Elian tenses, going on high alert. That brings me back to the moment real fast. Especially when he pulls a crotch knife from... wherever the hell they get those damn things, and palms it with practiced precision. "Someone is here. They just crossed the ward," he growls.

Reed shifts nervously on the back of his heels, and I turn my attention to him while the others swiftly burst into action. He looks guilty as fuck and my heart stutters. I can't take any more bullshit today.

"Is there anything you want to share with the rest of us, Red?" I ask, trying my best not to sound accusatory. The tension in the room is now aimed at Reed as everyone focuses on him. The others stop in their tracks to focus on him.

He wrings his hands. "Actually, yes. I may have called in reinforcements before we ever went to the challenge and told them to meet us here."

"What do you mean by 'reinforcements?'" Elian asks with

an edge to his tone, looking lethal with his blade in his hand. He doesn't fuck around when it comes to the safety of his Circle.

"She's a family friend and here to help us," Reed defends.

"Who is *she?*" Kaos demands, watching Reed closely. He expertly spins his karambit for emphasis.

"Well, that's no way to greet a lady, is it?" Just as the last syllable leaves her mouth the glow of a portal opens in the foyer and a small, silver-haired, older woman pops out of it. Her face is equal parts cunning and wise as she gazes around the room, taking all of us in with a single sweep. Interesting. She looks to Reed. "You rang, my King?"

"Uh, Red?" I interrupt. "Care to explain?"

Reed clears his throat. "Everyone, I'd like you to meet, Matilda. She's a master with portals and one of my family's biggest allies." His face sobers and turns haunted. "Thankfully, she is gifted with portals as she was able to sense the Elders coming that night, and grabbed as many Light Weavers as she could, shielding them so the Elders couldn't get to them."

That must be how some of them survived and sent him the letter.

"That I did," Matilda cuts in. "Good thing too, or the whole faction would be gone. Minus Reed. Those Elders though... I've never seen anyone with that kind of power. It ain't natural." Her face is pinched in distaste.

I take a moment to study Matilda, mentally sizing her up. Her stature leads me to believe she's strong. Her hands are calloused, which likely means she didn't sit around all day. No, this woman has seen some shit.

"Well met." I extend my hand for her to shake and, at first, she looks at it like it's going to bite her or something. Then a broad grin stretches her face, and she clasps my hand in hers.

Nothing about her sets off any of my intuition alarm bells either, which is a good sign.

Honestly, the older woman reminds me of Bedi before she transformed into a younger version of herself. And for her to appear to be this old… she really must be.

Speaking of which, where is that dang Seer?

I remember her grabbing ahold of us before Elian shadowed us out of the Elders' garden, but I haven't seen her since.

"Has anyone seen Bedi?" I ask. Knowing her, she's probably pulling the strings from behind the scenes somewhere, but dammit, she has some explaining to do. My uncle acted like he knew her, and I want to know how. Plus, what the Goddess and my parents said, I *need* to know more.

Kaos clears his throat. "She took off while you were… um, grieving. Said something about how she'd be back when you complete the mate bonds with all of us. I didn't stop her because I needed to tend to Elian." He looks slightly guilty for letting her go so I squeeze his hand, so he knows I'm not mad at him.

"Thank you for taking care of Elian, Steel. I appreciate you taking the time to heal him for me." Creeping up on my tippy-toes, I plant a kiss on his cheek before taking a step back so I can look each of my mates in the eyes.

Kaos' blue ones soften with understanding. Dante's green ones shine as he looks ready to go to battle for me at a moment's notice. Elian's emerald ones are exhausted looking, but he gives me a small head tilt. Reed smiles and his gray eyes are shining with unfulfilled promises.

We'll get to that, I project, knowing he'll understand my meaning.

And then I look over to Vinson who is coming down the steps after having quickly gotten dressed. My fifth mate.

Fucking hell. I have *five* mates. Five. I'm going to be so sore in the future. Kaos' healing ability may be put to the test.

I realize I'm probably being rude and turn back to Matilda. "It's nice to meet you, Matilda. Any friend of Reed's is a friend of mine."

"Likewise, Shadowbringer."

"I'm curious though, why are you here?"

That brings a cocky smirk to the older woman's face. "My King thought you would need my help. And since the Elders have been trying to find a way to bypass Elian's ward and portal in to kill you, I'd say he was right to call upon me."

Ah, hell.

8

SADIE

"Whoa. Say what now?"

My mates tense behind me and Elian steps forward, angling his body as if to protect me. The gesture is slightly jarring. I'll have to get used to seeing him act like this, instead of as a colossal asshole.

"Don't get your knickers in a twist, boy. Your wards are strong but, with this heightened state the Elders are in, *they* are stronger. It's only a matter of time. In fact, I'd say we have twenty minutes before they're slaughtering you like they did us."

Everyone jolts at the mental image her words cause. Shit. This is bad. Vinson lets out a growl that says *over my dead body*, while the others tighten their grips on their crotch knives.

Reed takes a deep breath, and I can almost see him mentally shoving his feelings down as he steps forward and draws our attention to him. "I know there's bad blood between Night and Light Weavers, and that won't go away overnight, but I have a plan. Let me explain."

"Then fucking explain it, Reed," Elian demands, his

patience with the whole scenario wearing thin. That man craves control, and all of this has been the furthest thing from it.

"Matilda knows her stuff with wards and portals. With her knowledge, your ability with wards, and the natural resistance of Light magic, I think we could fortify the Soleil family safe haven long enough to buy us the time we need to plot against the Elders safely. I also think Sadie's abilities will allow her to be a buffer between the different magics. She can be the conduit we need to bring it all together. The haven should be virtually untouchable by anyone who wishes us ill will."

I see Alpha Darren's face fall, and it makes my heart twist. "That sounds amazing, Red, but what about everyone else? The shifters, the Night Weavers who want change, and your Light Weavers?" I interject, waving toward Alpha Darren. "I'm not leaving anyone behind."

"That's what I admire about you, Love," Reed says with a broad smile, which I return with a small one of my own. "The safe haven is large enough to house everyone and then some. We could set it up as a refuge of sorts, taking in anyone that wants to defect from the Elders."

A *refuge.* That word hits me hard because it almost sounds too good to be true, and I've always been wary of things that sound a little *too* amazing, but if we could pull this idea off?

Ever since I found out about this community and met everyone, I knew it was going to be my calling to bring change, and now that it's here... It brings me immense joy. Honestly, this feeling is something that can't really be explained in words, but I'm looking forward to what the future holds for one of the first times in my life. Even after everything that's happened, a warmth spreads throughout my body at the prospect.

I give Reed a nod of thanks, hoping I'm conveying exactly

what I'm going to give him as soon as I can to further express my gratitude. He's seriously saving all our asses here, and I'm beyond ecstatic for this idea of a safe haven. "That sounds brilliant. What does everyone else think?"

Kaos nods, and I can tell he's having the same thoughts as I am, running through all the possible scenarios in his head. It's one of the things I truly admire about him. "I trust Reed, although I do think we'll have to iron out the logistics, but overall, I like the idea."

"Me too," Dante agrees. "I think it could work."

Vin is looking at me in awe. "I do as well."

Everyone's attention turns to Elian, and we watch as his jaw clenches. "I don't like it." I shoot him a look with my eyes narrowed. "Because of the safety aspect, but I also don't see another option. Matilda is right. The Elders are trying to sneak their way in here. I almost overlooked it with everything going on." His face is pinched like the admission pains him to say. He might as well have sucked on a lemon before speaking, but he's right. This is our best option for now.

"Then it's settled," I announce. "Everyone, get a move on. Grab anything essential." Kaos and Dante head up the stairs to grab our go-bags. Yep, I convinced them to make some of their own. They're definitely coming in way handier than I ever expected. I turn to Alpha Darren and Carter. "Can you have the shifters ready and back here in fifteen minutes?"

Alpha Darren's head snaps up as he looks at me, shock coloring his features. The same is reflected on Carter's face. "Wait, you really want us to come?" he asks in disbelief. I guess most Weavers would leave them to die or use them like they're expendable. Not me. Not anyone who aligns with us during this.

"Of course, I do," I respond gently, but firmly. "I won't leave any of our people behind. It's time to break the mold."

CHAPTER 8 | 63

I may only be a quarter shifter and may never have a wolf emerge as I haven't had any inkling of one yet, but they're my people now too.

Alpha Darren's jaw hits the floor as he stares at me in wonder and suddenly drops to one knee. Carter does the same. *Uh, what the hell is happening?*

"I pledge my life unto thee, Sadie Sinclair," they say in unison.

"If you have any need for us, then all you have to do is call and we will be there fighting by your side along with my entire pack at your back," Alpha Darren finishes. People bowing to me is so freaking weird. I probably look like I'm the one who just sucked on a lemon now.

Hemsworth snickers, sensing my discomfort, and I shoot him a dirty look to which he gives me those innocent puppy eyes. Ugh, can't stay mad at that face, dammit.

I realize they're still on their knees and probably waiting for me to say something. "Umm, wow. Thank you, Alpha Darren and Carter." *Really, Sadie? That's the best you could do?* I clear my throat to try again. "For now, though, go get the shifters ready. I know everyone won't want to go," I say, thinking of the traumatized shifters from the compound. "But I trust you can get them on board."

I'll process what the fuck just happened later.

They both stand. "You truly are the one we've been waiting for," Carter says in awe.

"And I'll do you one better," Alpha Darren says with a wink. "We'll be back in ten." Both he and Carter jog out of the house, letting out a long howl that I sense is a signal to the other shifters.

I return my attention to Matilda. "How many can you portal out at once?"

"My abilities are not infinite, but I'd say I can make it

wide enough to transport six through at a time. Maybe more."

Six at a time. It'll take a bit but we'll make it work. "Good, we can work with that."

There's a flash outside and then a knock at the door. My temper spikes when I recognize the signatures standing outside. "What the fuck do you want? And why are you here?" I call out.

"Mind if we go with you, wherever it is you're going? Since we're kind of disgraced for helping you," Adam says sheepishly, coming into view with his brothers and Emma in tow. They must've portaled in. Dammit, why did we give them permission again? Oh, right, because they saved Ash for me the first time.

"You have quite the fucking nerve, Adam," I snap, thinking of how he and his brothers fucking ditched us in the garden. "You were going to leave us there."

Guilt colors his features, true guilt too. He genuinely feels bad, but it doesn't ease my anger. "I'm so fucking sorry, Sadie, but we had to protect Emma above all else. Our mate means everything to us."

"Then why are you here and not somewhere safe? If you hadn't noticed, your fathers are outside trying to tear our ward apart."

"Because we have to protect Emma and you're our best shot at that," Nick, one of the twins, says, and his brother nods his head in agreement.

"We would do anything to protect her," Adam agrees. "And that meant leaving you behind."

Emma looks livid. She rears back and smacks Adam across the face with perfect form, just like I taught her. Adam's mouth pops open in shock as he rubs the spot, looking awestruck with her. Pfft, dude is pussy-whipped and she's oblivious. Not that I blame her for being cautious with who they are. Hell, even I'm extremely wary of them right now. I don't fucking trust them and their intentions.

"That's for leaving my friend!" Emma exclaims and walks over to our side. I give her a high-five. I know I haven't known her for long but I can see her becoming one of my best friends… Maybe once I forgive Ash, we can create a cross species women's fight club or something. Where we teach and inspire women of any species to defend themselves.

"Thanks, Em," I whisper.

"Anytime, Sadie."

"As cute as this is," Elian starts with an eye roll. "I think we need to discuss the trio coming with us. They're a liability, and I don't trust them. At all."

Kaos and Dante reemerge with our bags draped over their shoulders. Kaos takes in the scene in a single glance while Dante looks pissed.

"No, we are not," Nick counters. "We could help you."

"How are you not? You could lead them right to us," Elian snaps back. "How do we know they're not here right now *because* of you?"

Adam's face is devastated at Elian's words, and my intuition isn't giving me dishonest vibes. Godsdammit.

"They've disowned us completely," Adam says. "After everything went down, we received a fire message from their missive stating we are accused of treason. Since we are their sons, they are sparing our lives this once, but if they ever see us again, we're dead. We have nowhere else to go," he admits quietly. "Meeting our mate has completely opened our eyes. We've been so foolish."

"But we are not our fathers," Niall, the other twin, adds.

"No, you are not," I agree, something in my gut urging me to trust them. "Guys, they probably have inside knowledge that we may need. It could be vital. I'm not saying let's trust them implicitly, but maybe keep them on a short leash?"

"I'm prepared to swear a blood oath," Adam states and steps forward and the mood instantly changes. Swearing a blood oath in this community is huge and speaks volumes about Adam's intentions. "To prove to you that we are serious about leaving our fathers in the past."

Reed, who has been watching them closely, is the first to speak. "If the time comes, are you prepared to kill them, if need be?" he asks. That question is probably more personal for him, considering their fathers killed his father... and made him watch.

"Yes," Adam replies without hesitation.

I turn to my mates and pull us all into a little huddle. It's not like the others can't hear us, but it gives me a small sense of privacy. "I get it. It was one thing to let them into the estate under supervision to visit Emma after giving us Ash. This is different, but where do we draw the line? I don't think any of you would say you'd have done it differently if the roles were reversed."

Their faces turn slightly sheepish because they know I'm right. If I was in Emma's shoes, they would've shadowed me out of there faster than you could say *run*.

Adam looks to Reed. "I'm extremely sorry for the pain and suffering my father caused you and your people, but I want you to know we're with you, all of you, for this mission." He glances to Emma, eyes full of love. "I want a safer world for our future. One where we're not judged because of who our true mate is."

Elian is the one to break the silence, and his nostrils flare. "Fine, but you will swear the oath to me, Adam. Because if you renege on your word, you know I *will* hunt you down." The feral grin on his face shouldn't turn me on, but it totally does.

Adam gulps. "D-Deal."

"Wrap this up, kids," Matilda chastises. "We're running out of time."

Elian nods and drags his crotch knife across his palm then hands it to Adam who does the same. "I, Adam Adair, pledge an oath to Elian King, that I will not reveal or otherwise disclose any information to my fathers about you, your Circle, or anyone else. We will abide by your rules. So let it be bound."

"So let it be bound," Elian echoes, placing his palm against Adam's.

"Never thought I'd see the day this fucker pledged an oath to Elian." Dante snickers but covers it up with a cough when Elian shoots him a look.

Alpha Darren jogs into the foyer and announces, "I've gathered the pack. Everyone is waiting outside." He's slightly out of breath, but I'm glad he got everyone ready so quickly.

"Perfect timing," Matilda says gleefully, clapping her hands together. "Shall we?"

My Circle, along with Emma's, Alpha Darren, and Hemsworth, follow her out to the front lawn where all the shifters are gathering. I'd estimate there are around forty or so of them, plus the shifters from the compound who are huddled to the side, near the others, but far enough away for them to feel comfortable. It's certainly an improvement over when they feared everyone.

"Sadie," the brave one from the compound that usually addresses me calls out, and I head over to her with my mates and Hemsworth in tow. "What is going on?" she asks with worry in her gaze. "The Alpha wouldn't tell us much but said it's life or death."

I debate for a moment about cushioning the truth, but ultimately decide to tell them exactly what's happening. Even though it pains me because it's technically my fault.

"The Elders are coming here to slaughter us." Gasps ring out through the crowd as everyone hears and grows antsy. "And it's because I refused to bow to them," I say, addressing all of them this time. "But please, do not fear. As a Triad, a person of all three species, and the Shadowbringer, it's my duty to bring change and peace." The shifters start whispering amongst themselves. Someone murmurs about their family and a thought occurs to me that we haven't discussed yet.

I mentally reach out to the guys before saying anything out loud. *What about their friends and families that aren't here? We can't deny them that.*

Kaos ponders my question. *We'll find a way to get the word out. Anyone is welcome to join us.*

I could kiss you right now.

You'd have to plant one on all of us, Angel, and we're on a time crunch, remember?

Later then, I promise.

"If you choose to follow us," I continue, raising my voice to allow everyone to hear my words, "I will ensure your friends and family have a safe haven and a chance for a better future as well. One where everyone is equal. Not only am I a Triad, but I also have a mate from every part of our magical community, and I propose we start a new status quo."

My mates stare at me with pride in their eyes as every shifter raises their voice and say, "To the Shadowbringer!"

9

SADIE

Once my speech is over with, the whole crowd is buzzing, waiting for us to take them to the safe haven. We return to where Matilda is standing, and I swear I see a spark of pride in her eyes, but if it was there, it's gone in a flash.

Without warning, she throws her hands up in the air, conjuring a ball of light between her palms. She lets the power grow and grow until she considers it big enough and throws it beside her. It takes the form of a mesmerizing, swirling gold portal straight out of a freaking movie or video game.

The color is so distracting that I almost miss what she says. "It'll take a minute to get it ready for everyone to pass through," she tells me. "While I'm making it larger, feed your power into the ward. The Elders are... close."

Her warning isn't necessary, though. A sick feeling settles in my stomach, setting my intuition ablaze. A shock wave rolls through me, and I fall to my knees from the force of it. Vinson is the closest one to me and is by my side a split second later. He asks me something, but I can't seem to hear him. The only thing I can focus on is the ever-growing nauseating feeling that something is wrong.

Chaos erupts around me as everyone jumps into action. Matilda works her hands faster, feeding the portal. Alpha Darren starts barking orders to Carter, who runs off toward the women and children.

My mates circle me as another wave hits me. "I'm fine," I grit through clenched teeth. I feel like a damn live wire getting ready to blow. They're close.

"It's the ward," Elian declares to the others, his voice breaking through the fog. "She helped me strengthen it and now it's feeding off her to keep them out."

"How can we help her?" Reed asks.

He shakes his head. "We need to get her out of here. It's only going to continue to get worse the longer they try to get in."

"Matilda," Reed calls out. "I need you to hurry up!"

"What do you think I'm doing, boy, frying an egg over here? I am hurrying!" she sasses back.

If my brain wasn't foggy as hell, I might laugh at their banter.

The Elders batter against the ward again and the force undulates through me. Honestly, I'd be surprised if my hair wasn't flying in fifty different directions, like when you touch one of those static electricity balls.

"I've got it!" Matilda shouts. "Everyone, get through *now!*"

Reed grabs my elbow to help me from the ground and starts to shuffle us toward the portal, but I dig my heels in to stop him. "No, everyone else goes first!" I shout.

"Absolutely not," Elian snaps. "You are the main target."

"If we go through first that leaves the ward unpowered. The Elders will annihilate them. I'm not leaving them to get slaughtered." He grits his teeth and Reed stops tugging on my arm. "Go, help the others get through."

Adam steps up to my side with Nick and Niall not far behind him. "Stay with your mate," Adam tells my Circle. "We'll help the shifters get through." Then the trio takes off to do just that. I watch as they simultaneously work as a team to keep everyone moving in an organized fashion. With six people going through the portal at the same time, thankfully, it doesn't take long to get them to the safe haven.

Another shock wave breaks through me, and this time it renders a scream from my throat. Everything about the magic feels wrong. Vile. Evil.

They're here.

My fears are confirmed when I find the Elders standing in front of me with my Uncle Mickey in tow. The guys are facing me, so they haven't seen them yet. The assault on the ward is over, but I'm still nauseated by the sight of them and from the power they used to break in. I watch as their stupid cloaks billow in the unseen breeze behind them. I wish this were a superhero movie where they'd get sucked into a jet engine. It sure would make my life a hell of a lot easier.

"They're here," I tell my mates hoarsely, locking eyes with Reginald. That fucker stabbed my mate. A red haze descends on my vision and all I can think about is stabbing him in the heart then ripping it out and doing it over and over again. The shadows start rising off me like steam, sensing my need for vengeance.

He smiles and it's that same bone-chilling sort of smile from the first time we met. "Hello again, Mercedes." His eyes flick to my left where Vinson is standing, and his smile dissipates. "How? How is he alive?" he demands like a child throwing a tantrum.

"You know, you assholes are really starting to get on my nerves. Get fucked, Reginald."

My uncle snorts. "She always did have quite the temper. It was so fun punishing her for it. You know, I could've reanimated him for you if you really wanted him back that badly." His words are nothing more than cruel taunts, and I'm not going to give him the satisfaction of seeing his words strike me.

Instead, I flash him a sickly-sweet smile, teeth and all, wishing they were sharp like Keros'. "Don't worry, Uncle Mickey. You can get fucked too. You always were such a piece of shit. It's no wonder you've teamed up with the fucked-up threesome. What I still don't understand is why? What use are you to them?"

Vald steps forward like he's going to be the peacemaker. Yeah, like I'm buying that. How stupid do they think I am? "Must we fight like this?" he asks. "You know what to do to make all this go away, Mercedes. Say you'll bow to us and no one else will get hurt."

I snort. "That's the thing. You hurt people every day, and I won't stand for it any longer." I chance a glance at Matilda and the portal, which is about ten steps away. The Elders are about twenty. All the shifters have made it through safely, minus Alpha Darren and Carter. The two of them alongside Emma and the trio are going through now so that will only leave Matilda, me, and my Sworn.

It'll be close, but I think we all can make it.

"You mean the inconsequential shifters?" He laughs and it grates on my already shot nerves. "They're nothing. They mean *nothing*. Little more than pigs for slaughter." Vinson growls at him like *I'll fucking show you nothing* and it totally soaks my panties. Seriously, that's hot as fuck. I think I might be a tad fucked in the head.

On the outside, I keep my face blank even though I'm imagining clawing his eyes out. That's about the only thing keeping me from reacting to his words. "Well, as fun as this has *not* been, Reggie..." I pause, smirking when his nose turns up at my nickname for him. "It's time for us to bounce. I'm sure we'll see you soon enough."

Giving everyone a silent push through the bond, I make a break for the portal. I'm unsteady on my feet, but thankfully, Vin keeps me upright. Testing the waters, I throw a tendril of shadows over my shoulder at the Elders, hoping to distract them long enough for us to get through safely, but even with the blackness hurtling toward their faces, they don't even so much as flinch. My shadows glide over them like they're not even real. What the actual hell?

"You're right," Reginald agrees.

Right about what? Seeing them soon?

Then it dawns on me. They weren't here to kill me; they were here to taunt me. Unease skates down my spine, but the good news is, we're too close to the portal for them to retaliate. I guess this truly proves the theory about them being untouchable, though. And they fucking know it too judging by the look of triumph on their faces.

Matilda hops in first, keeping it open from the other side then the six of us plus Hemsworth are next and it's barely wide enough to fit us through.

"We'll find you, Mercedes, when it's time." Those ominous words are the last thing I hear before stepping into the portal, and it sends a chill through me.

The feeling of the portal overtakes me before I can really think about what they mean and then I'm sailing through time and space. I think. Not exactly sure how these damn things work. It's as if every molecule in my body is split apart and then rearranged on the other side. It spits us out smack dab in the middle of a meadow with small cabins surrounding us on all sides. It's a disorienting feeling to be in one place one moment and another the next. Handy, but confusing.

And why am I on the ground?

"Welcome to the safe haven," Matilda says, smirking when she sees my bewilderment and all of us on the ground, except for her and Reed who have likely traveled this way before.

Even Hemsworth seems a little woozy. "Remind me never to travel that way again," he groans.

Matilda laughs. "It's a little disconcerting at first, but you'll get used to it."

Reed helps me to my feet by my elbow, and I notice the shifters who were portaled in before us and the trio are exploring the meadow and the cabins. I'm glad we're surrounded by woods because I know the mated shifters are going to love to explore them in their wolf forms.

"Wow," I say, in complete awe of this place. "When you said safe haven, I thought you meant an actual house. Not *houses*. There have to be at least fifty cabins here or more."

"Aye, and with bunks in most of them. I'd say they're able to house roughly ten or twelve each," Matilda says.

"Which means—"

"We have plenty of room for anyone who wants to join us," she supplies with a small smile tipping the corner of her lips.

Excitement flows through me at all the possibilities. "This is incredible. Now we just need to get the word out safely."

"Indeed. But leave the world saving for another day, will ya? First, let's get you all settled. Seems like you've been through the wringer." Matilda walks off without another word. Wow, she's a firecracker, that one. I'd love to see her and Bedi interact. If only I knew where the latter was and what the hell she's up to.

I glance at the guys and they all have varying degrees of smirks on their faces with Reed's being the broadest. "We better follow her. She won't wait, trust me," he tells us, shaking his head.

And she doesn't either. Matilda doesn't even lessen her

brisk pace to let us catch up as she leads us through several rows of cabins, all of which look fully furnished until we reach a larger, central cabin.

In front of it is a circle of people, sitting around a small fire, chatting and laughing amongst themselves.

Most of them seem to be about the same age as us, with a few older. When they see us approaching, they seem excited at first, then their gazes move past Reed and onto the rest of us and their expressions morph into shock. I'm assuming these are the last of Reed's faction of Light Weavers.

A man with ruddy, brown hair and smooth facial features questions, "Wha–what are they doing here, Matilda?"

Matilda looks at me with a devious smile splaying across her lips and gestures as if to say, *you can handle this one.*

I step forward and clear my throat. Might as well rip the Band-Aid off, right? "Hey, my name is Sadie Sinclair and I'm Reed Soleil's mate. These are my other mates—"

A girl with bright pink hair to the left of the ruddy, brown-haired man scoffs, cutting me off. I notice she drops his hand when she stands, but I don't see a mate mark on either of their wrists, so I'm assuming they're not true mates. I don't initially sense anything off about her with my intuition, but she's definitely not hiding her disdain for us.

"That's impossible," the girl says and her voice is slightly nasally. "You're a Night Weaver. Your kind hates ours. It's your Elders' mission to wipe us from the face of the planet. How dare you suggest that you are our King's mate?"

Reed steps in front of me. "Don't, Merri. She *is* my mate and therefore you know how protective of her I will get."

Merri looks at the man beside her, back to Reed, and then sits back down with a huff. I can tell from where I am standing that she's biting her cheek to keep from saying anything else.

"Ignore Merri, darling. She and Jack have issues," A man

with well cared for golden curls stands and bows his head slightly to me. "My name is Auryen, and I can tell you, judging by everyone else's emotions, most of us are super intrigued about you. Even if we are a bit leery of Night Weavers."

That catches me off guard. I'm used to Weavers hiding their powers, but seriously, why all the secrecy? Why should they?

Oh, wait, the psycho Elders looking to exploit any and everyone.

"Mostly because of your intimidating mates though, but like, damn, girl. I'd eat the pissed off looking one for a snack." He's right too. Elian looks ready to stab someone. Then again when does he not? But even the rest of my Circle still has their crotch knives out as if they're preparing for a fight, and Vin is a weapon in his own right, now that he has his wolf. "Please, tell us more."

"Honestly, neither of us are really sure about the how's and why's," I say, indulging him. I need to win them over if we're all going to win in the long run. "But we aren't going to spit in the face of fate when we've obviously been paired together for a reason."

I give Reed a quick smile to find him already looking at me with a thousand emotions written on his face. He smoothes them out quickly, turning his leader aura back on.

Auryen full-on laughs at me. "Oh, darling, I don't care about the specifics! I meant for you to tell me about how you met. Was it love at first sight? Did he give you one of his shy smiles and you fell for it instantly? Gah, I'm such a hopeless romantic." He sighs dreamily, placing a hand on his forehead to really sell it.

"Oh, uh, actually, we met at the diner where I worked."

A blonde girl with soft features gasps. "You worked in the human world?"

"Yeah. I wasn't raised as a Night Weaver."

They all start gossiping amongst themselves, growing louder as they talk. I can't really make heads or tails of it so I just kind of stand there awkwardly while they cast strange glances at me like I'm the freak show in the room full of magic users.

"All right, guys, you can interrogate her later. We've had a hell of a day and it's not over yet. Elian and Sadie need to strengthen the wards and that's going to take a lot out of them," Reed speaks up, interrupting their chatter.

"Aww, fine," Auryen says with a pout. "We expect details sometime though." He winks at me, and they pack up their things. Two of the men stay behind but stick to the shadows. Guarding us, I presume. I am in the presence of royalty after all.

"Don't remind me." Reed groans, picking up on my train of thought, and I laugh.

"I think it's kind of hot, King Reed."

He casts a devious look my way. "Oh really, Queen Sadie?" he quips right back, and my face twists. I don't know how to feel about being a queen, but I guess it's technically my title.

Elian breaks up our banter, his nose crinkled at our display. "Come on. Let's go strengthen these damn wards before I gag. They're already quite strong, but we can make them better."

I reach out with my own power and find that he's right. Actually, I'm pretty impressed. The wards around this place feel strong, like they've been tempered by a multitude of different people and powers over the years, which should work in our favor in keeping the Elders out. Hopefully, Elian and I can bolster them even more. Guess we'll find out.

"That's enough for tonight, Elian," I tell him when I see the sun is starting to crest the horizon. "I'm beyond exhausted and I want to go crawl in a nest with my Circle and say fuck the world for *at least* twenty-four hours. Maybe forty-eight for good measure."

"I agree," Kaos says, wrapping an arm around me.

None of them have left my side. Even Vinson, who has to be the most drained of all of us. Matilda didn't leave either, giving Elian and I advice as we worked to strengthen the ward.

And boy, have we strengthened it all right. This damn thing is absolutely buzzing with power. I'm not a hundred percent certain it wouldn't fry someone with ill intent if they got within a few feet of it. No one that wishes us harm is getting in without us noticing, that's for sure.

"Matilda, if you'd show us to our quarters, please," Reed says, and she nods.

"Right this way." She leads us to the larger cabin I noticed earlier and opens the door, gesturing us inside. "This one belongs to the Soleil family. No one has lived here in quite a number of years. We cleaned it up as much as we could, but you might want to open some windows and let it air out. I'll bring over a fresh set of towels and linens." With that, she disappears.

Kaos lets go of my shoulders so I can walk inside, and the others follow suit, spreading out in different directions like they're looking for intruders. I don't even say anything. I can't fault them.

First, shower.

Then, bed.

Man, I'm more tired than I realized. I guess having a fight to the death, a standoff with the governing body of my secret magical community, and going to the In-Between to save one of my mates from death has really taken a toll on me.

Who would've thought?

"Where are you going, Love?" Reed asks. "The bedroom is this way."

"Shower," I mumble.

"I'll set a towel on the counter for you when Matilda gets back," Kaos calls out behind me. So thoughtful. He deserves a blow job, or five.

"Thanks, Steel," I respond.

Swinging the door open, I fumble for a light switch and grumble when I can't find one anywhere. The bathroom is pretty dark, but surely there's one in here somewhere, right?

"Here, let me help," Reed says, conjuring a ball of light in his hand. When I give him a look, he smiles. "We have the power of light at our fingertips, Love. Why would we pay for electricity?"

True fucking that. Electricity bills are outrageous. Smart Light Weavers.

"Wait, how do you power the water heater then? I need hot water, Red." I am one cranky bitch when I have to take a cold shower. I've taken many of them in my broke years, and it's not something I enjoy.

He chuckles. "Solar power, of course."

Thank. Freaking. Goodness.

Reed tosses the ball of light at the ceiling and the whole bathroom instantly illuminates. He kisses me on the cheek and then leaves me to it without another word, knowing I need a moment to decompress. I shut the door to help keep the heat in and turn the water to scalding. Because what's a shower if the water is not hot enough to melt the skin right off your bones?

This isn't the nicest bathroom I've ever been in, I think to myself, staring at the wooden walls, floor, and stone-tiled shower. I've been in much worse ones though, so this works perfectly.

I start stripping my dress from the Goddess off, already feeling the water calling my name. Since it's so beautiful, and I don't want to mess it up, I carefully fold it and place it next to the sink. Then I hop in the shower and let the warmth seep into my bones. When I turn to get my hair wet, I realize there's no shampoo, conditioner, or even bodywash. I sigh and resign myself to a water only rinse.

It's better than nothing, right?

Someone clears their throat, and I yelp. My eyes spring open to find Vin standing stark naked and holding three bottles behind me. Conditioner. Shampoo. Bodywash. Hello, my old friends!

I practically snatch the bodywash from his hands and squirt a shit ton into my palm. Then, it hits me.

"Wait, what are you doing in my shower?"

"I thought you could use a hand," he responds sheepishly.

I raise an eyebrow. "And the others let you come alone?"

He smirks, and the sight of it makes me want to see him do it more often. I take a moment to study his delicious body. He's lean but extremely toned from working every day. His brown hair is longer than usual and hits his shoulders in small waves. I glance at his chest and find it scar free, which makes me happy. I'm glad he's not scarred because of me.

"I guess I drew the long stick this time," he quips.

"Mhm, I see," I say, lathering the suds in between my breasts. His eyes drop to track the movement, then flash gold like his wolf is peeking through. He looks back up to my face and they return to normal. "So, there are actual sticks you draw then?"

Honestly, this is probably their way of welcoming him into the fold, and it makes me fall harder for each of them. They know what I need without me even saying it. Besides, who am I to argue with their hierarchy?

"Something like that," he says distractedly, watching me lather myself. "Here, let me help you. I know you're tired."

"Thanks." I hand him the bottle of bodywash, which smells surprisingly like Reed, and he squirts a large dollop in his hands. He motions for me to turn around and immediately starts on my neck and shoulders. I moan. Out loud. Very loudly. Because it feels so fucking good. I'd kill for him to do this all the time.

"That can be arranged, you know." There's a husky edge to his tone as his hands slide down my spine. I arch into him, loving the way his calloused hands feel against my skin that he's starting to build into sensual strokes and teases.

"Wait a damn minute. You're not a mind reader too, are you?"

He chuckles. "No, Luna. You do say a lot of your thoughts aloud. I think it's adorable." His hand grazes the top of my ass, but instead of actually touching it like I want, he skirts around it and his hands resume work on my shoulders. What did I say about needing to decompress? I take it back. I need Vin. Stat.

"Mmm. I think you missed a spot, Vin," I say, desire coursing through me and heading straight toward my throbbing clit. I can feel his own desire in my chest, foreign, but also not, and it amps up my own passion. We're bonded in soul, but we need to be bonded in flesh.

Vinson groans when he makes another pass on my back and I arch into him. "My Moon, I'm only so strong," he murmurs. "I don't want to take advantage of you while you're so exhausted."

"I suddenly find myself no longer tired." I turn back around to face him and grab his hands, placing them firmly on my ass cheeks. His own arousal is hot against my belly. "Now, would you mind?"

His dick thumps between us, and I glance down at it,

zeroing in on the giant's club like a beacon and I'm a ship lost at sea. I want nothing more than to wrap my lips around it and bring him to the brink of pleasure before he loses control and fucks me hard against the wall of the shower.

I'm fucking drenched, and it's not only from the water dripping down on us. His nostrils flare as he scents my desire. It draws a growl from his lips and he starts kneading my ass. I'm still distracted by his fucking Thor hammer down below, suddenly finding myself dying to know how he tastes.

So, since he's still hesitant, I decide to show him I'm not, and drop to my knees in front of him. My lips part as I lick up his shaft. He shivers, and I take the opportunity to put his enormous length into my mouth.

Vin hisses and drops his head back in pleasure, his long hair now wet from the shower. "Fuck," he strains to get out. I watch from my position on the shower floor and the sight of him losing control when he is always so careful to keep himself contained, and his wild almost feral sounds he's making spur me on even more.

I start bobbing my head up and down his cock, setting a steady pace. He wraps his fingers through my hair and grips lightly. Not enough to hurt, but enough to make me moan around his dick.

"Just like that, Sadie," he praises, his voice sounding deeper than before. "You're doing so good. Just like that."

His hips thrust a little—almost like he can't control it—pushing him further into my mouth. "Gods, you're so fucking beautiful. I love seeing your perfect lips wrapped around my cock, Luna. I've imagined this moment so many times."

I grip his ass and push him as far as I can take him into my mouth, encouraging him to let loose. He starts thrusting, making the most amazing half growl, half moan sounds as he does. He uses my head to control his pleasure and I fucking love it. I love seeing him like this. So utterly carefree. He was always meant to be this way—to be with me. Now with our souls and his pleasure mingling, it feels so right.

Vin suddenly stops and grips his dick at the base before pulling out of my mouth. Panting, he says, "I need to be inside you. Now. Is that okay?"

"Yes, Vin. Please. I'm so fucking wet. I need you."

"I need you too, my Moon." He helps me from my knees and hefts me around him like I weigh absolutely nothing at all.

"Fuck, Vin. The strong man thing is definitely working in your favor," I rasp as he adjusts his grip under my ass, positioning my core to his. He backs me into the wall and the tile is freezing which, in turn, makes my back arch into him, pressing my breasts against his chest. His eyes flash golden again, letting me know the wolf is peeking through. I love being able to feel his heart beating against mine when not that long ago, I felt it stop and thought I'd lost him forever.

"You're a fucking vision right now, Sadie. Absolutely gorgeous." He devours my mouth. No, we devour each other —our tongues clashing in our fervor. Claiming. Owning. My senses are alive from his touch, his kiss, his scent, his soul.

The warm water sprays onto us, little droplets hitting me in the face, but I don't care. Vin's fingers drop between us to find my center and he groans when he finds the wetness there. He startles me when he snarls and then pops those digits into his mouth, tasting me. The sight of it makes me gasp and then moan.

He notices the look on my face. "I'm a chef, darling, don't you think I've been dying to taste you?"

Fucking hell, we were made for each other.

"Please, Vin," I beg.

"Ask and you shall receive," he responds, lining up at my

entrance before pushing in ever so slowly to give my body time to adjust to his size, but that's not what I want.

Using my upward advantage, I push down until I'm fully seated on his dick, making him curse. My eyes roll to the back of my head from the pure pleasure coursing through me. Vin hisses and then starts to thrust, taking his sweet ass time with me. This time I don't rush him because I can tell he needs this, I can feel from our bond that he needs to feel me, needs to comfort himself with my body. Hell, we both need this. We lost each other and that was fucking scary.

"You feel so good, Sadie. You're taking my cock so well. Such a good fucking girl."

"More, Vinson. I need more. I need to erase the memory of him slamming my dagger into your chest. I need to feel that you're alive."

"I need the same, my Moon. I'll give you what you need."

Vin places his knee under my ass to help keep me stable and removes one of his hands to grip me by the back of the head, pulling my lips to his in a blinding kiss. One that I never want to end.

While his hands are busy, I increase the pace, bouncing on his dick until I'm seeing stars and I'm forced to break our kiss to scream my release. Vin wraps his hands under me again and his hard thrusts help draw out the sensation until he's coming alongside me, spilling himself inside of me.

Fuck, why does that turn me on more than it should?

An overwhelming need to claim him comes over me. "You're mine, Vinson. All mine," I pant.

"Mine," he echoes, dropping his lips to the crook of my neck as he continues to rock into me. There's a pinch of pain followed by pleasure as he bites down on my neck, marking me as his. The bond between us sings its praises, agreeing with his decision.

When I come back to earth enough to fully look at Vin, he

returns his gaze to mine, "I know you're not ready yet, my Moon, and that's okay, but I want you to know that I love you, and I can't go another minute longer without telling you how I feel about you." When I try to speak, he places a finger against my lips. "The connection we had was instant. We both tried to fight it and look where it got us. I love you, Sadie Sinclair, and I'm so grateful the Goddess placed me at your side. What we have, what we all have with you was always meant to be." His feelings of love and adoration swell inside of me through the bond, and it makes me giddy. "It was always meant to be like this, and now we need to convince everyone else."

"Fucking hell, Vin. How is a girl supposed to find words to live up to that?" He chuckles. "I'm falling for you, hard. I'm falling for all my mates hard, but love is complicated for me. It's not something I say lightly."

"Of course, Luna. Take all the time you need. I don't plan on leaving your side for the rest of my days. Not that I would anyway. We're soul bound. Besides, I don't need you to say it. I can feel how you feel about me."

This time, I kiss him and savor our slow brush of lips. We're just two battered souls trying to repair themselves. We both need it.

I'm coming to realize I need these men more than I need air some days.

And that's not always a bad thing.

10

SADIE

The next morning, I wake next to two hard bodies I know very, very well. Stretching my legs and letting out a yawn, I say, "One of these days, you two are going to have to put all that talk from the festival into action and show me this sandwich thing I've heard so much about. I'm starting to get a little miffed about it not happening." I wipe the drool from my face and Dante's arm. "Er, sorry."

He sits up and leans over to kiss me. His blonde hair is messy from sleep, but he totally rocks the bedhead look. "Don't worry about it, Angel. I see it as you claiming me with your sleep saliva. Now, what's this about a sandwich? It's like nine-thirty in the morning, so not really sandwich time yet, I'm afraid," he responds cheekily, and I roll my eyes. Fucker totally knows what I meant. Also, I can't believe I slept a whole day. I mean, I can, but wow.

"Don't play coy with me, Dante King. You know dang well what I mean."

Kaos splays a hand across my stomach and drags me toward him until my ass hits his hardness and that's when I discover they do know exactly what I mean by sandwich, and Dante's just being Dante.

"That can be arranged, Little Flame," he says huskily as his hot breath fans across the back of my neck.

"Oh, can it now, Steel? You know we wake up in bed like this a lot and it hasn't happened yet, should I be worried?"

They both growl and pounce on me in a coordinated attack. A hybrid laugh slash moan comes out of me as Kaos trails kisses up and down my neck while Dante goes for my lips.

Things are really starting to heat up and I think I just might get my sandwich after all when someone clears their throat from the direction of the door. "As lovely as this sight is, Reed has called us all into the living room for a meeting. I think it's time we all talk." I'd recognize that dark voice and his aura anywhere. Dammit.

I groan from being interrupted. "Now I remember why I haven't been able to have both my pipes plumbed—" I wince when they all shoot me a look with varying degrees of *what the fuck* and *ew*. "Yeah, it sounded punnier in my head. Anyway, we always get interrupted before we can get started."

With a sigh, I work my way out of the covers. After my very hot shower last night, Vin tucked me in bed with Dante and Kaos and took off outside. He wanted to let his wolf run, and I can't blame him. Though, I did ask Reed to keep an eye on him just in case. This whole multi-mate thing really does have its perks.

Elian grips me by the waist and pulls me to him instead of letting me walk past him. His erection presses against my belly, and I let out a small gasp. He leans in, brushing my hair aside to whisper, "Next time, I want to watch."

I'm so flabbergasted it takes me a moment to get my bearings. By then, Elian is already gone, walking into the living room like he's not sporting a massive erection. Although, I guess that will happen a lot around here, so they better get used to it.

The seating area, which I totally overlooked last night, is quite small. There are only five seats, but Elian chooses to be the wallflower and stand like usual anyway. I plop down in between Vin and Dante on the sofa. Reed and Kaos are in armchairs across from us and Hemsworth struts in from outside and lays at my feet. Kaos, Dante, and I are chilling in sleep clothes whereas Reed is dressed, and Elian is in his leather jacket and jeans. Vin is shirtless but wearing a nice pair of jeans.

Reed clears his throat and leans forward, placing his elbows on his knees. He steeples his fingers and, with his three-quarter length sleeves, it really highlights the veins in his toned forearms. Am I attracted to that?

The longer I stare the more I think I am. Plus, I'm *dying* to get him in bed.

Reed quirks an eyebrow at me, and I don't miss the heat flashing in his eyes. Dammit. Forgot he's a mind reader again. That is going to take some getting used to.

At least he doesn't call me on it out loud, though I'm sure the others notice our exchange. Man, when did I become so horny? I've always had quite the appetite, but Vin and I went three rounds in the shower last night, I almost jumped Dante and Kaos in bed this morning, Elian made me weak in the knees with his voyeuristic promise, and now I'm ready to head to hanky-panky town with Reed too.

"It's natural, Love," Reed tells me, responding to my thoughts. "Your body knows it has five of us to keep up with." He winks, and I stick my tongue out at him all super mature-like. Vin and Dante put a hand on me like they can't stand not to and it's totally fine with me.

"If you say so, Red." I shoot him a wink. "Now let's get down to business, shall we?"

"You're the boss." *Damn right I am.*

"Don't tell her that," Hemsworth pipes up from his spot beside us. "It'll go straight to her head."

"I'd love to give her head," Dante says with a husky chuckle.

Okay, so maybe I'm not the only one feeling the pull.

Vin shakes his head at our antics. "I would love to hear what happened while I was, uh… down." I appreciate him not saying dead, as it's still a fresh wound. "I'm a little confused on where this Triad thing came from," he says.

I nod and retell everything, starting with seeing my parents, to the Triad revelation, to giving Vin a piece of my soul, to seeing Ash's parents and what they told me about Mickey.

"Moons above. I wonder if you'll have a wolf?" he asks when I'm finished. "Since we soul bonded, have you had any new feelings? Can you feel another presence in your head?"

It totally sounds creepy when he puts it that way, but I don't comment on it. I shake my head. "No, nothing like that. I'm only a quarter wolf, so I don't know if I'll even have one."

Vin looks a little upset with that statement, but it's gone in a flash. "That's okay, my Moon. You alone are enough for me and my wolf."

Gah, swoon. Everything between Vin and I has been fast and hard. Falling for him is going to be no different.

"What about that creepy statement from the Elders?" Dante asks. "What the hell did they mean by, 'We'll see you when it's time?'"

Kaos shakes his head. "I don't know. I've been trying to work through what it could mean, but I have no idea."

"Something with the prophecy and Sadie, I'm sure," Reed says thoughtfully.

There's a pause as everyone trails off into their own trains of thought. "Is this where you grew up, Red?" I ask, changing the subject.

"No, this is only here in case of emergencies."

"Huh, interesting. Well, it's a good thing the Light Weavers thought ahead," I respond.

Vin clears his throat. "We talked a little about this in the In-Between but needed to get home before we could finish. Did you want to talk about the shadestone more?" he asks. "Maybe I can provide a fresh perspective? Or the others will know something I don't."

I nod. "Good thinking, Vin. What I was trying to make sense of and what I still don't understand is why, when Elron handled my dagger, it burned his hand and he was forced to drop it. I can't imagine it deemed Elder Reginald, of all people, worthy to wield it… yet it didn't seem to affect him at all, so what gives? My shadows also slid right off them."

Vin considers my words for a moment. "I'm not familiar with all types of magic, since there are so many, and most of the mechanics are hush-hush around my kind, but is it possible they've found a way to shield themselves from harm? All the assassination attempts I've heard about have also failed, so they either know they're coming… or they're protected somehow."

"That would make sense," Elian responds, pondering Vin's words.

"Yeah, it does," I agree. "But if Weavers and shifters alike have tried to kill them in the past, what the hell am I going to be able to do to stop them? Before I ran into Kaos—"

"Literally," Dante butts in with a chuckle. It makes us all dissolve into giggles. Thank the Goddess for his comedic relief.

"Before I *literally* ran into Kaos," I amend. "I was just a girl from Kentucky with a shit past. I wasn't anyone special."

Vin growls at that, Dante loses his smirk, Kaos scowls, Reed frowns, and even Elian looks like he disagrees. "You were always special, Angel. Don't ever forget that," Dante tells me fiercely.

"Damn right, Weaver," Hemsworth concurs, and I give him a little head pat for it.

"I don't want to lie and say I have all the answers, because I don't," Vin starts. "But I do trust in the Goddess, and I know she has a plan for you. Plus, you have us now, we'll figure it out together."

"Ha, yeah, we can thank her for that," I say, smiling brilliantly at them.

Reed sits forward, drawing our attention to him. "Vin, can you tell us what happened back at the estate while we were with the Elders? How did they manage to get to you all?"

A haunted feeling resonates down the bond and across Vin's face but he manages to pull himself together and nods. "The details are a little hazy as I was still dealing with the effects of whatever was in that orb I took for Sadie—" When I wince, he moves his hand from my leg and places it in mine. "And I wouldn't change a damn thing about that day either. Who knows what they would've done to you, my Moon."

"It's hard not to feel a little guilty," I whisper.

"Please, don't. I'd do anything for you. We all would."

"Fuck yes we would," Elian says while Dante squeezes my thigh in agreement and Kaos and Reed's eyes tell me the same.

Vin continues with his story. "I could tell something was off when I woke up. There was a crash, so I went downstairs to investigate and found Bedi fighting with Elian's father. There was an unknown man, which I now know is Sadie's uncle, standing to the side watching the whole thing with glee. Emma was passed out on the ground and Ashley was sobbing. She said something about how they weren't supposed to hurt us, and you were never supposed to know."

My heart pangs, but I motion for him to continue. I'm still upset with Ash, but at the same time, after having talked to her parents, I can almost understand. Almost. She was so close to them, and I know she did it because she thought she could bring them back, but I'm still extremely pissed at her for what her actions caused. That won't go away overnight, but her absence does make my stomach twist. I make a mental reminder to bring up a rescue plan with the guys later.

"He told her he lied and then hauled her from the floor by her chin." The others grunt their disapproval.

"Sounds familiar. He's done that, or worse, to me on several occasions," I tell them, which makes them all snarl or, in Vinson's case, full-on growl.

"I can't wait to rip his fucking heart out," Elian grits out.

"No, you leave that to me. That shit is personal, and he is mine." I give him a snarl of my own. We have a sort of mini standoff, his eyes bouncing between mine until he rolls them, admitting defeat. Or that's how I'm taking it at least. Hard to tell with Elian.

"Anyway, that's when I lost it," Vin continues, and I feel an echo of his rage in my chest. "No one hurts a woman around me and lives to tell the tale, but I was so weak. I did manage to get a punch in though, and it was so fucking sweet. I might've broken his jaw too." I grin at him and tighten my grip on his hand. "But in the end, I couldn't do much else. That's pretty much the last thing I remember before waking up with a dagger to my chest."

"We'll find a way to make them pay, Vin. I promise."

"I know you will, my Moon."

"Anyone have any ideas on where to get started?" I ask.

"I hate to be the bearer of bad news here, but not only do

the Elders have something protecting them physically, they also have something shielding their minds too," Reed says. "I couldn't get a single reading off any of them, or the servants while we were there."

"Dammit," Kaos grunts, rubbing his chin. "I was really hoping to gather some intel on them while we were there."

A thought occurs to me, and I smirk. "We do have some intel. Hell, we have the next best thing. Their sons. They have to know something, right?"

The door to our cabin opens and the trio walks in with Emma in tow. Speak of the devils and they shall appear. Adam, Nick, and Niall look tired and so does Emma, but they're at least wearing more casual clothes instead of the fancy ones the Elders require. I'm assuming they borrowed some because I don't remember seeing them pack anything.

Adam must've overheard my statement because he says, "Don't get your hopes up too soon, Shadowbringer. I'm afraid we don't know as much as you're probably hoping. As you can imagine, our fathers kept us at arm's length our entire lives. We've never been as cruel as them, although I can't say we were always saints."

"No one's a saint, Adam. We all have shit in our past that we regret. It's the future that defines you. I'm glad you're here, though."

"Do you have any idea how they're able to deflect attacks so easily?" Elian interjects, straight to the point as always.

"No," Niall responds. "We've been trying to find out for years."

"But I can tell you every assassination attempt we've witnessed, and there have been many, they've come out unscathed each time. Poison, blades, magic, bullets. It doesn't matter. Nothing harms them," Adam adds, rubbing his jaw. It has to unnerve them not knowing. I know it does me anyway.

"Fuck," I say, running a hand through my hair. "Okay, let's shelf the Elder conversation for today. We could spend hours going in circles about it and I'm getting a headache just thinking about their devious bullshit. Is there a way to get the word out about this being a safe haven for anyone who wants to defect?"

"Actually, I have an idea about that," Vinson says and stands up. "The shifters have figured out a way to securely get messages to those who have family or friends at different estates. I can get word to them about it. The problem is, I don't know if they will report us straight to the Elders or not. My gut says the majority won't, but the Elders have dirt on pretty much everyone. Then there's the issue of getting them safe passage here."

"I think I can help with that," Matilda says, joining our conversation as she walks through the front door. Huh, guess I was the only one who didn't get the memo about a meeting in our living room. "There's a little trick I learned a while back with paper. I can imbue some of my portal magic in the ink and if they have no ill will toward our cause, and accept the invitation, they'll automatically be transported here when they're ready. If not, the ink will catch fire, burning the only proof they have so they can't take it to the Elders."

"That's fucking genius," I breathe in awe, then turn to Vinson. "And you can get these invites to the shifters safely?"

He nods. "I have several connections, my Moon. We know how to be discreet and sneaky. We have to be."

Dang, it's handy having connected mates. "But what about the Night Weavers who wish to flee? Surely not everyone agrees with the Elders' bullshit."

Nick snorts. "That's an understatement, but they have just as many loyal followers as they do disloyal ones. It'll be hard to know who's friendly and who's not."

"I can help with that," Elian states. "I still have a connection or two in the Elites."

"Have you lost your ever-loving mind?" I demand. "Aren't the Elites super loyal to the Elders? It's their whole fucking job to do the bastards' bidding."

He shakes his head. "Not all of them truly want to be there. They are the best of the best though, and the Elders have *made* them loyal. But they're fixing to learn that loyalty has to be *earned.*" The bloodthirst in his eyes calls to my own, and I seriously want to jump his bones. Fuck me, I'm losing it. My shadows want to go caress him for it, but I hold them back. Just barely.

"He's right. Some of them are only a part of the Elites because our fathers are holding their families hostage or have some other depraved way of keeping them compliant. It's what they're good at—playing on people's emotions," Nick confirms.

"It's true," Adam agrees in disgust. "They live for the game."

"It's a start, anyway," Elian says thoughtfully. "I'll see if I can find any potential allies there first."

"Fine, but please be careful," I say to him. "I know our magic is bolstering the fuck out of this place, but we're responsible for a lot of lives here and I don't want any retaliation attempts."

"I will be, my Pet. Don't you worry." His nickname for me coming out in a public setting is a little jarring, but fuck if it doesn't turn me on even more, but I keep myself in check. If it weren't for the slight flush in my cheeks, and Reed reading my every thought, I'm sure no one would know.

"Make sure you check with your friend, Malachi, at the compound. He didn't seem to like the Elders any more than we do. And Oliver's Circle. They'll want to come," I say, and Elian's nose wrinkles.

"Who is Oliver?"

"You know, the scrawny guy I saved at the compound. Shrimp?"

"Ah, yes," he says as the memory comes back to him. "Okay, but I could use some help with all of this." He turns his stare to Dante and Kaos and waits for them to notice, which they do, but are as confused as I am. Elian, asking for help? The world really must be ending. "What? They respect you two. They fear me."

"Fair enough," Kaos responds with a sigh. "At least you can work on mending those relationships while we're doing this."

"Sure, I'll go," Dante says with a smirk. "But only in case you two fuckers scare them away with your frowny faces and reading their every move. Someone needs to have some flare."

"I can shield you from my fathers," Niall cuts in, and I remember him saying something about that the day they brought Ash back. He shielded them so the Elders didn't know they were with us.

"Right then. Anyone else have any business to discuss today?" I ask, motioning for anyone with something to add to go for it.

"Actually, if everyone doesn't mind, I'd like to properly introduce you to my faction. They're, uh, sort of dying to meet you all. Your names are legendary," Reed says to the rest of my mates. Then, he looks to me. "I think a few of them are speculating that the prophecy is about you."

That makes me nervous. The Light Weavers have been passing that down as a bedtime story. What if I don't live up to their expectations?

Regardless, I still say, "Sure, Red. I think we'd all love to meet your faction." Because I'm totally not facing this alone.

"Can someone remind us of this prophecy again?" Adam asks.

"Sure can," Matilda responds and starts reciting it from memory.

"Born from the night,
Into the shadows and darkness alike,
One with the power to bring them to their knees,
A force to reckon she shall be.
To right their wrongs,
And mete justice with ease.
She will be fate's guiding light,
She will be night's enforcing might.
Her heart so pure,
With the strength to endure,
Only she can unite us,
Only she can save us from them all."

While the trio is mulling it over, Reed smiles at me and pushes his glasses up his nose. "Come on. Let's go meet everyone," he says, getting up from his chair. He waits for me to walk past him before he whispers in my ear, "And you'll never be alone again, Love."

11

REED

Things went better with my faction than I expected, thanks to Auryen last night. Based on the shock on their faces and their confused thoughts, which I tried to be respectful of, they were leery, but also hopeful. There's a fine line I try to ride, as having the ability to read minds means I'm privy to some very personal thoughts that some people would rather I didn't know.

With my position and title now, I also need to know what my people are thinking so I can better protect them and Sadie. My ability gives me an advantage, but one I refuse to abuse.

Either way, most, if not all of them have heard the prophecy. Mainly as a bedtime story—something we thought our parents made up to give us hope. I don't think any of us thought it was real after all this time, but still. We carried the hope all the same.

Unfortunately, there is such a deep animosity between our worlds and in our communities that changing that is going to be difficult. But if anyone can do it, it's Sadie Sinclair.

Gods, I'm falling hopelessly in love with that woman. She's so full of beauty and grace and is such a fiery ball of passion. I wouldn't change a single thing about her.

Following the thoughts of my faction leads me straight to the training hall, which is perfectly outfitted with gear and weapons. The place is rather large and, besides the mess hall, the most updated. There are treadmills for running, weight racks for lifting, and even several punching bags. My ancestors really did plan for anything with this safe haven. Hell, maybe with the prophecy, they knew or expected we would need it one day.

Sensing my presence, my faction stops what they're doing and turn to me, bowing their heads slightly in a show of respect. Several pairs are lined up sparring, while others are utilizing the treadmills and weightlifting equipment.

Auryen's thoughts are full of hope for the future, while Merri is still wary of the Night Weavers with me. Several of them are, but I'm hoping to set their minds at ease today. Merri might prove to be a challenge though. She came from a semi royal line of Light Weavers and has always been vocal about her opinions. I spot one of my oldest friends, Hades, sparring with Jakob, and I shoot him a smile, grateful Matilda managed to get him out in time.

Nevertheless, I have no doubt Sadie's actions will speak for themselves. She has that way about her that draws anyone in. Including me. Before everything that happened with my father and my Elders, I was already trying to figure out how I was going to see her again… and then I fell through her porch. The memory brings a melancholic smile to my face.

Sadie is stroking Hemsworth's head absentmindedly, something I've noticed she does often, as she stares at the Light Weavers. Likely trying to size them up. Her thoughts are worried about impressing them, but as long as she's herself, I know she will.

"Good morning, everyone. I thought we should try a do-over on introductions since last night was kind of a shock for everyone," I announce, trying to make my voice firm. My father always had the heavy hand out of the two of us, and he tried to teach me, but I've always been softer spoken. More interested in books than people most days. Because of my ability, I preferred the alone time with books over the noise of being around people.

On the other hand, my father was always scheming. He wasn't quite as cruel as the Elders, but he did use me as his pawn, an asset to his reign. Yeah, our relationship was complicated to say the least.

Realizing I got lost in my thoughts, I clear my throat and motion to Sadie, showing her off. "This is my mate, Sadie Sinclair. She is a Triad, the first of her kind we know of and, as such, I expect you to treat her with respect."

Sadie gives a small wave. "Hello, everyone. It's lovely to meet you."

Merri rolls her eyes. "I wish we could say the same." My control over my power slips for a moment because of her strong emotions practically shouting it at me, and I hear her thoughts. *Who does this bitch think she is?*

Alongside Sadie thinking, *Tough crowd.*

Merri's comment pisses my fellow Circle off too, and if they weren't trying to play nice, they'd call her on her bullshit.

This is one of mine and therefore I'll take care of it, knowing I need to reaffirm my position as their leader in their heads. I haven't been around since the massacre, since my father was killed.

I level Merri with a look. "Speak to my mate, your Queen, with such disdain again and we will have issues. I let your shit slide last night, but I won't today. Don't forget who I am, Merri Duval."

She looks away from my gaze and reluctantly nods her head. I check her thoughts quickly, making sure she's going to behave before I continue with my introduction. "And these are my Circle mates, Kaos, Dante, and Elian, who are all Night Weavers. And Vinson, a shifter."

Several of my fellow Light Weavers gasp and stare at us with wide eyes. Their thoughts are all over the place and slightly overwhelming, which is exactly why I normally choose books over people.

Sadly, I don't have that luxury anymore.

"How is that possible? How is any of this possible?" Merri demands. "Where's your mate mark to prove it?" she sneers, looking at Sadie's wrist and mine.

Such mates they are if they don't even have marks, her thoughts tell me, and my hackles rise. But Sadie doesn't let Merri ruffle her tail feathers, though her shadows do rise around her—a show of her agitation. More than a few eyes bug further out of their heads.

"Reed and I have not bonded yet. All you need to know is that the Night Goddess blessed me greatly." Her short, clipped response brokers no room for arguments. Damn, I love her tenacity. Her admission of us not being mated yet causes them to whisper amongst themselves and a few of them shift on their feet, eyes bouncing between all of us like they don't know what to think.

Crap, I'm losing them, Sadie thinks, trying to sort through what to do.

"But that's enough with the pleasantries, don't you think?" Sadie asks, and I listen in once more to figure out what she's going to do. *Maybe if I can show them what I can do,* she thinks. It's a smart move.

Sadie shrugs off her shirt, leaving only her sports bra

underneath, and starts cracking her knuckles. "Would any of you mind if I spar with you? I'd love to get a feel for how Light Weavers train."

Merri's boyfriend, Jack, scoffs. They're not true mates, but they try to act like it. The others look at me, and I nod my approval of her sparring with them. Sadie's right. Sometimes when you're powerful, you have to lay your cards out on the table, but I also know Sadie is smart enough to ride that fine line like I do.

Hades steps forward with a cocky grin on his face, shooting me a wink before he extends his hand for Sadie to shake. "Why, hello there, lovely," he practically purrs, and I hear a rumble from Vin that Hades does not miss. I know he's a hopeless flirt though, so I'm not worried. "I'm Hades, and no, not like the God with blue hair. Just plain old Light Weaver, Hades. I'd love to spar with you."

"Hades, no!" Merri exclaims in outrage. "What if she's using this as a way to exploit us?"

"To what end, Merri?" Sadie asks.

My anger with her bubbles over. "One more outburst and I'm putting you on toilet cleaning duty for a month, Merri. Respect me and my mate or get the fuck out."

Hemsworth chortles. "Oh, he told you, bitch."

Damn that dog. It takes everything in me to keep from cracking a smile. I can't say the same for everyone else though. Several of them are covering up their laughs with a cough or chuckling behind their hands. Others have confusion on their faces. Right, I forget not everyone is used to Hemsworth talking. They'll figure it out eventually.

Sadie stares her up and down. "Trust me when I say I want to take the Elders down as much as everyone else. Take a ticket and get in line."

A tiny bit of respect flashes in Merri's eyes, but it's gone in a flash. Is she testing Sadie? Her thoughts are neutral at the moment, probably knowing I can read them. Either way, I'm going to have to keep an eye on her and Jack.

"Yeah, shut up, Merri. Only you and Jack have issues with this. What if she's the one?" Auryen asks, confirming my suspicions.

Merri throws her hands up in surrender and storms off the training mat with Jack trailing after her. Everyone else also leaves the mat, giving Sadie and Hades the room they need to spar, but secretly they just want to watch. Heavy doses of anticipation and thoughts of curiosity permeate the room.

Sadie looks Hades up and down with a smirk. He smooths his sweat-slicked, black hair out of his face, his blue eyes sparkling with mischief. "Let's see what you've got, Hades. Is magic allowed?"

He shrugs. "Sure," he says, essentially signing his death warrant. I barely hide my chuckle behind my hand.

The way Sadie's face lights up with an evil grin confuses him and he shoots me a quick look, but I school my features, not giving anything away. He shakes it off and they take their fighting stances across from one another.

"I bet I can take you down in less than five seconds," she tells him confidently, bouncing on her toes to get her blood pumping.

Hades scoffs. "Pfft. You're on, Weaver. Someone count us off?"

"I got you," Jack calls out with glee. He's a short, ruddy sort of dude that I've never really liked. Thankfully, we haven't interacted much until now. He and Merri watch from their spots on the far side of the mat, away from me and my Circle. "Take her down."

Hades taunts Sadie and lunges for her, going for a takedown straight away. Big mistake, bud. Sadie is light and agile on her feet. Not to mention has way more experience than I know Hades has. She's not going down so easily. The corner of my lip turns up.

"One," Jack shouts.

Sadie dodges expertly and he goes sailing past her, stumbling until he manages to catch himself. Meanwhile, Sadie is calling her shadows to her and they come slithering from the floor, solely at her command. She looks completely badass like this and hell if my dick doesn't awaken at the sight. I mentally scold it because now isn't the time or place… but soon.

"Two."

All it takes is for her to lift one tendril, wrapping it around his ankle for her to trip him. Hades' face morphs into shock as he hits the mat with an *oomph*. Every single one of her mates, myself included, is smug as fuck for her.

Until Jack says, "Three," in disbelief. "No fucking way! I call foul. That wasn't even sparring. She used her damn magic."

"Which was allowed, per Hades' rules," I remind him, barely keeping a snarl from my voice.

Hades pops up from the ground, rubbing his hands together. He laughs and extends his hand for a fist bump, which Sadie returns. "He's right, bro. Sadie won fair and square." Then to her, he says, "The real question is, can you spar without your magic?"

Sadie smiles. "Of course, I can. Ready for me to hand you your ass again in round two? I may need more than five seconds this time though."

Hades grunts. "I'm ready all right. This time I won't be taking it easy on you."

He shoots me a look and says, *way to warn a dude* to me in his thoughts. I chuckle and shake my head.

"Psh, that was me taking it easy on you, bro," Sadie taunts

and dives in with a jab that he barely misses. She smirks and says, "Prepare yourself."

Glancing around, I notice the room has shifted. Most of them are looking at her with varying degrees of respect. Some are even in awe already, and she barely tipped the surface of what she can with her shadow ability.

Just like that. She's already turning the tide in her favor exactly like I knew she would.

Sadie spars with the Light Weavers for hours, learning their moves and getting a feel for everyone's actions. Honestly, she's a fucking vision. If someone's takedown form is wrong, she corrects it. Their stance is off? She fixes it. Their thumbs aren't tucked in while throwing a punch? Oof. She chastises them about the possibility of breaking it. But honestly, she's learning as much from them as they are from her.

And more than a few of the men are jealous of me, and that makes me smug as fuck.

Vinson and Hemsworth left to go for a run to stretch their legs while Dante, Elian, and Kaos are doing some macho shit and doing three on one takedowns. I needed a break so I'm sitting on a small bench at the far end of the room, taking everything in while also keeping an eye on my mate.

I hear Matilda's thoughts coming before I see her. She's normally very open with them and they're hard to tune out. She sits next to me on the bench, quietly watching the action for a while before she speaks. "It's barely been a few hours and she's already winning them over. I can see why the Goddess chose her."

The noise level in the gym is loud enough for us not to be overheard.

A dreamy sigh escapes me. "She really is amazing, isn't she?" I can barely keep my eyes off her, watching her muscles burn and pull as she spars with Auryen.

"You love her? Truly?" Matilda asks quietly.

"I do," I respond without even thinking about it. "She stole my heart that night at the diner and refused to let it go. She's it for me."

"Then why haven't you claimed her properly yet? You know it's dangerous for her not to have finished her mate bonds. Her Awakening is coming soon and she's going to need you. All of you."

"I know."

"'I know' isn't good enough, Reed Soleil," Matilda chastises. "Does she even *know* about the Awakening?"

I shake my head. "No, none of us have told her. We agreed that we don't want to rush her into these mate bonds with us. Especially when Vinson just fucking died and her relationship with Elian is rocky at best. We've barely gotten time together either. Hell, I just got the others' stamp of approval."

"Boy, I raised you better than this. Tell the woman how you feel. Make her *yours*. If you wait for the world to fall in your laps, it'll pass you by. You know this."

She's right. Sadie's Awakening is upon us. We need to finish the bonds with her because a mated Weaver is always safer. Something about the magic of love puts an extra layer of protection on us. Not to mention bolsters our powers.

Her magic will also continue to push us together regardless, which is why I haven't said anything. I don't want her to think she has to mate with me. But then again, mates aren't meant to be separated. Usually, they bond instantly, and the Awakening happens shortly thereafter.

Matilda is right though. What the hell am I waiting for?

Knowing the whole fucking magical community is about to be divided, which means our Circle needs to be stronger than ever, I should tell her how I feel. Put myself out there. That gets the gears in my head turning about all the possibilities between us. I have to make it special. I want her to know how much she means to me. Maybe I could write her a little something… That really gets all the ideas swirling in my head.

I give Matilda a nod, catching on to exactly what she was doing—pushing me to be better, like always. "Thanks, Tildy," I say, using her nickname from when I was little.

She makes sure no one is watching us and then ruffles my hair like she would when I was fifteen and got caught sneaking a book out of the library against my father's wishes. "Sometimes you men need a little push." Then she portals away and leaves me with my thoughts.

12

SADIE

Dante waltzes into the kitchen and puts his hands on my waist. "Good afternoon, Angel," he says, pulling me into an expert spin. The sudden movement draws a laugh from me as Dante leads me around the kitchen. He's slightly sweaty from his workout, but smells delicious, like a campfire.

"Good afternoon, Blondie," I repeat, using his nickname. He stops for a moment then proceeds to dip me before giving me a searing kiss.

Vin chuckles at our antics from his spot at the stove, where he's preparing dinner. He gets this shit-eating grin on his face, looking at Dante staring at me like I'm a snack.

"Hey, Dante. What's your favorite food?" Vin asks.

Dante raises my hand and shoots him a suggestive eyebrow raise while waving his other hand up and down my body, stopping to gesture at my vagina. As if we didn't catch exactly what he was referring to.

That makes Vin full-on laugh, and he sticks his hand out for a fist bump. Vin's eyes roam from my legs up to my face, making a shiver traverse down my spine. "Yeah, I could eat that every day," he responds, desire flashing in his golden eyes.

Hot damn. Did the temperature just rise nine-hundred degrees, or is that my skyrocketing libido? Fuuuck.

Men who enjoy eating kitty?

How did I get so lucky?

"As much as I'd love to eat you on this table right now, Angel, I'm afraid I need a shower before dinner. Will you be okay?"

I chuckle. "How will I ever survive? Yes, Dante, I'll be fine." I get close to his ear and whisper, "But maybe later?" He shoots me a devious grin and a nod before waltzing right back out of the kitchen.

"Need any help?" I ask as Vin gets out some homemade pie dough he made earlier. Niall has been making grocery trips for everyone, using Matilda to portal him and his shielding ability to stay under the radar. It's been working well so far.

Vin expertly sprinkles some flour on the dough before smacking it with his hand and starting to roll. Moons above, why is cooking with Vin so erotic when it shouldn't be?

"Sure," he says, watching me over his work. His muscled arms expand and contract with each pass of the dough and my mouth waters. Not because of the food either. "Want to help me cut out mini circles so I can make individual apple cobblers?"

I nod and walk up to him, waiting for him to give me instructions. "I don't have any mason jar lids here so I've been using a knife to cut them. It doesn't have to be perfect," he tells me. Once he gets the dough to the right thickness, we work on cutting out the dough circles. He reaches into a bottom cabinet, and I get a fine view of his taut ass when he bends over and whisks out a cupcake tin.

"Huh, that's genius," I say, watching him line the tin with

the dough circles we made. "Now everyone can have their own serving and the crust will be perfect."

Vin smirks and boops my nose playfully, getting flour on my face. I attempt to wipe it off, but I only make it worse with the white powder all over my own hands. I reach up and swipe my thumb across his cheek, giving him his own floury battle mark. He chuckles and our gazes lock. My body sings under his appraising and inquisitive gaze. My nipples tighten and his eyes dip to them.

I'm not sure who moves first, but it doesn't matter. We collide in a bruising blend of fervor and passion, mini cobblers all but forgotten. My lips part and Vin's tongue rushes inside. He wraps my legs around his waist and deposits me on the counter, his rock-hard steel brushing against my core. A puff of flour explodes around us as he sets me down, but neither of us pay it any mind, too lost in the throes of passion.

Vinson

Kissing Sadie is like taking a breath of fresh air. One I find myself addicted to if I'm honest. An idea pops in my head and I pull back. She chases my lips and I chuckle, giving in to her demands. This time the kiss is slower, more exploratory, and damn, do I explore. Running my hands down her side, over the soft curves of her hips, then I draw her closer to me, pressing her body into mine. She lets out a moan and grinds her core against my dick. It's almost my undoing.

I pull back again and she looks at me in confusion. "Mind if I try something?" I ask, shooting her a mischievous look.

"Go for it," she responds, always down for anything. That's something I appreciate about her. She's so open-minded and always willing to try new things, which is so unexpected compared to the other Night Weavers. I'm glad she's breaking the mold. Well, I guess she's really a triad. A Triad raised as a human. What an interesting combo.

A part of me really wishes for her to have a wolf, but she hasn't had any of the usual mated wolf urges and she can't picture one in her mind like I can. It doesn't matter though; I'll love her all the same. Wolf or no wolf.

Sadie grinds against me again to hurry me along. *Yes ma'am.* Wrapping her around me securely and closing my eyes, I picture the clouds I took her to in the first dream of ours, weaving the threads in my mind until I feel the ground beneath my feet change. Sadie's mouth pops open in shock.

"Vin, this is fucking beautiful. How are you doing this?"

"Honestly, I'm not sure. I wasn't even sure if my powers would work while I'm awake, but I had to at least give it a try. I love being in the kitchen, but I think the scenery is much prettier here. What about you?"

"Uh, yeah," she says, wild excitement in her eyes. "Vin, you created this place within your mind. That's—that's—" I brace myself and wait for her to say shifters aren't supposed to have powers or something like that, but she doesn't. "—fucking amazing, Vin. This is truly spectacular. We have to show the others some time."

All I feel with her words is relief. This is something I've hidden from everyone my entire life, even my fellow shifters. No one except Sadie knows about my power, but I think it's time to change that.

Dying brought out my confidence, and I refuse to be soft-spoken anymore. I'm going to fight for what I want, especially where Sadie is involved.

"We will," I vow. I'm not sure how or when, but

eventually, I'll show them too. "Now, can I make love to you in the clouds, my Moon?"

"I thought you'd never ask," she says and punctuates her point by grinding against my core once more, drawing a moan from my lips.

This woman makes me feral. I run my hands down her clothes, debating on how to take the damn things off her without taking her out of my arms. It feels amazing holding her like this, and I don't want to let her go but fuck, I want her clothes to go away so I can feel her glorious, naked body against mine.

And that's when her clothes disappear. Poof, like they never existed.

She smirks. "Well, that's a handy trick, huh?"

I laugh, admiring her peaked nipples and flushed skin. "Apparently, the environment isn't the only thing I can control with my dream power."

As much as I don't want to let her out of my arms, my need to feel her overcomes me, and I set her on her feet. Tracing up her bare sides, I cup her gorgeous breasts in my hands before tweaking those tight, pink nipples between my fingers since they're practically begging for my attention. She lets out a gasp that shoots straight to my dick.

"If you can control this, why are you still clothed?" she asks cheekily before taking my lip between her teeth and biting softly, looking downright playful. Her eyes are brimming with desire, and I groan, picturing myself naked so my clothes will disappear too.

"Much better," she responds, reaching between us to palm my cock without warning and making it twitch in her hand. Fuck. She rubs her thumb through the bit of precum leaking out, using it as lube as she strokes me. But I need more. I reach down and tighten her grip, showing her exactly how I like it.

"Like that?" she asks, massaging me harder like I showed her. She looks absolutely radiant like this, skin flushed, pupils dilated because of the pleasure coursing through her.

"Yes, Luna," I groan. "Just like that." Not to be outdone, I swipe a finger through her sweet heat because I can't hold back any longer, finding her absolutely soaking for me already. My dick pulses in her hand. "Someone is excited, huh?"

"Less talky, more strokey," she responds, hips undulating as she seeks her pleasure from my hand.

"You got it, my Moon."

I give her exactly what she wants, finding my way to that sensitive little nub, no map needed, and drawing soft circles on it. The sounds coming out of her mouth are enough to make me come early, but I grit my teeth and hold it back because I want to be inside of her when I spill my seed. I want to fill her up with it like a fucking caveman. She makes me want to embrace my wolf's wild side.

I grip her hand to slow her pace on me, but I keep mine firmly on her clit and she continues to ride my fingers, silently begging for more. So, I slip one digit into her pussy and curl my finger, stroking that sensitive spot inside her. She tips her head back and closes her eyes. "Vin," she moans. One more stroke is all it takes for her to explode all over my hand, a choking gasp leaving her parted lips.

I don't even give her a second to breathe before I'm laying her down on the clouds and lining myself up to her entrance. I wait for her to look at me and then I slide the tip in, groaning when I feel her warmth embrace me.

"Goddamn, you're so tight for me, Luna."

"Fucking hell, Vin." I love the sound of my name coming from her lips. "You're fucking huge, you know. Your dick is monstrous. They sure weren't lying about shifter cocks." She mumbles the last part under her breath, and I laugh.

"Is that so?"

"Yesss. Now put that weapon to work and fuck me. Please."

"As you wish, Luna." I push myself in further, letting her body adjust to my girth until I'm buried to the hilt inside her. "Fuck, it's like you were made for me."

She starts moving her hips against mine, seeking the friction only I can provide. I require no further encouragement and rock my hips into her, loving the way her lovely pussy grips my dick like a vice. Her gaze stays on mine while I thrust into her, filled with adoration. It's thrumming down the bond too.

"More, Vin. Please, more."

I place my arm under her hips and lift her up to get a better angle, increasing my pace. She meets me thrust for thrust until we're both a tangle of limbs. I'm not sure where I end and she begins, and that's exactly how I want it. Fate brought us together and I'm so glad she is mine. I couldn't have pictured anyone more perfect. She challenges all of us in the most exquisite ways.

My spine starts to tingle as the pressure builds and builds. I reach a hand down to rub Sadie's nub and she cries out at the same time I climax, both of us reaching our crescendos together. My balls tighten and my seed spills into her in hot ropes.

I lean down and lick her pulse, biting down as I mark her again. Every fucking shifter in the world will know she's mine with my mark and my scent all over her, and it pleases the beast inside of me. Pleasure, unlike anything, explodes through us both, and I continue to rock inside her, letting her milk my cock for all it's worth until we're both sated—well, as sated as we can be, anyway.

I'll never, ever get tired of having her like this.

So perfect. All mine.

13

SADIE

It takes Matilda a week to get the portal invites ready, and in that time, we've had little to no contact with the outside world as the cell reception around here is nonexistent. Hell, I'm not even sure where we are exactly. All the trees look the same as they did back home so we're still local but in the middle of nowhere at the same time.

It's probably for the best that I don't know where we are though. No one really does. This place is invite-only and if some poor soul with bad intentions does happen upon the haven... Well, the wards will zap them faster than lightning.

Our plan for the day is for my Sworn, minus Reed, to leave the safety of the haven to inform everyone they know or find through networking, who aren't loyal to the Elders about the impending rebellion. They are bringing Niall as a shield but I'm still a nervous wreck over it.

They're powerful in their own rights, yes, and they're going to be super careful, but that doesn't ease the worry eating at me. Shit fucking happens. I know that better than anyone.

They're going to start with the shifters since their lives are in more danger than the Night Weavers. I'm afraid of the Elders doing something drastic since they know I have a soft spot for them—especially after what happened leaving the King mansion. Plus, Kaos still has family out there, so they need to get to them asap.

Speaking of which, I need to talk to Elian about rescuing Ash. Maybe he'll hear something about where she's being held during their travels. She's not dead, I know that much, but I don't know where she's being kept. Or why the Elders still have her.

The good news is Reed and I are searching for more information about Triads and my heritage today, so I'm really looking forward to that. Hemsworth is spending time with the compound shifters, but honestly, I think he only left to give Reed and I some alone time. Which I'm grateful for. The little shit totally knows my needs more than I do sometimes. I guess that's why he's my familiar.

"Are you ready to hit the archives?" Reed asks me after I say goodbye to the others. He pauses to take a closer look at me when I don't say anything, too lost in my thoughts. "What's on your mind, Love? Are you all right?" He has probably already read my inner turmoil so I'm grateful he gives me the choice to voice it out loud if I want.

"I'm worried about them. That's all."

"Trust me, they'll be okay. They have something so amazing to come back to, they won't jeopardize that for anything. Besides, they have Niall with them to help shield them from the Elders."

"Mmm. Something so amazing, huh? What might that be?" I ask coyly.

Reed raises an eyebrow and laughs. "I mean Vinson really can cook—" he starts, and I shoot him a look of mock outrage. "Of course, I mean you, Sadie."

"Aww, my King," I gush with all the sugary sweetness of syrup. "You're too sweet."

"I try," he says with a slight smirk, heat flaring in his eyes. He tamps it down and motions for me to follow him. "Come on, the books are this way. A book in your hands always cheers you up."

Leave it to my book loving mate to already know where the book stash is.

"Now that we know what you are, maybe we can find out more about you. Especially since the Light Weavers seemed to know more about this prophecy surrounding you than our counterparts."

"It's worth a shot. Maybe we'll find something useful," I agree.

Reed leads me to a small study. It's nothing like the one I'd gotten used to back at the King estate, much to my disappointment, but beggars can't be choosers. He looks around, then points to a two-tiered shelf crammed with books. The top row is filled with leather-bound journals while the second houses varying texts. I spy ones like, "A History of Light Weavers," "Sun Spells and Other Useful Powers," and "The Guide to Shifters," the last of which really captures my interest now that I have a shifter mate and have some inside me as well. I make a mental note to ask Vinson about their history at some point.

"You can take that one with you when we leave if you want. Actually, feel free to take anything you'd like. What's mine is yours, after all, my Queen."

"Ahh, a man after my own heart. The quickest way to it is by feeding my book addiction. Speaking of which, when the Elders are buried six feet under, you all owe me some signed paperbacks from my favorite authors."

"Your wish is my command, Love."

We smile at each other like fools for a minute, his gray

eyes darkening by the second as my thoughts take a less bookish turn. A flashback of the sexy times in the library flashes through my mind. Kaos' husky voice as he read, Reed's fingers trailing up my thigh, the way that orgasm rolled through me. Yeah, books will forever be a turn-on for me now. I clear my throat and look away before we get too distracted to focus on our task.

"So, what are the journals on the top?" I ask, bringing us back to the moment.

"Those are a collection of past Kings' thoughts, plans, ideas, anything from their time in power, really. That's why I'm hoping there will be something in here worth our while."

"Damn, Red, why didn't we read these sooner? You were holding out on us…" I try not to act hurt, but I kind of am. It's possible something in here may have the answers we've been seeking, and he didn't tell us...

"Wait, please don't look at me like that, Love. I didn't know about them, I swear. Matilda is the one who told me they were here. Apparently they have some sort of fail-safe put on them to protect the knowledge inside. When the current leader dies, they're transported to the study. And no one knows about this place because if this information were to fall into the wrong hands..."

"It would be extremely detrimental," I finish for him.

"Exactly."

"Okay, where should I start?"

"Well, I never met him, but my father always used to say I took after my grandfather with my love of knowledge, so I'll start there. You can take his father's and then we'll keep going down the list from there."

I NEVER REALIZED EXACTLY HOW BORING PEOPLE'S THOUGHTS were until now. Not all books are sexy, and it's a damn shame.

Being a leader is not all it's cracked up to be, that's for sure, but I do feel like I'm getting to know Reed's people more. "This is interesting. Your great-grandfather wrote about how a Light Weaver and a shifter fell in love under his watch. I wonder..." I trail off in thought then decide it's better to work through it out loud. Reed stands and reads over my shoulder. "My mother said she was part Light Weaver, part shifter. You don't think..."

"I don't know. What else does it say?"

I scan the page. "Nothing much, but it seems that he was convinced Light, Night, and shifters were interconnected somehow. He believed that it strengthened the Circle. Not weakened like we're led to believe." I flip through a few more pages and catch another interesting bit. "They had a child. A girl. Reed, do you think this means..."

"That these are your grandparents? Yes, I do. It's too much of a coincidence not to be."

"I really am a Triad... Holy shit..."

His breath feathers my neck when he chuckles. "What, did you think your mom lied?"

"Truthfully, I was half-convinced it was all in my head because I craved that interaction, but fuck, it was real, and she was telling the truth."

"You're the hottest damn Triad I've ever seen too," he says, brushing a piece of hair off my neck. The slight touch of his fingers against my skin is enough to set my nerve endings alight.

Fucking hell, he touches my neck and I'm horny. What the hell is wrong with me? I'm not some lovesick puppy. What is it with being in a library with Reed that turns me on every time?

Reed sighs and gently taps my shoulder, signaling for me to turn and face him. "There's something we need to talk about, Sadie."

Shit, he said my real name instead of Love. This must be serious. I try to tamp down on my rising nerves, but little good it does. When someone says *we need to talk* it usually involves bad news or a breakup, which I guess is a form of bad news. "Give it to me straight, Red. Is it bad news? Do you not want this life anymore? I know Light Weavers are usually monogamous and sharing me must be hard and—"

Reed cuts off my panicked babbling with a searing kiss and I thread my fingers through his hair. His mouth is demanding on mine, like he's trying to prove to me how wrong my assumptions are. It feels like forever before he finally pulls back a little, both of us breathless. "I'm not going anywhere, Sadie Sinclair. Don't you ever doubt that for a second. I'm here and I'm yours."

"And I'm yours," I respond, using the hand I put on the back of his head to bring his lips to mine once more. This kiss is still as steamy, but with a little sweetness mixed in and less dominating. But fuck, I find the demanding side to Reed extremely hot.

He must read that thought because he smiles against my lips and yanks my legs around him. I groan into his mouth and use my other hand to trail up his side while he explores my body with his own, dragging me even closer to him. Until recently, I didn't realize that Reed could be anything other than sweet but having seen his confidence come out as he's stepping into his new role has been nothing short of a turn-on.

When I drag his bottom lip through my teeth, he hisses and that's when I feel his length press against my core. Testing the water, I grind against him softly, but he pulls back, panting. "Sadie, we really should talk."

He eases my legs back to the floor while I pout. His hair is all ruffled and his glasses are crooked on his nose. As a punishment for pulling back, I send him a mental image of me riding his face, my head thrown back in wanton pleasure as he—

Reed growls, and it interrupts my thoughts. "Trust me, there's nothing I want more than to take you over this desk right now and let you ride my face while I plunge my tongue into your heat." The outline of his erection thumps against his pants and he runs a hand through his hair. "Seriously, I've imagined what it would be like worshiping you in a room full of my favorite things—you and books if that wasn't clear—so many times but there's something I need to tell you first."

"Fine," I relent. "But we are resuming this afterwards. M'kay?"

He laughs and pushes his glasses up his nose, then his face turns serious once more, but he remains silent. He's quiet. Too quiet.

"You're starting to scare the shit out of me, Red. Spit it out."

"One thing we were always taught about true mates is when they meet their partner, or all of their partners, the Link then goes through what's called an Awakening, but usually by the time it starts, all of the mates are already well… mated."

"I'm not following, Red. What's an Awakening and what does it have to do with already being mated?"

"Well, your Awakening is coming on and since you haven't finished the bond completely with Elian and I, I think it's hitting you a little harder than usual, pushing you to complete the Circle."

"Huh?" Then it hits me. The desire lately, the increased emotions in any of my mates' presence, the constant ache I've been ignoring. "Fucking hell, is this why I've been so horny? Why didn't you tell me sooner! I thought I was losing my mind."

"I didn't want you to mate with me because you felt like you had to, but the bond will continue to amp up our desires until it's completed. Plus, I know you and Elian have issues. Rightfully so. Although, it seems like he's slowly pulling his head out of his ass. Anyway, I want you to want me for me."

"Oh, Red. Of course, I want you for you. What's *not* to want about you? You're every girl's wet dream. A man who reads magic smut? A man so selfless and sweet he puts others first? A man who cares for my feelings and is willing to share me with four others? One who cares for his people? And who has been through so much but is still standing? I hit fate's fucking jackpot if you ask me." I can tell in his eyes he's still not truly convinced, and it hurts my heart. "Reed Soleil, I am falling hopelessly in love with you and it's not because of some bullshit magic. It's because of who you are as a person. Your heart is pure, Red. I just hope *I'm* not a stain on it."

"You could never be a stain on me, Love. And I'm falling in love with you too." My heart soars with joy at his admission and I make sure to keep my thoughts completely open so he knows exactly how much I mean it.

"Then let's complete our bond," I say with honest conviction in my tone. "What are we waiting for anyway?"

"Right here? Right now? But I—" He looks around and back to me, an unreadable emotion in his eyes.

"What's wrong, Red?"

"This may sound stupid, but I have so many plans and ideas on where and how to do this because I want it to be special for you. You deserve the best, and I want to deliver."

"What's a better place than here, surrounded by books?" I ask, sending him mental pictures of him laying me out on top of his ancestor's journals, desecrating them with my naked body while he slams into me, pleasure etched on his face. He groans.

"Us surrounded by smut I wrote specifically for you," he quips, and I laugh, but the thought of that severely turns me on. I need smut written by Reed in the future. Holy shit, what if he and Kaos co-wrote something? Might as well start picking out a headstone now because that might be my undoing.

Before either of us can overthink it anymore, I interlace my fingers with Reed's and the moment our palms slide into place, we both freeze. I stare into his eyes while my body lights up like a fireworks display. There's nothing but love and admiration in his eyes.

The power flowing through me is strong, stronger than with Dante or Kaos, but this time I refuse to pass out. Reed and I have some unfinished business to settle.

And by that, I mean sex.

Mind over matter, Sadie. You can fucking do this.

I take a few deep breaths, in through my nose and out through my mouth to help get through the onslaught of power coursing through my veins. The feeling intensifies, pulling a grunt from my throat. Reed's eyes shine with concern, but there's nothing he can do for me. We're still paralyzed, frozen in place.

I'm fine, I project to him and that seems to appease him slightly.

I'm here for you, my Love. Once the power evens out between us, it'll settle down. Just keep breathing. Reed coaches me through several more breathing exercises, calming me. Eventually, I feel the telltale burning of a mate mark appearing on my wrist, and our bodies unfreeze. Giddiness flows through me as I raise my arm to look at it. I can't wait to see what Reed's design is next to Kaos, Dante, and Vinson's.

A gasp escapes me when I find a beautiful symbol of the sun, with all its shining rays, now resting above Kaos and Dante's symbol. There's a small space on the right, the only gap in the design, which I'm guessing is where Elian's symbol will go.

If he can redeem himself that is.

Reed's voice pulls me from my thoughts. "Hello, mate." A shiver travels down my spine from the huskiness of his tone. "What do you say we consummate the bond?"

My nose wrinkles. "Never say consummate again, and my answer is yes."

"Deal," he responds, and I wrap my arms around his neck and pull him closer to me so I can kiss the living daylights out of him, ironic since he's a Light Weaver and all.

On instinct, his hands go to my ass and lifts my legs around him. He's already rock-hard, and I gasp into the kiss when his dick thumps against me. Reed pulls back with uncertainty in his gray eyes. "Look, Sadie. Before we do this. You should know, I've, uh—" He blows out a breath. Whatever he wants to say he seems nervous about it, and it makes me want to ease that tension from him.

"You know you can tell me anything, right?"

He smiles softly. "I know, my Love. It's not that. It's—I've never done this before," he blurts and promptly blushes.

The first emotion to hit me is satisfaction. Knowing that I'll be the only woman Reed has ever been with?

Pure satisfaction.

"I've been saving myself for my mate. For *you.* Does that bother you?"

"Does that bother me?" I ask and he nods. "No, of course not, Red. Hell, a short while ago I was also a virgin. It just never felt right with anyone. Until I met you all and now you've turned me into a fucking nympho." He chuckles and captures my lips once more.

"You have no idea how relieved I am to hear you say that. So, um, would you mind showing me the ropes?"

This is going to be so much fun.

14

REED

The look of pure desire on Sadie's face is an extreme boost to the ego. I can't believe she's my mate and we're about to have sex for the first time. The very vivid and colorful thoughts she's sending my way are going to make me lose my mind.

"First, I want you to strip for me," she commands, and it sends a white-hot jolt of lust straight down my spine. My cock jumps against her clothed core before I ease her legs down so we can undress. I carefully start taking my shirt off, watching as her eyes darken as she stares at me, tracing every movement with her eyes.

She reaches down and fumbles with the button on my jeans like she can't take not seeing me naked a second longer. Eventually, I reach down and undo the button with one fluid motion. Sadie makes a noise of disbelief. "How do men do that? Fucking hell, it's magic, I swear. You're not even looking!"

Once my clothes are in a pile on the floor, I lift her shirt over her head and her bare breasts greet me. "Fuck, Sadie," I groan, palming one with my hand. "You're not wearing a bra?"

"Hell no. Those damn things are the bane of women's existence everywhere." She says something else, but I'm distracted by the sight of her. So utterly beautiful. Her nipples are pebbled from desire and look ripe for sucking. Which is exactly what I decide to do. I lower my head and take one in my mouth, which makes Sadie gasp. "Gods, Red. I wasn't expecting that."

I look up at her and shoot her a smirk, or as much of one as I can give with her nipple in my mouth. While I may not have done this before in real life, I've read about it hundreds of times in the smutty novels I like so much. I think Sadie will be very happy with my creativity.

She brings my hand up to her other breast and shows me how to rub her nipple between my fingers. I tweak and suck, alternating between both of her tits until Sadie says, "My turn."

She palms my dick in her hand, using the bit of precum at the tip as lube, and starts to stroke. My spine tingles with desire and a moan falls from my lips.

"Let me hear you do that again," Sadie whispers and starts stroking me faster.

The pressure at my spine builds and when I feel like I'm going to come, I grab her hand to stop her. "I want to be inside you, my Love." Her jeans and panties are off in the next instant and then she's completely bare in front of me. "You're perfect," I whisper in awe, gazing at her beautiful, flushed body. There's a slight sheen of sweat coating her silky skin which adds to the appeal. "Such stunning perfection."

She chuckles. "Careful, Red. You keep dishing out these compliments and I'll expect them every day for the rest of our lives."

"And I'll deliver. Trust me, my Love."

The desire between us grows, singing down our newly formed bond. She practically jumps into my arms. I love the feel of her soft, velvety skin against mine. She wraps one leg around my waist, and I yank the other around me and walk her to the desk, depositing her on it, not caring in the slightest that all the books go flying. I'm intent on reenacting her dirty thoughts from earlier.

"Now, it's time for me to fuck you over this desk like I said a few minutes ago, but first, let me make you come." Giving her no room for thought, I descend onto her pussy with my mouth, devouring it like I'm a man starved and her juices are the sustenance I need to live. One thing about romance novels is they sure can teach you a thing or two. And because of them, I know exactly where to find her clit. I may have never done the actual deed before, but I know how to pleasure her.

She gasps and threads her fingers through my hair. "Gods, yes, Reed. Like that."

She rides my face like a champ, controlling my head with her hand, taking her pleasure, and I'm more than apt to give it to her. I'd give her the whole fucking world if it were possible. Alas, she'll just have to settle for as many orgasms as I can give her instead.

I need more, her mind tells me, and I oblige by sticking two fingers in her sweet heat before she can even ask, groaning into her pussy when I find her dripping.

"Curl them and act like you're stroking my inner wall," she instructs then throws her head back in pleasure when I hit that sensitive spot. She grinds against my face as I lick her nub then suck on it like I've read about before. That sends her screaming over the edge, her core spasming around my fingers. I pull them out and lick them clean.

"Reed," she gasps my name. *I need you inside of me. Now.*

"Yes, my Love." Sadie grips my dick and aligns me at her entrance. I push in slowly, savoring the moment, loving the way her sweet cunt grips my cock like a vice. "You feel like heaven."

"Reed, please," she whimpers, and it takes no further encouragement from me. I start moving, slowly at first and then building in speed. Sadie wraps her legs around me and pulls me in closer to her.

Lifting her ass, I start to piston into her harder, loving the wet slap of our bodies joining and the mewling sounds coming out of her mouth. Our pace becomes frenzied, and Sadie meets me thrust for thrust.

My spine starts to tingle with my impending orgasm, so I reach a hand between us and pinch Sadie's nub, sensing from her thoughts how close she is to coming. That action sends her hurtling over the edge. Her pussy ripples around me and sends me over next. I can't help the grunts and sighs that escape my lips as my cock spurts, and I fill her with my seed.

Utterly spent, I lay on top of her, still inside of her, and relish the comfort we bring each other. "That was... Wow," I say, and Sadie's chest shakes with a silent chuckle. We collapse to the floor in a pile of limbs, cuddling each other.

"I could say the same," she says with a dreamy look in her eye. "Definitely lived up to the fantasy in my head." With smug satisfaction, I smirk, and she traces one of my dimples with her finger. At some point we must fall asleep, wrapped in each other's arms.

15

KAOS

Slow. That's how this day is going. By now I was hoping we'd be finished with the list we compiled of possible allies, but with the secrecy involved in trying to keep this quiet, it's going a lot slower than any of us expected. Which means it's going to take several days to do this. Possibly even weeks.

Which also means time away from Sadie, and I don't like it.

But this needs to be done. The Elders have numbers on their side, along with their ability to deflect any attacks. If we're even going to have a chance at winning this thing, we're going to have to fight power with brains, and that means getting people on our side.

A strong undercurrent of energy jolts through me and I grunt from the force of it, tightening my grip on the steering wheel. Yeah, we're doing this the old-fashioned way, trying to stay under the Elders and Elites' radar.

When another forceful blast rolls through me, and I let out a breath through my teeth, Elian gives me a weird look from the passenger seat. I'm surprised he even let me drive, honestly. The fucker craves control like he craves Sadie's wildness. Even if he's still too afraid to truly embrace the latter.

All of us were shocked at the turn of events the night of the challenge, especially when Elian killed his father. Elron was a vicious bastard and deserved to die, but Elian kept his feelings about him locked up tighter than Fort Knox. Seriously, the dude rarely ever expresses anything, even with us. I've been able to learn some of his tells over the years by observing and getting to know him, but not even I suspected he'd actually kill his own father. In front of the Elders no less.

Don't get me wrong though, the asshole definitely deserved to die. Now, with him gone, the Elders are struggling to find a new leader for the Elite. Good. It feeds into our plan to take them down perfectly.

Another surge of power rolls over me like a wave, and it takes everything in me to focus on the road long enough to pull over and ride it out.

"What's happening? Why are we stopping?" Niall asks. "And why does Dante look like he's in pain?"

"It's Sadie," I grit through clenched teeth. "Something is feeding her power."

"Or someone," Elian responds, jaw clenched. Since he and Sadie aren't bonded yet, he's only getting residual bits from his bond with Dante and I. Nothing like the full force of raw power streaming through us, although he's probably feeling something akin to a high. "The Light Weaver and her have just bonded." Something about his tone seems bitter, and if I didn't know any better, I'd think he was jealous of that fact.

"Boned more like it. Fucking hell, the bastard is strong," Dante wheezes from the back seat as more power hits us.

"Is this how you felt every time?" Vinson asks, gritting his teeth. We nod. "Damn, our girl is strong too."

I chuckle slightly. "Good news is, no one will want to fuck

with us today. All this extra juice riding us could be a blessing."

"Let me drive so we can get a fucking move on, Kaos," Elian snaps. "We're sitting ducks here." I'm so used to his prickly personality that I don't even bat an eye as I get out and trade places with him.

I catch Niall's envious glance when I hop back in on the other side. A part of me feels bad for the dude because it would be hell if Sadie hadn't accepted us, but then again, Emma is justified in her feelings. If I were a shifter and I suddenly found out I had three Night Weaver mates, the Elders' sons no less, I'd be terrified too.

Thankfully, by the time we reach my family, the power is starting to level off and isn't quite as distracting.

I haven't seen my parents since I met Sadie, so I'm nervous, but also excited to hear their thoughts about her. My mom, especially, is going to love her as they're pretty much one and the same. Full of fire and passion. Not taking any shit whatsoever. To be honest, I've missed them dearly, but another part of me has stayed away on purpose. The Elders will use any outlet in their arsenal to get to us. I'm surprised they haven't already come for them. What are those bastards planning?

My mother and father are both standing on the porch of their small house when we arrive. They live in a tiny suburb on the outskirts of town, filled with other Night Weavers.

My mother is a streak of brown hair as she launches herself at me. "My son, I have missed you so much," she says and kisses me on the cheek before repeating the process with Dante and Elian.

Even Elian can't resist my mother. She'd tan his hide if he tried to push her away, and he has come to accept her need for hugs over the years.

My mom gives me the look. The distinctly *mom* look that says, *you're in trouble for not calling.*

"It's good to see you too, Mom," I say with a nervous chuckle.

"What's this I hear about you challenging the Elders, being disgraced, and having a *mate?*" she demands, placing a hand on her hip.

Yeah, she's definitely pissed at me for not telling her all this sooner. Might as well apologize now and get her scolding over with because I know it's coming. "I'm sorry I didn't call you to tell you all this, but things have been extremely... hectic lately, to say the least. Not to mention, I was afraid to drag you into my mess for fear the Elders would use you against me."

Okay, that didn't help my case any. I think she's frowning even more now.

"Kaos Remus King, you should know better than that. I am your mother. Screw those pretentious bastards. Speaking of which, why is *he* here?" She directs her venom toward Niall.

"He's helping conceal us from his fathers. They have also met their mate, a shifter, and have sworn off the Elders," I explain, and her eyes widen.

"A shifter? Oh my," she says. "Come, come inside. We shouldn't stand out here in the open much longer."

My mother leads us through the entryway and into the small living room. They downsized a few years after we were old enough to take on the estate and I don't blame them. Keeping up with the estate is a huge undertaking.

The scent of her lavender and honey cookies permeates the space, bringing me back to my childhood. Dante, Elian, and I squeeze onto the sofa while she sits across from us on the bay windowsill. Niall and Vinson choose to stand beside the sofa.

I clear my throat, feeling sheepish. "I really am sorry, Mom. We've had a lot going on lately."

She sighs. "You should have come to me, son. Your fathers and I would've helped you."

"With what?" I ask gently. "We met our mate, our true mate, who was immediately challenged. Then we were told we might lose her. The Elders were going to stick us with someone none of us could stand unless Sadie won, which she did. I just wanted to enjoy all the time with her while I could. Meeting her was such a surprise and a huge shock. You know how much true pairings have been dwindling lately."

She nods and her face softens slightly, but I can tell she's still upset. Although nothing really keeps her down for long. Something else she and Sadie have in common. "I feared with them dropping off, you wouldn't be as lucky as I was and wouldn't find yours. So, tell me about her. What's she like?"

"Feisty. You're going to love her," Dante chimes in.

I debate telling my mom the Triad revelation, but she's going to find out sooner or later. There's no sense in hiding it. "Yeah, she's a firecracker," I agree. "She's also a Triad and carries all three races in her."

My mom gasps and her blue eyes, much like my own, light up. She squeals and I cock my head at her in confusion. "My son's received such a powerful match! I knew raising you boys right would pay off. Did you hear that, Chris, and Gerrard?" My mom calls out to my fathers in the kitchen. Then, to us, she says, "You know, I've never liked those blasted Elders. Sorry, Niall."

He waves his hand. "No offense taken."

"A Triad, huh?" she asks, and I nod. "Wow, this is huge. It's going to blow this community apart." Her tone is serious, yet there's glee in her eyes.

"I know," I respond, rubbing my chin. "I think my life has been in danger more times than not lately."

And that puts the frown right back on her face. "Tell me everything," she demands. "Oh, I made your favorite cookies. Gerrard should be pulling them out of the oven any second."

I delve into everything that's happened to us since the night of the festival and my mother listens intently. At some point, my fathers, Gerrard, and Chris walk in and follow the conversation after depositing the cookies on the coffee table. When I'm finished, she takes a deep breath and snags a cookie.

"My sons are starting a revolution," she says around a mouthful, pride shining in her eyes. "I'm so damn proud of you. But—" There's always a but isn't there? "—I sense something more is going on today. Elian looks like he sucked on a lemon."

"When does he not?" Dante quips, and Elian elbows him playfully.

"I'm fine, Viola, honestly," Elian responds, dismissing her concern.

"Yeah, right. He's upset that the Light Weaver bonded to Sadie before he did," Dante says, calling him out. "If he'd pull his head out of his ass already, he could bond with her too. Somehow, she still seems interested in the prickly fucker."

My mom swats at Dante and levels Elian with one of those signature *mom* looks. "What's holding you back?"

"Nothing... not anymore," he amends. "I just don't know how to repair the damage I've done."

"Talk to her," she says to him, and the look on his face is like she told him he needs to jump through a ring of fire, naked. Yeah, Elian is not a talker. "Oh, don't look at me like that. From what you've told me, she seems like a very sensible woman. I'm sure you can win her over. And apologize. That's the main thing."

Something about my mom always brings out another side to Elian, and he suddenly looks a tad more relaxed than before, but still guarded like usual. "I'll try," he responds and looks at his pocket watch. He never talks about it, but I'm pretty sure it was a gift from his mom. "As much as we'd love to keep chatting, we need to get going," Elian says.

"Yeah, we stopped by to drop off this invitation for you all to come stay at the safe haven with us. Well, actually, to tell you you're coming to the safe haven." I reach over the coffee table and extend the portal-infused paper, explaining how it works and why we're doing it. "Gather your things and then accept. It'll take you straight to where we're staying."

"Not so fast, Kaos," my mother says before I can get up. "When will your fathers and I get to meet Sadie?"

"I, too, would like to get to know the woman my son is so smitten with," my birth dad, Gerrard, adds, watching my mother with such love in his eyes. When she's happy, he's happy, and that's something I've always said I would do for my mate one day if I ever found her. One can only hope I look that way when outsiders see me looking at Sadie.

Honestly, she's my whole world, and I'd be lost without her.

"Yeah, we would!" Chris, my mother's other mate adds.

"Soon. She's at the safe haven, but I'd rather be the one to introduce you, so don't go looking for her," I say, giving my mom a look. She tries to look innocent, but I know better.

Dante smirks. "Trust me, you'll know when you see her."

That's for sure. Even Elian cracks a smile at Dante's comment—one my mother doesn't miss.

"She's had a bit of a hard life, and I'm not sure how she'll feel about meeting my family," I explain. "So let me talk to her first, okay?"

"Okay, no worries. Tell her I won't bite her head off or anything and that I'm looking forward to meeting her," my mother says. "I know you're under a bit of a time crunch here, so I won't keep you any longer." She rises and the rest of us follow suit, trailing out of the house.

After saying goodbye, we move on to the next target on our list and then the next, and the next, until we're all so drained and exhausted that we have no choice but to call it a day and head home. I'm not complaining though. I'm so ready to see Sadie, it's not even funny. Her presence is like a balm to my soul.

Tomorrow, I'll introduce her to my parents. If she wants to meet them that is.

No pressure.

16

SADIE

Two words.

Morning. Wood.

Actually, make that ten words.

Morning. Wood. Poking. Me. In. The. Ass. From. Both. Sides.

Ahh, a girl could get used to this.

"Mmm," I say, trying to clear the tiredness from my voice. "You two were so sleepy last night, I didn't get a chance to ask, but now that you're here and hard—I mean, awake—I have a question to ask." I sit up so I can see Kaos and Dante better without having to turn and look.

"Go for it, Little Flame," Kaos mumbles, opening his bright, blue eyes still hooded with sleep. Dante merely grunts his acknowledgement. He's not a morning person. His penis is definitely a morning person, however.

"When were you going to tell me about this Awakening I'm apparently about to go through?"

That sends both of them shooting up, wide awake, and scrambling to face me. Now we're all sitting crisscross on the bed, me with my back to the headboard and them facing me.

The sudden commotion wakes a sleeping Hemsworth at our feet, who grumbles something about *Damn, Weavers and their damn sexual needs. When do I get some sexy times?* He hops down and says loudly, "I'm going to go bug Vin for something to eat. Maybe he can keep it in his pants." Before he saunters out the door, he shoots a wolfish grin over his shoulder, letting me know he's not actually that upset about it.

"We need a bigger bed. I want all of you in it. Comfortably," I say absentmindedly.

"Agreed, maybe we can push one of the others against this one." Kaos pauses to ponder the logistics of it for a moment but then realizes he's distracted. "Back up, did Reed tell you about your Awakening?"

"Yup," I say, popping the P. "He sure did."

He doesn't look upset at all. In fact, he looks relieved. "Congrats on bonding by the way. We felt the power surge while we were handing out portal-invites. Hopefully, it wasn't too bad for you? That was a hell of a rush."

"Nothing I couldn't handle," I respond. "Back to the Awakening. Why am I just now hearing about it?"

Dante sighs. "We didn't want to scare you, Angel. Or freak you out and make you think you were being forced to bond to us."

"Yeah, you found out about a hell of a lot really fast and took it very well all things considered. Not to mention our accidental bonding, that I wouldn't trade anything for, but you did freak out about it there for a while," Kaos says.

I should probably be mad they kept this from me, but I'm not. Not really. They're right. I did react badly at first.

"Point taken. Thank you for taking my feelings into account and for always thinking of me first. I lov—I appreciate you for it." I pause, eyes widening as my hand comes up to my mouth. I was totally about to tell them both I love them.

I take a moment to ponder my feelings. Is that really how I feel?

Do I love these men?

The warm fuzzies in my heart and stomach tell me yes.

Ah, to hell with it. If I've learned anything these past few months, it's that life is short. Too fucking short. I'm in love with these men, both equally. And it's about damn time I tell them how I feel.

Thankfully, they're both super patient, sensing I need a moment to gather my thoughts. Dante reaches out to play with a strand of my hair while Kaos grabs my wrist and turns it over, caressing our mate mark. A shiver runs down my spine from the tingly feeling their touch provokes. "You two keep doing that and this is heading in a totally different direction."

Dante's smile is devious. "What were you going to say, Angel?"

"I love you," I blurt before I can think about it any harder and talk myself out of putting myself out there like that. It's hard for me to be vulnerable. "I love you, Dante King. I've loved you from the moment you didn't let me leave after Savannah showed her ass. And, Kaos, I love you. I have since I saw the devotion in your eyes when we bonded. I love both of you so fucking much."

Broad smiles crest both of their faces, pure joy etched across their features. "You told me you loved me first," Dante boasts and preens like a peacock stretching his feathers. He and Kaos look at each other and pounce. Dante reaches my lips first, searing them in a bruising kiss, giving me all his fiery passion. When he lets go, he whispers against my lips, "I love you too, Angel."

Then Kaos is shoving his ass out of the way and yanking me into his lap. He kisses me all over. From my cheeks, to my lips, to my forehead, peppering me with his love and that same devotion. It makes me laugh, and I've never felt more carefree, despite all the bullshit happening around us and everything that still needs to be done. "And I love you, Sadie Sinclair. The fates sure knew what they were doing when they gave you to us. I thank the Goddess for you every single day."

Their words strike a deep chord inside of me, one I thought I'd locked away after everything I've been through. I wipe a stray tear from my eye, one of pure happiness, and dive in for a hug. Dante's heat at my back lets me know he's not going to be left out and I wouldn't want it any other way than to be wrapped in their arms.

Kaos clears his throat and puts me into Dante's arms so he can look at me fully. Why the hell does he look so sheepish?

"My parents are here and can't wait to meet you, Little Flame. I explained your situation when we dropped off their invite, and I think my mom might wring my neck if I don't introduce you to her and my dads. Would you be all right meeting them?"

My eyes widen and a spike of fear shoots through me. I'm loud and boisterous, way too opinionated, and totally not the kind of girl a guy brings home to their parents.

Or am I?

I've come a long way from the girl I was at the festival.

I can do this... right?

"I can see the gears turning in your head from here, Little Flame. You don't have to, but I want you to know that it would mean a lot to me if you would. I know they won't replace the family you've lost but I'm hoping this can be the start of a new, slightly larger one."

The understanding and hope in his eyes are enough to make me agree. *Turn over a new leaf, Sadie. You got this.*

I already met with a whole faction of Light Weavers who were technically supposed to be our enemies, and that seemed to go well. Meeting parents should be a walk in the park compared to that, shouldn't it?

How hard can it be?

Not hard at all apparently. Kaos' mom, Viola, was ecstatic to meet me. Seriously, she threw me straight into a bear hug when she saw me, and the rest was history. We've been gushing about little Kaos, Dante, and Elian for at least an hour now.

Yep, much to my mates' chagrin, she brought her entire arsenal of Kaos' baby pictures and some of the others after they bonded as a Circle. And let me tell you... they are pure gold. Part of me is sad that my mates will never know my parents like this, but the other is glad I'm not being tortured with baby pictures like they are.

"This was when Elian first learned to harness his fear magic," Viola says, handing me a picture of them sitting on the floor.

Kaos has healing magic in his hand while Dante has flames in his. Elian on the other hand has a bright smile on his face, one I've never seen him make, while Kaos' dad, Gerrard, has a horrified expression in the background. He looks seconds away from peeing his pants. But I'm barely able to focus on the photo. Viola's words about Elian's fear magic are swirling around and around in my brain.

It makes so much sense—why he's so afraid to get close to anyone. Combine that with what I've been able to deduce about his father and... I think I'm finally starting to understand the man behind the icy mask.

"Viola!" Gerrard protests and tries to yank the picture away, but Viola prevails with a pterodactyl screech and tucks the picture into her pants. Kaos looks so much like his birth father it's almost uncanny. From their face structure to their blue eyes. Not to mention Weavers don't age much, so that's kind of taking some getting used to. I'm also sensing he probably inherited the people watching from him too. "I told you to burn that picture, woman. Elian caught me off guard that day."

"That's what makes it such a gem, darling. Your expression was hilarious. Look at Elian's smile too! Oh, to go back to those days."

"All right, mother," Kaos interrupts with a chuckle. "I think that's enough embarrassment for today. How are you all adjusting?"

His mom sighs dramatically and shoots me a wink before packing the pictures up into the album. "It's a little strange being around so many Light Weavers," she admits. "But I think we're going to adjust just fine, and it seems like things are going smoothly for the most part. Everyone here is tired and ready for change. It's refreshing."

"Honey, I'm home!" A man calls from the direction of the doorway with a plate full of food from the mess hall. He sees all of us and a grin breaks out across his face, but his focus isn't on me or his sons, or anyone else for that matter. No, his gaze zeroes in on Hemsworth who is chilling by my feet.

"Chris!" Viola scolds. "You'd be late to your own damn funeral. Come, meet Sadie, Kaos' Link."

Chris glances at me then back to Hemsworth. His eyes are alight with a childish wonder despite his age. Do I look that way when I see dogs too? Eh, probably.

Hemsworth stands and wags his tail and that's all it takes.

Chris crosses the room, setting the all but forgotten plate of food down, and immediately starts petting Hemsworth.

Hemsworth, like the little attention seeker he is, eats it up. Especially when Chris starts with the butt scratches. He's a goner for sure, melting into Chris' touch.

I look around at everyone like, *are you seeing this?* Dante looks seconds away from bursting out laughing, so much so his face is turning red from holding it in. Kaos' face is morphed with shock and the others seem stunned like I am.

Viola reaches over and swats at her mate playfully, snapping him out of his dog fog. "And just who is this little fella?" Chris coos.

Even I can't deny the irony of their names.

"Nice to meet you, Chris. The name's Hemsworth," my familiar says, startling him. Chris yanks his hand away and clutches his chest. Then he looks to all of us like *you heard that, right?*

Hemsworth chuffs. "I'll never get tired of doing that."

And cue the laughter. Dante can't hold it in anymore. A guffaw so loud it's contagious bursts out of his mouth, and we all dissolve into peals of laughter. Once someone stops for a second, someone else wheezes and gets them going again. It's a never-ending cycle.

Eventually, Viola pulls herself back together to put her hands out. "Okay, okay," she says between breaths and wipes a tear from her eye from laughing so hard. "If we don't stop, I'm going to pee myself. My bladder isn't what it once was before pushing a baby out."

Kaos shakes his head and chuckles despite himself. "We should get started for the day anyway. Plus, Sadie has a date with a certain Weaver to begin her training with light, and we need to resume our campaign for allies."

Viola grips my hand in hers. "Welcome to the family, Sadie. I can see why my sons are so taken with you." We stand and she pulls me in for another hug. This is like the third or fourth one since I've been here. I'm getting the impression they are a very touchy-feely bunch. Which is fine, but more than I'm used to. It'll take me a bit for my people-o-meter to get back to normal after this endeavor.

"Yes, it was very nice to meet you," Gerrard adds.

"It was nice to meet your dog. I mean you. Ah, hell. You know what I mean," Chris says.

I can't help but chortle again. "Thank you, Viola. Likewise, Gerrard. I'm glad my familiar could bring some entertainment for you, Chris."

After everyone gives another round of hugs and goodbyes, Kaos takes my hand and leads me outside. "Come on, Little Flame. Let's get you to your training."

That wasn't bad at all.

17

VINSON

When Sadie puts her mind to something, she puts her whole self into it. Since my part of getting the shifters the message about the safe haven is over, I'm watching her and Reed train from the sidelines, and wow. She's breathtaking.

Even when she's frustrated, like now, because she's having a hard time working with the light, she's still so adorable it makes my heart ache. And knowing I have a part of her inside me, and she also has a part of me inside her?

Words can't quite describe the feeling of utter joy.

Every time I shift into my wolf, or I look down at my wrist, or even when I look at her, I'm reminded I hold that piece of her soul. Sometimes I don't feel worthy of her soul, to own the truth, but I don't let my insecurities stop me from getting closer to her either. She willingly gave me that part of herself.

For Goddess' sake, she didn't even let death stop her from coming to get me.

Dying has completely changed my outlook on life. Even now, I can feel my wolf starting to exert Alpha qualities.

CHAPTER 17 | 147

Which haven't gone unnoticed by Alpha Darren either. He approached me last night and offered to show me the ropes. He wants me to take over the pack one day, which completely shocked me. Meeting Sadie has changed my life in so many ways, and I wouldn't do a single thing differently.

Sadie's frustration bubbles over into an irritated growl which is when I decide to step in. I cross the gym and put a hand on her shoulder, inhaling her sweet scent, and she shivers under my touch.

"Hey, Luna," I whisper, giving her a peck on the cheek from behind before spinning her to face me. "What's wrong? Can I do something to help?" I can't stand to see any other emotion on her face than happiness. That's what I strive for —to keep her happy all the time.

Her green eyes find mine, her face pinched into a small frown. I want to kiss every inch of that frown until it smoothes away. "The light refuses to cooperate with me," she responds with a huff. "It's like all my sides are fighting one another for dominance. Reed keeps saying I need to draw the light out of me, but I can't. It doesn't work like that for me."

Reed gives me a grateful look over her shoulder and I return his gesture with a nod.

"It's okay, my Moon. That's understandable seeing as you're a Triad and things are probably different for you. I want you to just breathe for a second, okay?" She nods and takes a deep breath and then another. "When shifters are lucky enough to find their mate and learn to shift, the very first thing we're taught is patience. You want to know why?"

"Yes," she responds.

"It doesn't always happen overnight," I tell her. "Or easily for that matter. Usually, only Alpha's have smooth shifts. What I'm trying to say is everyone is different and that's all right."

She shakes her head. "I have to master this, Vin. I have to

be the best or everyone is going to die because I'm not strong enough. Everyone is depending on me to save them. *I can't fail!*" She screams the last part in frustration and looks down, scuffing her shoe on the floor, her teeth clenched. Damn, that won't do. My wolf gives an internal grumble in agreement. We both want our smiling, confident Sadie back.

Reed and I share another look, and he motions for me to continue.

"There might be some prophecy about you, Luna, but that doesn't mean you have to put all the pressure on yourself. Let us help carry the burden. And if you do fail, at least we tried. At least we can say we went out knowing we fought our damnedest. Let us carry the weight for a little while. We're your pack," I pause. "I mean Circle. We carry your emotions, your soul, and therefore we share all of the responsibilities together. You will never be on your own again."

She still looks uncertain. I can tell this is tough for her because I feel an echo of the worry she carries in my own chest, her soul telling me more than her expressions do. So, I don't push her more than that. She's stressed as hell, but like I said, it's not only her burden, and I'll gladly carry every single one for her if she'll let me. The others would do the same. It's why we work so well. We work as a team.

Reed clears his throat. "Stop worrying about all the what-ifs, my Love. We'll cross every single bridge as we get there. Together. Because that's what mates do. Okay?"

I can still feel echoes of uncertainty and insecurity through our bond, but she says, "Okay. I'm sorry I freaked out on you both, but I've never really cared about anyone this much and it scares me knowing what all I stand to lose if this doesn't go right…"

I brush a strand of hair behind her ear and Reed puts his hand on her shoulder from behind in support. "We'll get those bastards, Love," Reed says. "Don't you worry."

She sighs. "Can we do something else for a little while? I think I need a break."

A smile tips the corner of my lips because I have the perfect solution. "I have an idea, Luna. How would you like to hang out with the pack? We're having a big meeting with the new shifters tonight to welcome them into the fold. We're even going to run, mated shifters and not. Darren wants to start a new tradition."

Her face lights up in excitement. "Mated or not? So, everyone is going to run together?"

"Yes, my Moon. How would you like to run with the wolves?"

She grins broadly and takes my hand. "I'd really love that, Vin. Plus, I'm intrigued by this new tradition idea. Would it be all right for Reed to tag along with us?"

Before I can respond, her stomach rumbles loudly, and I take that as a personal offense. No mate of mine is going to go hungry while I'm around. I'm a chef for crying out loud.

"Of course, my Moon, everyone is welcome. But first, let me cook you something and take your mind off things. The meeting doesn't start for another hour, anyway."

"Oh, that sounds delightful. You know how much I love your cooking. Do we have some stuff to make your famous BLT-jelly sandwiches?"

"I think I can make it work." I wink at her and she smiles.

I'd do anything for that smile.

Sadie

I will never get tired of Vin's cooking. Seriously, this man is a wizard. He might not be a Weaver, but he definitely cooks like he puts magic into every single ingredient, every motion, every spice. He makes every meal with precision... and love.

Moaning around the mouthful of his homemade sandwich, I realize Reed and Vin are watching me instead of eating.

"What?" I ask, covering my mouth while I chew. It's not like they haven't seen me completely ravenous before, but a lady does have standards. Kind of. "I can't help it. It's so good," I say when they continue to stare at me hungrily. I wipe the corner of my mouth, and thankfully there's no jelly or crumbs stuck there.

"Fucking hell, I want to hear you moan like that around my cock," Vin responds cheekily, and I swat his arm.

"Me too," Reed agrees, eyes banked with desire. Vin's are too, glowing gold meaning his wolf is watching. Their lust floods through the bond, momentarily distracting me, but ultimately the food wins out.

"And I thought I was the insatiable one," I quip with a wink before taking another bite. "So good," I reiterate in case they didn't hear me the first time.

Reed takes a bite for himself, and his eyes widen. He gives Vin a nod of approval. "It really is delicious," he says. "You sure can cook, bro. Thank fuck. I'm a book person, not a food person."

Vin laughs and starts to enjoy his BLTJ alongside us. We sit in companionable silence while we eat, savoring the food and the company. This is how I wish our lives could be all the time. Carefree.

Once we deal with the Elders, I remind myself. *Then it can be.*

When we're finished, Vinson takes our plates and washes them off. I help him dry them and then he takes us over to where the shifters are staying. Much like the first time I went to a shifter party, they're all standing around enjoying themselves. Dancing, talking, having a wonderful time. I'm surprised at how many of them there are, and it warms my heart to see them happy and most importantly, safe.

Some of the mated shifters are in their wolf forms, running around and playing with each other. There's a small gaggle of children scampering in circles around their mothers. All in all, everyone seems like one big happy family —like this is any other BBQ on the block or something. I truly love their dynamics.

I spot a Night Weaver or two in the crowd, namely Oliver's Circle and Malachi. They're socializing with the shifters with broad smiles on their faces. I make a mental note to speak to Viola about how to get everyone else involved also.

Emma and her mates are here too. Adam, Nick, and Niall look slightly awkward chatting with a few shifters who appear to be Emma's friends. I'm sure it's strange for them but they're doing well, all things considered.

And much to my surprise, some of Reed's faction are here, mingling with the shifters. Hades is holding a ball of light in his hand and doing tricks for them and he's amassing quite the crowd too. That man is a handful, but he definitely cracks me up. I'm glad he's on our side.

When Reed sees his faction members, he smiles and waves to them. To us, he says, "It's so nice to see everyone mingling together."

"It really is," I respond. Reed takes my hand in his while I take Vinson's in my other and we walk into the throng of people, getting lost in the crowd.

18

SADIE

They really aren't lying when they say time flies when you're having fun. Especially when you're getting to know everyone and making new friends left and right. Usually, Ash is the charismatic one, but tonight, I feel like it's me.

The next thing I know, it's dark outside. The shifters gather around a large fire as it's finally starting to get cool at night. Not that I think it would stop them from having a fire anyway.

Alpha Darren came to us earlier and said he wants to make every shifter that seeks refuge with us a part of his pack instead of the separate ones that form by different households. I couldn't think of a better idea, or Alpha, so I concurred that this is for the best. We're still working on a pack name, but it gives me hope for the future.

Standing around, the fire illuminates everyone's faces, casting them with an orangish glow. Hades throws up a few balls of light to help brighten the space. Anticipation mingles in the air as we wait for Alpha Darren to give us his big speech.

Speaking of which, he walks to the center of the giant circle we've got going around the fire and claps his hands. "If I could have everyone's attention," he calls out with a serious expression on his face, and everyone hushes.

He smooths his hands down his dark jeans, which pairs nicely with his red flannel shirt before beginning. "To start with, I'd like to welcome you all and say we're glad you're here. For the first order of business tonight, I want to induct every shifter into my pack who wants to join us. I also want to reiterate that it is not required, but we'd love it if you would."

The shifters start murmuring quietly but from what I can tell, their talk is positive. Reed squeezes my hand so that must mean he concurs from hearing their thoughts.

Darren waits for the whispers to stop before continuing. "As most of you have heard by now, our Shadowbringer and first Triad endorses my idea. We should no longer be separate. We are one. We are a pack!" He lets out a loud howl that's followed by several others. Some of the ones close to me even give me a nod of approval, looks of awe on their faces.

"To the future!" Carter, his beta, shouts.

"To the future!" we repeat as one.

One by one, Alpha Darren calls the new shifters up and inducts them into the pack. The process is fascinating. He cuts their palm before saying a few words then placing theirs and his together, and bam, new member of the pack. I've noticed palms are important in the magical community. They connect mates and they connect packs. It's interesting, to say the least.

"This is fascinating," Reed says in agreement, watching everything with wide eyes.

I glance at Vin and feel an echo of pride and hope thrumming through our soul bond.

When the new shifters have been introduced into the pack Alpha Darren clears his throat to get everyone to focus on him once more. "If everyone doesn't mind, I'd like to do something a little different. We have someone among us who is family, even part shifter, but is not an official part of the pack yet." He pauses and looks at me. Several other heads whip in my direction, following his line of sight. "I say it's time to bring her into the fold, what about you?"

The resounding *yes* echoes around us as Alpha Darren points to me and smiles. "Sadie Sinclair, our Shadowbringer, you are one of us. Would you like to officially join the pack?"

I'm too stunned to speak. Logically, I know I'm part shifter so I don't know why I wouldn't be accepted into the pack, but I hadn't dared to dream.

Vin nudges me softly. Crap, they're waiting for me to respond.

Alpha Darren walks over to me and lowers his voice so only the two of us will hear. "If you're worried, you shouldn't be. I won't have access to your thoughts or anything like that, but I will be able to sense you and send you messages if need be."

"It's not that," I whisper. "I don't have a wolf…"

He shakes his head, amusement in his eyes. "You might not have a wolf, but you are one of us. You're also Vinson's fated mate which means you're pack." He turns, addressing the crowd once more. "I think I speak for all of us when I say we'd love nothing more than for our champion to join us."

"One of us! One of us!" the crowd chants loudly as one, stomping their feet on the ground. The energy radiating is infectious and washes over me. I can feel the rightness of it in my bones. I want to belong. I want to unite everyone and forget our differences and erase the injustices. I want to be a part of the pack.

My heart fills with joy at the feeling of being wanted. So

many times I've thought about everything I've been through in life and wondered what it would've been like if I had made different choices, but everything has led me here and I wouldn't change a damn thing. All of this has led me to my mates, to here, to save this world.

My world. I belong here.

Reed squeezes my hand, and I realize he's probably listening to my thoughts, but I don't care. I'm glad he knows how I feel.

"I would love to join the pack, Alpha." Alpha Darren nods and holds out his hand for me to place mine in. The crowd whoops and hollers in victory, clapping their hands. Their excitement makes me laugh. Vin's joy is shining as bright as mine. I refocus on Darren's hands which are extremely large and calloused. Like his fingers are the size of two of mine put together. Definitely finger-fuck worthy.

Reed nudges me, and I snap my gaze away from the Alpha's too-large-to-not-be-mini-dick fingers and place my hand in his. He turns my palm over and shifts one of his massive fingers into a claw. There's a prick of pain before he's mixing my blood with his, slamming our bleeding palms together. I feel it the moment the Alpha bond snaps into place.

The bond is completely different than with my mates, in the sense that it's more of an echo, not as strong, and feels like camaraderie with my fellow pack. I definitely don't want to bone every single one of them like I do my Sworn.

Pack, my mind registers.

I'm a part of the pack.

The crowd cheers again, shouting and dancing while banging their chests. It's wild and I fucking love it. Some of the mated shifters even start howling, joining their voices in with the rest of them.

Once the crowd settles, I watch as Adam, Nick, and Niall

approach. Emma is behind them, looking confused. "Alpha Darren," Adam begins, and I notice him shift his gaze so he's not staring directly into the Alpha's eyes, deferring to his leadership. He clears his throat. "As a show of our goodwill toward our mate, we would also like to request to join the pack, if you will have us." There's nothing but complete sincerity on his face and in his voice.

Whoa. Can Weavers even join a pack of shifters? I project to Vin.

He shakes his head. *I'm not entirely certain.*

Darren stares at them so long that even I start to squirm and I'm not even the one under the gun. Time continues to tick by, and I wonder if he's going to speak. Eventually, he casts his gaze over the crowd. "These three Night Weavers would like to be a part of the pack," he announces. "What do we say?"

Murmurs erupt through the shifters, and everyone turns antsy. "What are your thoughts, Shadowbringer?" Darren asks.

This a monumental decision, one that could be a turning point for Weavers and shifters alike. I mull it over and decide to speak from my heart. That usually seems to work in my favor over blurting things out. "I think we should let them join," I respond. "They're mated to a shifter, and I suspect they won't be the last. Let them prove to Emma they're serious about her." The trio gives me a grateful look, and I check them with my intuition. They're doing this for the right reasons.

"Besides, if we remain a separate unit, separate people, would we be any different from the Elders?" Vinson asks. The crowd mulls it over and most of them shake their heads *no*.

"All right. Unless there are any objections, I agree," Alpha Darren says and pauses in case anyone disagrees. No one says anything. "I'm not sure how the bond will work between full Night Weavers and shifters, but I suspect it will be a tad different," he says, getting ready to slice Adam's palm.

"That's fine. We want to prove our worthiness to our mate and to this cause," Adam responds.

The Alpha nods and quickly slices Adam's palm, repeating the process for Nick and Niall. They have a dumbstruck look on their faces when it's finished, and it mirrors the one on Emma's. Yeah, she's totally falling for them.

I waggle my eyebrows at her and mouth, *get it, girl.* She giggles and returns her attention to her mates.

"We're a pack for all!" Alpha Darren boasts loudly, and everyone cheers. "Now, let's have our first run as a whole pack!"

That jolts everyone into action, even me. Vinson shifts into his enormous, black wolf in a split second, my shadows surrounding him like the first time he shifted, and then we're off, my hand in Reed's so I don't lose him in the chaos, sprinting through the woods surrounding the safe haven.

My hair billows behind me as I run, my feet slapping the ground as I go. The leaves are starting to change into their fall colors so everything around us is beautiful, especially with the moon's light gracing everything with its presence.

Vin's wolf tilts his head back and gives a carefree howl, which several of the other wolves return. Even Reed joins in, so I say fuck it and do the same until eventually, everyone, no matter their race, is howling alongside us.

This is how we were always meant to be.

19

SADIE

"You're up late," I comment as I walk into the study to find Elian nose deep in one of Reed's ancestors' journals.

To be honest, I can't sleep because the guilt of leaving Ash, even after the heartache she caused, and not knowing what happened to her is gnawing at me. I come to a stop at the edge of the desk and take a moment to admire Elian's physique. His sharp jawline, his muscular, tattooed arms, his pursed lips. "I didn't take you for the studious type," I say when the silence drags on too long for my taste.

He lifts those emerald eyes to meet mine and everything unsaid stretches between us. We haven't had alone time like this since the night against the tree, and he definitely didn't want to talk then. Not that I minded. Thinking about him between my thighs has my toes curling and my heart rate accelerating.

"There's a lot you don't know about me." His voice is husky, likely from lack of sleep. He takes a sip of the whiskey sitting on his desk and my nose crinkles when the scent hits my nostrils. My body wants to freeze, to react to the smell as memories try to surface, but I force myself not to panic like I did at the festival with my ex, Tyler.

Elian may be an asshole, but he would never harm me like that, and my brain knows it. Elian doesn't miss my reaction either, even with me tamping down on the trauma that tries to make itself known.

"Viola told me about your fear ability," I blurt.

Elian tenses and looks away from me. From this distance, I can just make out what looks like an inked scythe with roses wrapped around it sprawling up the side of his neck. How have I never noticed it before?

His tattoos are stunning. One of these days, I want to inspect all his ink. Thoroughly. Maybe even get one of my own.

"So, you know what I can do," he says.

"Yes," I respond simply, picking up the journal he put down. I was right, it's another of the Light Weaver's past leaders, but one I haven't read yet. "What I don't know, or rather, understand, is why you want to hide that from me."

He grunts and his gaze returns to mine. "Let's be honest, Pet. We aren't exactly on the best of terms most of the time." The self-deprecating quality to his tone seems to say *and it's all my fault.*

"And yet, you've been inside me."

Those few words are enough to set his normally icy gaze ablaze. "That I have," Elian says, rubbing his jaw in thought. "Sadie. I—" he pauses and runs his hands through his hair, tugging. The next thing I know, he's towering over me—his mask completely gone. Other than that night we fucked or in the Goddess' realm, I've never seen Elian look this vulnerable. He cups my cheek with his tattooed hand, bringing my eyes to his. "Fuck, why is this so hard to say?"

"I don't know, but you've never minced words before. Why start now?" I ask gently, trying not to smell the whiskey on his breath. My heart races despite knowing he won't hurt me.

He blows out a breath and the scent of alcohol hits me, but I hold my breath. "You're right. I want to apologize for the way I've treated you. When I first saw you at the concert, I knew by your aura that you were our Link, and I still pushed you away. If you hadn't bonded to Kaos, I probably would've let you walk away because every woman in my life has been killed—*murdered*—because of me."

He drops my cheek and turns to pace back and forth in front of me. "I'm powerful, Sadie, but my father was more so. My ability to control fear was child's play compared to his, and that man has never loved anyone but himself."

I've heard some powers can be passed down from parents, but it doesn't always happen. Still, I'm not surprised Elron could control fear. Fitting for a man like him.

"Screw him, Elian. He's dead. Don't let his ghost continue to haunt you." Pot calling kettle black here with my aversion to whiskey, but I digress.

Elian shakes his head, still pacing, before glancing over at me. "You don't understand. My mother and sister got caught in the crossfire of one of our fights." He pauses to take another deep breath, and I let him, allowing him to work through all the emotions I can see storming in his eyes.

"Unlike Dante, I wasn't allowed to live with Kaos' parents full-time. My father still demanded my presence most nights. One day, I finally decided I'd had enough of his shit. It was after a particularly gruesome night, one he spent three hours marking me with his razor. That was when I hit my breaking point. Since I wasn't perfect in his eyes, I had to atone for every single imperfection. A hair out of place? Mark. Said the

CHAPTER 19 | 161

wrong thing at dinner? Mark. A second too late to anything? Mark. You have to understand... I was fed up. Done. I decided then that I was going to kill him."

I have a feeling I know where this is going and it's killing me for him. My own past with my uncle threatens to wield its ugly head, but I shove it down, knowing I need to focus on Elian right now and not be stuck in my head. That dark part inside of myself feels a sort of kinship with him. "Oh, Elian..." I whisper, not with pity but with sympathy.

"Don't. Do not pity me," he snaps, misreading my expression. "I made my bed with my choices and now I have to lie in it—even if you hate me forever because of it. It's time you know the truth about me."

"Elian..." I try again, but he stops pacing and puts a finger against my lips to stop me from saying anything else.

"I had it all planned out. Once he was finished marking me, I was going to steal his razor and slit his throat with it. I'd learned how to mask my fear around him and I was good at it, or so I thought. I convinced myself that my ability had finally surpassed my father's. What a fucking fool I was..." The pain radiating off him is almost enough to choke on. I want nothing more than to wrap my arms around him, but I know he's not that kind of guy. He'd shut down and close off and that's not what I want. I want him to finally let it all out. To let me help carry the weight he holds constantly. So, I stay quiet and wait for him to continue.

"My mother and sister weren't supposed to be home that night. If they hadn't been home... They might still be here."

"You don't know that."

"It doesn't matter either way because I failed them. My father played me. Gods, I still remember his smile—the look of triumph in his eyes when he marched them down to the basement and slaughtered them in front of me in retaliation for my actions. I swore after that I'd never get close to anyone else other than my Circle. I'd bide my time until I could murder the bastard, even if that meant turning into what I am now. A cruel, cold-hearted bastard, and it worked... until you waltzed into my life."

I can't help myself when I blurt, "What about Savannah?"

Elian snorts. "As if that wretched bitch could hold a candle to you. She was a means to an end—expendable. I didn't give a fuck about her so if my father used her to get to me, he wouldn't get very far."

"Elian... I—I don't even know what to say." I expected his life to be fucked-up, the others have told me so several times, but this? Well, this is more than I imagined. Maybe we are more similar than I thought...

"You don't have to say anything. But there it is. My ugly truth. In my quest to bring him down, I lost my way. It wasn't until you started calling me on my bullshit that I realized I was becoming like him." He looks disgusted with himself, so I reach up and smooth the frown from his brow. He leans into the touch like I'm his lifeline. It's my turn to be his life raft.

I have so many questions. I want him to tell me everything, but instead, I ask, "Is this why you have so many tattoos?" I watch him closely, trying not to say the wrong thing. This is the most he's ever opened up to me, and I'm terrified of losing our footing again. His expression is the most open I've ever seen it and he has the same look in his eyes the night I found him jumping off the cliff.

"I'd rather be covered in ink than reminded of those scars," he says.

I can definitely understand that.

I know I have to be careful not to push him away or push him too hard, but I can tell he's seconds away from slipping his mask back on and I don't want that. I want *him*. Every-fucking-thing about him. Ugly truths and all.

"Elian, you know their deaths aren't your fault, right?"

"How could they not be? If I had been—"

"No," I interrupt, tone firm. "None of that. It was not your fault." I punctuate my point with a jab to his chest. "Look, there's something I've been meaning to tell you, but I haven't really had you alone until now."

His hand returns to my face, and he grips the back of my neck but not enough to hurt. Just enough for him to feel in control. "What is it?"

"Your mother and sister weren't in the In-Between," I admit, and his face drops. I reach a hand up and tilt his chin until his eyes are back to mine. "That means they'd already crossed over. They didn't feel like they had unfinished business in their life. And even though they weren't there I still told your story. I know, in my heart, they heard me. They know, Elian, and they're not mad at you."

His eyes shine with unshed tears, the emerald color far more vibrant than usual before he blinks them away. When he reaches up with his other hand to tuck a stray strand of my hair behind my ear, I catch a glimpse of a tiny piece of bare skin on his wrist... in the exact place a mate mark would go.

Quick as lightning, I snatch his wrist and pull his sleeve down so I can further inspect the tattoo-free patch of skin there. Sure enough, there's a spot just big enough for a mate mark.

"You—I thought... Your skin is blank here?" The last part comes out as more of a question.

He watches me inspect his skin. "It is," he says.

"You saved a spot for a mate mark?"

"I did."

My eyes search his. "Even though you didn't know if you'd ever meet your Link?"

He nods. "I always dreamed I would even as much as I

dreaded it because of my father. I still held hope and here you are."

Something inside of me shifts. I let go of the part of myself I've been holding back from Elian, deciding to say to hell with it. If he burns me then so be it. I can take his heat. If he freezes me out, I'll thaw his ice. I'm done keeping him at arm's length. I'm ready for *more* from him.

Hell, I've been imagining him on his knees worshiping me since the night in the woods. And that memory is enough to make my nipples tighten and my core clench.

"Get over here and fucking worship me, Elian. That simple apology for your actions earlier isn't enough. I need you to *prove* it to me. Prove to me that you're serious," I respond breathlessly.

He has a similar reaction to mine, his face morphing from sadness and heartbreak to heat and possessiveness. He's going to own me, possibly even damn me, I can see it in his eyes, but I don't care. I want this.

"With pleasure, my Pet."

The control he always keeps so tightly wound snaps. His lips descend on mine, and he makes no hesitation, sticking his tongue in to tangle with my own.

The taste of whiskey invades my mouth and I almost freeze, my mind trying to slip into the past, dredging up Mickey's face. Elian senses me about to panic and bites my lip. The slight pain works to bring me out of the past and I refocus my attention on him, savoring his lips on mine. His taste mingles with the whiskey, and I find I almost like it, but only because of who I'm with.

The kiss is over way too soon when he suddenly drops to his knees and looks up at me with his gorgeous eyes still storming, but with heat this time—no mask either. This is all him. Raw, unfiltered Elian.

CHAPTER 19 | 165

"You know, I quite like seeing you like this," I tease, threading my hands through his hair.

Elian places a kiss at the apex of my clothed thighs and says, "You are the only woman I would ever get on my knees for, Sadie Sinclair. Now I want you to watch as I worship you like the absolute Goddess you are."

Shock tumbles through me. "I'm surprised you remember me saying that the last time we had sex."

"I remember every moment with you."

His words send a jolt straight to my clit. My vagina puts her thinking cap on and goes to work, instantly flooding my pussy. Elian yanks my sleep shorts off and shreds my panties, stuffing them in his pants pocket with a wicked grin. This must be his thing. I don't protest because I know it won't do me any good, but I do make a mental note to buy him some more panties to shred.

Next thing I know, he's spreading my thighs and licking me from my clit to my ass. A gasp escapes my lips from the sensation.

"Elian," I breathe and tip my head back. If he wasn't holding on to me, I'd probably collapse from the surprise and utter pleasure. One lick and I'm convinced my cocky asshole has a magic tongue.

"Yes, my Pet?" When I'm too shocked to say anything else he smirks up at me. "Don't worry, you'll be screaming my name in a moment. I'll have you writhing before me and then, and only then, will I spear you with my cock."

My pussy practically weeps from his dirty words, but thankfully, he doesn't keep me waiting long. Instead, he dives in again, scraping my clit with his teeth before sucking on it and then sliding a finger to my back entrance to tease me.

"Fuuuck." My eyelids flutter close from the sheer bliss.

"Eyes on me, Pet," he growls, and my gaze instantly

returns to his, the commanding tone too sexy to resist. "So obedient. So good. So delicious. This pretty pussy was made for me."

He dips his head between my thighs again. My fingers thread through his hair tighter, and I use that to ride his face. He relishes in it too. By the time I feel the pressure start to build in my core, I'm fairly certain he's licked every fucking inch of me down there. He sticks one finger inside of my ass and the other in my heat, curling that digit. That's all it takes for me to come on his face.

"Oh Gods, Elian!"

My knees almost give out from the pure pleasure coursing through me, but he holds me up and refuses to let me fall. Once he's satisfied he's licked me clean, he pulls back, grinning with my juices covering his chin. His smile is feral when he says, "You taste divine."

I'm still weak in the knees, but somehow I manage to yank his shirt and pants off when he stands, and I admire his inked body. "You're stunning," I whisper when I realize he's waiting for me to say something. When we fucked in the woods, it was dark, but here in the study, there's enough light for me to see him. All of him. Something flashes in his eyes; insecurity, maybe? But it's gone before I can really be sure.

"Even with my scars?" he asks, his posture rigid, like he's waiting for me to reject him.

"Even with your scars," I confirm.

A squeal escapes my throat as my feet suddenly leave the floor. Elian wraps my legs around him and deposits me on the desk. He aligns himself at my entrance and pushes into me with one hard thrust. A gasp escapes my lips as he starts thoroughly fucking me. My fingers find his back and I rake them down his skin, hard. He groans and starts fucking me harder. At some point, my shadows come out to play, twirling and dancing around us.

He pinches my nipple, drawing a choking gasp from me, then he puts his lips over mine and kisses me senseless, all the while thrusting inside of me.

In fact, he's fucking me so thoroughly the desk underneath me starts to creak and groan, shouting its protests at us. It's a pretty solid wooden desk too. Elian growls and hefts me up, keeping himself inside of me while walking backwards.

I yank his mouth to mine once more, needing his lips against me. I can still taste a hint of whiskey on his tongue but it's mixed with the taste of me, and I'm honestly surprised at how much it doesn't bother me as he walks out of the study and hurries down the hallway. He shakes his head suddenly, laughing into our kiss, like he's suddenly remembering something. I feel the familiar cold surrounding us from his shadow magic as he transports us elsewhere. Huh, seems like I distracted him so much he forgot he could shadow us.

"Where are we going?" I ask breathlessly.

"I'm taking you to my bed, Pet, so I can worship you better. You're going to ride my cock and take every single inch inside of that gorgeous pussy."

I groan. "Elian... please." My back bounces against his soft bed, which creaks when he throws me down on it. I miss his fullness when he slips out of me. "Shit, be careful!" I shout. "You're going to break the bed."

What is it with unsturdy furniture around here?

He smirks. "Who fucking cares? As far as I'm concerned, if this bed makes it through what I want to do to you then I wasn't doing enough."

And that's one of the hottest things anyone has ever said to me. If vaginas could purr then mine would definitely be rumbling Elian's praises.

Deciding to test the waters, I say, "Then quit talking and

start fucking me again, Elian."

He pauses and makes sure I'm listening before saying anything. "Before we go any further, you should know, I'm never going to give you up after this. Do you understand? You are mine from this moment on. There's no going back. Is this what you want?"

"Yes," I respond with complete conviction. "Damn me, Elian. I never want to go back to the way things were. This is so much better."

His eyes implore me, like they're searching my very soul. "I may not always say or do the right thing. I'm still an asshole at heart. Can you live with that?"

"I want you, Elian. Asshole and all." My shadows spank his ass, and he jolts, looking at me with pure lust on his face.

"Then kiss me, my Goddess," he responds.

If this moment wasn't so serious, I'd ask if that's considered blasphemous, but considering Elian is flipping our positions and pulling me on top of him so he can align his giant cock at my entrance, I decide to let it go. For someone who craves control, this is huge for him.

He lets me set the pace and I sink down on him tortuously slow just for all those snide and dickish comments he's made to me since I've known him. My teasing is effective judging by the way his hips shift slightly underneath me and the way his eyes roam my bare skin. His fingers dig into the skin on my hips so hard I know I'll have bruises tomorrow. Fine by me.

I begin to notice more and more of his tattoos. On his chest is a beautiful, fallen angel surrounded by shadows and more roses matching the ones on his neck. On his shoulder is a compass leading to the north star, which is really cool. The other shoulder houses a pocket watch with the clock hands stopped at a specific time. They're perfect and fit him so well.

"Sadie," he says impatiently, and I smirk. The thing I'm

not counting on is how me torturing him ramps up my own desire as well. I'm already turned on from him fucking me on the desk and a part of me wants to savor this moment because I've waited for it for so long.

Eventually, I give in to what the desire zapping between us wants, lowering myself until he's buried to the hilt inside me, loving the sound he makes when I do.

"Gods, Sadie. You're a fucking Goddess," he rasps. "Take your pleasure from me. I'm yours to own tonight."

And sploosh. I'm a fucking goner. I know he's a glutton for control so for him to say that? It takes a lot.

Ever so slowly, I start rocking on Elian's cock, building the pressure and passion between us, taking him how I want. When slow becomes too slow, I start moving faster and faster, using my hands on his chest to help control my movements. Staring down at Elian like this while his eyes are so banked in lust makes me truly feel like the Goddess he thinks I am.

"How does it feel, Pet?" he pants, watching my every movement, his grip on my hips still firm.

"You feel so fucking good inside me, Elian," I respond, or at least I think that's what I say. I'm barely able to stay coherent, so lost in the pleasure that is Elian King. For all I know I might've told him he's the fucking God of Cock or something. Either way, it makes him smug as fuck.

He places his hands on my ass, no longer able to keep them to himself, and starts smacking me down on him even harder. The wet slaps of our coupling echo through the bedroom, and I swear I hear someone that sounds suspiciously like Dante, cheering us on before Elian adjusts my angle and starts hitting me in a spot that makes me see fucking stars. No, supernovas.

Hell, let's be honest, there's not even a word for what I'm experiencing right now.

"Come for me, Sadie," he beckons and smoothly flips our positions in a move I'm jealous of. He pistons into me like his fucking life depends on it. Harder and harder, hitting that sweet spot inside of me over and over.

"Yes!" I yell as my pussy flutters and clamps around his dick. With a few more hard strokes I take him over the edge with me and he spills his hot seed inside of me as the bed beneath us snaps and collapses, making me squeal in surprise.

The sound of it echoes throughout the cabin, and the thump, thump, thump of several pairs of feet reach my ears as the rest of my mates slam into the room throwing the door open with wide eyes searching for threats.

When they find us naked with the bed broken beneath us, they calm down. I'm slightly embarrassed for all of five seconds before I start laughing. Elian seems cocky as fuck on top of me. Kaos' stare is super intense and more than turned on. Reed blushes and pushes up his glasses, but he doesn't look away.

"Mind if I join?" Dante asks, waggling his eyebrows to which Elian chucks one of the pillows at him.

"I'll fix that tomorrow," Vin says, gesturing to the bed with a salute and a wink.

I can feel myself turning red when Kaos herds everyone through the door and they leave as quickly as they came, but not without Dante loudly protesting the whole way.

Completely and utterly spent, Elian wraps his arms around me, and I lay my head on his chest. It takes ages for me to come back down to earth, which is fine by me. It gives me a moment to relish the feeling of being in Elian's arms.

A part of me expected him to take my hand and complete the bond, but he didn't, and I want *him* to be the one to take *my* hand. He's the one who has struggled through all of this, so I want it to be his decision. I know where I stand on the idea.

I open my mouth to ask about it when Elian says, "Now, why don't you tell me why you really came to see me tonight?"

Shit.

20

ELIAN

"How did you know?" she asks, scrambling to look at me, as if I couldn't sense her nervousness earlier. Her aura shows me exactly what she's feeling, which for an asshole like me, really works in my favor.

Although I do quite love this game we play, bantering back and forth with each other. She does too, even if she won't admit it out loud. Maybe after this shift between us, she will.

"I'm a smart guy, Pet. Tell me what it is you want."

I stroke the silky skin of her side, loving the goosebumps that appear afterward. From the way her pupils dilate even after she already came, she also likes the feel of my skin against hers.

I'm waiting for her to take my hand and complete the bond, but she hasn't, and I know I'm not deserving of it so I don't push it. I can't believe I'm the last one either. I'm pissed at myself for it. For letting the guys complete the bond with her before me.

Logically, I know it's my fault, but fuck. It infuriates me

that the shifter and the Light Weaver bonded to her before I did. Even so, I want this to be wholly her choice. I don't want to take anything else from her which is another reason I haven't jumped at the chance. I did mean what I said earlier about not going back from here and she agreed which placates the caveman in me a fraction.

She takes a deep breath. "We need to rescue Ash."

My eyebrow raises at her words. "And what makes you think I'm going to risk my hide and yours for that traitorous bitch?"

Sadie bites her lip. "Well, as you know, I had the chance to talk to her parents while I was in the In-Between. Mickey is reanimating them to make her think he brought them back. Look, I'm still angry with her, that won't go away overnight, but I'm also trying to understand. I can't sit here and say I would've reacted differently had that fucker reanimated Skylar or my dad and put a geas on me. She's as new to this world as I am and doesn't understand they're not actually back. Apparently, Mickey can only bring them to life for a short while, dragging their consciousnesses from the afterlife to the In-Between, and it's painful for them. We have to make her understand."

That bastard is pulling them from the afterlife?

Fucking hell.

"That's messed up and one of the most disrespectful things you can do to the dead."

"Yeah, it's no wonder he has the Elders' full support," she quips with an eye roll, making my lips twitch. "I still wonder how that happened."

"Good question. Something I'm sure we'll find out eventually. If there's anything those fuckers like to do, it's brag. Have you told the others you want to find her?" I ask, and I'm betting the answer is no.

She worries her lip between her teeth again. "No." *Bingo.*

"But I will after this. I'm only worried they won't understand like I know you will. You do some sketchy shit to protect your Circle brothers."

Gods, if she only knew how true that statement is. The lengths I'd go to protect her—to protect all of them. Every decision I've ever made, good or bad, has been to protect them. And now her.

"Ah, so you brought this harebrained idea to me first, huh?" I smirk on the outside but on the inside, I'm honored. It's a big deal she came to me, trusting me to come up with a solution. The thought she believes in me soothes the metaphorical beast inside of me, so much it's almost preening. Moons, this woman drives me wild.

"Yeah, I did," she admits. "I'm hoping you might have some intel on where she's being kept or how to get her back. It's not right what they're doing to her family. They were once my family too, you know."

"Sneaky, little Pet," I purr. "Sure, I can try to get that information for you, but it's going to cost you."

A devilish grin spreads across her face. "What did you have in mind?"

I'm terrible at expressing my feelings, always striving to be the leader and protector. But I can show her every minute of every day how much I am willing to give up and the lengths I'm willing to go for her. How much I'm hers, and I intend to show her that right now.

"You," I growl and flip us over. "I'm nowhere near done worshiping my Goddess."

21

SADIE

Throwing on a tank top and some workout shorts, I get ready for my training with Reed, throwing my hair up into a loose ponytail before exiting our room. The guys, minus Vinson, are out recruiting again today, leaving Reed and I to train.

Vin is in the kitchen when I walk in. He's wearing a black apron on top of his gray T-shirt and jeans, and his muscled arms look as scrumptious as the food he's whipping up smells. He has training with Alpha Darren today, shadowing him on Alpha stuff. He's fitting into the role rather nicely. I've noticed while we're out and about more and more shifters are deferring to Vin.

When he finds me looking, he grins at me and says, "Good morning, Luna," before returning to the stove. The man takes his cooking seriously, that's for sure. I don't think I've ever seen him burn anything. "Are you hungry?" he asks, stirring what looks like sausage gravy.

Gods, how did he know I've been craving biscuits and gravy?

See? Part wizard, I tell you.

"Extremely," I respond, and my stomach gives an answering growl to punctuate it.

"Don't worry, my Moon. I'm making plenty. I'll take good care of you." The last of his words send a spike of lust straight down to my clit, which I have to mentally tell to calm the fuck down.

"Mmm," I start, thinking about the almost possessive way he likes to take care of me. "Speaking of which, is that a shifter thing?"

"Which part?" he asks. "Me wanting to take care of you?"

"Yeah, it seems like the male shifters are always taking care of the females. Like when you let us eat before you."

"It is," he confirms. "Once a male shifter is mated, he's overcome with the urge to take care of his mate. It's a little different for us because I'm sharing you with the others, but yes."

I watch as he brings the steaming spoon to his lips to taste the gravy and it distracts me for a second. His eyes flick over to me, and he grins before returning it to the pot to keep stirring.

"I love the shifters' customs," I tell him truthfully. "It seems like you really cherish the women and children, even the other males. I've seen a few scuffles, but most of the time you all get along so nicely."

"Pack is family," he says simply. "We may bicker sometimes, but at the end of the day, our bonds are thick."

"What does it feel like having a wolf?" I ask softly, catching Vin's eye.

He turns off the stove so he doesn't burn the gravy and gives me his full attention, pondering my question. "It's like a comforting presence that's always in my mind. Even before I shifted, I could see him. Right now, he's prancing around in circles, preening under your attention. Oh, and he's fucking horny. Seriously. Dude never wants me to keep it in my pants."

I crack a smile. "Is that so?"

He nods and not so subtly adjusts himself under his apron. "Extremely."

What I wouldn't give to have a wolf of my own, I think wistfully. But that doesn't seem to be in the cards for me.

"I've had no inklings or even a feeling of a wolf inside me," I admit. "I wish I had though." That's an understatement. I long to run as beasts with Vin, but he can likely sense my feelings about it through the bond, so I don't voice it aloud.

"It's okay, Luna," he says, rounding the island to give me a kiss on the forehead before pulling me into a hug. "You're special in so many other ways." He returns to cooking, but not before giving me another peck on the lips.

Reed walks into the kitchen freshly showered, wearing dark gray sweatpants, which highlight the outline of his dick, and a blue tank top that makes his gray eyes pop. He makes his way over to me, stopping beside me at the small counter we turned into a bar area of sorts. I'm totally distracted by him because he looks delicious, so delicious that I sort of want to lick the water running down his neck even though that probably wouldn't be appropriate.

He kisses me on the cheek shuffling over to make us some coffee when he realizes no one has started any yet. "Good morning, Love," he says while turning the machine on. I can practically smell the bean juice already. "Are you ready for today?"

Working with the light is gradually becoming easier for me, though it's much finickier than my shadows and likes to elude me a lot, but I'm guessing it's because my Light Weaver powers aren't as strong. Reed is also helping me master healing and fire while the others are out recruiting.

"Psh, I'm always ready. Have we learned any more about

my family?" I ask. I'd like to know more about my grandparents or even anything that could help us take down the Elders.

He shakes his head. "Unfortunately, no. I've read his journal front to back and besides what we've already read there was no mention of it again. Although, I did discover later in the journal that he was planning on going public with this information. Before he was killed, anyway. Some kind of training accident."

I gasp as a chill immediately runs down my spine. "Reed, you don't think he was murdered to cover this up, do you? I wonder if that's why my family went into hiding…"

Reed's eyes widen and he almost over pours the coffee. He quickly grabs a towel and cleans up the dribbles he did spill. "It's possible, I guess," he responds in thought. "But who would do such a thing and why?"

I take a moment to ponder, but I've got nothing. It doesn't make sense. "I don't know. My next question is, why does no one remember this happening? It couldn't have been top secret with a shifter and a Weaver walking around."

"Matilda is definitely old enough to remember," Reed agrees. "But she says she's never heard of it happening before us. Maybe their memories were altered?"

"My father," I say, working it over in my head. "He did mention in the In-Between that he could mess with memories."

"You're powerful, so it stands to reason your father was as well…"

Vin sets a plate piled high with delicious looking biscuits and gravy in front of us. "Speculating on an empty stomach won't do anyone any good. Dig in."

My mouth waters immediately at the sight and my fork rips into a biscuit before anyone can say anything else. "Soo good," I say around a mouthful.

Reed chuckles. "Gods, I love the way you can put food down," he admits, watching me before diving into his own plate.

"Ever since we got back from the Goddess' realm I've been starving. More so than usual," I confess.

"Ah, yeah. Another thing you can thank your impending Awakening for. I think the time difference between our world and the Goddess' realm affected you more and is speeding up the process. Speaking of which, how are things with Elian?" Reed blushes, and in turn, my cheeks turn crimson, thinking about how they all rushed in when Elian and I broke his bed.

"We're... getting there, I think. Truth be told, I thought we might bond that night, but he didn't take my hand. I want it to be his decision, so I haven't said anything yet."

"That's understandable," he responds. "On your end. Personally, I don't understand why he hasn't bonded to you yet."

"I think it terrifies him," I admit.

As I take another bite and my taste buds explode, I thank the Goddess the training Reed and I have been doing lately isn't too strenuous or I'd be puking this all up later and that would be a shame. At some point, we need to work on Reed's fighting form, but he's leaps and bounds from where he was when we first met, so I'll take that as a win.

"So, what are we going to work on today?" I ask, changing the subject.

"I thought we could work on drawing your light out again. See if we can get your shadows to play nicely together."

Outwardly I groan, but internally I'm picturing visions of a certain Light Weaver *playing nice* with me and my shadows to tease him instead. Yeah, I might be slightly evil if the outline in Reed's sweatpants is any indication.

Sitting across from Reed with my eyes closed, I peek one open to find him deep in concentration. I close it again and take a deep breath, letting myself get lost in the soft rock music playing. It always helps me concentrate and he doesn't make me turn it off like Elian does.

"Whenever you're ready, I want you to pull your shadows to you in one hand and in the other, call the light," he says.

My shadows come to my call instantly, which makes me giddy. The training with Elian on the side has really paid off. Especially now that my shadows come to me easier, and I don't have to solely rely on my heightened emotions. I'm also proficient at healing and using Dante's fire, but they aren't my powers, so I don't think I'll ever be as good as who they belong to.

Now if I can just master the fucking light. You wouldn't think something that is all around us would be so hard to control. Then again, my shadows used to be the same way. I need practice, which is why I've been training with Reed almost every freaking day. Gods, the patience of this man.

Focusing on that bright ball of energy in my center, I call it to me slowly. I decide to try something different and instead of pulling it to me like I do my shadows, I hold my hand out and ask for it to come to me. Ever so slowly the air starts to shift. The hair on my arms lifts as the light comes to me. It feels like I'm holding electricity in my hand, which is completely different from the almost sentient shadows.

A breeze enters the room and lifts my hair from my shoulders. Reed gasps and it makes my eyes pop open. From the mirror across the room, I see myself with my hair splayed every which way holding a swirling ball of shadows in one hand and white energy in the other. Maybe my frustration plays a part in it finally working or maybe it's my determined grit. Either way, I look powerful, and it makes me feel like I actually have a chance at coming out on top in the end.

But my concentration slips, and the light leaves me once more. "Dammit," I curse and rise to my feet. "I had it! I totally had it."

Reed tugs on my arm and spins me into him, capturing my lips in a daring kiss. When we're both breathless he pulls back and says, "You did. I'm so proud of you, Love."

Staring into his blue eyes, I find butterflies filling my stomach and giddiness flowing through me. I cup his cheek in my hand, bringing his gaze to mine. "I love you, Reed Soleil. My glorious Light Weaver. Thank you for everything."

The smile that overtakes his face could rival the sun. "I love you too, Sadie Sinclair. I would do anything for you, give you anything, including the sun if I could. I'm so glad the Goddess paired me with you."

I shoot him a cheeky grin and beckon him to follow. "Now, let's work on your fighting form for a while," I say, flipping the script on him.

He groans but follows me anyway. "Do we have to?"

Payback is a bitch, I project, and he rolls his eyes with a smile on his face.

"Yep. So get your cute ass over here. I think you're going to like this fight training," I say, pulling my tank top off. "Good thing we're the only ones in here right now, huh?"

His eyes widen and darken with lust. "As you wish, my Love."

22

SADIE

The days are passing quickly, far too quickly to be honest. I know it's only bringing me closer to my inevitable showdown with the Elders and my uncle. They've been quiet lately too, which makes me nervous. What are they plotting?

Surely, they have to be pissed that we're taking their precious shifters and Night Weavers.

Silence in some situations is good, no news is good news as they say, but I fear in this case, no news is bad news. They're not the type to go silently into the night.

Good thing neither am I.

Don't think about that now, Sadie. Focus on what you can control.

Now that we're amassing some numbers at the safe haven, I figured it was time to go around and meet everyone, give them a feel for who I am and what I can do. I'm nervous about what they will think but I also know it needs to be done. As much as I'd like to stay cooped up in our cabin, these people view me as their savior, and I need to meet with them.

Hemsworth nudges my leg. "What's up with you? You look like you're strung tighter than a guitar string."

"You know me, worrying over things that haven't even happened yet. What if they don't like me? Or try to shun me because I'm a Triad?"

His brown eyes soften, and I bend down so I'm closer to eye level with him. "Then it'll be their fucking loss. Change is brewing and they can either get with the program or get left behind." He lets me stew for a moment before continuing. "Not that I think that will happen. You have a way with people, Weaver. Even if you don't see it yourself. Stop fretting over things you can't control."

"Thanks, Hems," I say with a sigh. "I needed a good dose of your wisdom today."

"That's what I'm here for," he responds and lays down so I can give him belly scratches. See? Sucker for tummy rubs. When he's had his fill, he gets to his feet. "Let's go knock these new Weavers dead." He winces. "Not literally though. Try not to kill anyone, yeah?"

I chuckle and finish lacing my combat boots then head toward the living room, smoothing my hands down my ripped jeans. Yep, I've graduated from Converse to combat boots. I call them my shit-kickers. Never know when you might need a bit of ankle support these days.

Almost all the shifters Vin managed to get the portal-invitations to have joined us. We've started working with Matilda and the new shifters to get more out to the harder-to-reach shifters. Though no one has been able to get to the ones who work directly with the Elders.

I get to meet with the new shifters at our weekly meetings, which is nice. Except for when they bow to me and call me Shadowbringer. Still getting used to that. Better than Malachi and his *Shadow Girl* greeting though.

The guys are waiting for me in the living room and all

heads turn to find me when I walk in. Dante is in the middle of an arm-wrestling match with Vin, which he's losing. Kaos and Reed have what looks to be a fairy porn book between them that they're discussing, and Elian has a smirk on his face despite himself. All of that is forgotten when they look at me. Each of their stares are steamy, and I want nothing more than to devour each of them, but alas, we have an obligation to uphold.

"Ready to go?" I ask.

"You look amazing, Little Flame," Kaos says and kisses me on the cheek.

"Uh, thanks?" I look down at the random blouse, jeans, and boots I pulled from the closet. "But I'm just wearing normal clothes? I figured I'd look less intimidating this way. Plus, I'm not really a formal person anyway—" I ramble and Elian cuts me off with a kiss that has my toes curling, all tongue and possessiveness. When he pulls back, I catch a few of the others adjusting themselves.

"You're hot, Pet. Take the damn compliment."

"Yes, sir," I respond and his eyes darken with lust.

Reed steps in between us before we can attack each other and rip our clothes off. "We need to get going. Everyone should already be in the mess hall for lunch. We don't want to be late." He directs that last bit at Elian with a pointed look.

Holy hell, assertive Reed makes my core clench. A daring daydream of him bossing Elian around in the bedroom and looming over him pops into my mind, but alas, it would never happen.

And damn, I hate it when he has a point. He reads that entire thought process, though, and his lips twitch, shooting me those dimples and shaking his head.

Definitely not happening, Love. I'd love to boss you around a little though, Reed projects. *Let's get going before I say to hell with it.*

"Fiiine," I huff and waltz out the door with an extra sway in my hips that none of them miss, judging by the growls and groans behind me.

Responsibilities suck, huh? I project down the bond.

Hemsworth is right on my heels, giving me one of his doggy chuckles. "I love how you tease them."

Alpha Darren and Matilda are waiting outside for us when we approach the mess hall. It's probably the largest building here, minus the gym, and also recently renovated.

"How are the shifts working out with the mess hall?" Reed inquires in lieu of pleasantries. None of us are the type to beat around the bush anyway.

Matilda smiles, which I'm taking as a good sign. "Everyone has been pitching in, shifters and Weavers alike," she says proudly. "It's gone well so far."

Reed, Matilda, Alpha Darren, and Viola made up a schedule and whoever lives in the chosen cabin are the ones who make the food for everyone that day. I'm glad to hear their system seems to be working nicely. In addition to the nonperishable foods that were already stockpiled here, the guys grab fresh food and supplies while they're out doing their recruitments. We'll be set up for a while.

Alpha Darren nods his agreement to what Matilda said. "Thankfully, there has only been a bit of bickering here and there, but nothing I couldn't break up or handle. Other than that, everyone seems to be playing along rather nicely." He seems kind of surprised at the notion and to be honest, I am too.

"That's wonderful," I respond as they usher us inside.

The smell that hits me reminds me of a typical cafeteria, though less hospital-y and more school cafeteria, which I don't mind. The long, communal tables are crammed full of supernaturals, most of them mingling between kinds.

The Weavers sitting at the table closest to the door notice me walk in, whispering quickly to their friends and it seems to have a ripple effect, leaving silence in its wake. Everyone stops eating and the silence is slightly awkward. Forks are paused halfway to their mouths, other's jaws are dropped open in surprise. They're acting like I'm on some sort of pedestal, and I don't like it. I'm one of them.

I catch sight of a familiar head of red hair when a Night Weaver stands. Oliver, the guy I saved during the training exercise at the compound, drops to a knee, placing his hand over his heart in a show of respect. The other member of his Circle does the same, echoing his motions. "Shadowbringer, we have all heard of you and what you're doing for this community," he squeaks out, looking nervous as all get out. He clears his throat. "I would like to offer you my Circle's allegiance should you ever need us."

Ah, hell. I don't like this. I don't want anyone indebted to me. What if I let them down?

What if they die because of me?

I'm not like the Elders and I refuse to make these people follow me like that. I open my mouth to say as much when Elian puts a hand on my shoulder and squeezes, telling me with that simple touch to stay quiet.

For some reason, I do as he says.

As one, every Night Weaver in the mess hall stands and drops to a knee, offering me the same oath. Fucking hell, this is intimidating. My skin starts to feel itchy, and it takes everything in me not to twitch or finger my necklace for strength. Somehow, I manage to keep it together enough to place a hand over my heart and slightly bow my head, returning the gesture with my thanks.

One of my mates, Kaos if I had to guess, ushers me

toward the kitchen, behind closed doors. "Fucking hell, do you know how important that was?" he asks, rubbing his hands up and down my shoulders.

"No?" I respond, and it comes out as more of a question because I'm still slightly shell-shocked.

"That was insane, Angel!" Dante agrees, eyes filled with hope. "Usually, oaths like that are reserved for whoever is in power."

"Then why do I feel so fucking sick about it?" I snap. "I don't want their lives on or *in* my hands."

Elian pushes Kaos out of the way and gets in my face. "You're afraid you're going to let them down." Isn't that what I just said? "The first step to being a good leader is knowing that. You know what's at stake and it scares the fuck out of you. It's not a bad thing. It means you actually give a damn about what happens to them. Which, if I had to guess, is why they're so willing to follow you. Now, snap out of it and get back out there, Sinclair."

Jesus, Elian really knows what to say to get me out of my funk. He may be an asshole most of the time, but he's smart. It does the trick though and I find myself taking a deep breath before exiting the kitchen with a small smile on my face as I greet everyone.

Oliver wraps me in a hug when I make it to his table and receives a few growls from my mates. He chuckles, eyeing them warily.

I roll my eyes at their antics. "Don't worry about them. Their bark is worse than their bite."

"Hey, I take offense to that," Vinson grumbles.

"Anyway," I say with a laugh. "How have you been? How's life at the haven?"

There's a gleam of hope in his green eyes. "Better than I ever could've expected, to be frank. No one here has forced me into a fight or beat me up. I mean, yeah, sometimes there are pissing contests between Circles or between the shifters and Weavers, but mostly, it seems to be going great." His grin is contagious.

"Is there anything happening I should know about?" I ask.

Oliver contemplates for a second. "I can't think of anything. Although, I do think some of us would benefit from a training session or two with you."

That brings a smile to my face. I love training, and I'd love to help the others. Total win, win. "I'll see what I can do."

He nods. "Well, I'll let you get back to it. I know you still have a lot of people to talk to. Thanks for dropping by, Sadie. It's good to see you."

"Anytime, Oliver. It's good to see you too."

Malachi finds me next. "Hey, Shadow Girl. Long time, no see."

"Hey, Malachi. I'm glad you're here."

"I'm all for bringing down the patriarchy." He winks at me, and I laugh. "Have fun schmoozing the masses," he says, and I give him a small wave before moving on to the next table. And the next and the next, until I'm exhausted from having to people so much.

It's nice to meet everyone though, even if so many of their stories break my heart. So much death, lies, and deceit. So much tragedy. Too many with family members stolen from their homes to work for the Elders. It's too much for one community to handle to be honest. And it all swings back to the fucking Elders.

Someone grabs my Circle's attention, but I need some air, so I quietly slip out the door, inhaling several deep gulps. Why am I sweating so damn much?

After I feel like I've finally caught my breath, I spot Emma and the trio outside, sitting on a giant picnic blanket near their cabin, and start to head their way. Emma glances at the guys while they eat, but when they look directly at her, she quickly averts her gaze, and they do the same.

Psh, they are so stricken with one another and none of them will admit it. I, too, used to be that way. Hell, I still kind of am with Elian. Sometimes the game is worth it, but with everything going on... I've realized exactly how easily life can change on a dime, and I'm no longer the person I once was.

Hemsworth catches up and nudges my thigh. "Hey, why'd you leave?"

I stop and ruffle his fur. "I just needed some air. Some of their stories are really heavy, and I needed a minute."

He ducks his head in a nod. "That's understandable." He catches my line of sight and shoots me one of his toothy smiles. "It's good to see them finally getting along."

"Yeah, it is. Let's give them their privacy. I don't want to interrupt them while they're actually being civil."

Niall must say something that pisses Emma off because her face turns red.

"Who would've thought little Emma would be so feisty?" I almost move to step in when she moves to tackle him from her sitting position and screams something about, *I'll show you!*

Hemsworth and I chuckle. Well, he chuffs, and I laugh. "She's certainly got some fire in her," he responds.

"That she does."

Suddenly, my body temperature spikes like ten degrees. It feels as if I'm on fire, burning from the inside out. I cry out in response, doubling over with my hands on my knees. The fierceness of the heat wave takes my breath away until I feel like I'm choking on it. What the hell is happening?

"Sadie? Sadie! What's wrong?" Hemsworth demands poking the side of my thigh with his nose, but I can't focus on him. I think someone might also be shouting, but I can't hear them over the roar in my ears.

Next thing I know my mates are there. Elian places both hands on my cheeks and pulls my attention to him. His lips are moving, but I can't make the words out. No, all I can focus on is his ice-cold hands on my cheeks and the other hand around my wrist and on my shoulder from my other mates.

I sigh and lean into Elian's touch which makes him look at me like I'm insane. He looks behind me to where my other mates are and then backs away. I cry out again when his hands leave my face, but thankfully, Reed takes his place.

Sadie, Reed says into my mind, breaking through the fog. Having a mate bond with him is so amazing. I can literally feel him inside me.

Wait, why isn't he inside me? That would be wondrous. Am I drunk or something? Did someone spike the lemonade? I mean it did kind of taste funny, but I figured it was because it's powdered. Squeezed lemons are so much better...

Sadie, focus! he says sternly. *Your Awakening has started.*

My eyes widen comically. *Is that why I'm so Godsdamned hot and* horny?

I mean suns blaze, I feel like I could jump every single one of them right now in the middle of the safe haven. In front of everyone. And my kink is not voyeurism like Elian's. Well, I take that back, I might be slightly voyeuristic but for my mates only. I want them all to watch *me.* Then again, that might be the lust talking.

Reed says something about all hands on deck and then there's a lot more skin touching mine than there was a few seconds ago. I'm fairly certain Vinson took his shirt off to wrap himself around me from behind while I'm wrapped around Reed's front and it feels glorious, which is saying something because Vin feels like a popsicle, and shifters normally run *hot*. They're the damn antidote to my heat, but it's still not enough.

My skin still feels like it does whenever I'm making contact with one of my mates but like it's on steroids. The buzzing feeling is intensified by a million. I bet if I focus closely enough, I could even feel the little electrical currents under my skin moving.

Nope, that just seems weird. Not going there.

Yes, Reed responds mentally. *You'll feel increased horniness until the power settles between us.* He levels me with a serious look, and I try to fight the fogginess of heat and lust to focus. *You will have to complete your bond with Elian so he can take some of the power, is that going to be okay?*

I want Elian to want it. It has to be up to him.

A moan escapes my lips when Vinson starts rubbing his cool hands up and down my back. That's when my mates decide to make this matter private, and I'm lifted into Reed's arms as they hurry us back to our cabin.

Matilda is on the doorstep, concern etched on her face. "I heard something was wrong. What's happening?"

"Her Awakening," Reed responds, brushing past her to make a beeline for the bathroom.

"Oh, have fun!" she calls out after us, cackling like she knows something I don't. It makes me slightly suspicious about what an Awakening truly is. Reed explained it like a division of power between mates. Not a heat wave sexathon.

This bathroom doesn't have a tub, but that doesn't stop Reed from turning the water to absolutely *frigid* before stepping into the spray with me in his arms.

"What the fuck, Reed!" I screech and try to bail out of his grasp. Vinson left us somewhere along the way and I'm not sure where the others and Hemsworth are.

"Suns blaze, stop squirming. I need you to come back down to earth for a moment."

Something about his tone makes me stop and when I do I

find that the cold really isn't that bad. Plus, it's bringing some clarity to my mind once more. "Holy hell. Thanks, Red."

"My pleasure," he responds and turns off the water before stepping out of the shower with both of us sopping wet. He doesn't even stop for a towel before depositing me in the bedroom with Elian and then shutting the door.

"Uh, what the hell?"

Elian shoots me one of those chilling smiles of his, and I notice his eyes are not iced over like usual. He's not shutting me out. He's allowing me in, to see him fully. "It's time to complete our bond, Pet. Are you ready?"

My eyes widen and suddenly, I'm thankful for Reed tossing me into a cold shower because I want to be fully alert for this moment.

"Are you?" I question, thinking back to our moment the other night, and brace myself for the answer. I know we talked about not going back, but this is more than just sex. This is forever. This is huge.

Three months ago, if you had asked me if Elian was capable of forever, I would've said hell no. Now... Well... I think he is, but the question is, will he *let* himself be capable of it?

When it boils down to it, he's the one that's been holding himself back all this time. Even when he acted like a complete dick, I still felt insanely attracted to him.

"I want nothing more than to finally complete our bond," he says, and I let out the breath I didn't realize I was holding. His expression is soft, the softest I've ever seen it, and vulnerable. "If you'll have me that is. I want it to be your choice." There's a flash of insecurity in his eyes that he doesn't hide from me.

He wants it to be *my* choice?

"My choice?" I question aloud, and he nods which makes me snort. He tilts his head in confusion. "I wanted it to be *your* choice! I've been waiting on *you*. You stubborn, stubborn idiot."

His own eyes widen, and he chuckles, shaking his head. Then he focuses all that attention on me. "So, we've been waiting on each other. I guess we're both stubborn idiots, huh?"

"I guess so."

His emerald eyes shine with affection. "I want nothing more than to place my hand in yours and complete our bond with you. I want to feel you inside of me and all the shit that comes with bonding."

A soft smile overtakes my face. "It's about damn time." My feet carry me to him of their own accord and I wrap my arms around him. He startles, and I laugh. "It's a hug, Elian. No different than the ones you give Viola. Wrap your damn arms around me."

He envelopes me in his embrace and for a moment we relish in each other's company before he's pulling back. "Obviously, it's a hug," he growls but there's no real bite to it. "I still wasn't expecting you to say yes for some reason."

The vulnerability of that statement makes my heart clench. "I meant what I said, Elian. I want to bond with you. I feel like I've been waiting for this moment forever. I'm already yours, but make it official. Please?"

He pulls back to look at me with his hands on my shoulder. Ever so slowly, he trails one down my arm, leaving a path of fire in its wake until his hand rests next to mine, buzzing. His pinky barely brushes mine and the anticipation is already killing me.

Elian and I are about to bond. This is really happening.

"This is probably going to hurt you," he says softly.

"It always has with you, hasn't it? I'm not afraid of a little pain, Elian. You're worth it. You're all worth it."

"I love you," he whispers before slipping his palm into mine.

There's not a chance for me to respond before we both freeze in place. Elian's eyes are full of an emotion I've never seen from him before—love—then concern as my entire world goes black without so much as a warning. Hopefully, that means I won't feel the pain, or else this is really going to suck when I wake up.

23

SADIE

My head feels like it's been shoved into a cloud of fog that's swirling around in my brain, not letting me fully process anything. *Something is off,* that's one thing my mind registers. My fingers dig into the softness beneath me. *Am I in one of Vin's dreamwalks again?*

No, those are definitely sheets, I decide when it curls in my hand.

I'm in bed, but why?

The power inside me roils and bubbles. There are sparks flying everywhere, igniting against one another like they're trying to fan the chaos inside of me.

Think, Sadie.

I remember going to the mess hall and meeting all our new allies and then... the heat wave... and Elian. There's a light underneath my eyelids, like my crazy powers are somehow manifesting on the outside of me. I slowly pry my heavy eyes open and catch a glimpse of black and white magic shooting out of me like lightning before it snaps back and fades under my skin once more. *What the hell?*

Now that my eyes are open, I'm feeling much more aware. Taking a glance around, I find I'm in bed with Kaos and Dante plastered to my sides like any other morning, except today there's an ache between my thighs that's downright painful, and I'm absolutely soaked with slick. My legs shift, seeking that friction I'm craving but it's not enough. A whimper escapes my lips and both Dante and Kaos shoot up, looking at me in concern.

"Hey, Angel. You were out for a while, are you feeling okay?" Dante asks, running a hand through his messy hair.

"No," I whimper, shifting my legs harder. The sight of him shirtless and in bed with me, along with his gruff, sleepy voice sends a zing straight to my core.

Kaos pushes his healing magic into me, thinking I'm hurt but that's not it. Not at all. I'm fine, merely horny as hell. His eyebrow crinkles in confusion when his magic doesn't find anything to heal, and the feel of his magic is enough to make my clit pulse again. The magic snaps out of me, and I grab Kaos' hand as more lust washes over me. Using his power on me only served to amplify *everything.*

Dante sees me shifting my legs and lifts the cover. His eyes widen when he sees my undulating thighs and probably the wet spot underneath me.

"Oh, Angel," he purrs, his nostrils flaring like he can scent me. "We can take care of that if you want us to?"

I love how they always ask for my consent. It drives me wild.

Weird, freaky power stuff all but forgotten, I say "Please, yes. I need this ache to stop."

I feel like one of those omegas from the knotty stories I've read in heat, practically begging for them. Their touch is the coolness to quell the flames raging inside me. They're the balm I need to cure this ache and my vagina knows it too.

And their smell. Gods, their smell. Have they always smelled like this?

Inherently masculine... musky, but in a nice way that makes me want to rub myself all over them and have my scent on their skin.

"Oh, Little Flame. I hate to break this to you," Kaos says, voice husky from desire. "But that ache isn't fully going away until after your Awakening is over."

Surprisingly, that thought doesn't bother me. He sees the excitement on my face and grins wickedly. One that could even rival Elian's, but not quite.

"Get over here and fuck me then, dammit," I whisper-growl. "I want you to make me so wet, I'm dripping, got it? That way it'll be easy to take you both inside me at the same time. It's time for a sandwich."

Groans are my only answer as they both strip naked and then work on removing my clothes. Thankfully, I don't seem to be as hot as I was earlier, but now I'm battling a different kind of heat.

Lust.

Pure, unadulterated lust.

Dante's blond head dips between my thighs as he settles on the bed, putting his arms under my thighs so he can pull my heat to his mouth. He licks up my slit, drawing a hiss from my lips, and takes a strong whiff of me like he finds me irresistible. My head falls back in pleasure as he starts tasting me. I slip my fingers into his hair and pull, which makes him moan into my pussy.

Before I can really focus on it, Kaos is there, kissing my lips as he takes my breast into his palm and tweaks my nipple. I buck on Dante's face, and he smacks a hand down on my stomach to stop me from squirming before resuming trying to suck my soul out of my cunt. RIP my insides because that was fucking hot, and I'm even more drenched than before. I might just drown him down there like the sunken city I grew up near. That, apparently, might house a portal to the In-Between. Why am I thinking about this right now?

Totally blame the sex hormones.

"You're absolutely divine, Little Flame," Kaos murmurs, watching me. His eyes are laser-focused on my face like he's reading the pleasure coursing through me.

He snakes his other hand down my belly, sensually drawing out the sensations and making me pant into his mouth before rubbing my clit. I lose it, coming all over Dante's face. A choking gasp escapes me as Kaos presses in harder, never stopping his circular motions on my nub, and extending my climax, sending little aftershocks throughout my entire being.

Dante pokes a finger at my back entrance, and I tense on instinct. He clucks his tongue and rubs his digits through my wetness and then circles me again. "Relax, Angel. Let me in. I'm going to get you ready to take my cock."

Taking a deep breath, I do as he says and relax my muscles as much as I can. With as slick as I am, this time he slips right in. The sensation is a bit strange at first, like with Elian in the forest and the office, but once he starts to move and stroke, the more I find I like it. Plus, I'm dying to take both of them at once.

It's my time for the promised sandwich, dammit.

"Who says you get her ass first?" Kaos growls, his lips leaving mine.

Dante smirks from his place between my legs, stopping his motions to which I protest with my own growl. "You claimed her first and were the first to bond. So I'm claiming this for myself." Dante's tone is smug.

Kaos' expression morphs from inquisitive to pure possessiveness. "I don't care who was first—"

CHAPTER 23 | 199

I grab Kaos' dick to shut him up and start stroking his silky skin, pulling a groan from his lips. The possessive mumbo jumbo is hot, don't get me wrong, but I need a cock in me more than I need coffee to not be a monster in the mornings. Which is saying a lot.

"Don't worry, Kaos," I murmur. "I can assure you if it feels good, this won't be the only time. Now shut up and fuck me." My power punctuates my statement by sending different colors of our magic shooting in different directions of the room. Like earlier, it snaps back to me and settles under my skin again. Kaos and Dante give my magic a strange look before returning their attention to my face.

"Yes, fucking, ma'am," Kaos says and nudges Dante out of the way. "If you get her ass first then I get her delicious pussy. Keep working on her while she rides me."

Dante chuckles. "Got it, boss."

Kaos tugs me into his lap and then lays back, letting me decide how I want to ride him. I make no hesitation to align him with my entrance and sink down on him. He's thick, stretching my walls, but with as wet as I am, he glides in nicely until he's buried to the hilt.

Gods, he's huge. They all are, but Vinson is definitely the biggest with his monster shifter cock. Elian is probably a close second, tied with Kaos. He completely fills me up and I have to take a second to let myself adjust to his girth. Filling me up eases the ache but now I want more. Always more.

When I start to move, Dante trails his fingers down my backside once more. "Lean forward, Angel," he instructs. "Put your hands on his chest. I want you to use them to ride your other mate's cock while I finger your ass."

"Fucking hell, why are all of you so good with words?" I mumble, but there's no time to think about it further before Dante slips a finger into my ass and Kaos is thrusting into me from beneath.

Pleasure.

That's what this is, pure pleasure.

When Dante's satisfied I'm loose enough, he slips another finger inside. He matches his pace with Kaos' and I can feel his fingers rubbing Kaos' dick through the sensitive wall separating my two holes.

"Fuck!" I scream as I feel my next orgasm building, but before I can reach that peak, Dante withdraws his fingers, and I'm so stunned I stop riding Kaos.

"Dante! What are you doing?" I demand.

"One sec, Angel," he says and reaches into the nightstand drawer, pulling out a giant bottle of lube that I have no idea where it came from, and I don't really care enough to ask. I was about to go feral on him for stopping, but lube is cool. Lube your tube before you do the doob. No idea if that's a word or not, but it is now.

Dante squirts a handful into his palm before slicking his cock with it. I watch him stroke himself while I grind on Kaos.

"Gods, that's hot," I say breathlessly.

Dante smirks. "You like watching me pet my dick, Angel?"

"Of all the words, you seriously used 'pet?'"

He merely chuckles in response, and now that he's properly lubed up, he returns to his spot on the bed, situating me where he can align himself at my ass.

Kaos groans after my magic zaps out again. "Hurry the fuck up, bro."

"Aye, aye, captain," Dante quips and pushes the tip of his head into me. I tense again, and Dante smooths a hand down my back. "Loosen up, Sadie," he murmurs, brushing some of the sweaty hair from my shoulder as he licks my thumping pulse.

Kaos groans from the gush of wetness Dante's action

induces. "You can do this, my little mate. You're going to take both of us and you're going to do it so well."

"I'm going to take both of you," I repeat like a mantra, mentally psyching myself up to take them both. I unclench enough for his head to slip inside, and my eyes roll to the back of my head from bliss as a hiss escapes me.

"That's it, Angel," Dante coos. "You're doing perfect. Just a bit more."

The sensation is quite hard to describe. Somewhere between pleasure and pain, but still oh, so good. "Moons above, you're so damn tight. I could live back here," Dante praises, sinking into the hilt inside my ass.

"Oh Gods, please," I whine, feeling fuller than I've ever felt in my entire life. "Both of you start moving now. I need to come." My magic is doing its haywire thing again, and I instinctively know orgasming is the way to settle it down.

"Your wish is our command, Little Flame," Kaos says and starts to move. Dante waits a second, so their rhythm is slightly off.

I was wrong before. *This* is pleasure.

Pure fucking pleasure.

Godsdamned ecstasy.

Bitching bliss.

Once again, probably not a thing, but I'm so lost in lust I don't care.

I'm so fucking full I don't think I could handle anything else. And yet, when I open my eyes and find Elian standing in the doorway, his pants on the floor with a fist around his dick, stroking it nice and slow, I know I need more. My cheeks heat as his eyes find mine and his pace starts to increase. He's staring at me like I'm a gem and he's lucky enough to have found the rarest one. It's empowering and hot as hell.

"Ahhh. Fuuuck!" I scream as my walls clench around

Dante and Kaos, bringing both of them to their climax alongside me, and drawing grunts and gasps from their lips. Their hot seed shoots inside me and it's like some of my power that's acting completely bonkers settles a tiny fraction.

See? Orgasms. The cure to life's problems.

Also, totally called it on the sex stuff. We may not have needed it to bond, but it definitely seems like we need it to get me through this Awakening.

"Holy fuck, Angel," Dante says, withdrawing from me and sliding me off Kaos so they can cuddle me. I miss their fullness already though. "That was..."

"Amazing," Kaos finishes and leans up to kiss my lips. "You are fucking amazing."

"I told you next time, I wanted to fucking watch," Elian growls near the doorway, but there's no real heat behind his words.

"Mmm, from where I'm standing, it seems like you did get to watch. Especially seeing the mess you made," I respond, gesturing to the cum leaking from his tip and on the floor. "Thank the Goddess there's a rug down or else that'd probably leave a stain," I say, thinking out loud.

"Careful sassing me, Pet, or I'll give that mouth something else to do."

"And who says I wouldn't like that?" Now that I'm not entirely overcome by lust, I glance around. "Wait, where are Reed and Vin? Oh snap, and Hemsworth?" I think back to mine and Kaos' first time and Hemsworth popping up afterward and the thought makes me chuckle.

"Hemsworth decided to visit Chris, Viola, and Gerrard." Smart dog. I'm sure Chris is gushing over him too. "The other two fucks are sitting in the living room sporting massive boners," Elian responds, stripping the rest of his clothes off. I love watching his inked fingers work. Too bad they're not inside me... *Whoa, calm down, girl. We just orgasmed.* "They're far more chivalrous than I, wanting to give you your moment with Kaos and Dante."

My cheeks heat from embarrassment... or desire from seeing Elian in his full glory and knowing the other two heard everything. Take your pick.

"Reed! Vin! Get your asses in here," I holler, and then chuckle when I hear one of them trip over their feet and curse in their haste to get to me.

"I'll get more blankets!" Vin shouts as Reed scrambles past Elian through the doorway and Vin slides past them, heading for the linen closet.

I eye the bed we're on dubiously. "We seriously need a bigger bed." Even with two pushed together, fitting six of us on it is a challenge.

"We do," Reed agrees. "We'll worry about that when we have somewhere permanent though. For now, we'll make it work." He winks at me.

"So, what's up with this Awakening?" I ask. "I was under the impression that I was coming into my full powers and sharing them with you all."

"That's correct. A Weaver's Awakening is the full surge of a Link's power coming into fruition and then a division of that power between her mates." Reed responds. "The way you do that is through—"

"Sex," I supply when it hits me. The palms connecting is the spark... and this is what solidifies it. "This makes so much more sense."

Vin runs through the doorway with every single blanket we have in this damn cabin and smiles. "Fuck nest!" he announces and goes to town on building... well, whatever a fuck nest is, I guess.

Not for the first time, I wonder what the hell I have gotten myself into.

24

SADIE

"Sorry, but what the heck is a fuck nest?" I question once Vin is satisfied we're all cozy-burritoed and cocooned enough in the massive blanket fort he's built on the bed. There has to be at least ten pillows surrounding us too.

Our connection sizzles with the echo of his need to provide and fuss over me. I like the attention too, if I'm honest. I've never had a man wait on me like this before. Now I have five. Well, four because I doubt Elian would. Maybe if I begged...

"You know," Reed starts, "like a sex fort, rut hut or... oh I know! A boink bunker! I know you've probably read about them before."

"A boink bunker?" I echo. "Like a nest?" I ask and he nods.

"Technically, according to Urban Dictionary, it's an abode consisting of several layers of blankets and pillows. But this is what you're going to need while you're going through your Awakening," Vin says and works on straightening a part of one of the blankets in my *boink bunker* until it's perfect. "Which I'm assuming is like a mated shifter's heat. Except without the magic... and you know, power leaking out of you," he responds, tilting his head when my magic goes all wonky and shoots out of me again. At least it's not harming me or them.

Dante cracks a devious smile. "No, bro, that's my cum leaking out of her currently."

"Dante!" I screech and smack him with a pillow. With my heightened emotions, my magic goes on the fritz again and snaps out of me. It's such a strange sensation.

Reed watches it happen and says, "Looks like you need a few more orgasms to help the power settle, Love." His eyes are banked in desire.

And sure enough, as soon as the words are out of his mouth, I suddenly feel warm and horny, like speaking the words into existence was enough to throw a signal up to the part of my brain that processes sexual desire that reads, *Yes, all the orgasms, please! So many may kill me, but who cares.*

Death by orgasms sounds like the right way to go if you ask me.

"Would you like that, Love?" Reed asks, and his husky tone sends a zap straight down to my clit. When I nod, Reed takes off his pants and his dick springs to life like it's happy to see me.

I see Vin in my peripheral still clothed. That won't do.

"You too, Vin. This is a no clothes party."

Moons above, where is this wanton woman coming from?

For Goddess' sake. I blame the Awakening. Yep, totally that and not my own fantasies. That's my story and I'm sticking to it.

"In a second, my Moon. I'm going to grab you a warm washcloth to clean you up with first." With that he disappears into the bathroom, presumably to get said cloth. My heart squeezes and I swoon over his need to take care of me.

Gah, what did I do to deserve him? All of them, really.

Reading my thoughts, Reed pulls me into his side and kisses my forehead. His glasses are missing today, which is likely a smart idea since they might get broken in our tumbles. I love being able to see his lovely gray eyes undeterred.

"You're *you*, Sadie," Reed tells me, and I shoot him a dubious look. "In all things, you're always you. Your feelings are real and you're vocal about them. It's why people respect you so much. It's why we love you—why I love you."

"I love you too, Red," I respond and capture his lips in a passionate kiss that quickly turns into something more. My lips part and he eagerly slips his tongue inside, plundering my mouth like I wish he would my pussy. Dante lays a sensual kiss on my shoulder while Kaos strokes my other side.

Vin returns and wipes me clean with a warm rag. I pull away from Reed's lips so I can watch Vin between my thighs. "You're perfect," he rasps before settling to the side so he can watch Reed and I.

Reed kisses a trail down my jaw and to my throat before adjusting so he can settle between my legs, aligning himself at my entrance.

"Wait," I say in a voice I barely recognize from my lust. Reed is tugging on my earlobe with his teeth while his hand... *Dante's hand?* is playing with my left nipple. I can feel the tip of Reed slowly sliding between my already drenched folds, despite the cleanup.

"Isn't this weird for you all?" I turn my head to the side to take a peek at the others while Reed doesn't let up with his kisses and nibbles down my neck. Dante is definitely the one playing with my nipple and smirks at me but looks seconds away from pushing Reed aside and taking his spot. Kaos is watching us intently, like he's learning everything I like.

Elian and Vin are further down the bed, eyes smoldering at the scene.

Kaos chuckles huskily in response to my question. "Not at all, my Little Flame." His eyes are hooded and his dick twitches like it's agreeing with his statement.

We should have no clothes parties more often...

"Yeah," Dante agrees. "Let yourself enjoy the hell out of this and try not to think about it so hard. Let us worry about ourselves, okay?" The truth in his eyes is enough to soothe my worries and it makes my vagina shout, *hurray!*

"Okay," I agree. It might be greedy to want all of them focusing on me, but my cunt does not care at the moment.

The anticipation of them all wanting this has my magic shooting out of me again, but instead of entering me like I expect, Reed moves to his knees then and captures my lips once more. He simultaneously runs his hands up and down my sides, over my stomach and breasts, between my legs, wait... might be Dante's hands too. His kisses lead away from my lips to my cheek then to my neck, drawing a moan from me when he hits a particularly sensitive spot.

Damn, he's a fast learner. Must be all those romance books.

My body hums with desire under his touch and he hasn't even gotten to the really sexual stuff yet. Ever so carefully, he traces my curves down to the apex of my thighs, drawing circles along my skin.

"Reed," I beg when my clit starts throbbing with anticipation.

He chuckles against my skin. "I'm getting there, Love. Don't worry."

Vinson smooths my sweat slicked hair back from my face and scoots Reed and I further down the bed so he can place my head in his lap. He proceeds to use his thumb to work out some knots in my neck while Reed continues to tease me. Neck massages should be considered foreplay.

A girl sure could get used to this.

And that's when Reed takes the opportunity to slide a finger through my wetness before returning to rub my clit. "Shit, Red," I breathe, desire wreaking havoc through me. Not to be outdone, Dante tweaks my nipple, sending another wave of my magic cresting out from me.

"That's it, my Love," Reed coos. "Are you ready to take my cock now?"

"Yes, please," I respond eagerly to which he obliges, sinking into me gradually. Slow may have been what I needed earlier to get my mind off things like having five fucking mates watching me get railed, but now I'm so Godsdamned wrecked with desire that I couldn't care less who's watching.

Besides, these are my mates, and they love me unconditionally. It's reflected in each of their gazes as I glance over to them. Even though Kaos and Dante already came, their cocks are standing at attention again. Same with Elian who's watching Reed and me.

It hits me then that I want all of them. I want their hands all over me, their kisses, their heat. Every fucking thing. I need this. I need all my mates. I have no idea how I'm going to take five fucking cocks, but I'm going to do it or die trying.

"Seems our mate is worried about how to handle five cocks at once," Reed says to the others after reading my thoughts. Hell, I probably projected them to him. "Let's give her what she wants, yeah?"

Dante bursts out laughing. "Angel, you don't have five holes, but you have a mouth and two hands." He winks, and then they all scramble over to me.

"Vinson, you and Reed switch," Kaos says in his bossy bedroom tone that makes all my bits excited, taking charge

CHAPTER 24 | 209

of the scenario. For some reason, Elian lets him too. "The shifter's cock is too big for anal right now. We don't want to hurt our little mate, do we?"

"Of course not," Vin responds, smug as shit with them acknowledging the size of his monster cock as he and Reed switch places. Vin puts me on top of him and I settle onto his enormous member, loving the way my walls grip him the whole way down. "Fuck, Sadie. I'll never get tired of having you," he says, looking up at me like I'm his very own Goddess.

Dante tosses Reed the bottle of lube and he squirts a hefty dollop in his hand before slicking his dick with it. He pushes two lubed up fingers in my ass, pumping in and out before replacing them with the tip of his dick. He slides in slowly and easily, my body so ready for him, them. All of them. He gives a groan and a curse under his breath, his hands gripping my hips, and I watch Vin's head fall back at the feeling of everything getting even tighter.

I feel so full. The sensation between the stretch of Vinson's huge cock, and the stretch of Reed's also big cock in my ass, both of them pushing against my inner walls almost too much and yet not enough. Reed starts to move, making Vin roll his hips upward, trying to match his thrusts.

Moons, Vinson's dick is so big. Judging by his grin, I'm pretty sure I said that out loud too.

When Reed and Vinson get a steady rhythm going, I open my mouth and lean forward slightly, beckoning Elian forward. I lick the sliver of skin under his tip and his dick bounces and hits me on the cheek. "Sorry, that felt really good," he rasps.

I let out a chuckle that turns into a moan when Reed changes angles a bit then take Elian further into my mouth, using my saliva to get him nice and wet so I can use the momentum of Reed and Vin fucking me to bob up and down

Elian's cock. He hisses and throws his head back in pleasure, threading his fingers through my hair and pulling slightly. The sting sends a whole other sensation running through me.

When the three of us settle into a good rhythm, I reach my hands out and take over for Kaos and Dante where they are stroking themselves, slicking their precum down their shafts as I caress their velvety steel. They both groan and rock into my hands, saving me from having to think with both hands, mouth, and holes, and letting me enjoy taking them all like this.

I'm on fire with the six of us connected. My entire body is buzzing, humming every place we're making contact. The heady scent of our pleasure mixing makes me want to devour everyone.

I wonder...

A delicious idea pops into my head when my magic snaps out of me again like it's reaching for my mates, so I beckon my shadows to me. They heed my call and I release my hands from Kaos and Dante. There's not even a moment for them to protest before my shadows take over my pace.

"Fuck, fuck, fuck," Dante curses. "Your shadows know exactly how to grip me, Angel."

"Moons above," Kaos chokes out in agreement.

Damn, that was a good idea.

With my shadows, I feel rather than see Kaos and Dante being stroked by my magic, Reed and Vinson piston into me from underneath, and Elian dominating my mouth. This is where the true magic is. In the love and devotion I can feel thrumming through our bonds, which are finally complete.

Elian taps the back of my head twice, letting me know he's about to come so I suck him into my mouth deeper, allowing his head to hit the back of my throat as I also call my shadows to stroke the sensitive part between his ass and balls. He grips the back of my neck in an utterly possessive gesture that has ripples shuddering through me as he comes down my throat with a roar, his hips jutting with tiny thrusts, and I swallow everything. The feeling is so erotic that I feel my own walls start to tighten.

An orgasm so strong, it might as well be a landslide, tears through me as I clench around Reed and Vinson's dicks and lean back so I can shout my release.

Kaos and Dante finish next, my shadows bringing them to their completion. Their cum hits my sides in hot ropes which is sexy as hell. Reed spills himself inside of my ass with Vinson right alongside him in my cunt, both of them continuing to thrust, drawing another mini orgasm from me.

Their emotions flood down the bond. I'm overwhelmed by everything, all their emotions and my own. Connected as one like this makes the power under my skin flare out in a colorful tidal wave, snapping into my mates instead of me, mixing the different streams of magic.

"Did you feel that?" I whisper.

There's an awestruck look on their faces.

"I think we just got a power up," Dante responds, and I feel the truth of his statement as the magic settles in my chest.

Breathless, we stare at each other, the desire between us already building again and I already know I'm going to need more. Always more with them. It might as well be my new favorite drug. I belong with them—my five fated mates—and I'm going to make damn sure they know it.

25

SADIE

Five days.

It takes five *glorious* days of nonstop orgasms before the power finally settles between us and clicks into place inside me, and honestly?

I've never felt this whole before.

It's as if every single missing puzzle piece is inside of me, waiting for me to explore the new facets of myself. I feel strong and empowered like this is what I've been waiting for this entire time. I'm cautious not to let myself feel too cocky though, because that's when people start making mistakes, and I can't afford to let anyone get hurt on my watch.

On the second day, Reed and Vinson left to check in with everyone and discovered the trio decided to take over my mates' recruiting duties while we were—ya know, out of commission. They even managed to rope in a few of the other Circles to join them. With their help, our numbers are growing nicely, but I'd say we still have less than half of the Elders' forces. Which is more than what we started with, but I'm worried it's not enough.

Who would've thought so many people wouldn't want to

follow murderous tyrants that have no regard for the lives they hold in their hands?

When will the bad guys learn?

Oh, wait. Never.

There must be a balance. Where there's light... there will always be evil lurking looking to smother it.

"Are you okay, Luna?" Vinson asks from his spot over the stove in our tiny kitchen. We emerged from our cocoon around noon, and I miss it already. It's been so nice to be sequestered away from the world's problems for almost a week. And the sex was nice too.

Reed places his hand over his chest like I shot him. "Just nice? I'm wounded, Love."

I shoot him a smirk because I figured he'd read my thoughts. Judging by the looks on the others' faces, he projected it to them too. He's gotten really good at that, using the bond they share as a Circle to clue everyone else into my private musings. I figured it would bug me, but it doesn't.

Reed leans over and gives me a kiss over my mug of coffee. Yep, I'm totally drinking coffee at noon. I need caffeine like I need life.

"It was nice," he whispers, and I know he's talking about more than the sex. It was nice to not have anyone constantly pulling us away or needing our attention for five days. Alas, it's time to get back to work.

But first—food.

Godsdamned delicious food judging from the smells wafting off it as Vinson finishes up with the final touches. He's sprinkling some kind of spice onto the steaks when a familiar orangish-blue spark of fire shoots out alongside it, setting whatever seasoning on fire as it travels down and hits the pan, combusting into a much larger flame. Vin's wide eyes find mine and then travel to Dante.

"Uh, guys?" he says in confusion. "Did I—Did that just happen?"

"No way," I breathe. "You used Dante's fire!"

"Would one of you mind putting it out?" he asks, pointing to the fire in the cast iron. "Unless you like well-done bricks for steaks?"

My nose wrinkles at the thought of a tough steak, but Dante beats me to it, extinguishing it with a flick of his fingers. Totally not jealous at all of his range of control.

"You used my power without half a thought…" Dante says in amazement. He turns to Reed and puts a finger on his head, concentrating so hard he looks like he's constipated. Reed's expression morphs from mystified to horrified.

"Dammit, Dante!" Reed growls and shakes his head like he's trying to physically shake him out of it. "Why are you using me as your guinea pig?"

Dante drops his finger and stares at it in wonder. "Sorry, bro, I didn't think it would work. Elian's powers are usually so finicky. We've all experimented with borrowing each other's abilities before but nothing on this level. Usually it drains us too much, but I don't feel any strain at all," he says, staring at his body like it holds all the answers.

"Why can I suddenly hear things I've never heard before?" Kaos chimes in, focusing intently on the leaky faucet in the kitchen. "I swear it's like I can hear the water in the pipes."

Elian's nose crinkles. "And why the hell can I smell wet dog everywhere?"

They turn to Vinson who smirks. "Shifters do not smell that bad," he counters. "But I'd say it's because you have shifter hearing and sense of smell now."

Now that I'm paying attention, I can hear and smell things that I'd never been able to before. There are three little thumps and then several smaller ones as something bounds up our steps. The front door creaks open.

"Is everybody decent?" Hemsworth calls out.

"Yeah, we're in the kitchen!" I respond.

His nails click against the wooden floor—something else I've never really noticed before. Not on this floor anyway. "I smelled steak," he says when he comes into view, nose high in the air as he struts into the kitchen. "So naturally, I came running."

Vin laughs. "I made one for you too, buddy, don't worry." Then he addresses the rest of us. "Let's explore the whole power shift thing after we eat, yeah? I don't know about you all, but I'm fucking starving."

"That tends to happen after you survive on sex for five days," Hemsworth supplies helpfully. I choke on my coffee.

"I love this little shit," Dante muses dreamily.

"Of course, you do," I say with an eye roll. "Your terrible jokes are on par with one another." I give him a smile over my coffee mug, sending how much I love his jokes down the bond so he knows I'm messing with him.

"He's my spirit animal," Dante defends.

"Nope, he would be mine. Literally."

That makes everyone dissolve into peals of laughter.

"I'll fight you for him," Dante says, holding up his fork like we're about to joust with kitchen utensils. I raise mine and dive in, slamming my fork against his. The cling vibrates through the kitchen.

Hemsworth chuffs. "As much as I'd love for you two to fight for my honor, I'm with Vinson. I'm fucking starving. Food now, fight later."

"Fine," Dante huffs and pulls me out of my chair and into his lap. "But not before I give the pretty lady a kiss." His lips brush against mine in a sweet kiss that makes my toes curl.

He releases me and I float back to my seat with a smile on my face. Vin sets a plate in front of me piled high with various meats, including the steak which looks cooked perfectly, and sauteed veggies. "Fucking hell, Vin. When did you have time to get all this stuff?" I ask.

He wipes down the counter with a rag before walking over to the table to join us. "I didn't. The trio brought it back for us yesterday, knowing we'd need the extra calories."

I take a bite and groan as all the flavors hit my taste buds and travel all the way to my synapses because it is so damn good. We've mostly been snacking the past few days, using orgasms as our sustenance, but this... This food is almost better than those orgasms.

Almost, I reiterate, knowing Reed is listening to my inner monologue, and he chuckles in response.

"Ugh, someone tell the trio I love them," I say around a mouthful of another bite. The table shakes from the force of my mates' combined growls, and I look up from where I'm shoveling in my divine meal, only to realize what I said. "Not literally, you fucking cavemen. I'm only thankful for their foresight for the *food*."

Vin stops suddenly as if realizing what he's doing then clears his throat and nods in agreement. "It was thoughtful of them," he admits, and the others concede. It's so nice to see Vin completely unburdened like this and not weighed down by some fucked up duty or blackness crawling through his veins because of me. He looks happy and healthy, and he cooks for us because he *wants* to. Not because he has to.

"It was," Kaos says, forking down his own meal. My mates could give me a run for my money in a food eating contest, that's for sure.

"It's nice to have people like them around, period," I confess. "For so long, it was Ash and I against the world, so long I'd forgotten what having a family—people who utterly support you in every aspect of life—was like." My heart pangs at the thought of Ash, and I sigh, placing my fork on my plate, which draws my mates' attention to me. They know how much I love food so if I'm stopping, it's serious.

"What's wrong, Pet?" Elian asks, watching me with those emerald eyes of his. The mask he normally wears is gone this morning, although I have a feeling it will come back when he goes out to take care of business today. The real Elian is for our eyes only.

I rub my necklace for comfort and decide to come right out with what's bugging me. "I'm worried about Ash," I admit. "Has there been any word on her whereabouts or how she's doing?"

He shakes his head. "I'm sorry, but no. The Elders must be holding her close because there hasn't even been a whisper of her anywhere. I even asked the trio for their help." He rakes his fingers through his sex-mussed hair. "I thought I'd be able to find out her location by now."

I sigh, having figured as much but hoping all the same. "It infuriates me that they still have something of mine in their grasp. And her poor parents…"

"Don't beat yourself up, Sadie," Reed says softly, taking my hand in his. "She made her choices."

"I know, but she was my best damn friend, my family, and for some reason, I miss her despite what she chose to do," I say quietly.

"She doesn't deserve you," Dante snaps.

They're still pissed at her for her actions, but I keep coming back to not knowing if I would've done things differently if I was human and it were my parents or Skylar on the line. I was supposed to protect her from shit like this, and I failed.

Kaos' eyes soften like he can sense my inner turmoil. "We'll get her back, don't worry," he says, taking my other hand from his position on the other side of me. Dante huffs, but nods. I'm grateful for them and their understanding, even if they're still angry.

I decide to pick my fork back up and eat because I know the guys won't finish without me, and my sad bullshit isn't fair to them. Plus, it would be a shame to let Vin's cooking go to waste.

"What's on the agenda for today?" I ask, trying to distract myself.

"Matilda needs my help on some policy shit," Reed says with a sigh. I know he's been having to handle a lot lately assuming his new role as King. "I'm trying to abolish some of my father's ridiculous rules. Unless someone is directly attacked and has to defend themselves, there will be no more fighting. I'm also getting rid of the rule that shifters and Light Weavers can't mix. We may not have treated them like the Night Weavers did, but we also didn't do anything to help either."

And that reminds me. "There's something I've been wondering, Vin," I say out loud, turning my attention to my shifter. "What are the Night Weavers holding over the shifters? Elian once said something about a life debt?"

Vin sighs and rubs his temples. "To understand the whole story, I have to start at the beginning." He pushes his plate away and settles back in his chair. "The story has been passed down for generations. Like a story we tell each other at pack meets around the campfire. They say that shifters were once wild and free. We lived in packs and roamed wherever we wanted.

"Until some of the packs decided to band together to help strengthen our numbers. That pack grew and grew until almost every shifter had joined forces, but it was mainly a verbal agreement. Then one day a powerful shifter emerged, and he became our Alpha, the Alpha of all Alpha's."

My eyebrow raises. "So must have been really powerful

then?"

"He was," Vin agrees with a nod. "So much so, he convinced every shifter to join his pack. By doing so, my forefathers had to share blood with him, that way the bond was stronger. Everything went well for many years it seems. The story says that things changed when the Alpha's mate was captured and taken right after he found her. That poor man had been searching and searching for his equal and when he finally found her... she was ripped away."

Anger eats at me, but I don't say anything so he can finish his story.

"He went on a rampage and was desperate to find his mate. So, when the Elders offered a deal to find her and bring her back... he did the unthinkable and accepted. What he didn't realize is he was damning us all to a life of servitude. He thought he could kill the Elders after getting his mate, but it didn't work out like that."

"Oh Goddess, Vin. That's awful. I can't imagine," I whisper.

"The shifter community turned the Alpha into a villain. He became the reason for the shifters' oppression. Chose his mate over his people when the choice should have been different. But after having met you..." He fixes me with a searing look. "I don't think I could've made a different choice."

"Vin..." I breathe.

"No," he says. "I'm serious. I'd do anything for you." The look in his eyes tell me he means it too.

"We all would," Kaos agrees, and for a moment I'd forgotten the rest of them were here.

I shake my head. "No, not at the expense of others, right?"

Elian grips my face, forcing me to look at him and it startles me. *Shit, when did he get so close?* "He said anything, Pet, and he meant it. We all do."

I breathe in his leathery scent that's mixing with mine, needing it to ground me as I think about if my mates were captured or in trouble and I had the opportunity to get them back. Would I be able to put everyone else above my mates?

I'd like to think yes but… would I?

Fuck.

What does that make me?

Elian lets go of my face and steps back, but not too far. "What happened to the Alpha and his mate?" I ask, returning the focus to the story and off that dangerous line of thought.

"The Alpha plotted to kill the Elders, but his attempt backfired. The magic binding him to their servitude killed him and his mate for conspiring against it. It was already too late, anyway. The packs were separated, and they were bound to the bastards in blood and magic, and the following generations after that. You can see where it has gone since then. No one is really sure how the magic works, but it's effective."

All I feel is rage and sadness at the previous Elders' actions and ours for perpetuating it and using their tyranny to make it even worse when they could've done something about it. "Thanks for adding yet another reason to my list of reasons why they have to die," I grit out.

"Death is too easy for them," Elian responds, venom threading every syllable, and he's right, but what do we do?

That answer is still a mystery to me.

"Enough of that for now," Kaos says, changing the subject. "Besides Reed, the rest of us aren't going anywhere today, Little Flame. We can go train with the others if you want? Oliver said some of them really need the help."

I nod, bottling up that anger and saving it for when I can actually use it. Because that day will come, and if the churning in my gut is any indication… it'll be sooner rather than later. I just hope we're ready for it.

26

DANTE

After the couch is moved out of the way, I plop down between Sadie and Kaos, completing the mini circle we've got going on in the living room. Reed is on Kaos' other side, while Elian is across from us and next to Vin.

"All right, who wants to go first?" Sadie asks, looking at Elian who has a scowl on his face. Sometimes I wonder if he even knows he's doing it or if his face is permanently fixed that way from the years of frowning. I've always heard it causes wrinkles too, and he's one grumpy bastard.

"Careful, Elian. You keep scowling like that and your face is going to get stuck. Or all wrinkly," I quip.

He stares back at me totally unimpressed, but there is a slight curvature to his lips as he glances at Sadie.

Man, I wish I knew what's going through his mind at times like this.

Suddenly, the mental image of him slamming into Sadie against a desk, her bare breasts bouncing from the force of their coupling, her eyes on his, and sweat slicking her skin invades my mind and shoots straight to my dick, who rises to say hello.

"No wonder he's pissed the majority of the time. He's probably sporting a massive hard-on ninety-nine percent of the time!" I shout, instinctively knowing I'm somehow borrowing Reed's ability to read his mind. There are other thoughts and flashes. All about her. Even about giving up his love of whiskey for her.

Elian growls at me for invading his mind but that's the last thing I hear before other thoughts overwhelm my mind. They're too fast and loud for me to catch or focus on. A hiss escapes my lips, and I put my hands up to my head like that will make the voices stop.

"Put a mental shield up," Reed says, his voice breaking through the others. I barely register it, trying to sort through the thoughts zooming through my mind. He says it again, louder this time. I do as he asks, building a mental fortress, brick by brick, focusing on stacking each one in my mind, but fucking hell, it feels like I'm sluggishly wading through mud trying to do it. Eventually, I get it up, the voices trickling away, and breathe a huge sigh of relief when my head is blissfully silent again.

I turn my attention to the Light Weaver. "Moons above, dude. Is this what you deal with all the time?"

Reed nods. "Yeah, pretty much. Although with years of training, I can now let thoughts trickle in and sift through without getting overwhelmed. However, your thoughts are always crystal clear and much louder than everyone else's," he says with an eye roll.

Oh Gods, I'm always thinking about Sadie in every single capacity I can have her. I'm slightly obsessed with my mate, to be honest. But what isn't there to love? She's fucking perfect. And fuck, that mouth. I love how she goes toe to toe with me, or anyone for that matter, no matter what. My thoughts begin to spiral into an endless sea of Sadie and all the parts of her I like naked.

Reed clears his throat like he's saying, *Um, hello?*

Sadie grabs my hand, stroking the completed mate mark on my wrist, which makes my whole body hum happily, including my cock. "Are you okay? You looked like you were in pain."

"I'm all right, Angel. But I definitely have a new respect for the damn Light Weaver," I respond, rubbing my temples. A headache is already trying to form behind my eyes. I can't imagine dealing with this every day. People think too damn much.

She leans over and kisses my forehead, and I smile. Fuck, she's so beautiful. "Much better now. Thank you, Angel."

"Anytime," she responds with a wink. She looks away to focus on everyone else, making me want to grab her face so her gorgeous eyes are only looking at me.

I want to know what she's thinking every minute of every day which means I'll have to ask Reed to train me so I can decide which thoughts to hear and how to block out everyone else. "I'm curious how far this power sharing thing goes. Like, can you all use every ability?" she asks.

"I doubt it," Vin says, scratching his chin in thought. "I doubt you all suddenly have wolves now, but maybe we can use the abilities we need when we need them."

"Yeah, I don't feel a wolfie in my head telling me to piss on everything to mark my territory or anything," I respond. "So no need to worry there." Vin actually laughs. I'm surprised at how well the shifter is fitting into our Circle. And how well he's going to fit into an Alpha role. Darren has been teaching him on the side and eventually, he's going to take over the pack. I can feel it.

"Either way, it's handy," Kaos says, watching all of us like he does in that keen way of his. He's always more concerned with the rest of us than himself, but it is nice to know someone is watching our backs.

Handy for sure. Seems like our new upgrades might be what we needed along with our new bond to get those fucking bastards who took my parents from me.

Like Sadie can sense the direction of my thoughts, she reaches out again and strokes my wrist. I'll never get tired of seeing her mark on me. I'm so in love with this girl that I'm enamored with her. My thoughts further dissolve into seeing her delicious body, the way her waist slims and then curves into her hips. Her ass is divine.

The others groan, letting me know I projected all of that to them. Yeah, my mental shielding abilities are horrible. We've definitely got to work on that. I watch as Elian fixes a papercut on Reed with Kaos' healing magic and a smile breaks across my face.

This is going to be handy indeed.

SADIE

"Hands up, Oliver! Protect your face," I snap for the third time since Oliver and his Circle mate, Wyatt, started this sparring match. "Use your intuition," I add softer this time. I forget not everyone is used to grueling training like I am.

Apparently, Oliver's power is the gift of intuition, which is handy—I would know. My intuition is my first line of defense. It tells me something is wrong before it even happens, but he doesn't know how to use his or how to listen to it at all. No one has ever taught him how to lean into those gut feelings which is a shame because he could be a really great fighter if he knew how to implement and adjust to what it's telling him. So that's what I'm working on with him.

Oliver nods at me, his red hair a blur as he and Wyatt circle each other. "Yes, like that!" I praise when he senses a hit before it happens and avoids it.

Wyatt has the ability to know what time it is at any moment. It's… not the greatest power, but I'm not judging. Their Circle seems to be comprised of Defensive magic, so

I'm hoping their true mate has some Offensive magic. When or if they finally find her, that is. Hopefully they will.

Both of them need some serious work when it comes to training, but they'll get there. Especially if I'm able to keep working with them.

I glance over to where Emma and Merri are sparring beside Wyatt and Oliver. I've been keeping a close eye on the latter since all the things she said when she first met me, but there haven't been any more outbursts. I'm hoping that means I've managed to prove myself to her. Either way, I give her space and she avoids me.

Malachi is working with a shifter on technique. He sees me staring and mouths, *Hey, Shadow Girl,* before correcting the shifter's form, and teaching him how to shift his weight to the balls of his feet before fighting.

Dante, Kaos, and Elian were pulled away to deal with some mouthy Night Weavers so I'm trying to watch the whole gym by myself. Which is fine, but I only have two eyes. I'm focusing on some shifters sparring when out of the corner of my eye, I see Emma throw Merri in a chokehold and take her down to the mat. It takes everything in me to remain neutral and not to cheer her on, but I do shoot her a wink when she looks at me, which she returns with a broad grin.

Apparently, when her mates aren't out recruiting, they're in the gym teaching. Which makes me feel a little guilty. I should be here more often. I've spent half of my life training in a gym, and I miss it. The gym used to be my second home.

Emma suddenly clutches her shoulder and drops her hands from protecting her face. Merri's eyes widen but it's too late to stop the fist that connects with Emma's cheek, though she does pull her punch a little.

"Shit, I'm so sorry, Emma!" Merri exclaims, but Emma shakes it off like a champ.

"I'm fine," she says, brushing the loose strands of her sweaty black hair out of her face. "I think."

I start to make my way over to them to see what's going on but Hemsworth bursts through the gym doors and bounds straight over to me with a wild look in his eyes. He and Vinson decided to go for a run today and stretch their legs so for him to be back without him...

"Where's Vin?" I ask, crossing to the center of the gym and meeting him halfway. Everyone turns to watch us, but I wave them off. "Keep sparring!"

Hemsworth is totally out of breath and it's starting to worry me. "Sadie, you need to come to the cabin," he pants.

"Whoa, slow down, Hems. What's going on? Where is Vin?"

"Vin is fine," he responds, and the fist around my heart eases a little. "He went to round up the others while I came and got you."

"What's going on?" I try again.

He glances around like he's suddenly realizing we're not alone. *The trio was attacked. Adam was hurt in the scuffle, and he said he needs to speak with you urgently. He found Vin and I while we were out on our run,* he projects to me.

Emma gasps and doubles over. "Something is wrong," she says and takes off running.

Dread begins to unfurl in my insides like a dragon waking up from a nap. Something more is happening, and it makes me uneasy. My intuition is tingling, and my shadows come out to play, flaring around me because of my heightened emotions.

"Keep sparring!" I shout behind me again as we hurry out of the gym. Before we pass through the doors I say, "Oliver, you're in charge while I'm gone!" His comically wide green eyes and his pale face are the last things I see, and it almost makes me chuckle, but I'm too worried about Adam and what the hell is going on.

Hemsworth and I are right on Emma's heels as we jog. I work on trying to rein in my shadows until we reach our cabin. When we walk in, I find Adam leaning against the wall, breathing heavily and my eyes widen at his appearance. His hair is completely disheveled, which is totally out of the norm for him, he's covered in dirt and bleeding from a cut on his shoulder. Frankly, he looks like plain shit-on-a-stick. Kaos is already there healing him, working his magic over the wound on his shoulder.

Elian, Reed, Dante, and Vinson are standing to the side. Thankfully, they're all here.

"What the hell happened to you?" I ask, walking over to Adam.

Emma beats me to him, and I stop when I realize she's crying softly. Adam strokes her cheek and whispers something too soft for me to hear, and Emma nods.

Adam grunts when Kaos' magic starts stitching the wound together. I forgot that for anyone outside our Circle, Kaos' ability can be slightly uncomfortable, but it's better than remaining injured. Adam knows that too, judging by the way he grits his teeth and bears the feeling.

"We were ambushed while out recruiting this morning," Adams says, still slightly out of breath. "We barely made it out of there alive. Nick and Niall went to find Emma as they came out better than I did in that fight, but they could probably use some of your magic too, Kaos. They should be here soon now that I know Emma is here."

Kaos nods his agreement but keeps his focus on healing Adam's wound.

Hemsworth asks the question on the tip of my tongue. "How did they know you would be there?"

Adam shakes his head. "I don't know, but there wasn't any

sort of warning. None of us suspected anything. We knocked on the door and as soon as it opened, magic started flying. One of them managed to nick my shoulder with their knife during the scuffle."

That's more than a little nick, I think, staring at the gaping wound pouring blood out of his shoulder.

This is not good. Not good at all. It means the Elders are retaliating, upping the ante. I wonder if this has anything to do with their creepy statement, and the time they mentioned is creeping up on us.

All of us are spinning, round and round on the same meteor that is currently hurtling onward, stuck on a collision course that will split it apart. There can only be one side that wins and I'm going to make damn sure it's ours.

"You all are going to have to start being more careful," I say, voicing my concern out loud.

"You're telling me," Adam responds and grits his teeth.

"What happened to the people you were there for?" Vinson asks.

Adam's face twists with anger. "Dead. Their throats were slit. From what I could tell, they had been dead for a few days."

My gut churns with unease and guilt for the dead Weavers I don't even know. I may have some deaths on my own hands, but not anyone innocent, thanks to my built-in crime-o-meter from the Goddess. Those Weavers didn't deserve their fate.

Kaos finishes healing Adam's wound, then runs his hands over the rest of his body, checking for other injuries. When he doesn't find any, he steps away and says, "You're all good."

"Thanks, man," Adam says, rubbing the smooth skin of his shoulder and then stretching it.

"What I don't understand is why ambush you and kill those people?" I ponder.

Adam looks at me, and from the glint in his eye, to the tick in his jaw, to his clenched teeth, I instantly know I'm not going to like what he's going to say. "Apparently, it was to leave you a note. I found this on one of the attackers." So, the Elders knowingly sent those Elites that attacked the trio to their deaths, knowing they'd be killed. They didn't want to kill whoever stumbled upon them, they wanted to toy with us.

Adam fishes a letter with a wax seal out of his pocket and hands it to me. It's slightly crumpled, and the outside is blank save for the seal on the back, which isn't broken. *At least they didn't read it.*

A chill skates down my spine when I flip the envelope over to get a closer look at the symbol embossed in the wax. "Recognize this?" I ask, showing it to Kaos.

His forehead crinkles. "Isn't that the same symbol from your apartment that night?"

Dante leans in to also get a better look. "And the one from Ashley's parents' house?"

I shiver, thinking of the blood on the walls that day. "Yeah, it is. What does it mean?"

"Well, I've never seen that *particular* symbol before," Adam responds, watching our exchange. "However, it does remind me of my fathers' official seal. Although slightly different. See how the star has four points? My father's only has three."

"Yes, I noticed that as well," Elian says, staring at the letter in my hand.

The more I hold onto it, the more my stomach roils with anxiety.

"Speculating about a symbol will get us nowhere. We need to open it and see what the bastards want." Wasting no more time, I crack the seal and slip out the letter. It feels like an omen in my hands. I carefully unfold the paper and start reading the scrawling handwriting I recognize as Mickey's.

Hello, darling niece of mine.

This letter is to inform you of my official acceptance into the Circle of the Elders.

As you will soon find out, we are outlawing any worship of the Goddess. Anyone who chooses to break that rule will be swiftly dealt with. Including your little gang of rebels you're trying to hide.

Time's ticking, little Mercedes. You cannot save everyone.

I can almost hear him chuckling as he writes that line. I glance at the last few words, steeling myself for what I find there.

I bet that's eating you up, isn't it? Knowing you won't be able to rescue them all. That your heart will ultimately be your undoing. You even abandoned your little friend who will soon be dead.

That's fine with me though. I can't wait to suck that mixed-breed power right out of your rotting corpse.

-M.S.

Shell-shocked, I hand the letter over to my mates. I feel slightly light-headed, so I head to the couch and plop down on it, dropping my head between my knees to breathe for a moment. My shadows wrap around me comfortingly, knowing I need them.

Seeing my mate mark on my wrist distracts me and I stroke it, lighting it up silver. My mate bonds hum in my chest, and I love the way it looks with Elian's full moon symbol completing the intricate design. It brings me a small amount of comfort, along with Hemsworth licking my knee.

"They can't seriously outlaw Goddess worship, can they?" I finally ask, raising my head once they finish the letter to find several stricken faces looking at me. I stroke Hemsworth's fur, letting the feeling distract me. "For fuck's sake, she created us."

Kaos shakes his head, anger radiating off him in waves. "What do they care about that? They've shirked her at every step. With the fake mate pairings, amongst a multitude of different things, and now adding Mickey to their Circle without her blessing. It's clear they don't give a fuck about the Goddess."

He's right, and it doesn't make what they're doing any less shameful.

All of us pause for a moment to think about everything. I replay my uncle's words in my head. *You won't be able to rescue them all. You even abandoned your little friend who will soon be dead.* The guilt renews my need to find her with an all-new sense of urgency.

"They're starting to make their move," Adam says, wiping sweat off his forehead and trying to fix his hair, but there's no use. Emma is glued to his side, leaving no empty space between them.

"We need to start upping everyone's training," Reed says decisively, and I feel—rather than see—everyone agree, the foreboding feeling settling over us. The air is charged with grave anticipation, permeating throughout the cabin.

"We also need to come up with a plan, but how do we do that when we still don't know how to defeat them?" I ask.

The sound of our cabin door opening has us on high alert. The guys reach for their crotch knives, but the sight of two familiar faces stops them. It's just Nick and Niall. They immediately head over to Emma, and she throws herself into their arms. So maybe she is coming around after all. Good, I'm glad.

My mates and I give them that side of the room to have a little privacy. The door opens again, and I sigh. *Who the hell is coming in now?*

Imagine my surprise when I find Bedi walking through the door like she didn't disappear on us at a really shitty time. I open my mouth to give her a piece of my mind, the anger I've been reserving bubbling up, but that's when I see the first drop of blood splatter onto the wood beneath her feet.

Bedi collapses to her knees, holding the wound at her side. Her red hair is wild, splayed around her head in every direction like she's been running from something.

"I sure know how to make an entrance, huh?" She groans from the pain. "Good news is, I'm back. Bad news is, I'm not feeling so great."

Once again, I say, *fuck*.

28

SADIE

Kaos and I rush over to Bedi's side. I grip her hand while Kaos works on her wound. He and I have worked on healing a billion times… I know how to heal, but it's like all that knowledge flies out of my brain. Flashbacks to Vin bleeding out in the estate's foyer are at the forefront of my mind, and I'm slightly panicky. I have to tell myself to inhale and exhale several times before I calm my racing heart enough to come back to the moment.

"Lie back," Kaos instructs, and she does as he asks, wincing as she goes down. The blood is flowing freely now. "I need to get a better look at this," he says in frustration. "Is it all right if I lift your shirt?"

Bedi nods and grunts with the movement of Kaos lifting up her shirt. "Gods, that hurts." Her breathing is erratic and every time she draws in a breath, there's a wet gurgling sound coming from her mouth. I'm guessing she has a punctured lung. This is not good. Not good at all. Dammit.

"What happened to you?" I ask.

Bedi squeezes my hand, gritting her teeth against Kaos'

magic. His hands are glowing black like usual, but it doesn't seem to be doing anything yet.

"Futures are finicky things, you know?"

I shake my head because no, I don't know. I'm not a seer.

"Well, they are. Yours especially. Almost every little detail in your life matters. Things change here and there and it's exhausting to keep up with." She winces and tries to take a deep breath. "The thing is, the more you know about your future, the more it changes." She looks at me, imploring me to read between the lines. I know what she means from my mom telling me in the In-Between.

"Is this why you've been avoiding us?"

She nods. "It hasn't been for naught, though. I've been spying on them." The blood running out of her doesn't seem to be slowing, but she draws my attention back to her face with her next ragged breath. Her freckles are prominent today and her eyes are wild. "I got too close today. I didn't sense the asshole sneaking up behind me until it was too late. He was already on me by the time I turned around and caught one in the side."

Kaos' jaw clenches and his face falls, but I ignore him for now, sending some magic through the bond to help charge him up, thinking that's what he needs after healing Adam.

"What did you find out, Seer?" Elian asks, watching our exchange with a calculated eye. His mask is firmly in place right now. Which is okay. This is a serious situation, and I know he needs it.

Bedi draws in another long gasping breath. "First... there's something I need to tell you, Sadie. I need you to understand."

Why isn't Kaos' magic working already?

He healed Adam's shoulder wound so easily.

I nod. "Sure, what is it, Bedi?"

"I've been lying to you almost your whole life." She pauses

and grimaces against the pain again when she pushes up to her elbows. I don't stop or interrupt her, but my intuition is seriously tingling. "Your mother and I were friends." She smiles like she's remembering something, and then her face falls. "When she saw that she was going to die... she asked me to watch over you, and I did. I've been there at almost every step of your life, even if you don't remember most of it. I have a unique ability to morph my appearance, which you already know, but it's been more than that. I've watched you blossom into such a strong, young woman and protected you when I could. I even helped you get that job at the diner. I know you hated it, but it was money." I laugh, thinking back to that wretched place. I guess it wasn't all bad though. "I couldn't interfere too much without changing your future."

A thought occurs to me, and my mouth is moving before my brain fully processes it. "Were you there when I was with Mickey? What about Skylar?"

She nods.

"What the hell, Bedi?" I snap. "Why didn't you stop him?" The questions pop out of my mouth rapid-fire and then I feel guilty at the look of anguish on her face.

She coughs and blood comes out with it. My brain refuses to register what that means. "I'm afraid I couldn't take him on alone. I never thought the magic on Skylar's power would snap... By the time I realized it, it was too late. I'm sorry, Sadie. But unfortunately, that's not what I need to tell you." She looks at Kaos, they share a look, and he shakes his head.

Kaos lifts his hands away from Bedi with sadness etched into his features.

"No, please!" I cry out, my voice breaking with the panic building in my chest. My heart feels like it's a butterfly trying to escape its cage. Said heart knows the reason, but my brain refuses to accept it all the same.

"I'm sorry, Little Flame. There's nothing I can do for her.

The wound is mortal. The blade must've been imbued with magic." He begs me with his eyes, and I see a thousand emotions mirroring my own flash in them. They can probably all feel my turmoil broadcasted over the bond. He reaches out a hand to me, but I flinch away and place my own hands over her side.

"No," I whisper and push all my power into trying to heal her wound. Nothing happens. "No, no, no." My magic tries to enter her, but it won't sink into her like usual. This can't be happening. My magic should fix this. It should fix her. I'm the solution to everything, aren't I?

I'm the reason she got hurt, so I should be able to fix her, right?

I can't lose anyone else to those bastards.

"Sadie, look at me," Bedi demands, garnering my attention. From the look on her face, it's not the first time she's called my name. "It's okay."

"No, it's not!" I shout, trying again and again to force healing magic into her. Still, it does nothing and I feel fucking useless. Despair creeps up my spine as tears leak down my cheeks, and I don't stop them. She's been there, protecting me from the beginning, looking over me. And now she's going to die. Because of me.

Mickey was right. I can't save everyone.

Bedi pulls in a ragged, gasping breath. "Listen to me, child. I've been spying on your uncle's nefarious plans. He has gone off the deep end completely, seeking power in every way possible. He's unhinged. He's gathering people to slaughter."

She grabs my hand and pulls me closer to her and visions fill my mind. At first, it's Mickey joining forces with the Elders, then it's of them ranting something about taking over the world and how Night Weavers will reign supreme. Then it's him killing a shifter and absorbing his life force. The sight makes my stomach churn and anger spreads from my chest to my limbs.

The visions she's showing me shifts again, but this time it's much lighter. She shows me all the times she protected me or watched over me from afar. Hell, she even impersonated a few teachers of mine to get closer to me when I was having a rough time in school. She shows how she found Hemsworth and kept him safe for me.

And then there was her persona as our neighbor. I can tell from her thoughts she loved being so close to us and viewed me like her own daughter, but she couldn't tell me any of this without risking the future.

Bedi has always been there. In so many ways. She's family, and I didn't even know it. And now I'm going to lose her.

She draws in another wet breath. I'm sobbing freely now as I watch the life leak out of her, knowing there's not a damn thing I can do. "Every person he kills, every life he takes, makes him grow stronger. He's going to kill them all, Sadie." I'm not sure who exactly she means, but I don't interrupt. Her voice is barely a whisper now, her strength failing her. She must mean the Night Weavers and shifters they employ, if I had to guess. "Including Ashley."

All the wind is knocked out of my lungs with that statement and panic starts scratching up my throat. My shadows burst to life, flaring around me. They're as tumultuous as my emotions.

Bedi grips my hand harder with what might be the last of her strength. "It's up to you now to stop them. Find the source of their power and take it from them." Her elbows give out and she flops to the floor. Luckily, Kaos cradles her head, so she doesn't smack it against the wood.

"Okay, Bedi. I will," I choke out through my tears, even though I'm not clear on what she means exactly. "Thank you for finding that out for me," I whisper brokenly, needing to say something, anything, as I watch the vibrance fade out of her.

She's normally so radiant, but her skin is turning white with all the blood leaving her body. There aren't any second chances here. I'm going to lose someone else. My chest tightens and my magic rears up inside me.

"You have to stop him before it's too late. You have to finish this. I know you can—" She gasps and then her mouth stops moving. Her body goes limp, and I don't have to check her pulse to know she's gone. Her bubbling presence that normally lights up a whole room is gone. *Gone, gone, gone.*

Your fault, a dark voice in my mind whispers.

I lay down beside her and sob, letting out all my feelings as I break down. My shadows create a bubble around me, soothing me softly. Tears, so many tears. So much heartache. So much pain. I'm tired of it. How far will this go?

How many others will those pricks take from me if I don't stop them?

They took yet *another* person I care about from me. The faces of all the shifters, Night and Light weavers I have met since joining this community drift through my thoughts. The pack meets with the children running around, laughing, carefree, seeing them all mingle, get to know one another, help each other. This is what the world needs to look like. This is what every one's life should be like. Instead of fear, death, and tyranny under power hungry assholes.

Well, no fucking more.

I rise from the floor, where I realize all my mates are too, sitting around me in a show of solidarity. Close enough to be there, if I need them, but far enough away to let me grieve because they know I need to. My shadows accepted them into my bubble easily, caressing each of them.

As I look at each of my mates, I can feel them sending me support through our Circle bond. I feel all the hope from

Reed, for something better. The resilience from Vinson, always unwilling to give up despite the odds. Strength from Dante, my funny mate who has overcome so much. Courage from Kaos who is willing to leap into every battle for those he cares for. And love. So much fucking love coming from Elian, my surly, grumpy mate that it almost knocks me over. I dry the tears and snot running down my face with a tissue Vin hands me.

"We have to end this before more lives are lost." They nod, somber. "But first, let's give Bedi and those Night Weavers a proper burial. Then we're going to rescue Ashley."

"After that?" Elian asks.

"We're going after those motherfuckers and we're going to end them."

29

SADIE

The Weavers believe that the dead should be returned to the earth, given over to it so their bodies can bring new life before joining the Night Goddess in her realm. I think that idea is fitting.

Matilda came and collected Bedi's body for us shortly after she passed and took her somewhere to prepare her for the ceremony that will take place under the moon, which is where we are now. The stars are out in full force in the meadow tonight, the bright moon illuminating the path to the altar where Bedi and the other Night Weavers are waiting to descend to their final rest.

It's beautiful, but I'm having a hard time focusing on it. All I see is her face when I close my eyes. Then it morphs into Vin's face, and Skylar's face, and everyone else I've lost or failed.

My feet are moving on autopilot.

I'm numb.

Actually, I'm angry, pissed as hell about losing someone else but I'm trying not to let that emotion show because tonight is about honoring the dead. Tomorrow though… Well, let's just say hell hath no fury like a pissed off Triad.

Vinson places his hand on my back to help guide me through the crowd and I appreciate the gesture because it reminds me, he's here and I'm not alone. Yes, there is a crowd tonight. All the Night Weavers, Light Weavers, and shifters are gathered in support. Two of our own are dead and so is the last seer.

My heart is heavy with grief, but I still try to give a small smile to the people staring at us with admiration. They know something big is coming. I can tell by the slight tang of anticipation in the air as I pass by face after face.

My attention returns to the altar where Bedi and the two Night Weavers are wrapped in simple cloth. It's all I can focus on as we get closer. Their faces are uncovered, and they look so peaceful. If I didn't know any better, I wouldn't even know they were dead. But I do know better.

Elian is leading our small group and he comes to a stop at the front of the crowd where six chairs have been placed for us to sit in. I stare at them for a moment before shaking my head. "I'd prefer to stand like everyone else," I say quietly.

Kaos and Reed nod, immediately clearing the chairs, dispersing them to some of the women around us instead. It warms my heart to see them so caring, but it still doesn't ease the ache of the loss.

Viola, Kaos' mom, offered to lead the ceremony tonight. As per Weaver customs, the dead need to be honored and sent off. I'm glad she offered because I wouldn't have the slightest clue on where to begin. She looks regal in a long, black dress, similar to my own, as she ascends the steps to a podium someone set up beforehand. Everyone quiets and waits for her to speak.

She looks at me and gives me a sad smile before starting. "Merry meet, everyone. Thank you for showing your support to our Shadowbringer and her Circle by being here for our seer, Bedi. And in the honor of the two Night Weavers we lost."

She continues by thanking the Goddess for bringing us life. I tune it out, all of it. I should probably be listening, but all I can think about is Bedi's last words. She believed in me, but do I believe in myself?

I still don't have all the answers, but I guess life isn't always wrapped up in a nice little bow and handed to us on a silver platter. I should know that better than anyone with the cards fate has dealt me. We don't always get to know everything or have things wrapped up nicely because the world doesn't really work like that.

Tomorrow we're going to mete out the justice this world deserves.

But for now, I look at my mates. With each of them dressed in black, they're stunning to look at. I find Kaos watching me, sensing my inner turmoil. He's always attuned to me. My gaze moves down the line. They're all looking at me instead of paying attention to the ceremony. Elian wraps his inked fingers around mine and Kaos does the same from my other side. Then Reed takes Kaos' hand, Dante takes Reed's, Vinson takes Dante's, and it connects us as a Circle. They push all their love and their light into me until I don't feel so deep in my despair.

I'm not alone.

I have them to lean on.

Now I just have to protect them.

"Sadie," Viola calls, and I realize everyone is staring at me. "Would you like to say a few words?"

I nod and start walking toward the podium with Hemsworth at my side. *You can do this, Weaver,* he projects to me.

I take a deep breath and think about what I want to say

then decide it's better to let it flow from my heart. I give a nod to the Light Weaver amplifying my voice to let him know I'm ready to begin.

Recalling how Viola greeted everyone, I start with that. "Merry meet, everyone and thank you for coming tonight. Most of you likely know by now that the last seer, Bedisa, was killed by the Elders' forces tonight. As were the two Night Weavers who were completely innocent, and in the wrong place at the wrong time." I blow out a breath and try to keep my tears at bay.

Hemsworth nudges my leg. *You're doing great,* he projects.

"Did you know that Bedisa means fate?" I ask, and most of them shake their heads. "I didn't either until recently, but I believe it was fate that brought Bedi into my life. Just like fate brought me to my mates and all of you. I also believe it was fate leading me to this exact moment, even as shitty as some of it has been. Bedi watched over me, protected me… and I failed her," I admit, and my voice wavers. I clear my throat. "But no more. No more saying goodbyes like this." My voice is stronger now than I expected it would be. "No more. Because tomorrow, we will start our plan to take down the Elders once and for all."

The night is quiet, only a faint breeze rustling through the trees, as if even the birds and animals of the night decided to pay homage to our fallen. Until all at once, every shifter, Night Weaver, and Light Weaver, place their fists over their hearts and drop to their knees as one, silently showing their support. My heart skips a beat, and I swallow thickly, the sight leaving me in awe. All these people, united against a common enemy.

One Weaver even starts drumming his fist over his heart. Others slowly begin to join in until all around us there is an echo of thumping, fists against chests. I can feel it reverberating through my body, fortifying my need for vengeance for these people. For Bedi. For my parents and Skylar. For Dante's family. For Elian's mother and sister. For Reed's faction. For everyone who has ever lost someone because of the Elders' need for power.

At some point, they rise from their knees but continue to drum across their chests. Some of the shifter's merge into their wolves and start howling alongside them. Light Weavers send up twinkling orbs of their magic, giving the meadow a majestic feel.

With one last glance at Bedi, I step down from the podium and allow the Elemental Weavers to do their job. They maneuver their hands, working their magic to open three plots of dirt for them to be buried in. A Telekinetic Weaver lifts their bodies off the altar and gently deposits them into the earth.

Another part of the ceremony is to send them off with flowers, so every Weaver and shifter alike walk by the three graves and deposit a few petals. When the last person is finished, I realize we're the only ones left besides the Elemental Weavers. Much like human funerals, the shifters believe a meal is in order afterward, so they all likely went to the mess hall.

"Are you okay, Angel?" Dante asks quietly when I don't walk over to deposit flowers.

"No," I respond. "But I will be, eventually."

He squeezes my hand and gives me a peck on the cheek. "I love you," he says.

"I love you too, Dante. I love all of you."

I'm still not ready to say goodbye, but I don't think anyone ever is when death takes someone from your life too soon. Walking over to the altar, I take a handful of petals from the basket and head to the open earth. I loosen my grip on the petals and watch them float down, down until they lay peacefully atop Bedi's body.

"Goodbye, Bedi. Thank you for everything." Somehow, those words don't feel like enough, but words are all that are left when one is dead, and the other isn't. A stray tear falls from my eye and lands with all the petals.

I repeat the process for the two Weavers, because even though they have no family here that we could find, they deserve the same respect. Technically, they probably died *because* of us. That sends a fresh wave of anger through my already tight chest.

Once my mates finish, I let them lead me away from where the Elemental Weavers are working to cover their bodies. "Come on, Little Flame. Let's get some food in you and then we can start going over the game plan."

My stomach rumbles in response. "Food would be nice."

"Agreed," Hemsworth says, licking his chops. It makes me chuckle slightly. Hemsworth is the only one I know besides my mates that is hungry more than I am.

"The shifters cooked a feast for everyone," Vin says, leading us over to the mess hall. He opens the door for me, and I step inside, my gaze immediately snapping to the delicious looking meal spanning the entire length of a long table.

Vin's shoulders shake with barely contained laughter. "I think they wanted to impress you."

"Consider me impressed," I respond, watching as the males in the room, no matter the race, fix the plates for the females. They work as a team, getting everyone fed until there are only a few left.

"Huh, that's one shifter custom I'm glad everyone is taking on," Dante says, to which my other mates agree.

I spot Oliver to the left of the mess hall and smile at him. He returns my smile with a grin of his own before he focuses on what he was doing once more. I watch as he shyly hands a plate of food to a badass looking Light Weaver who is sitting next to blue-haired Hades. I've seen her around before, and I think her name is Nova, but never really realized how gorgeous she is with her jet-black hair and bright blue eyes and *don't fuck with me* vibes. The total opposite of Oliver's quiet demeanor.

Oliver's hand brushes hers and his eyes widen. He looks from the plate in his hands to her several times before dropping the food. She looks as surprised as him when it clatters to the table, but neither pays it any more mind when Oliver places his hand in hers and they freeze.

"Holy shit," Hemsworth whispers, seeing exactly what I'm seeing. "Is what I think happening really happening?"

"Oh my Goddess, they're mates!" I exclaim excitedly.

A little too excitedly because everyone in the mess hall turns to look. Several people whoop and cheer while Oliver and the Light Weaver stand there, bonding. The shifters add their howls to the cheering voices. When it's finished and their new marks are in place… the smile on their faces… I will never forget that look.

Another true pair.

"What does this mean for mates, Shadowbringer?" someone calls out.

"Yeah, are true mate pairs coming back?" another asks, and I pull my attention from the newly bound mates.

There's a light, fluttery feeling in my chest, and I instantly know what I'm supposed to say, guided by the Goddess. "In the Goddess' eyes, we did right by honoring the dead tonight and as such, she decided to bless a few of you. The more we cleanse this community of the evil plaguing it, the more the true mate bonds will return."

Whispers start up amongst them and a few even drop to their knees and start thanking her. The sight makes me smile. Even in death, there can be light.

My heart is still a tad heavy, but it already feels lighter

than earlier. Bedi would want me to mourn her, yes, but she would also want me to be happy and enjoy life. So, that's what I'm going to do, because who knows what the next few weeks will bring.

Tonight, we're going to eat, drink, and be merry as fuck, because tomorrow will start the hardest part of this all. I don't think any of us will come out unscathed, but looking at the hope in everyone's eyes…

At least we have something worth fighting for.

30

SADIE

After tossing and turning for at least the tenth time while hearing the rest of my mates snoring softly, I decide to get up and go work off some of my restless energy. Getting out of this bed without disturbing them is going to be quite the challenge, though.

As carefully as possible, I rise and inch out of the covers, then I crawl to the end of the bed and slide off. No one seems to notice, which is a miracle when you have six people in a bed. We pushed a third mattress against the other two to have enough room for all of us, because none of them wanted to be without me tonight. Fine by me, because I didn't want to be away from them either.

My pajamas consist of one of Dante's band T-shirts and some gym shorts, so I decide to roll with it, figuring since it's super late, no one else will be at the gym anyway. Then I slide on my converse, loving the comforting feel of them as I head into the living room. I stare at the entryway where Bedi came through and collapsed. I don't realize I'm frozen there until a voice startles me.

"Penny for your thoughts?" Hemsworth asks, raising his head from the couch.

"I thought your thoughts were worth more than a penny?" I fire back.

He shoots me one of those doggy grins I love so much. "They are, but you look like you could use them." Moons, I love this dog.

I blow out a breath. "I'm going to miss her, Hems. Even though I was angry at her for bailing on us, I felt safe knowing she was likely out there pulling the strings somewhere, and I was right. Spying on my uncle and the Elders…"

"Yeah, that was really brave of her to do."

"It was," I agree. "Did you know she was my mother's friend?"

He shakes his head. "No, I never knew much about her at all to be honest, save from her drawings, she was always quite secretive—something about preserving the future. Anyway, what are you doing up so late?"

"I'm heading to the gym. Want to come?"

He hops down from the couch and bounds over to my side. "You never have to ask, Triad," he quips, using my new title. "I'm always down to stretch these legs."

"Let's go then. I need to work off some of this restless energy before trying to strategize tomorrow, and the punching bag is calling my name."

The night is calm, almost peaceful as we walk. The skies are clear and there's an owl hooting in the distance. Everyone is in bed sleeping. Apparently Hems and I are the only crazy ones out and about at this hour.

The gym is blissfully empty when we arrive, and I immediately hit play on my rock playlist, blasting it from my phone's speakers. Music is the only thing that it's good for anymore and the sole reason I keep it charged.

While Hemsworth starts running on the treadmill, using his freaky, familiar powers to turn it on himself, I head over to the punching bag, wrapping my hands. With Memphis May Fire's song, *Make Believe,* blaring, I start punching the bag.

Right jab, left hook, right kick, rotate, left kick.

I'm in the zone.

The sound of my fists and kicks hitting the bag, my music, and my breathing as I work up a sweat are the balm I desperately need.

Working my muscles beyond anything... It's euphoric.

I let the bag absorb everything I'm feeling. All my emotions, all my pain, all my guilt. Everything, and it takes it too.

Someone calls my name, and it brings me out of the depths of my mind. "Sadie, are you okay?" they ask again.

It's then I realize I'm crying. Tears are freely pouring down my cheeks. I turn and find all my mates there, all with bed hair and sleepy faces, but they're here. Reed opens his arms for me, and I walk over to the middle of them, letting them surround me in a group hug that even Elian participates in.

The bond hums with the emotions I'm feeling, alongside the comfort they're sending back. They embrace all of it and makes me feel grounded in a way I never have before.

After a while, everyone breaks apart and Elian levels me with a look. "Think you can take us all on?" he asks, somehow knowing exactly what I need as always, and wanting to push me past my limits.

A smile broadens my face. "Hell no but bring it on anyway. I'd love the challenge."

This is what I love about them. There is nothing conditional about their love like there was with my ex. They love my flaws, my quirks, hell, even my attitude. These men love everything about me, and I'll be damned if I give this up easily. Either I go out in a blaze of glory… or we win this damn thing.

For everyone's sake, I hope it's the latter.

31

SADIE

My arms are deliciously sore the next morning from sparring and so is the spot between my legs. Not that I'm complaining. Not one bit. My mates know exactly what I need to get my head in the game, or out of it, really. They know I could spend forever in my mind coming up with worst-case scenarios. Or I could be getting dicked down.

I know which one I'd rather be doing.

Currently, my mates, Hemsworth, and I are standing around our dining room table with Matilda, Alpha Darren, Beta Carter, Malachi, Emma, the trio, Oliver, Wyatt, and their new mate, Nova, plus a few other Night Weavers and Light Weavers figuring out our game plan on how to rescue Ash. It's cramped in here because this cabin definitely isn't large enough for all of us, but it's the best place to meet with a semblance of privacy.

With Wyatt's new bond, he noticed an increase in his power. Not only can he tell what time it is anywhere, he can also use his power to get a general location on anyone. They came to us first thing this morning to tell us about it. One minute they were exploring their bond and the next he was thinking about someone and immediately knew where they were. It's handy, and we're going to use it to find Ash.

"Since I've never met her before, I'll need to see a picture or something to find her," Wyatt says, brushing a piece of his curly brown hair out of his face.

"Sure," I respond, pulling my phone out of my pocket. I guess music isn't the only thing it's good for anymore. I pull up one of the pictures I snapped the night of the festival, and our smiling faces greet me. The grief smacks me straight in the chest. "Here you go," I choke out, showing him the picture.

He glances from me to the picture in concern, but he doesn't comment on it which I appreciate. Instead, he takes the phone and studies her face, trying to commit it to memory. When he's satisfied, he hands me the phone back. "I think I've got it."

Wyatt closes his eyes in concentration. The entire room is so silent you could probably hear a pin drop, maybe even a feather. Everyone waits with bated breath as Wyatt's eyes scrunch. Suddenly, they pop open, and his pupils are dilated. "I know where she's at. Seems like some kind of outpost on the outskirts of the Elders' property."

Relief pours through me.

"Being on the Elders' property is not ideal, but at least we know where she's at," Vinson says.

"Where do we go from here?" I ask, looking at everyone. If it were up to me, I'd have Matilda portal us in and snatch Ashley's ass, but I'm no longer just one person. I have a whole team and community backing me up.

"I say we just portal straight in, snatch her, and portal back out," Dante says with a huff, thinking exactly what I'm thinking. I shoot him a small smirk.

Adam shakes his head, using the paper in front of us to draw a map of the Elders' property. "If it's where I'm thinking, that won't work." He points to a building on his map. "The place will be heavily guarded. None of us were ever allowed in there and we'll need something to get past the inevitable built-in security measures they'll have in place. I can guarantee you can't portal in either so someone will have to go in through the front and disable the protections."

Have I mentioned it's good to have insider knowledge?

Too bad they still aren't certain what their fathers are using to remain invincible. That would've been nice info for the Elders to share with them, but alas, we weren't that lucky. No surprise there.

"What will work then?" Kaos asks. I can tell by the look on his face he's running through all the scenarios in his head.

"You're not going to like my answer," Adam replies, rubbing his chin in thought.

"Spit it out," Elian snaps. Ah, there's that famous temper.

"Patience, young Padawan," Hemsworth quips. Elian almost smiles. *Almost.*

"Have Matilda portal Sadie, Niall, and Malachi to the outskirts of the building. Then they go in to get her. Malachi can disable any electronics such as cameras or any other security measures. Niall can mask their presence long enough to get Ashley and hopefully find out where the others Bedi mentioned are being kept."

"Meanwhile, we create a diversion elsewhere that grabs their attention. Matilda will stay hidden and as soon as the protections are down and they have Ashley can portal everyone out," Nick finishes for him.

"You're right, we don't like it," Vinson growls, eyes flashing gold. His wolf is peeking through the surface. I can feel his inner turmoil radiating through the bond.

"We're not risking our mate," Reed agrees, and I glance at

him, feeling the vehemence against this plan the same way as Vinson's. Kaos, Dante, and Elian are on the same page as Reed and Vin if the scowls on their faces are any indication.

"If you want the girl back, what other choice do we have?" Niall asks gently but firmly. "We can't send in the cavalry without drawing too much attention. I know how my fathers' heads work. Malachi can disable their system, and Sadie is fucking powerful in her own right."

"Plus, I need to be the one to rescue Ash. I feel it in my bones." I look at my mates. "I love you guys, but we have to get her back, and then figure out where the others are that they're going to kill. Lives are at stake here." I send them lots of comfort and reassurance, but I'm still met with unease.

"I'll go in with them," Elian announces after a pause. "I'll protect our mate."

I shoot him a grateful look.

"Even with you there, I still don't like it," Kaos says. "We all should be there, we are stronger together, as a Circle." Reed, Dante, and Vin murmur their agreement.

"I don't either, but what choice do we have?" I sigh. "Niall is right. We don't need to draw attention to ourselves. What if they kill the others before we can find them? I wouldn't be able to live with myself if something happened to Ash while our friendship is in shambles, and I never got a chance to talk to her. There's been enough death in this community, don't you think? It's up to us to stop it."

"You are wise beyond your years, girl," Matilda says, watching me with fondness before turning to my mates. "Let her do this. You know she's more than capable."

Reed's jaw clenches and unclenches. He knows this is our best shot, but he doesn't want to admit it. "Watch over her for me, Tildy. You know how much she means to me."

Matilda nods. "Now, who is going to create the diversion?"

"I think we can help with that," Alpha Darren says, gesturing toward him and Carter.

A shifter clears their throat, their eyes shifting from Vin first to Alpha Darren. "You're the Alpha, though, sir. Should you really be the one to lead this?"

I pause, thinking about Alpha Darren's sweet mate, and I'm inclined to agree. "He's right, are you really the best choice?" I ask.

"It's my pack and my people. I'm not going to sit idle when I could do something. Besides, Carter and I are the only ones other than Vin who are battle ready. And he needs to be here in case something happens to you. You're more important, Shadowbringer."

As much as it makes my gut churn and as much as I hate to admit it, he's right about being the only one's battle ready. Do I really let them take on that responsibility, though?

I know it's not easy, Reed starts, *but you have to let them, Sadie. It's a good plan. Sometimes being a ruler means making hard decisions.*

They're already continuing the conversation, unaware of the emotional turmoil currently raging inside me. "We'll shift and lead them on a chase through the forest. There are plenty of places to hide until we can be portaled out."

One of the Light Weavers nods. "We can assist, and I think I can shield us too."

"We need to make sure everyone else is ready in case something happens, and this goes sideways," Adam says.

Vin nods. "We'll gather everyone and have the masses ready, just in case."

My spine tingles with awareness and a sense of urgency settles in my bones. "If this is what we're going to do, we need to get started soon. I just got one hell of a feeling that we need to act now."

Kaos clears his throat. "Everyone go, get ready. We need

to have a talk with our mate really quick." The others, including Hemsworth, disperse, and then it's the six of us alone in the room.

"Am I in trouble?" I ask sheepishly.

Kaos shakes his head. "No, Little Flame. We're protective of you, that's all."

"We'd do anything to keep you safe," Dante agrees.

"But we also know when you're needed, and in this case, you are," Reed says.

"We have something for you before you go," Kaos mentions, lips tipping up on the corners. He reaches behind his back for something, and I stare at him, confused. "We had it remade for you."

The glint of a blade catches the light as he pulls a dagger from the holster on his hip and hands it to me. I carefully inspect the silver blade, inlaid with intricate designs, and in the center, running up the length of the blade are pieces of shadestone embedded in the metal. I don't know why but tears spring to my eyes at the beauty of it.

"Are these—"

"Pieces of your shadestone? Yes," Vin says, and I look over to him. "Unfortunately, we couldn't make that blade whole again, but we wanted to remind you that some beauty can come from loss. Yes, that shadestone pierced my heart, but it was your blade first. Reginald never should've been able to wield it. The Goddess wanted you to have it for a reason, so we fixed it and made it better. The crafter even warded it against any ill intent and attuned it to your energy. It's all yours, Luna."

"It's beautiful," I whisper, admiring the handiwork in the blade. "Thank you." I slide it into my thigh holster, moving my other blade to my boot, and pull everyone in for a hug one by one.

"Now you're ready to kick some serious ass," Dante says with a wink, making us all laugh as we head out to regroup with the others.

He's right. I am.

32

SADIE

Portals are so strange. I'm not sure I will ever get over the feeling. It's like riding one too many rollercoasters in a row, combined with having your body mesh out and then phase back in while traveling through time and space.

Yeah, it's not exactly fun. Interesting, but not fun. Maybe I'll get used to it one of these days, but I doubt it.

With Adam's advice, Niall, Malachi, and Elian in tow, the portal Matilda casts lands us about fifty feet away from a small, brick building. Niall gives us a head nod to let us know his cloaking spell is working. It's colder tonight than I expected, but with my adrenaline pumping, I'm practically impervious to the cold.

The moon is high in the sky, not quite full, but almost there which means it's easier to see. But it also means the enemy can see us easier as well.

I pull my shadows to me and wrap them around us, giving us a cloak, then I return my attention to the building. From what I can see there's a door on the left end, guarded by a beefy dude carrying a magical gun, and another on the right side. They're decked out to the nines in tactical gear, and I roll my eyes at the sight.

Elite? I ask, projecting the thought to Elian. He nods.

Using my intuition, I try to get a read on the two guys, and *murderer of innocents* is the first thought that pops into my brain. So, they have blood on their hands, innocent blood at that.

I'd rather not kill anyone and draw unwanted attention to what we're doing if I don't have to. But I also know it's a possibility, and I'm guessing all the guards here are probably guilty of unspeakable crimes.

The back door is bolted shut. We're not getting in that way, Elian projects to me and motions for me to follow him. Niall and Malachi stay close, but none of us speak for fear of being overheard. Weavers also have a great sense of hearing, although my Circle's and mine are probably far superior now.

As quietly as possible we make our way through the trees to the front, careful to avoid twigs or anything else that would give us away, and find three more Elite guards carrying the same weapon as the two around back. They take turns walking the perimeter at different intervals. Suns blaze, that has to be a boring job. Sucks being a lackey. Though I don't feel sorry for them. Not really.

Reaching out with my intuition I find these three are even more guilty than the other two. The need for vengeance begins to rise in my chest, and I don't know if I can ignore their crimes. I am the Goddess' bringer of justice after all.

We're not here for that, I remind myself. *We're here for Ash and for information on the whereabouts of the other innocents. These assholes will get what's coming to them, but not today.*

I can warp their fears and make them see a threat that's not there, so they'll leave the door unattended, Elian says, watching the guards closely.

Do it. I don't think we're getting past them any other way, I respond.

Niall gives us a look, and I tap my head then point to Elian. Niall nods.

Elian puts a finger to his forehead and closes his eyes, tapping in on his fear power. I watch the guards for any signs. At first, nothing happens, but then one of them starts to look over their shoulder more often and one of the other's steps start to falter. Suddenly, the three of them stop, looking at each other in confusion.

Elian pushes a little more power into them until they unshoulder their guns. One of them whistles three times and then they silently stalk off in the direction of the woods, looking for threats that aren't there.

Thankfully, they walk in the opposite direction of us. When they hit the tree line and disappear Elian's eyes pop open. "Come on, this is our chance."

We cross the distance to the front door, and I use my shadows to give us extra cover in case there is anyone in the trees watching. I expect to pass through a ward or two, so I'm surprised when I don't feel anything. Malachi pushes the door open and then we breach the inside. I'm also expecting more guards, but so far, I'm not seeing any. Yet. I know they're here, but the question is, where.

The floor is concrete, which is fine as our footsteps are more silent and don't squeak like they would on linoleum or something. The entryway leads into a room that houses several cameras showing the feeds of the lower levels. What is it with these dudes and basements? Didn't they get the memo they're creepy?

And where are the guards?

Just as that last thought occurs to me, an Elite pops up to our right with a drink in his hand. *Rapist,* my intuition whispers. Immediately, my shadows slither from the ground and swallow him whole. Like, poof... gone. One second, he's standing there and the next he's nowhere to be found. Hopefully the Goddess drags him straight to the depths of the underworld where he belongs.

So much for being inconspicuous, though.

When I look over at the guys, I find them staring at me with comically wide eyes. You'd think Elian would be used to my magic doing weird shit by now, but apparently not. Honestly, he looks kind of turned on too. Looking down, I confirm my thoughts when I see a bulge there. Strange motherfucker. Either there's a crotch knife in his pocket or he's super happy to see me.

Dammit, Sadie. They're going to notice him missing, Elian projects.

I can't help it, I mentally hiss. *My magic does what it wants sometimes. We'll just have to find everyone before they notice him gone and kill the hostages.*

"Remind me never to fuck with you, Shadow Girl," Malachi whispers in awe and then gathers himself with a shiver. "This room houses the security system. I'm going to work on disabling the cameras and any wards I can find." He ducks into the security room without another word with Niall on his heels like I lit a fire under his ass.

Heh, I'm a scary bitch when I want to be.

My face is tingling from the intensity of Elian's eyes on me, so I refocus on him, only to be ensnared by his emerald eyes. He reaches out and yanks me to him roughly, cupping my cheek. "There's something I need to tell you, Pet."

"Uh, is this the best time?" I ask, glancing at our surroundings in this dungy building. He growls softly and brings my focus back to his face. "Okay, what is it?"

"I love you." Elian doesn't say it with any fanfare or frilly words. Three words is all he needs to take my breath away.

The look in his eyes says it all for me. He means it, though he does have really bad timing.

"I love you too, Eli," I respond and place my lips against his. He greedily meets me with his own lips and devours me, slipping his tongue inside my mouth. Every brush of our lips is a daring reminder that we belong together.

Two broken people finally found their way to one another.

All too soon, Niall and Malachi are emerging from the security room, saying, "We're good to go."

Elian and I break apart, but not before he squeezes my hand reassuringly. He takes the lead, and we follow the path the security guard came from, finding a staircase leading down to the lower portion of the building.

"Judging from the security cams, I'm guessing she will be on to the right at the bottom. The left looks like a dead end," Niall informs us as we descend. "I didn't see any other guards on the cams, but I'm certain there will be more."

The air is stale from the lack of fresh air, and it makes me miss the open outdoors of the safe haven. The further we go, the more the anticipation in my gut brews, a silent reminder of what's at stake here.

At the bottom of the staircase, Elian looks left and right before heading in the direction Niall recommended. To the left is only a single door. I stare at it for a second too long and Niall bumps into me, which in turn, makes Malachi bump into him.

"Sorry," I whisper out of habit before I catch up to Elian. We're in a long hallway of sorts and on either side are glass doors with people—shifters and Weavers from the looks of it—trapped inside.

"Holy shit," I breathe. Either they think we're Elites or they can't see us because none of them start begging to be let out or really give any indication they know we're here.

Most of them are sitting or pacing the tiny length of their cells.

"These must be the people Bedi was talking about," Niall murmurs.

"Yeah, must be," I respond and continue walking. Ash must be here somewhere. We'll worry about getting everyone out after we find her.

"Did you hear something?" a gruff voice says somewhere ahead of us.

Elian stops in his tracks and puts me behind him with one swift move, then he's pulling the four of us into the shadows. Next thing I know two guards round the corner in front of us stopping under a blinking overhead light, their eyes searching the shadows with weathered faces that are harsh and angry, but they won't find us. The shadows are where we thrive, fuckers.

Torturers, rapists, murders, my mind whispers. My magic reacts to the call of the vengeance in my veins, and the light the men are standing under becomes their worst nightmare, engulfing them whole. Intuitively, I know wherever they're going is much worse and it brings me a tiny bit of satisfaction.

I could fucking devour you right now, Elian says into my mind at the same time Niall says, "Holy fuck," in awe.

I'm all about getting their jaws to hit the floor today, I guess. It gives me the tiny confidence boost I didn't realize I needed.

The four of us continue searching for Ash. Eventually, the hallway turns to the right where the guards came from, essentially going in a giant square. We come to a stop before one of the last rooms, and all the breath leaves me. "Ash," I whisper.

Ash doesn't seem to notice me. She's laying on her side on a tiny cot, and the sight of her curled up in a ball tugs on my heartstrings. Seeing the button on the side panel of the door, I press it and the glass door slides open.

"It's not my time yet, assholes. Go fuck with someone else," Ash snaps, rising from the bed. She hasn't looked at me yet and for some reason, I'm frozen in place. The last time I saw her was when she walked in behind my uncle before Vin was killed. Minus the atrocious gray jumpsuit she's wearing—that she somehow still looks good in—she looks about the same as the last time I saw her, maybe a little more haunted.

When her eyes find mine, they widen. "Sadie?" she breathes in disbelief like her eyes are playing tricks on her.

From my peripheral, I notice Elian, Niall, and Malachi step away to give us some privacy and to watch our backs in case any other guards get curious and come running.

I nod. "Hi, Ash."

It's like time between us stops as we stand there and stare at one another, both lost in our emotions. Ash's eyes well with tears, and I feel mine do the same before we burst into action at the same time, throwing our arms around one another.

"I'm so fucking sorry, Sadie," she wails into my shoulder, the sound muffled and broken. "He promised he wouldn't hurt anyone… and Vin…. I got him killed. It's all my fault." She hiccups, the regret and guilt pour out of her. I pull back to look her in the eyes, which are definitely haunted.

SEEING HER LIKE THIS, MY FRIEND, MY FAMILY, THE ANGER I'VE been holding simply dissipates in this moment, leaving only the need to patch things up with my bestie. She doesn't know that Vin is okay, and she doesn't know about her parents and the twisted way Mickey is using them.

"We have to find my parents," she says brokenly.

"Oh, Ash, I know how much they meant to you. But you have to know that it's not permanent."

She looks at me in confusion. "What do you mean? They're back! I've seen them with my own two eyes, but they keep me locked in here, and I never get to see them."

I rack my brain for the best way to describe this and decide the best course of action is to be blunt. Ash has never been one to sugarcoat things, and I won't either.

"It's a long ass story. One we don't really have time for currently." I look behind me to Elian and he nods, telling me we're okay for the moment with his eyes. "I'll tell you the full version as soon as we get out, but here's the cliff notes version. I had to travel to the In-Between to rescue Vin, which is where souls go if they have unfinished business before heading to their final destination. Your parents found me while I was there and wanted me to tell you that what you're seeing isn't actually them."

More tears leak down her face and she shakes her head. "They're real. I saw them, touched them. They're real," she repeats. "I know it's them, Sadie."

"They're real," I agree, and she looks at me in confusion. "What you're seeing is real, babe, but your parents truly are dead. Mickey is a necromancer and is reanimating them. Every time Mickey reanimates them, it's causing them pain. They told me themselves."

"But... how? Why?" she looks so devastated, it shreds my heart. "What about Vinson? I don't understand."

"That's what I'm trying to tell you. I rescued Vin from the In-Between. The Goddess helped me get him back. He's alive. That's where I saw your parents." I pause, searching her eyes to see if she's understanding what I'm saying.

"You can do that?" she rushes out with a gasp. "What about my parents? You could bring them—"

I cut her off before she gets too carried away. "No, Ash, I

only saw them in the In-Between. They should not have been there in the first place. They were at peace, babe, and Mickey pulled them out, using his twisted magic to make you believe they were back from the dead. But it doesn't work that way. They want you to know they want to stay, but they can't, and gave me a message so you would believe me. Do you remember what they were talking about before the accident? The last conversation you had with them?"

She sniffles, wiping her tears with a sleeve. I check over my shoulder again and Elian makes a speed it up motion. Right. We are running out of time.

"They told me to tell you about their debate over which brunch food is the best: pancakes or waffles. And your dad's argument was that pancakes are better because waffles are—"

"Pancakes with abs," Ash finishes. She gives a watery, sad chuckle and looks at me. "He always had the worst dad jokes." She chuckles again and I join in, remembering the many times she and I rolled our eyes at his antics.

"Listen, they love you, Ash, but they want you to move on and be happy. It's okay to want them back, but not at the cost of suffering."

"I've been such an idiot," she cries out, shoulders slumped in defeat. "Everything that happened was all my fault. I'm so sorry. Will you ever be able to forgive me?"

My heart is still hurt over her actions, but she's also my best friend, and if the tables were turned... I don't know if I would've acted differently. We've been through hell and back together and I think it's worth making amends. Both of us have done things we regret. It's a part of life.

I take a deep breath, thinking through my words carefully. "It will take a while for me to feel like I can trust you again," I admit. "But yes, I do think I can forgive you, Ash. Recently, I've realized exactly how short life can be and how important forgiveness is. I love you even when you're an idiot."

"Hey, I take offense to that!" she says in mock outrage then grows serious again. "I love you too, Sades. I'm so sorry."

I shoot her a look. "Next time though, come to me." She starts nodding vehemently. "I don't give a fuck what it's about. I want to know. We both have a guy now," I say with a wink, referencing our conversation at the concert when she thought my mates had hurt me.

"Yeah, in this case, the geas made it a little hard to come to you. I tried to spill everything as soon as I came back but the words wouldn't come out of my mouth."

I think about when the trio brought her to us and remember her mouth moving, but nothing coming out and then chalking it up to whatever she went through. Dammit, I should've pushed harder. Not that it would have mattered, I guess.

"Still. We'll come up with our own code word or phrase so I'll know something is wrong, but first let's get out of here, yeah? What did you mean earlier by 'it's not your time yet?'" I ask.

"Oh, fuck. We have to get everyone out of here! Your damn uncle and those Elders have gone off the deep end. They're taking people out in groups and none of them are returning," she says with a shiver. "I heard one of the guards say they're building an army when they brought in my tray of food this morning and told me which group I'd be called with."

Unease slithers down my spine. "You're right. We need to get these people out of here." I turn. "Elian, did you hear that?" I ask.

"Yeah, we need to get word to the guys and Matilda to expect more people. We weren't counting on finding them all at this exact moment, though it seems like it's a good thing we did."

Reed, can you hear me? I ask mentally, reaching out to him through the bond.

Loud and clear, Love. What's happening? he responds.

We found Ash and the people Bedi mentioned. We need to get word to Matilda to expect to portal out way more people than our original plan, I tell him.

I'll figure out a way to get word to her. Maybe Dante can send a fire message, he says, quickly working through the options. *We also found another Night Weaver who can make small portals, so we'll get him and Nick involved.*

Sounds good. Thanks, Red.

You got it, Love. I love you. Stay safe, he responds and cuts off the mental connection.

"Okay, the guys know," I tell them and turn to Ash. "Do you know how many guards are normally down here?"

She shakes her head. "No, all I know is two deliver meals to me every day and there's usually another two behind them handing out food on the other side."

At least they feed them, I think, but I don't voice that thought aloud. That begs the question though, why *are* they feeding them?

You only feed prisoners if you want to keep them alive.

"At least four then," Elian notes, looking around. "Sadie has dispatched three which means there could still be a fourth."

"Or more," Niall adds.

"Yeah, we need to proceed with caution," I respond. "Let's start opening these cells and getting these people out of here. Ash, do you think you can keep an eye out for us?"

"You got it, babe," Ash says and moves to watch our backs while Elian, Niall, Malachi and I start letting people out of their cells.

Most of them are extremely grateful once they figure out we're not here to harm them, a few of them are still quite fearful of us, but calmed down when they found out who I am. Apparently, word has spread, even to them.

From what I can tell there's a mix of shifters, Night Weavers, and even a few Light Weavers. Which is strange, as I thought the Elders wanted them all dead. I don't have time to question their motives right now, though. We need to get these people out of here and get the hell out of dodge before the Elders figure out what's going on.

When the last of them are out of their cells, I motion to head up the stairs. Niall and Malachi take Ash and lead the group while Elian and I bring up the rear, herding the fifty or so shifters and Weavers outside.

Before we make it to the stairs, a bright blue light begins to glow under the door to the left of the dead-end hallway and captures my attention. I feel a tug in my chest and my intuition comes alive with a burning curiosity that I don't understand where it's coming from but doesn't matter. Something is urging me to find out what's behind that door. Like a mosquito to a blue light trap, I'm powerless to resist.

"Sadie, where the hell are you going?" Elian hisses, confused when I take off in that direction like my ass is on fire.

"The door," I whisper, feeling like one of those stupid heroines in scary movies who die because of their curiosity as my feet carry me over to it. The door itself is nothing special, but the power emanating from behind it is... something else entirely. Yet it feels familiar somehow.

What the hell are they hiding?

Let's find out.

As soon as my fingers touch the doorknob, it shocks the piss out of me and I gasp, but I don't let go. Instead, I push my power into it, telling it to fuck off mentally. It takes more juice than I'd like to admit before I'm able to twist and fling it open.

The first sight to greet me is a guard, who looks surprised as fuck as he drops his sandwich on the ground in shock. I don't spare him another thought, letting my magic handle his fate as I stare at the bright blue swirling glass case in the middle filled with souls.

Oh, shit.

We were so wrong about what is going on.

33

SADIE

So many souls.

The circular glass encases them from all sides so there is no escape for them. The way they're moving reminds me of the portal to the In-Between. The real question is, how did the Elders manage to get this many souls?

And why?

Is this what's keeping them invincible?

Guess that was more than one question.

"Holy fucking shit," Elian says, trailing in behind me, studying the room.

At the sound of his voice, the swirling souls become agitated, knocking against the glass, desperately trying to get out.

"We have to do something," I say, getting closer. It's like I can feel their pain and agony inside of me. There's no telling how long these poor people have been trapped in there.

My hand almost touches the glass when Elian yanks me back. "Have you lost your mind?" he demands. "You have no idea what sort of protections the Elders have put in place to protect this thing."

Admonished, I shake myself out of the trance the souls put me in. "Fuck, you're right. I don't know what happened. It's like they are calling to me. I couldn't stop myself..." I turn my gaze back to the souls, unable to look away.

Elian brings my face to his and looks leery for a moment before it's gone, and his normal mask is in place. "We'll come back once we get everyone out and try to determine a way to let them free, okay?"

Elian leads me from the room and the souls try harder to escape. My own soul aches for them, but I know Elian is right, we have to think of the living first.

When we emerge from the building, we join everyone outside and find Matilda is already working on portaling everyone out. The guards from earlier are nowhere to be found so Elian's fear trick must've really sent them on a wild goose chase. Part of me hopes they lose their way out in the woods. It would serve those assholes right.

"Hey, Matilda. Glad Reed's message made it," I say, crossing the distance to her.

"I'm just glad you found them all in one piece. I guess we can say that's one plan foiled, right?" She shoots me a wink and it dissipates some of the heartache and uneasiness created by our discovery downstairs.

I laugh. "I guess so."

The line seems to be dwindling rather quickly and so far, there's no indication that anyone is any wiser about what we're doing.

I should know better than that by now though.

There are about thirty or so people left when a terrible feeling strikes me straight in the gut. I wrap my arm around my stomach. Elian winces, feeling an echo through the bond, and immediately leaves his conversation with Niall to come check on me.

Even Malachi cocks his head and asks, "You okay, Shadow Girl?"

Elian rubs his hands up and down my shoulders. "What is it? What's wrong?"

"Something's not right," I respond when another awful feeling washes over me.

The ground beneath us begins to rumble, slowly at first. There's only a slight quake beneath our feet, but it's enough for us to notice. I look from Elian to the ground in confusion. Then out of nowhere, a crack splits the earth. It starts from the building everyone was housed in and heads straight for us and where Matilda is hurrying people through the portal.

The patch beneath my feet cracks open and instinctively, I jump off it. It grows wider, like it's trying to swallow me whole. I don't panic, but I do catch Matilda out of the corner of my eye. Her concentration breaks and she's forced to shut the portal down as chaos begins all around us and people begin screaming as the crack splits even more.

Everyone scatters like ants and runs in opposite directions. Elian is laser focused on me and grabs my hand as we run. When the ground eventually stops rumbling, I look back and find a giant abyss separating us. Somehow Elian, Ash, Niall, Malachi, and I end up on the opposite side from Matilda and her portaling abilities. *Fuck.*

The next thing I know, the building explodes, and the glass case of souls shoots out of the hole before the place implodes on itself. The souls hover menacingly above the wreckage, and the blast is enough to knock us off our feet, sending us flying. I hit the ground beside Elian with an *oomph,* and he throws up a shield, using Kaos' magic to protect us from the debris. He recovers faster than me and says something, but I can't hear anything over the ringing in my ears.

That's when the panic starts to set in, but I don't let it control me. I take a few deep breaths like Elian taught me, and when the earth stops shaking, I get to my feet alongside him and help Ash to hers. Niall is knocked out cold, but the rise and fall of his chest indicates he's still breathing. Malachi bends to check on him.

This is bad. So fucking bad.

Carnage is all around us. Most of the remaining shifters and Weavers are laying on the ground. A few of them are dangling off the edge of where the earth split and as much as I want to help them, my focus is on the three figures emerging from the cloud of dust with not a spec on them, those stupid robes of theirs billowing in the breeze.

Elder Vogt has his hand in the air, controlling the ball of souls as he walks. Reginald has a gleeful smile on his face, which I'm sure he thinks is seductive, but it merely turns my stomach. Vald is impassive and looking ruthless as usual. The moon shining on them gives their already ominous features an even more sinister look. None of them spare Niall a glance. He's truly dead to them.

"Isn't this a surprise?" Reginald calls out, his expression filled with malice. "Mercedes Sinclair, caught red-handed with her hand in our cookie jar," he tsks. "Do you want to know what we do with people who stick their hands in places they don't belong?" He pauses for a beat but doesn't give me a chance to respond. "We cut them off."

Elian grabs hold of my hand, and I grab onto Ash when I realize what he's about to do. He tries to shadow us the hell out of here, but he goes nowhere, and his eyes widen. I think he also tries to reach me mentally, but there's nothing but static between us when I try to send him a mental message as well.

"Not so fast," Reginald says with a smirk and cackles like a stereotypical villain. It makes me want to claw my eyes out. Or claw his out. That would be much preferred. "We learned our lesson the last time you used that pesky little trick to get away from us. Not this time, I'm afraid."

From my peripheral, I see Matilda and a few others working on saving the dangling shifters and Weavers, so I focus my full attention on the Elders. I attempt to pull on my own magic, but nothing happens. Figures.

I let their hands go and slip my newly reformed shadestone dagger from its holster and palm it, then hand one of my other knives to Ash. This is why I always come prepared. Locked and loaded. Looks like we're going to have to do this the hard way, but Gods do I wish the others were here. Mentally, I try to reach out, knowing the Elders have done something to block our connection, but I have to try something even if nothing comes of it. Same as Elian, there's only static.

I do feel some panic in my chest that's not entirely my own though, so it gives me hope that Vinson knows something is wrong through our soul bond.

Reginald, Vald, and Vogt are still a ways away, but they're steadily making their way closer to us, though it seems Vogt is struggling with the souls. They're writhing and slamming against the glass trying to escape and it's making the ball shake.

Keep them talking, Sadie. You know how they like to rant, I tell myself mentally, trying to sort through my options like Kaos would do. Maybe if I keep them talking, they'll slip up, and I can figure out a way to get us all out of here in one piece.

Like the night of the challenge, their slimy, awful magic tries to burrow under my skin, seeking to find a way in, but training with Reed has taught me how to protect my mind. I mentally layer shield upon shield over it while I rack my brain for what to say.

"What's with the ball there, Reggie?" I ask. "Didn't have any balls of your own so you had to construct one of glass and fill it with souls to feel big and bad? Don't you know glass is fragile?"

Reginald scowls. "You've got quite the mouth on you, girl. Didn't anyone ever teach you to respect your damn Elders?"

"I do respect them, Reggie. The ones that are deserving of my respect, anyway." I shoot him a wink and try to think of something else to get him talking because that didn't work. "I heard you joined forces with that uncle of mine. Speaking of which, where is he?"

That brings that malicious look back to his eyes. "That we did," he responds. "Is that burning you up inside, knowing we let the man who murdered your entire family into our ranks?"

I don't dignify that with a response, but I do notice he carefully ignores my question of where Mickey is. Instead, I ask a question of my own. "What'd he offer you, huh? What does that piece of shit even *have* to offer?"

They're getting closer. So fucking close. I chance a glance behind us and find a barrier almost like the one in the arena surrounding us entirely, including where Matilda and the other hostages are. Which means none of us are getting out that way.

Elian squeezes my hand in a silent show of support. He's also worked through all of this in his head and he's telling me we either get out of this alive, or we go down trying.

Surprisingly, Vogt is the one to answer my question this time. "You," he says, his tone menacing. A shiver runs down my spine at his words because that could be taken in many ways—all of which I refuse to find out about.

Reginald shoots me a smirk, but honestly, he just looks

constipated. Now that they're a tad closer, I see how rough they're looking. They look drunk, mad at the thought of getting ahold of my abilities.

"Don't look so upset, Mercedes. He means your power." No chance in hell I'll ever let that happen, but I let him continue. "Yes, your power is going to be the final boost we need to finally take over this world."

I groan and resist the urge to face-palm. "World domination? That's your master plan? Can't you assholes ever be more creative?"

Vogt flicks his fingers and an invisible slap lands across my face. My head snaps to the side and pain blossoms across my cheek, making Elian growl beside me, but I ignore it because that action was extremely telling. The glass ball hovering above him drops slightly and he has to quickly push more power into it to stop it from careening into the ground. The souls are fighting him every step of the way, and I find myself even more drawn to them than before. They must be the key to ending this. I just need to figure out how.

If only someone could give us some more time because as it is, they're closing the distance between us. They want us, or me at least, alive for something, but I refuse to let them get their hands on anyone else.

"Ash," I whisper. "I want you to run. You're human so you should be able to pass through the barrier without issue since you don't have any power."

"Hell no," she snaps. "I'm not leaving you again, bitch."

Judging by the look of determination on her face and the fierce grip she has on her dagger, there's no stopping her. I don't have time to debate with her. The Elders take a step forward and we take a step back. They've got us cornered, with no magic, and they damn well know it.

I want to wipe that victorious look off their faces so bad.

"A mouse caught in a trap," Vald whispers with glee. His

beady eyes travel up and down my body. It makes me feel like ants are crawling all over me and I hate the feeling.

"That she is, and you know what's funny?" Reginald asks, and once again, doesn't wait for me to answer. "If you had never gone into that room, never touched that doorknob, we probably would've never even known you were here until we found the missing guards. You could've slipped back to your little safe haven and saved the day. But as they say, curiosity killed the cat."

I remember the zap the doorknob gave me and curse myself for being so stupid. Of course, they had that room rigged so they'd know if anyone entered it. Probably had it attuned to my energy too.

"That's the thing, Reggie," I say, forcing my voice to be more confident than I feel. "We would've had to deal with you cocksuckers at some point anyway. No more hiding. It's time to end this."

Our backs are almost to the barrier and that's when I see Vald flick his hand. The barrier behind us flickers for half of a second. *Is he... struggling to maintain it?* I glance down at my dagger, embedded with shadestone, and that's when an idea pops into my head.

I give Matilda a look to be ready from across the divide that I hope she sees, and then I burst into action. Pivoting, I sprint the remaining distance to the barrier and slam my dagger into it before even an utterance of protest can happen. The force of it reverberates up my arms and through my body, but Elian is there, protecting my back with his knife in one hand. I put both hands on my dagger in an attempt to tear this barrier apart.

Come on, come on, come on.

I scream, forcing power into my arms as I shove the dagger down through the barrier as hard as I can, the magic fights me the whole way, but I push and push until I blow it wide open.

As soon as the barrier drops, I start to see the Elite running through the trees, heading this way as backup. Shit.

Testing my connection with my mates, I find it open once more, so I send out SOS's left and right down the bond to them, pleading with the Goddess for them to hear it. Because in this case, SOS doesn't mean *save our ship*. It means *save our Sadie*, and I'm going to need all the help I can get.

34

SADIE

Panting from the exertion of breaking through the barrier, I turn and shout, "Matilda!" But the woman is already on it, working her magic into a swirling portal. I don't have a chance to see who walks through, or if anyone does, because the Elders descend upon us with rage in their eyes.

Vogt is keeping the orb of souls safe, but Reginald and Vald aren't tied down by it. I call the shadows to me as Reginald readies to attack me but forget that they slide right off him. Shit.

How do you fight someone who can't be harmed?

You don't.

Elian! I think the souls are the key. We need to get to them, I project to him mentally.

He grunts his affirmation as he and Vald start fighting, and damn, Vald is ruthless. Elian has his knife in hand and they're sparring, going blow for blow, but I don't get to watch them fight any longer as Reginald is now aiming his own dagger at me. I'm forced to return my attention to him as I raise my shadestone in defense. The force of us colliding vibrates down my arms.

Using all my might, I shove Reginald away from me, hoping to make him stumble. He doesn't, but he is forced to take a few steps back, which gives me a little breathing room. I know I'm going to need it.

Elian

All hell breaks loose around us after Sadie knocks the barrier down, and that fucker, Vald, heads straight for me. He never liked me, and I can tell by the look in his eyes he's going to enjoy killing me. Good luck trying, asshole.

From my peripheral, I see the shifters and Weavers we were trying to rescue jump into the fray, trying to hold off the Elites for us. The level of respect they have for us stuns me.

I keep Sadie and Reginald in my line of sight as much as I can while attempting to use my fear power on the Elders, but it slides right off them like I'm not even trying. Sadie must be right about the souls being the source of their invincibility.

Vald manages to nick my arm with his blade, but I ignore the pain. I've dealt with far worse, from my own father no less. "You're a fucking disgrace to your family, I hope you know that," Vald says venomously.

He leaves his right side open, and I dive in but he manages to block me at the last second. Vald has always been the Elder I've kept an eye on the most. There's something completely unhinged about him in a completely different way than Reginald's crazy stupid.

"My mother and sister would be proud of me and that's

all I care about," I retort, throwing up a shield when he goes for my side. The look on his face makes a cocky smile spread across mine.

We could do this twirl and dance all night, but sadly, judging by the ones falling around us—because honestly, a ragtag bunch of Weavers and shifters are no match for the Elite—we're not going to last long, unless something happens. There's magic being thrown everywhere but the Elite are quick and thorough.

There's a tug in my chest and from the corner of my eye, I see a portal open and four hulking figures I'd know anywhere step through.

Bring it on, fuckers. The cavalry's here.

Sadie

"SADIE!" MY MATES BELLOW AS ONE, AND MY EYES FIND THEIRS from across the divide. Thank the Goddess they're here, but they're on the other side, and Elian is over here which means he can't shadow them to us.

I'm distracted by the sight of them a second too long because pain blooms across my shoulder as Reginald slices me with his blade, and I jump back at the last second to avoid getting impaled. *Fuck, that hurt,* I think as blood drips down my arm. *No more getting distracted. They'll figure out how to get to me. They always do.*

I circle Reginald, making him follow my movements. He's good, but he's also rusty. I can tell by the slight fumbles in his steps. They're small, but they're there. This is someone who is used to having their battles fought for them. I can't help but feel like I'm water circling a drain, getting closer and closer to it before being sucked down the pipes, or my doom. Too bad I have no intention of going down those pipes with him.

What I don't understand is why they aren't using their magic. The first time we met their magic, it was so strong it was almost choking, but I'm not getting that same feeling now. They look like they're decaying, and I wonder if they even realize it.

"Why aren't you using your magic, Reggie? I thought you were some all-powerful badass," I say, deflecting another harsh blow.

The frown that mars his face as we break apart is so severe that for a second, I think his face might get stuck that way. "It seems the power given to us by the Goddess is fading, but it doesn't matter." I shoot him a devilish smile at that knowledge, but he raises his dagger and attacks, the clinging of metal against metal rattles my teeth. "When we capture you and your mates, we'll absorb yours and become the most powerful Triad Circle in existence. Then all our plans will come into fruition."

He grins like a loon and a tingle shoots down my spine. One of Kaos' shields pops up and protects my back from a faceless Elite. I reach down and grab the other knife out of my shit-kickers and watch Reginald and the Elite. Thank the Gods Kaos taught me how to dual-wield. *In more ways than one,* my mind whispers. I'd laugh at myself if all our lives weren't at stake here.

Chaos is raining down all around us from every angle. Shifters and Weavers alike are pouring out of Matilda's portal and running into the fight, facing the Elite that keep popping out from the trees. Bodies are starting to pile up and it makes me sick to my stomach not knowing whether they're allies or enemies.

Niall must've woken up at some point and is now helping

defend Ash. I catch a familiar face emerging from the tree line. Carter makes a beeline for Ash like he's her lifeline. Distantly, I wonder where Alpha Darren is, but I don't have time to dwell on it or the strange hollow pain in my chest, because I have to deflect an attack from both Reginald and the Elite.

I need to do something—anything to end this shit. My entire consciousness is screaming at me because this is it; our last chance, the final showdown. But whereas Reginald is slightly rusty, the Elite is not, and between the two of them, they're keeping me on my toes.

Elian and Vald are still going at one another. I see a path to the souls when they shift and make a split-second decision to change my tactics and start going on the offensive instead of defense, leading Reginald and the Elite closer to the souls as I slash, punch, kick, and parry the whole way.

The Elite tries to shove his knife into my stomach, and I jump back just in time. Crap, that was close. I keep the orb of souls in my peripheral, but I don't directly glance at it for fear of them catching onto my plan.

My arms burn from the exertion, but I can't think about that. I also can't think about everyone I see getting cut down around me. My mates are safe, I'd know if something happened to them, but there are so many Weavers and shifters around me that I can't see anymore.

We're about ten feet away from the orb when the Elite suddenly charges me. We're too close to do anything, and I'm forced to hold on to him as he slams us into the ground. He's too big for me to roll so I keep a firm grip on my knife, and when we come to a stop, I immediately slam it into his side. He grunts but doesn't move from on top of me. I buck and struggle against his hold but he just doesn't budge. He cracks me across the cheek, but I ignore the pain, sorting through my options.

My shadows rear up inside of me at the exact moment I catch a blur of black to the side. Vin's wolf tackles the Elite off me and immediately rips off his head.

VINSON

As soon as I felt the panic in my chest and our mental connection cut off, I knew something was wrong. The forces were already rounded up, so it was just a matter of getting a portal open to Sadie and Elian. Except, we couldn't, no matter how hard we tried.

I don't know what suddenly changed and allowed us through, and I don't care. We all heard Sadie's mental call for help and came running. I was expecting carnage, but this is next level. Shifters and Weavers are charging the Elites, using brute force and numbers to take them down.

My wolf paces in my head. *Must get to mate,* he growls.

I'm working on it, I respond.

My eyes find the giant gap separating where we landed and my heart stutters in my chest when I find Sadie all the way across the divide, facing off with an Elite. He tackles her to the ground, and I don't have time to alert the others. I have to get to her. My instincts take over and with half a thought, I shift into my majestic black wolf. Sadie's shadows flare out around me, snapping and blending into the night. An Elite looks at me and his eyes widen when I snarl at him. He takes off running. Smart man.

My paws pound against the grass, and I don't question myself or my wolf as I get closer and closer to the gaping hole. I let my need to protect my mate fuel me as my wolf leaps. The distance is larger than I expected, and at first, I don't think I'm going to make it, but a gust of wind hits me and carries me to the other side. I find a Night Weaver staring at me, panic in her eyes and her hands in the air. I give her a nod of thanks before returning my attention to Sadie.

With my wolf's large gait, we're on her in seconds, and I tackle the fucker off her. The nasty tang of his piss-poor blood hits my tongue as my wolf bites his head clean off. *That's what you get for taking on our mate, asshole,* my wolf snarls.

Sadie's wide eyes are on me, shining with love and pride that's only for me before focusing on the fight once more. I'll do anything to keep that beautiful face alive.

Anything.

SADIE

MY SHADOWS DO THE REST AND THE ELITE'S BODY DISAPPEARS. Thank the Goddess, Vin got here in time. For a split second, I wonder how he made it across the divide, but I don't have time to ponder it because Reginald is readying to attack me again. If I can't disable whatever is protecting the Elders physically, we'll never be able to defeat them. Which is also why I'm trying not to expend any more power than I already have.

Vin, distract Reginald for me! I mentally shout, and he rounds on him, snarling. Reginald's eyes widen, but I turn my back on them and focus on the souls.

Unfortunately, the Elders' lackeys have other plans. Those that are still loyal to the fucks are starting to pour onto the makeshift battlefield alongside our allies. There are so many more of them than there are of us. We're completely outnumbered.

The Marsh Circle makes a beeline straight toward me with that bigheaded bully named Hunter, who was beating on Oliver at the compound, at the forefront of their little gang. For fuck's sake. I don't have time for this.

"What? You assholes didn't get enough of a beating that day at the compound? You want more?" I ask, palming my shadestone as they approach. Unfortunately, my other knife is still buried in the Elite that Vin took down for me, but this one will do just fine. Actually, I prefer it, knowing the work that went into it.

"Fuck you, you stupid bitch," Hunter snaps. "You're going down for defying the Elders. Imagine the glory we'll get for being the ones to do it, too."

I roll my eyes, but a part of me knows I need to say something. "No, you are going down for defying the Goddess by placing your Elders on a pedestal where they don't belong." My voice is doing that weird projecting thing again, and I instantly know the Goddess is with me. She may not be able to intervene, but I have her blessing. "Do any of you wish to change your path?" And I'm not only talking to his Circle anymore.

"As fucking if," one of Hunter's Circle mates growls, the Water Weaver, if I remember right. His entire Circle nods their agreement with him.

"So be it then," I respond to them, and then to everyone else, I say, "Let their foolishness be a lesson." Some of the loyal ones stop to look at me as my shadows rise to my call, and I blast them at Hunter's entire Circle. There's not even time for them to scream before they disappear, but even so, I begin to feel a drain on my power.

But that's what was needed. A wake-up call. The tides of battle start to shift as whispers of *the Shadowbringer* echo all around me. My allies start chanting it until the roar of it is deafening.

A glint of light in the night sky catches my eye, shining brighter than the moon's glow, and I find Reed looking as determined as ever as he works his hands in large circles, weaving a trail of light for my mates and Hemsworth to ride on across the divide. They look fierce, their faces lined with determination as they drop on our side in a crouch. Our bond sings between us, and I find myself more amped now that they're here.

The other Light Weavers pouring through the portal stare at him in awe. Then they begin to do the same, transporting as many as they can via the light beams until the score starts to even out to our side, but my focus is on my mates. My fierce mates.

Reed

The battlefield is absolute pandemonium when we step through the portal. Magic whizzes by my head that I barely duck in time to miss. Bodies are hitting the ground faster than I can count and a piece inside of me wants to shatter at the sight—the faces of my dead faction morphing with the ones I see now.

I shake myself out of that train of thought as I catch a glimpse of Sadie fighting with Reginald and an Elite across a huge crevice and the blood in my veins boils at the sight. The Elite fucker tackles Sadie and they hit the ground hard. Vinson is already pounding across the battlefield in wolf form, frantic to get to her.

I watch in amazement as he takes a running leap, pure

grit and determination fueling him. My heart stutters when it looks as if he's not going to make it, and I take a step forward, trying to think of anything to get him across safely when an Elemental Weaver shoots a gust of air that carries him across. Relief pours through me but it's short-lived.

"We have to find a way across!" I shout to be heard over the chaos wreaking havoc around us.

"How do we get over there safely?" Dante asks, deflecting a blow from an Elite off a shifter nearby.

"We'll find a way," Kaos responds, analyzing the scene with his critical eyes.

I raise my own dagger and call my light to me. It's then that I realize it's different. Light Weavers can pull light from just about anywhere, but this is inconsistent. The light that comes to me has more of a silvery hue than my normal daylight, and I glance up at the moon shining down on us.

In olden times, the Light Weavers would supposedly use the sun's rays to travel. I wonder…

Weaving my hands in large, looping circles, I attempt to form a moonbeam. If they could do it, surely I can. I've never practiced it before but it seems pretty straightforward. Satisfaction flows through me when a solid beam starts to take shape.

Hop on, I mentally project to my fellow Circle mates.

Riding a moonbeam is sort of like riding a wave, tumultuous and a tad bit scary, but I'd do anything for Sadie. As soon as our feet hit the ground, we land in a crouch, standing as we redraw our weapons.

"Let's end this," I say as we fight our way to our mate, defending anyone on our side who is innocent as best as we can. We get separated in the battle, but that's okay. We'll eventually make our way to our mate. Let anyone try to stop me.

Kaos

Reed is a fucking genius, and he definitely does not get told that enough. Using a moonbeam to travel across the divide? Absolutely fucking brilliant. I'd already sorted through every single option in my head and hadn't come up with anything yet, so I'm glad he figured out a way.

Nothing, and no one, is going to get in our way of protecting our mate. This whole damn day might've gone to hell in a handbasket, but it was inevitable. Eventually, we were going to have to do this song and dance.

So, let's fucking do it.

I land in a crouch, hopping off Reed's moonbeam, and dart into the fight. I throw shield after shield up, protecting those around me as I clear a path to Sadie. I even send my healing magic out to patch up our allies so they can keep fighting. They thank me with their renewed vigor toward our enemies.

A familiar face whizzes by me in the crowd. Malachi is a storm as he fights his way through enemy after enemy. He's a seasoned fighter and it makes me proud to see our friend fighting on our side.

Hemsworth works alongside me, going straight for people's jugulars and ripping them out. He's ruthless and effective. Then I catch a glimpse of Sadie through the crowd and my heart stutters and stops when I see a figure I recognize pop up behind Elder Vogt. *Shit. I have to get to her. Now.*

35

SADIE

Chills explode down my spine when I hear a familiar sound, a throat clearing, announcing their arrival. My head snaps in his direction and my intuition screams *danger*. My fears are confirmed when I find Mickey smiling at me with a triumphant look on his face and a dagger pressed against Vogt's throat.

What the hell? I thought they were working together...

"Well, well, niece. It looks like you're holding your own quite nicely," he says, and every single part of me wants to recoil at the sight of him.

He's never been normal looking per se, but right now he looks plain mad, drunk on power as he holds the knife to Vogt's throat, who is too weak to defend himself because he's been busy zapping all his power to protect the orb. He hasn't let it go though, as it's still floating, hovering above the ground.

Something about Mickey is... off. More so than usual. Which is saying something. Borrowing Elian's ability to read auras, I look at his and find it's a sickly brownish-green color. There's a gold cord running from him to Vogt, Vald, and Reginald and my stomach churns when I realize what that cord is doing. He's siphoning their magic. No wonder they look like death.

"I hate to break it to you, Uncle," I say, refocusing on the moment. "But the Elders are untouchable, remember?"

I don't clue him in that I know he's taking their power. Yet.

Hemsworth bursts through the crowd and sits beside me, snarling at Mickey in a show of support. With the blood dripping from his snout, he looks wild and menacing. He definitely deserves ten steaks after this.

"Darling niece, you've forgotten they've allowed me into their Circle and that will ultimately be their downfall." Oh, so we're going there, huh? Guess he doesn't care if they know he's sucking them dry anymore. "I tried this whole playing nice business, but it's no fun. I don't want to have to share power with these idiots."

Vogt startles like Mickey slapped him. "What the hell are you doing?" he hisses and steadily lowers the orb to the ground beside them. "We had a deal, Sinclair."

"And I'm reneging on it, you fucking fool," Mickey says simply. He shoves Vogt to the ground and heads for the orb.

I burst into action, the draw of the souls tugging at me, making me move faster than I ever have before as I pump power into my legs. I reach the orb before Mickey does and bring up the hilt of the shadestone dagger down to shatter the glass, the need to free the souls overwhelming me and making me act without thought.

The souls rise out into the night, beginning to scatter, and it's like all the tension I've been feeling around them fades. The draw they were holding on me snaps in one go—my heart feeling as weightless as those souls.

I send up a silent prayer for them. *Goddess, help them find their way back to the afterlife.*

The souls are finally free from their prison.

But I should know better by now things are never that simple.

Instead, Mickey laughs, fucking laughs as his sickly green power bursts out of him. He starts absorbing souls before they can get away. They fight to escape him, but he's like a damn vacuum, sucking them to him.

"Mercedes, Mercedes, Mercedes. You always need to save everyone, don't you?" His mouth twists in what should be a smile but looks more like a grimace. "But you couldn't save Skylar and now you can't save these souls. You see, I needed you to release them. No one else could do it. It had to be you and how easily you played into my plans, you stupid fucking girl."

Shit, fuck, shit. He tricked me.

Panicked, I glance around the field and find my mates, trying to figure out what to do next, but they're facing off with Vald and Reginald, buying me time to sort through what to do with my uncle. I cock my head at the sight of the Elders' movements slowing. It doesn't look like my Sworn are going to have to do much.

"Now you get to watch me kill each of your mates one by one," Mickey snarls. "And there's nothing you can do to save them either, *Shadowbringer*." He spits out my given title like it's a curse and turns his attention to the Elders and my mates battling them, glee dancing in his eyes.

Now that the souls are free from their prison, the Elders look like they're withering away, all the color draining from their bodies, and I realize I was right, and the souls must've been their power source or protection. Mickey is draining them dry on top of it, absorbing their life source and powers.

"No!" Reginald screams as Mickey ups how much power he's taking from a trickle to a full-blown waterfall. Reginald's face goes from young and youthful to old and wrinkled in a matter of seconds. "How dare you"—he coughs—"betray us."

Vin's wolf tackles him to the ground and bites off his head before he can say anything else. I find it extremely fitting that he's the one to take Reginald down. Elian rams his dagger into Vald's heart while Reed lights Vogt up from the inside, much like I did to Savannah at the challenge, and his burned husk slumps to the ground. Their deaths are over far too quickly in my opinion, but there's no time to dwell on it.

The souls scream and recoil when they touch Mickey's nasty green magic as he sucks them into him. And as if that's not bad enough, Mickey immediately reanimates the Elders' corpses, including a headless Reginald and Vogt's burnt husk. He spreads his arms out wide, cackling as that same green power spreads out over the battlefield—raising the dead from all directions. They're mindless, soulless husks, but they're relentless.

With grim looks on their faces, my mates make their way to me. *What Mickey is doing is wrong, vile, and it's up to us to stop him,* I project to them, watching as more and more of the dead rise around us.

"Why are you doing this, Mickey?" I ask and sneakily try to feel him out with my shadows, but they slide right off him much like with the Elders. I'm assuming he found a way to steal their invincibility through their Circle bond. This maniac knew exactly what he was doing. How long has he planned this?

Mickey laughs again and the sound of it grates on my nerves. "Since you'll be dead soon, I guess it won't hurt to tell you everything."

While he's distracted, I turn my focus to the chaos around us. Most of those loyal to the Elders are either dead or have decided to jump ship since Mickey is reanimating everyone around them, and they're forced to fight the people they once knew to stay alive. It doesn't matter how they cut them down, Mickey's magic reanimates anything left. It's twisted, honestly. The screams and cries are going to haunt me for the rest of my life.

A fierce need for vengeance stirs in my belly, the strongest one I've ever had. I must figure out a way to get us out of this. I have to. I tune back into Mickey's words. "Your father and I were blood, and he threw me away for some half Light Weaver bitch?" He breathes in the power he's taking in, so much so, his eyes turn green like the magic he's wielding. "He thought he could alter my memories, he made me think he was dead," he snarls. "Imagine my surprise when something triggered my memories and I found him alive, shacked up with some fraud he called a *mate*."

Kaos, Dante, Elian, Vin, and Reed keep the dead off me while Mickey rants. I feel their anguish radiating down the bond as they fight people they know and the Elders' mangled corpses. I think I catch a flash of Malachi and Merri's faces among the dead and my heart squeezes.

"My mother was not a fraud," I respond, watching him carefully, searching for any openings he might give me, but I'm at a loss.

"Do not interrupt me, girl," he snaps, and a small part of me is young again, remembering when he used that tone of voice and the pain that came after, but I'm no longer that girl. I'm no longer defenseless, and I am no longer alone, but I let him continue anyway because I need to think of a plan. *Think, dammit.*

"Your father tried to send me off again, like I was nothing, so I killed his mate and fled with my grief. My only family shirked me like our bond didn't mean *anything*."

Mickey begins to pace. "I plotted my revenge on your father and that's when I found out he had two kids. Triads at that. Your mother and father went through a lot of trouble trying to erase your existence so you would be safe. But they couldn't erase everything. I found out about you both and how much stronger you are because you're a Triad, and I thought to myself... What if I took that from him? It would be the ultimate blow."

The souls are slowly trickling into him now. He's almost absorbed them all, and I really don't want to find out what happens when he finishes. Another wave of the undead surge upon my mates and Hemsworth leaves my side to help them. It's just me, Mickey, and my ever-growing tide of vengeance.

Mickey scowls. "But they thought ahead and had your powers locked away. I thought you both were useless for so long... until that fateful night Skylar's powers emerged to protect you, and I sucked them right out of his lifeless body."

That admission is a blow straight to my heart and he knows it. Grief sweeps me up into its toxic embrace, even though I know he was fine in the In-Between. It doesn't matter. I feel his loss all over again, remembering his blond hair splayed around him, his angelic face. I'm drowning once more, feeling the same emotions of when I first lost him.

"That's right," he says. "I took your brother's magic, but he was nothing compared to you and your stupid Goddess-blessed powers. That damn prophecy won't mean shit when you're dead, will it?"

The grief and the blackness swirling inside me is replaced by vengeance, far more blinding and stronger than before. It makes me more confident. I must do this. For everyone we've lost. "Or it could be your downfall."

"What did I say about interrupting me!" he shouts and pulls at his face. He has taken in so much power that even his veins are starting to glow green underneath his skin, casting an eerie glow around him.

I'm running out of time. "See, this whole plan of yours doesn't work for me, Mickey. You can straight get fuc—"

He flings his hand toward me, sending out a bright blast of his magic. It hits me straight in the mouth, cutting off my sentence and choking me simultaneously.

"I've been wanting to do that for so long. You never knew your place. How does it feel to be at the bottom of the food chain? Goddess-blessed, and I still have more power than you." If I thought my uncle looked mad before, he is absolutely insane right now. The veins crawling up his neck are pulsing green. He has too much magic for any one person to have.

My own magic flares up inside of me in my defense and tries to protect me, but everything slides right off his slimy, green magic. I struggle against the bind around my neck, but nothing happens, and I can't breathe.

Looking around I find my mates and Hemsworth desperately trying to get to me. Their movements are coordinated, corded muscles moving in sync with one another, magic flying. Hems' teeth are lashing, snarling, but they're vastly outnumbered, completely surrounded by the undead. Every time they cut one down another appears in its place.

With Mickey's magic reanimating everyone, they're fighting literal hordes of people. Malachi and Merri among them, even though I never really liked the latter, she didn't deserve to die. And Malachi... I'll never hear him call me Shadow Girl again.

My chest constricts when I feel my mates' pain and worry through our bond. I continue to claw at my throat, the edges of my vision starting to grow darker with the lack of oxygen.

Closing my eyes, I fight the rising urge to freak out as the need to breathe becomes stronger and stronger. My heart feels like it's going to pump out of my chest. *Think, Sadie, think.* Dammit. Of all the ways I thought this day was going to go down, this wasn't even a thought.

"Sadie!" a familiar voice screams. *Ash.* My eyes pop open, and I spin toward the direction of the sound. One of the undead managed to get through my mates and is gunning straight for me.

Time seems to slow as Ash dives for him and tackles him straight to the ground. The undead asshole is stronger than I expect for him to be, well, dead, and flips their positions. I make a break for her and stumble, but Carter appears with a battle cry, soaked in blood, and cuts his head clean off.

That doesn't stop the body from getting right back up, but at least he can't see anymore. We stare at each other, and he gives me a nod like *focus on yourself, I got this* before diving back into the fray taking Ash with him.

Mickey laughs, drawing my focus back to him. He's no longer paying attention to me, too lost in the madness because of the sheer amount of souls he has inside him. The man is drunk on it, though you'd think he'd be used to the feeling. His feet leave the ground as he pulls in more and more of them. Instinctively, I know he's about to let out another blast, and I can't let him do that. Something tells me he won't just be reanimating the undead with it.

The Elders wanted me alive, Mickey doesn't. Apparently, he can take the power straight out of my corpse, per his letter. He wants us all dead, but I would very much like to live. I have so many things left to live for. Five mates I love more than anything, a best friend I need to make up with, a snarky familiar who deserves way more steak. So much that I didn't have six months ago.

But life doesn't always work the way we want it to. Sometimes life is unfair and unjust, and my air has run out. Fate is wonderful but can also be a cruel bitch. My feet carry me closer to Mickey and the path I need to take suddenly becomes clear.

If I'm going down, he's going down with me.

Dante

If I'm going down, he's going down with me. Sadie's thought pops into my mind, interrupting my fight with an undead Elite. It fuels me to fight harder, to swing faster, to send more flames flying in every direction I can without hitting an ally. The need to get to her is overwhelming. I can't lose her. I can't.

But first, I have to take this fucker down before he kills me. I don't recognize him, but it doesn't make it any easier, and I can't say the same for the others. Reed clashes with that Light Weaver who didn't like Sadie at first, Merri, I think, while Kaos cuts down Malachi for the second time, looking more and more haunted.

Sensing my distraction, Hemsworth leaps, his powerful jaws wrapping around the dead Elite's throat as he rips it out and I do the rest, cutting his head off his body. It's harder than it looks, but it's easier this way. The body still fights but they can't see anything and are more clumsy.

Another wave of the dead surge on us and it makes me feel helpless. And I fucking hate feeling helpless. I'm supposed to be the happy-go-lucky guy, but nothing about this is fun. It's fucked up in so many ways, I know it's going to scar all of us.

The only thing on my mind is getting to Sadie, but I don't know how we're going to because if we turn our backs for a second, we'll die.

I love you, Sadie projects to us, and I know she's about to end this. The need brewing in my chest to get to her amplifies and a blast of my orangish-blue fire erupts from my core with a battle cry and a roar. I will my fire not to harm anyone who is on our side, and it does the trick, but we need more... and I'm running out of juice.

I love all of you, Sadie says again, and my heart squeezes painfully.

This can't be happening.

Sadie

Tears leak down my cheeks as I force one foot in front of the other. My vision is turning black around the edges, wonky from lack of air, but I put my trust in my magic and my intuition because they've never steered me wrong.

Mickey is levitating, cackling like a complete madman, but it doesn't matter.

One foot in front of the other, I tell myself. *Right foot, left foot, right foot, stop.*

I slam my hand into the power stream that he's feeding into the undead. The spark inside me ignites, bursting to life with a brightness that's almost blinding. I completely unleash my magic, trusting it to do whatever it needs to do to stop the flow.

Like a rising wave crashing into a shore, it bursts out of me in a tsunami that smacks everyone. Still, I let it go. I open myself up completely, letting wave after wave crest out across the battlefield. The undead stumble, and Mickey's power stutters. I feed more into taking it down. My insides feel like I'm sticking them in a live socket, but I continue despite the agony.

It's not enough.

Using the rest of my energy, I trust what my instincts are telling me to do and call a burst of shadows to lift me from the ground until I'm standing at Mickey's height. I scream as an overwhelming blast of light erupts from my chest and an equal parts light and dark spectral wolf bursts free.

The wolf—*my* wolf, I realize—clamps its teeth around the green magic Mickey is pouring into the ground, effectively cutting off its flow, and then sends her own power storming through him.

Mickey bellows a roar and jerks against the foreign magic inside him as it flickers from green to black to white.

"How?" he roars as he crashes to his knees. I'm not entirely certain either, but I'm guessing it has to do with the magical resistance of shifters.

All of this happens within a few seconds, but when you can't breathe, it feels like hours.

Elian suddenly appears behind my uncle and claps his hands around his head just as my vision darkens around the edges, and I collapse to the ground, clawing at my throat. My heart is thundering, roaring in my ears.

Pounding agony is all I can feel as my wolf absorbs Mickey's power. I need air. I need this to end. I need it to be over.

Distantly, I hear someone, or several someone's screaming my name, but I don't take my eyes off Mickey, relishing at the horror in his eyes as Elian pours his fear into him. All of it. He looks fierce and badass as my savior.

So many times, I've wished for Mickey to know the fear he instilled in me and Skylar and he's finally getting his fucking comeuppance. If I weren't dying, I'd take more pleasure in the thought.

Someone—Kaos, I think—is standing over me with his calm but collected energy. My other mates are here too. Reed with his quiet but resilient presence. Vinson with his strong but sweet personality. Dante with his firm but funny attitude. I feel every single thing they're feeling through the bond, and our love is strong, despite my magic waning.

Elian crosses the distance between us, my uncle face down on the ground behind him, staring at me in that way of his—concern and panic etched on his face. *Finally, all my mates are with me,* I think to myself as they place each of their hands on me and connect us as a Circle.

My vision darkens further, my energy fading, barely able to keep my head up, but I feel more than see the glow surrounding us. All our magic twirling and intertwining... it causes a small smile to form on my lips. It's so beautiful. They're all so beautiful. My mates. Mine. Even if it wasn't for long.

There's a black glow emanating from Kaos' hands that overshadows the rest of the light, but the dreaded darkness takes over, and I'm lost to it completely. The last thought I have before all the fight leaves my body is, *we did it.*

We fucking killed them all.
But at what cost?

36

SADIE

Pain.

My whole body feels like it was run over by a truck, backed over, and then tossed through a light socket or two. My throat is so tight and sore, I don't think I could swallow even if I wanted to.

Why am I in so much pain if I'm dead? They've sorely misled us if this is what death feels like. I expected an all-knowing sense of presence or some shit like that. Definitely not slight agony. And why is it so dark? I've been to the In-Between and it was at least light there, and no one was writhing in misery…

I peel my eyes open and find myself in our bed at the safe haven, golden light filtering in through the window like nothing even happened. *What the hell?*

"She's awake!" someone exclaims, and Reed's face pops into view and all the air is sucked right out of my lungs. "You're not dead, my Love," he says, likely prevalent as he reads my thoughts and confusion. His dimples are out in full force, his glasses crooked, and he looks so damn handsome with the light hitting his face just right.

Dante moves into my line of sight beside him. "Yeah, sorry, Angel. You can't get rid of us that easily, I'm afraid."

Leave it to Dante to crack a joke at a time like this. It makes me chuckle slightly, but that hurts like a bitch so I just kind of clutch my throat in agony.

Dante winces. "Sorry, Angel. I'll go get Kaos. He's been healing you as much as he can, but it may take a bit to get back to full stamina. Something about your wolf being an extension of your soul and her taking on Mickey's power completely zapped you."

I feel like I was roundhouse kicked by a horse, I project through the bond.

A split-second later, three more men and a familiar are bursting through the door to get to me. Kaos and Vinson are at my bedside seconds later. Vinson grabs a glass of water with a straw and holds it out for me to sip while Kaos runs his magic over my body. Reed soothes the hair back from my face, Hemsworth licks my hand, and Dante sits at the edge of the bed.

The cool water feels amazing going down my parched throat while Kaos' soothing magic heals me from the inside. When he's finished, I feel a lot better than before. "Thank you," I croak and take another sip of water.

How long was I out? I ask mentally.

"Two days," Elian responds.

My eyes find him in the doorway, and he looks... stoic, his arms crossed over his chest as he leans against it. "What's wrong?" I ask and wince at the pitch of my voice. I sound like I literally ate nails for breakfast. "What happened after I passed out?"

"We almost lost you," he says and his mask drops. His gaze is intense, and if he weren't my mate, he'd scare the shit out of me, but as it is my heart gives a little flutter at the sight. "I almost fried that fucker's brain trying to get him to release the power he was holding over you. It worked. Then I trapped him in his worst fears, which he is still reliving." His expression is aglow with glee at that thought.

But that statement has me shooting up from my pillows, which sends a jolt of pain through me, but I don't care at the moment. "That fucker is still alive?" I demand.

Elian nods. "The power he took from the souls is still protecting his body, like it did the Elders, but don't worry. He's not going anywhere other than his own mind until it wears off. You weakened him enough for me to slither in and anchor a hold."

Then I'm going to rip his fucking heart out, I mentally respond, forgoing talking out loud this time.

"He's all yours after that, Pet," Elian agrees.

That fucker killed so many Weavers and shifters, Malachi and Merri among them, and countless others I didn't see or know. He killed my parents and Skylar and turned my bestie against me. I plan on ending him as slowly and painfully as possible. If I were a necromancer, I'd probably bring him back to do it all over again.

"How's Ash?" I ask, thinking back to her fighting beside us on the battlefield and her diving in to protect me.

"She's fine," Reed responds, putting my curiosity at ease. Thank goodness. "She's been staying with Carter. Apparently they've taken quite a liking to each other."

Good for her. *Get that shifter D, girl.*

A thought occurs to me that sobers me right up, and I'm not sure how to voice it because I'm not entirely sure if I want to know the answer. "Did we—" I clear my throat and take another sip of water, which Vin is happy to provide. "Did we lose—" I don't have to complete that sentence for them to know what I mean.

The energy in the room turns somber instantly, and I

brace myself for the answer. "We lost several great shifters and Weavers," Kaos tells me gently, squeezing my hand.

"Malachi and Merri," I say, wanting to speak their names out loud. Reed squeezes my hand comfortingly.

Vin blows out a breath. "We also lost Alpha Darren and his mate," he says, sadness etched on his features, and it resonates down the bond, making my heart ache for him. I know how close they were, and I can feel how hard this is for him.

"Fuck," I curse and run my hands over my necklace, thinking of Skylar. I'm glad I could bring my family justice, but I hate that it was at the expense of others.

"Don't blame yourself. They knew what they were agreeing to," Elian says fiercely, surprising me.

I nod. "But it doesn't make the grief any easier."

"Maybe not, but they view you as their savior. Most of them are already calling to name you and the five stooges here the next Elder council," Hemsworth tells me, jumping on the bed to curl in my lap.

My nose crinkles at that title, and I shake my head vehemently. "Absolutely not. There will be no more Elders. Nuh-uh, I fucking refuse to be called that."

"We thought you might say that." Kaos chuckles. "Which is why we've already declined that idea."

"Oh, thank the Goddess," I say, the weight lifted off my chest with that admission.

"But," he starts. Should've known there would be a but. "We did have another idea..."

"And what's that?" I ask.

"What if we made a supernatural council where we all vote and decide on matters pertaining to our community together? Shifters and Weavers alike. We'll let the people elect who they want on the council," Reed responds. The idea is surprising but in line with what the Goddess would want for us. Reed sure is stepping into the role of King and it fits him well. Even if he's still my nerdy, fairy porn lover.

I take a moment to chew on the idea. "That's... actually a brilliant idea and a step in the right direction."

"Then it's settled."

"So it is," I whisper.

The ideas and possibilities of a council are endless... The people will get a say in how things are run and how their future will pan out. The world will no longer be divided by archaic bullshit started by people who festered hate in their hearts. And it's crazy to think my journey with this world started with a lake and a concert.

Trouble has always seemed to follow me like smoke to beauty, but for once, I am grateful that said trouble has stuck around. It's brought me into a world where I feel more at home than ever before and found me five mates who complete me in every way imaginable. A family.

Fate always has a plan for us, even when we're not always ready for it. She damn sure has a funny way of showing you exactly everything you need.

And I wouldn't change a single thing.

EPILOGUE

SIX MONTHS LATER

My hand slides down as I slowly caress my stomach and a contented sigh escapes me. I sink further into the chair, running my fingers over my bulging belly.

Vinson made the most delicious feast, and I definitely overate. Now I'm nursing the giant food baby he put in me. I glance at my empty plate, wishing I could magic a second helping of Vinson's homemade mashed potatoes. They paired excellently with his fried chicken. But alas, I'm too full. If I eat anything else, I think I'll go into a food coma.

Speaking of babies, one of Hemsworth's pups comes bounding into the dining room. His motor function skills aren't quite all there yet, and he goes sliding into my chair when he tries to stop. It doesn't even phase him as he dives for a crumb that one of us dropped on the floor. A chuckle escapes me and then a groan. Food babies are no joke.

Shortly after the final showdown with the Elders, Emma found her own familiar. A gorgeous, fox-red Labrador Retriever named Jane, and Hemsworth fell instantly in love with her. They bonded, did the deed, and now here we are.

EPILOGUE | 311

Six puppies later. They're breeding the next hellion league of familiars.

Truth be told, a lot happened after the final battle. Starting with picking up our damaged selves and burying the dead—respectfully. We decided to make the safe haven our home and are currently building additions to house everyone.

So many memories happened at the Kings' estate and while I'll cherish those memories forever... The haven was our chance to start fresh and where our unity as a community really began. None of us needed that lavish lifestyle. Kaos, Dante, and Elian handed the vineyard and estate over to some locals who have turned it into a wedding venue and touristy wine tasting area.

Vinson took over as Alpha for Pack Haven—a role he's fitting into quite well if I do say so myself. It's hot being mated to the Alpha. All the raunchy shifter novels I've ever read are coming to life—my life. And when Vin gets bossy and growly? Ugh, I love it.

My entire Circle was elected as a part of the new supernatural council, alongside Emma, Nick, Niall, Adam, Matilda, and surprisingly Hades, who found out his Circle's mate is a shifter. There's no more division between Light and Night Weavers. We're all simply Weavers now.

Weavers and shifters.

Since that fateful night, more and more mate bonds have been happening across all three races. Each and every pairing is different, and that's what I love about them. They're unique.

Oh, and we added cell phone towers and internet lines to the safe haven property. Because while I'm content living in nature, I'm not content to miss out on Ash's new lifestyle.

My phone rings and I glance at the caller ID. Speak of the

devil. She may be human, but I swear she has ESP and knows when I'm thinking of her.

"Hey, Ashes!" I say, putting the phone up to my ear. I hear a lot of chatter and music in the background so I'm assuming she's at work. Our relationship is a lot better than it was. Her betrayal still hurts, but I forgave her because our friendship knows no bounds, and ultimately, I love her. Everyone makes mistakes; it's what we do about it to fix them that matters.

Like I said, fresh start.

"Hey, Sades! How are things with the puppies?"

"They're as rambunctious as ever," I say with a laugh, glancing at one trying to eat Dante's shoelace. "They certainly take after their dad. How's the job going?"

"It's wonderful," she responds, a dreamy quality to her voice. "I mean the dick is great too, but being on tour? I fucking love it."

Oh, Ash. Always hankering for the D.

Yep, that's right. The hot rock star, Brandon Luck, was so taken by Ash, he invited her to become his personal designer. Apparently, before they fucked on his tour bus, she told him about her love of design… and well, he remembered.

Secretly, I think he just wanted her there with him. They've been touring around the US for the past three months and she's been sending me pictures. I'm definitely not jealous at all.

There's a husky laugh in the background and then two male voices talking about her ass. Did I mention she took Carter, the beta shifter, with her too? Brandon's into some kinky shit according to Ash. I didn't ask the details. I know more about her sex life than any friend should ever know.

She tells me all about the newest outfit she designed for Brandon, the tour, the sex—much to my chagrin. They're totally rocking the ménage à trois vibes.

We still have plans to open a cross species women's fight

club, but it'll have to wait until she's finished touring and settles down. Besides, I'm getting plenty of training in with all the Weavers and shifters around, but I don't plan on letting my passion die. It'll happen one day when I'm ready.

"Ow, *fuck!*" Dante yells when one of the pups accidentally bites his finger while he's petting it. "I know I taste like chicken, but you can't eat me!"

I chuckle, and he shoots me a playful death glare. "Sorry, Ash. Gotta go deal with the latest craziness! Love ya!"

"Eat some dick for meee!" is the last thing I hear before I end the call to focus on the chaos currently breaking out around me.

"Ow, fuck!" the pup repeats, talking for the first time, making my jaw drop and a snort escape. Then I inwardly cringe because Hemsworth is going to be *so* pissed at those first words. They've been waiting to see if they'll talk for weeks now and his first words were *ow, fuck*.

At least it wasn't my doing. Dante makes an outraged face when he hears my inner thought, and I stick my tongue out at him like a mature adult.

"Oooh, you're in trouble now," Kaos says, grabbing our empty plates so he can do the dishes.

"The pup started it!" Dante defends.

Elian cracks a small smile, watching the scene unfold. Vinson shakes his head at Dante's antics, and Reed looks up from his pen and paper. He's been writing a smut book for me to read, and I'm trying to convince him to publish it. He says it's for my eyes only but won't let me read it until he's finished. I'm dying to get a peek at it. Even Kaos has read his draft and helped here and there. It's totally not fair.

The only thing placating me is the thought of when I actually *do* get to read it and the hot steamy sex that will come after.

Hemsworth waltzes through the doorway with the other

five pups crawling all over him. "Eat dick!" the trouble-making pup under Dante's feet calls out.

My eyes widen, Hemsworth's eyes widen, and then he narrows them on me. "It's not my fault, dammit! Blame Ash's big mouth," I defend before he can say anything.

"Did my... did my pup just say 'eat dick?'" he asks calmly, too calmy.

"Run for it!" I holler and hop out of my chair with the others on my heels. Minus Elian. He's not afraid of anything. Not even a pissed off dog dad.

The food baby makes me a bit slower and Hemsworth catches up easily, pouncing on me. I collapse onto the grass with him on top and laugh, ruffling his fur. I manage to get my hand on his ass where he loves to be scratched and he goes limp, all the fight fading out of him.

"I can't believe my pup's first words were eat dick."

I wince and he doesn't miss it. "Actually, it was 'ow, fuck.'"

He shakes his head and heaves a long-suffering sigh. "Better than eat dick, I guess."

He hops off me and Vinson helps me to my feet. My mates each put a hand on me as we walk back to the cabin. A chorus of "fucks," "eat dicks," and "stubborn pricks," reaches our ears, alongside a ripping sound and we burst inside to find utter pandemonium.

The trouble-making pup has ripped open one of the couch pillows and is throwing stuffing everywhere which two of the other pups are going to town on. The other three pups are sitting to the side, practicing their howls alongside their newfound vocabulary.

Elian's phone rings and he shoots me a look before stepping outside to take it. Uh-huh, leave the mess for the rest of us, I see how it is. I snatch up the rowdy pup tearing into the pillow while Kaos grabs another. Hemsworth boops the last one playing in the stuffing, and he stops.

Jane, Hemsworth's mate, walks in and sees the mess. "Pups!" she growls, using that motherly tone that all mothers have. Even Hemsworth snaps to attention. "Our room, now!" she says, and they squeal. Kaos and I put the ones we're holding down so they can go.

Once they're gone, I collapse onto the couch with a sigh. Dante works on cleaning up the stuffing while Kaos sits beside me and pulls my feet into his lap. Reed sits across from us with Vinson plopping into the other chair.

"Has the council heard any more about those disturbances in Hale Springs?" I ask, moaning as Kaos pulls my shoes off and rubs a particularly sore spot on my foot. When I'm not dealing with council business, I'm training the Weavers and shifters, which is something that is really important to me, but leaves me sore on occasion. They're getting good though, and it makes pride bloom in my chest.

Kaos shakes his head. "No, not that I'm aware of."

"You don't think someone is trying to imitate what the Elders did?" I ask, voicing the question that's been on my mind since we received a fire message from Keros, the gate guardian.

"No, there's no way," Reed responds, but even he doesn't look certain.

Not everyone is happy with the new routine, I guess, but I essentially told them to get in line or get fucked. After the fight, if my magic deemed them as unredeemable, they were banished. Or they were judged by my shadows and light and went where they deserve.

"Even if there is," Vinson begins, "we'll tackle that hurdle when we get there like we always do."

"I love you," I say to him and turn so the others know I mean it as well. "With all of you at my side, I feel like anything is possible."

Dante comes back from throwing the stuffing away and

places a soft kiss on my lips. "Because it is. Don't worry your little head over things we can't control."

Elian returns from his phone call with a strange look on his face, spinning his crotch knife in his hand. They still won't tell me where they put those damn things, but a part of me doesn't want to ruin the mystery, so I've given up on trying to figure it out.

"What is it?" I ask, pulling my feet out of Kaos' lap so I can sit up.

"That was Keros. There's been a disturbance at the gate. He's requesting our help. There was more, but the line cut out before he could say anything else, but I could hear fighting in the background and maybe a woman screaming?"

Holy shit.

"Well, what are we waiting for?" I ask with a determined grin. "There are adventures awaiting us, asses that need kicking, adversaries to gain," I say, getting up from the couch to go find my shit-kickers.

Fate always has a plan for us indeed.

The End

AFTERWORD

Phew. I'm totally sobbing right now. This is hard for me to write because I want these characters to live on forever, but this is where Sadie's journey ends. Have no fear though, I do have spin-off ideas for this world. Some of them will be with characters you've met and others you haven't. If you're interested in that, please feel free to tell me in my reader group! That's how I'll be able to gauge interest.

As always, thank you for reading. If you enjoyed this story, it'd mean the world to me if you left a review saying so.

ALSO BY DEMI WARRIK

Burning Chance

"Destiny bites but I bite harder."

A paranormal reverse harem - featuring shifters, witches, vampires, coming fall 2022! You can expect three, hot as hell shifters, and one dark vampire loving their witch, Rue, and their pursuit to keep her safe from the Blood Curse. **Blurb and cover coming soon!**

(BC is set in a different world than Sadie's. <3)

Fates Mark Series

Marked by Night (Fates Mark Book One)

Bound by Light (Fates Mark Book Two)

Called by Fate (Fates Mark Book Three)

ACKNOWLEDGMENTS

Holy. Shit. I can't believe I just wrapped up my first series. If you're reading this, thank you. Thank you, thank you, thank you. Without you, none of this would be possible. I'm forever grateful to my readers for loving this series. You rock!

A special thank you to my husband for putting up with my emotional ass throughout the end of this series. For allowing me to daze out when a plot idea came to me in the middle of a conversation. For supporting my dream—even when the times were tough. They still are, but like Sadie, with you, we'll tackle these hurdles.

To Lysanne, my Lys, for all the suggestions and help. For pulling me out of the pits of despair when I wrote myself into a plot hole and was ready to torch the whole damn thing. For always being there for me and being one of the very best friends I've ever had. You're my Ash. Minus the whole betrayal thing. The bond thing. You totally get me, right? Flove youuu.

To my beta team for all their hard work and ideas. Thanks for sticking with me and taking time out of your schedules to read when this deadline was so tight even a boy scout couldn't tie a tighter one. Without you, this book would not be the same. #Mooners4eva

To my editors, PollyAné and Raven, for always being kickass ladies and being there when I need them. You guys are the butter to the bread of this series.

To my ARC team for being the amazing group of people

they are! I truly appreciate you reading this and always being hyped for every book.

To Big Stabby, aka Rory Miles, for helping my sanity. Always.

And a huge shout out to Melanie Rhoda for being quick on the draw and giving me Wyatt's name!

Peace, love, and cock, Weavers

- Demi.

ABOUT THE AUTHOR

Demi Warrik is an emerging romance author dedicated to giving you stories you can ditch reality with. In her free time, she enjoys writing romantic shenanigans that will leave you laughing for days. Most of the time you can find her with her nose shoved in a book or plotting someone's demise… in a story, of course! Join Demi on her journey to finally write down the plethora of characters swirling around in her brain demanding to have their stories told. She'd love it if you would.

Join my newsletter here: www.demiwarrik.com

Printed in Great Britain
by Amazon